For the Love of

WHISKEY

The Whiskeys

•

MELISSA FOSTER

Cover Design: Elizabeth Mackey Designs
Cover Photography: Rob Lang Photography

WORLD LITERARY PRESS
PRINTED IN THE UNITED STATES OF AMERICA

A Note to Readers

It sounds cliché to say that I am the ink to my characters' pens, but for me, it always holds true, and I hope that never changes. I started writing Sullivan "Sully" Tate's story in 2013 and fell in love with her quiet strength, but I had to set the manuscript aside because I didn't know who her older sister was, and I hadn't yet met the right hero for her. That changed in 2020. While writing SEARCHING FOR LOVE and HOT FOR LOVE (The Bradens & Montgomerys), I met Jordan Lawler, who had been searching for her younger sister for many years, and Callahan "Cowboy" Whiskey, a fiercely loyal, overprotective cowboy and biker whose heart had belonged to his family, his motorcycle club, and Redemption Ranch, and I knew I'd found the people who were meant to be in Sully's life. Cowboy's heart was as locked down as Sully's, and I believe he needed her as much as she needed him. I am thrilled to finally give Sully and Cowboy their happily ever after and give Jordan the closure she so deserves. I hope you love them all just as much as I do.

If you'd like to read a detailed account of Sully's escape from the Free Rebellion, pick up FREEING SULLY, the short prequel to this story.

Please note that I have taken fictional liberties while writing Sully and Callahan's story. In the real world, their timeline could have taken much longer, but I'm a believer in spiritual connections and knowing when you've met the One. I have every faith that together Sully and Callahan will weather whatever storms come their way.

All my books are written to stand alone and may also be enjoyed as part of the larger series. If you'd like to read Jordan's story, pick up THEN CAME LOVE, a fantastic forbidden-love story and a Braden & Montgomery novel.

If this is your first introduction to my Whiskey world, when you're done reading Cowboy and Sully's story, you can go back and read Billie and Dare's story in THE TROUBLE WITH WHISKEY and then enjoy my other Dark Knights series, The Whiskeys: Dark Knights at Peaceful Harbor and The Wickeds: Dark Knights at Bayside.

The Whiskeys, Wickeds, and Bradens & Montgomerys are just three of the series in my Love in Bloom big-family romance collection. Characters from each series make appearances in future books, so you never miss an engagement, wedding, or birth. A complete list of all series titles is included at the end of this book, along with previews of upcoming publications.

Download Free First-in-Series eBooks
www.MelissaFoster.com/free-ebooks

See the Entire Love in Bloom Collection
www.MelissaFoster.com/love-bloom-series

Download Series Checklists, Family Trees, and Publication Schedules
www.MelissaFoster.com/reader-goodies

If you prefer sweet romance, with no explicit scenes or graphic language, please try the Sweet with Heat series written under my pen name, Addison Cole. You'll find many of the same great love stories with toned-down heat levels.

Remember to sign up for my newsletter to make sure you don't miss out on future releases:
www.MelissaFoster.com/News

WHISKEY/WICKED FAMILY TREE

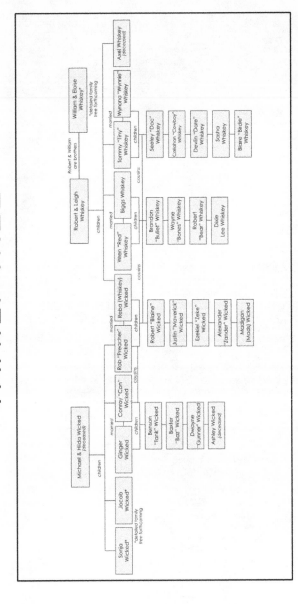

New York Times Bestselling Author

MELISSA FOSTER

Chapter One

CALLAHAN "COWBOY" WHISKEY took off his Stetson and dragged his forearm across his brow, squinting against the late-afternoon sun as he looked out over the property that had been in his family for generations. His heart had always belonged to Redemption Ranch, where they rescued horses *and* people, giving ex-cons, recovering addicts, and other lost souls a second chance. The ranch had live-in facilities and a full therapeutic staff run by Cowboy's mother, a licensed psychologist. His father managed the ranch, and Cowboy and three of his siblings worked and lived on the property. Cowboy was as deeply rooted to that land as he was to his family and to the Dark Knights motorcycle club. His father had founded the local chapter of the Dark Knights well before he and his four siblings were born, and giving back to the community had been a part of their lives for as long as he could remember.

Today the ranch was bustling with activities for the kickoff of the Ride Clean anti-drug campaign run by the Dark Knights. Every fall the club kicked off the event with a motorcycle ride and rally, followed by a day of fun and fundraising at the ranch. Families came from several neighboring towns to take part in the festivities. Kids learned about caring for horses and enjoyed yard games, paintball, horse and pony rides, and hayrides. This afternoon Cowboy was overseeing horseback rides in the lower corral with Simone Davidson. Simone had come to the ranch almost two years ago, after completing rehab. She'd thrived in their program and had remained on as an employee while taking classes toward becoming a substance abuse counselor.

Three giggling kids ran past as Cowboy's cell phone rang with his father's ringtone. He put his hat back on and stepped away from the corral to answer it. "Yeah?"

"Gather the Knights. Emergency meeting in the main house." His father's gruff tone left no room for questions. When they were at events, alerts were passed personally rather than having forty phones going off with texts at the same time.

"Yes, sir." Cowboy pocketed his phone, wondering what the hell was going on, and headed for Simone.

"Uh-oh, the big man doesn't look happy." Simone's thick auburn hair framed her pretty face and bright smile. With her arms covered by her flannel shirt, the only visible reminder of all she'd been through was the scar running down the left side of her face. "If it takes all day, I'm going to get a smile out of you."

Not likely. Especially now. "I need you to take over. My old man needs help with something." They had a hard-and-fast rule that club business went no farther than club members. For their families' protection, even wives weren't privy to club business.

Simone's smile faded at his tone. "Is everything okay?"

"Yeah. I'll send someone over to help you. I'm taking Sunshine."

"It wouldn't hurt to let her name wear off on you a little," she called after him as he mounted the sweet-tempered palomino they'd rescued a few years back.

He waved as he rode off, scanning the crowds for black leather vests with Dark Knights patches on the back, like the one he wore. All the club members and their families were helping run the event, but they had plenty of volunteers to cover things while they were called away.

Cowboy rode by the barns and riding rings, discreetly alerting members to the meeting. In turn, each man went on to notify other members. They were well versed in discretion. They had to be. Too many Dark Knights walking purposefully in one direction would attract attention. Instead, they acted jovially, sauntering up to each other and clapping their buddies on their backs, like two guys just shooting the shit, and then they took separate routes toward the main house, careful not to stick too close together.

As Cowboy made his way around the grounds, he spotted his younger brother, Dare, running the pony rides and felt a familiar gust of gratitude, as he often did these days when he saw him. Dare had been a daredevil since he was a kid, and Cowboy was forever trying to rein him in. A couple of months ago, a horrendous accident had damn near killed Dare and his fiancée, Billie Mancini. It was the most terrifying thing Cowboy had ever experienced, and it had shaken Dare up enough to make him start changing his daredevil ways. That didn't mean he'd stopped doing crazy shit. It just meant he'd do a little less crazy shit.

Dare lifted four-year-old Gus Moore off a pony and carried him over to his father, Ezra. Dare and Ezra were both Dark Knights and therapists at the ranch. As Cowboy rode over to them, he spotted his sister Sasha, an equine rehabilitation therapist, heading their way.

Ezra looked up, and Sasha pushed her long blond hair over

her shoulder, flashing a flirtatious smile. *What the hell, Sasha?* They had rules against employees dating each other, and she knew better than to flirt with a co-worker. Especially Ezra. He had enough trouble with his ex, so much so that he wasn't interested in getting mixed up with another woman. Thankfully, Ezra broke their connection, as Cowboy had thought he would. He made a mental note to have a talk with his sister and nip that in the bud before it had a chance to cause any trouble.

"Hey, Cowboy!" Gus waved excitedly, his mop of dark curls bouncing around his face as he wiggled in Ezra's arms. "I rode a horse, too!"

"That's great, buddy," Cowboy said.

Gus began talking a mile a minute, and Cowboy gave Sasha an imploring look and a curt nod. Having grown up around the club, she was used to their impromptu need for private discussions, and she'd honed her ability to read their silent cues.

She reached for Gus. "Hey, Gusto, how about we play in the bouncy house and then get one of Birdie's yummy chocolate pony pops?" Their quirky youngest sister, Birdie, was the co-owner of a chocolate shop in a neighboring town, and she was at the event selling chocolates to raise money for the club's drug-free campaign.

"Yeah! Bye, Dad. I'm going with *Sugar*!" Gus had a major crush on Sasha, and he'd picked up on Dare's casual use of the endearment *sugar* when speaking to female friends.

The guys chuckled as Sasha carried Gus away, but the amusement was short-lived. They swiftly turned their attention to Cowboy.

Cowboy was acutely aware of the families milling around them and was careful not to alarm anyone. "Our old man needs help carrying some stuff from the main house. I'm on my way to grab Doc and the guys from the paintball field." Doc was their oldest brother and the ranch's veterinarian.

"I'll let Mom know we're going to help," Dare said casually. Their mother would alert the other club members' wives and girlfriends and make sure no attention was brought to the club gathering.

Ten minutes later Cowboy stood among the Dark Knights brotherhood in their largest meeting room in the main house. All eyes were on his father, who stood at the front of the room. Tommy "Tiny" Whiskey was a mountainous man at six foot four and three hundred pounds. He had a pendulous belly, long gray hair, and a bushy gray beard, and he wore a black-and-gold bandanna—the colors of the Dark Knights—tied around his forehead, along with his leather vest boasting club patches, which he was rarely seen without. Tiny didn't put on airs for anyone, and he was the toughest and the fairest man Cowboy knew. He was a strong leader, and he was well respected by every man in that room and damn near every resident three towns out for his groundbreaking efforts to help others. He was also as fearless and ferocious as a grizzly and one of the most lethal weapons the club had.

"We've got a situation," Tiny said sternly. "A young gal escaped from a cult in West Virginia and was picked up by a trucker who was heading this way. They need a safe haven for her while DNA tests are run and they figure out what's what. Her name is Sullivan Tate, and she goes by the name Sully. She's in her early twenties, and I hear she's tough but scared. She's refused to go to a doctor or to the police for fear of being taken back to the cult. We're bringing her to the ranch tonight after dark, where she can undergo therapy and be seen by one of our doctors. This girl needs *complete* protection. *Nobody* can know she's here until I get word that it's safe. Not even your wives, or you could be putting our entire family, and everyone on this ranch, at risk. Hazard, this needs to be kept *off* the records." Hector "Hazard" Martinez was a police officer. Like Cowboy, and most of the other men in that room, he went by his road name.

"You've got it," Hazard said.

"Cowboy, you're taking the lead on this," his father said. "I want you to have eyes on her at all times. No exceptions. Hyde, you're taking over Cowboy's duties until we know she's safe."

"Yes, sir," Hyde and Cowboy said in unison. Cowboy had no doubt about why he'd been chosen to watch over the girl. All the Dark Knights were protective, but he was known to be fiercely responsible, overprotective of everyone in his circle, and not easily distracted by a pretty face.

His father told them that the girl had been staying with the trucker and his wife for three weeks and had been too afraid to leave the house. He filled them in on what he knew about the Free Rebellion anti-establishment cult and their compound and said they supposedly had connections with dirty cops and other people of power, the bastards. "I alerted our other chapters to keep their ears to the ground about this, and it looks like the girl has a good reason to be scared. Biggs said the word on the streets is that the cult is searching for her." The Dark Knights had several chapters across the United States with connections to informants in various seedy, underground operations, and Tiny's brother Biggs ran the Peaceful Harbor, Maryland, chapter.

"The trucker who picked her up and his wife are going to a safe house, but I want eyes on their house from a distance, in case anyone connects the dots." A few of the members volunteered to watch the house. "If you see anyone sniffing around, we need to know about it." When they nodded their understanding, his father said, "When today's event ends, take your families home, and then I need everyone to come back and stick around. We need extra security around the ranch for the foreseeable future. And remember, when you step out of this room, it's business as usual."

His father went over the plan to utilize decoy trucks when they picked up the girl and to form boundaries around the ranch that would be watched twenty-four-seven by club members in case the media got a whiff of her escape and where Sully was staying. Manny Mancini, Billie's father and the vice president of the club, was putting together a schedule for security. His father's serious eyes locked on Cowboy as he said, "Sully will be staying in cabin six."

Strategically chosen, no doubt. That was the only cabin Cowboy could see from his own home. "What're we telling the staff and residents about who she is and where she came from?"

"She's here to heal," his father said. "Nobody needs to know more than that."

After the meeting, Cowboy walked out with his brothers, their cousin Rebel, Ezra, and their buddy Hyde.

"Damn, that poor girl." Doc's jaw clenched, and he shook his head. The pain in his eyes was palpable. He was the deep thinker of their family, and conversely, a charmer with the ladies when he chose to be. But his relationships were like an extended-stay motel, never lasting more than two or three months. "She's got to be brave as hell to have escaped a fucking cult."

"Brave and strong," Dare agreed.

"That's a hefty dose of perspective right there," Ezra said, as if he needed any. He'd first come to the ranch years ago as a

7

troubled teen. After completing one of their programs, he'd gone on to intern there while he was in college and graduate school, and now he was one of their therapists. He'd followed in his father's footsteps and had become a Dark Knight. Like the other Dark Knights and the ranch employees, Ezra had become family.

"No shit," Rebel agreed.

"Yeah, while we're dicking around wondering what girl is going to land in our beds tonight, that poor girl's scared for her life." Hyde had come to the ranch a few years ago as a belligerent ex-con and went through the program with Dare as his therapist. He'd since become one hell of a ranch hand and a trusted friend.

"Kind of like any girl who ends up in your bed," Rebel teased as they pushed through the doors and walked outside, doing as they were told: going back to business as usual.

The guys chuckled, but those sounds were heavier, weighed down by their new reality as they shifted gears from club business to upbeat campaign hosts.

Something had bothered Cowboy during the meeting, and he didn't shift gears quite as easily. As the guys shot the shit and began to go their separate ways, he pulled out his wallet and withdrew the missing-person flyer they'd been given at a club meeting a couple of months ago. Cassandra "Casey" Lawler had been missing for more than twenty years. She and her parents had been on their way to pick up her older sister from a camp in West Virginia when their car hit a tree. Authorities found her parents dead, and Casey had been missing ever since. Her sister had hired a private investigator over the summer to look into the case, and the little girl's picture had been all over social media ever since.

Cowboy studied the image of the blue-eyed four-year-old who had burrowed beneath his skin the first time he'd seen the flyer. She wore a flannel shirt, leggings with dirt stains on the knees, and little construction-style brown work boots. Her golden-brown hair was tangled and frizzy, like she'd been running around all day. He'd never seen a four-year-old with an edge, but those baby blues with impossibly long, dark lashes said, *Watch out, world, here I come.* He studied the age-progression picture of a young woman with those same bright, tough eyes and felt the clutch in his chest he'd gotten every damn time he looked at the flyer.

"Dare, where are you heading?" Doc asked, drawing Cowboy's attention away from the image.

"To the one person who can put a smile on my face." Dare nodded in the direction of Billie, who was talking with Birdie by the table where she was selling chocolate. He glanced at Cowboy. "Dude, you okay?"

No, I'm not fucking okay. Cowboy nodded.

"Better get that look off your face, or you'll scare off the women around here," Doc teased. They were always giving him shit for being too serious.

"Right." Cowboy rolled his shoulders back, cleared his throat, and stroked his beard, forcing a smile. "Better?"

Dare grinned. "Now you just look like you've got a wedgie."

"Maybe I do," Cowboy said with a laugh. "Asshole."

"You know you love me." Dare headed for Billie.

Cowboy looked at the flyer again, his gut fisting.

"You've been studying that thing for weeks," Doc pointed out.

He met his brother's serious gaze. "I can't shake the feeling that she's out there somewhere. She went missing in West

Virginia, and that girl Sully escaped from a cult in the same state. What are the chances they're the same person?"

Doc's brows knitted. "Dude, that little girl's been gone for more than two decades. Chances are she's no longer breathing."

Cowboy gritted his teeth against the visceral and surprising anger rising inside him. "If Sasha or Birdie went missing, I'd *never* give up hope."

"If she were our sister, I wouldn't either," Doc said sternly.

"She's *someone's* sister, and they're looking for her."

Doc lifted his chin. "Why're you so pissed?"

"I don't fucking know." Every time he looked at this flyer, it ate away at him like nothing ever had. "Sorry, man. I just..."

"Look, I know you're worried about that girl and the sister who's looking for her, but sometimes when someone's gone, they're just gone."

Cowboy couldn't swallow that jagged pill, but he held his tongue because, years ago, Doc had fallen for a politician's daughter who had interned at the ranch over the summer, and it hadn't ended well. Cowboy knew Doc's follow-up texts and calls had gone unanswered, and he didn't want to reopen that Pandora's box. His brother hadn't been the same since, and that was why they now had rules in place about not dating co-workers.

"Yeah, I guess you're right. Time to pretend we're not facing a ticking clock." As Cowboy's gaze swept over crowds of happy families and carefree kids, he wondered what kind of hell the girl heading their way had been through.

Chapter Two

SULLY KNEW WHEN to count her blessings and when to fear the hand that fed her. Chester Finch, a portly man with a warm heart, scraggly brown hair, and a near-constant cigarette hanging from his lips, and his pleasantly plump and perpetually kind wife, Carol, were definitely blessings. They'd been kind enough to let her stay with them for the last few weeks without asking many questions or pushing her to see a doctor or go to the police. She would give anything to be able to stay with them longer, but she'd been so afraid to leave their house, she was hindering their lives by making them keep her existence a secret, and when she'd finally agreed to go to the ranch, they found out the cult was looking for her. She might have *already* put Chester and Carol in danger.

As moonlight streamed through the windows of their modest living room, Chester paced by the fireplace in jeans and a button-down, and Carol, in a pretty fall dress, watched him with worry. Fear and regret clung to Sully like a second skin. They had opened their home to her, cared for her, and now because of her they had to leave their life behind and relocate to a safe house. If only she hadn't gotten into Chester's truck, they wouldn't be forced to leave their home.

If I'd never gotten into his truck, Rebel Joe's men probably would've found me.

She closed her eyes against clashing waves of heartache and gratitude, remembering the night she'd escaped and had flagged down Chester's eighteen-wheeler. She'd been terrified that he might know Rebel Joe, the leader of the Free Rebellion. She'd been told that everyone in a hundred-mile radius knew Rebel Joe and was loyal to him. But Chester had been her only way out, and she'd drawn courage from the fact that her best friend, Ansel Rhodes, had taught her how to fight, and more importantly, how to act like she wasn't scared, even when every inch of her screamed with fear.

She drew upon that strength now, as she waited to be taken to the second-chance ranch Chester and Carol swore would keep her safe. For weeks they'd been singing the praises of Redemption Ranch and the family who owned it, the Whiskeys, as well as the Dark Knights motorcycle club, who they said would protect her.

A rumble of engines sent her nerves into a frenzy. She turned to look out the window just as headlights appeared on the long driveway.

Carol sat down beside her on the couch and patted her hand reassuringly. "It's going to be okay, honey. The Whiskeys are good people. You'll be safe with them."

"What about you and Chester? You have to leave your home, and you can't even tell your family or friends where you're going."

"Don't worry about us," Chester said. "You just take care of yourself, sweetheart. You're finally free, and you got a lotta livin' to do."

"But—"

"No buts," Carol insisted. "We're going to be fine. Our relocation is only temporary, until the authorities are sure nobody's looking for you. We want you to have a beautiful life, and that's what you should be thinking about. A bright new future."

Sully had nothing to her name but a stolen duffel bag with a few items shoplifted when she'd escaped, toiletries and other necessities the Finches had given her, and fourteen dollars—and in a few minutes she was going to leave the only two people she knew outside the cult. She didn't feel *free* yet, and she didn't need a beautiful life. She just needed her *own* life, and she had no idea what that could or would look like. In all her planning, she'd never thought past getting far away from the compound. Now that she was faced with it, she wasn't sure how she could have any type of life at all without relying on others, but she was willing to fight for a chance to figure that out.

A knock on the door made her heart race. Carol patted her hand again and pushed to her feet, following Chester to the door. Sully knew how she'd been taught to act around strangers, but she'd promised herself that if she was ever free from Rebel Joe's reign, she wasn't going to hold her tongue or go against the way *she* believed she should act ever again.

She rose to her feet on trembling legs, but she was unable to see the gruff-sounding man Chester was speaking to at the front door. A minute later, a large, heavyset man with a long gray beard and a bandanna tied around his head, wearing a black leather vest over a T-shirt, weathered tattoos covering his arms, walked in with a pretty blonde with short, layered hair. They looked to be in their fifties, and they were followed by a younger bearded man wearing a cowboy hat and a similar black leather vest and T-shirt. A chain ran from the younger man's belt loop into the front pocket of his jeans. He was just as tall as the older man, his shoulders equally broad, but while the older man's stomach hung over his belt, the younger man's stomach looked as hard and flat as concrete. His beard was light brown and trim, and he had muscles upon muscles with no visible ink. He was as beautiful and powerful as a summer storm. Sully had never seen a man who looked like him, but she'd been around enough arrogant men who used their size to intimidate that she held her breath, her stomach churning with worry, as she tried to figure out how to get out of going with them.

The younger guy was the first to look into the living room. His gaze collided with hers, stealing her breath and causing wild flutters in her chest, as if butterflies had been roosting there and their visual collision had scared them to life. She'd never felt anything like it, and she couldn't look away. But she wasn't afraid—not of *him*, anyway—even though the underlying fear of the unknown lingered. She didn't know how to define what she felt about this man who made her heart race in a way it never had. Ansel's mother, Gaia, had been the closest thing to a mother Sully had ever had, and her voice whispered through her mind. *Never judge a person by appearance alone. Kindness and evil live in their eyes, their actions, and their inactions.*

The guy took off his cowboy hat and held it to his chest, revealing light brown hair a shade darker than his beard. He nodded once as he put his hat back on, the compassion in his eyes and the warm smile curving his lips unexpected balms to her nerves.

"Let me introduce you to Sully." Carol led them into the living room. "Sully, this is Wynona and Tiny Whiskey, and their son Callahan. They run Redemption Ranch."

Wynona stepped forward. "Hi, Sully. It's nice to meet you." She had friendly eyes and a soothing voice. "You can call me Wynnie."

"Hi," she said softly.

"We're so pleased you're going to be staying with us. I'm sure it's unsettling to go someplace new, but we have a nice cabin all set up for you," Wynnie said.

"Who will I be sharing it with?" she asked.

"Nobody. It's all yours," Wynnie said.

"We assumed you'd want privacy and a place to call home for however long you're with us," Tiny said in a gruff but reassuring voice.

Half of Tiny's face was hidden behind his beard and mustache. His eyes were serious but not cold like Rebel Joe's. Was he the leader? The person she'd have to *thank* for using the cabin? She glanced at Callahan, standing behind his parents, the muscles in his jaw bunching. Was he a dutiful son or a silent serpent? It didn't matter. Her body was *not* currency. Her nerves caught fire. "What do you expect in return for use of the cabin?"

"We don't expect anything, honey," Wynnie said gently. "We're here to help you, and the cabin is yours for as long as you need it."

Sully pressed her lips together, wanting to believe her but knowing better than to take people at face value.

"We know you have concerns about members of the Free Rebellion looking for you, so we've arranged for extra security around our ranch," Tiny said. "Don't you worry, darlin'. Nobody's going to get to you."

Her mind raced. She'd always thought the people in the cult posed the greatest threat. Now she wondered if she should fear these people and others on their ranch.

"Tiny and I need to speak with Chester and Carol for a moment, and then we'll take you back to the ranch. Do you have your things ready?" Wynnie asked.

Sully glanced at her duffel bag by the couch. "Yes."

"Okay. We'll only be a few minutes." Wynnie reached for Tiny's hand, and they went with Chester and Carol into the kitchen.

That simple act of reaching for his hand was so different from what Sully was used to, she found herself staring after them as she sat down on the couch, all too aware of Callahan's presence looming across the room. She didn't have to look to know he was watching her. She felt it in every cell of her body. After a lifetime of being watched and having her every move analyzed, she was sick and tired of it. She wanted to push to her feet and demand he look away. But she was doing her own analyzing of his family's every move, breath, and word out of their mouths and thought she might learn more by watching him.

Callahan stepped toward her, and her pulse quickened, memories of whispered threats by Rebel Joe and his overbearing underlings pummeling her. She refused to cower for anyone ever again and lifted her chin, meeting Callahan's gaze.

He took off his hat and got down on one knee beside the couch, bringing them eye to eye. He was even broader up close, his chest impossibly thicker. His jaw was square, his nose straight, and he had angular cheekbones, as if he'd been carved from stone. But there was something merciful in his eyes, something that drew her in and held her there, making her want to trust him, and *that* was terrifying.

"Hi, darlin'. I'm Callahan, but everyone calls me Cowboy.

I'll be helping you learn your way around the ranch. You doing okay?" His voice was deep, low, and coaxing.

About as okay as a mouse in a trap at the moment. She nodded.

"I know my old man looks scary, and you don't know me or my family, but we've been helping people around these parts since I was a boy."

"Why do you help people?" It might seem like an odd question, but she didn't care. She'd lived behind a wall of secrecy, picking at what little information she could gather to figure out people's motives, and she was never going to be kept in the dark again if she could help it.

"That's a good question. The quick and truthful answer is that it's the right thing to do."

It took everything she had to fight the habit of accepting surface-level answers to avoid getting into trouble. "I need more than that if I'm going with you."

"I suppose you do. My father was raised to believe men were meant to protect everyone and everything around them. But for him, protecting wasn't enough. You see, beneath that rough exterior is a heart the size of the moon. He's stepped in to put an end to some horrific wrongdoings, and having been judged by his appearance his whole life, he knows people aren't always what they seem. Sometimes good people do bad things, and other times good people get caught in the webs of bad people and don't know how to get out. He found that with the right help, those who wanted to turn their lives around could do it. So he made it his mission, and the mission of the Dark Knights, to know the difference and help the ones he could."

She tried to process all he'd said, but something was missing. "What about women?"

His brows slanted. "What about them?"

"You said men are protectors, but you never said how your family sees women."

"I don't know how men and women were viewed where you came from, but I assume it was a lot like the way my grandfather saw women, as if they had their place, and that place was *below* men."

A chill ran down her spine. She curled her fingers around the edges of the couch cushion. "That's pretty much how it was."

"I'm sorry to hear that. But rest assured, that's not how we do things on the ranch or in our motorcycle club," he said earnestly. "My father is proof that we are not the sum of the people who raised us. Women are the heart and soul of our ranch, and my mother is the center of our world. She will shut down my father as often as she loves him up, and she's not afraid to shut down any other man."

"Are there punishments for that?" Gaia had told her that life was different outside the compound, and she'd seen that firsthand living with Chester and Carol. But Gaia had also explained that every household was different, and sometimes what you saw wasn't what was happening behind closed doors.

"For speaking her mind? Hell no." He cocked a grin. "Although I guess getting yelled at by my mother is a form of punishment for my father for saying something stupid."

She felt herself smiling.

"I don't know what you've been through, Sully, but in our world, women are our equals. They have voices and opinions that are often far stronger than ours. We might bicker, but that has nothing to do with gender and everything to do with stubborn minds. As men, we might physically protect the women in our lives, but we're under no misguided belief that we're any better or stronger than they are, and I know my sisters and the women on our ranch would attest to that."

His words were earnest and heartfelt, and she wanted to trust them, but she needed more. "And children? How are they treated?"

His gaze softened. "I don't have children of my own, but I can tell you that one of our therapists and his four-year-old son live on the ranch, and little Gus has got everyone wrapped around his finger. My mother will tell you that children often have valuable insights that we adults have long ago forgotten. That said, we have horses, equipment, and vehicles all over the ranch. It can be a dangerous place if kids aren't careful, which means we have to teach them how to be safe and watch out for them. But we all believe that children are meant to be curious and get dirty and to challenge authority so they can learn and grow and hopefully come out on the right side of the law."

She felt a flicker of something bright and new inside her, but she was afraid to trust it.

Tiny and Wynnie came out of the kitchen with the Finches, and Cowboy gave Sully a reassuring nod, settled his hat on his head, and pushed to his feet.

"Okay, sweetheart," Wynnie said, her gaze moving between Sully and Cowboy. "I think we're ready to head back to the ranch."

Sully couldn't tell who she was talking to, but her nerves spiked, because either way, this was it. She was leaving Carol and Chester.

"We'll wait in the foyer while you say goodbye." Wynnie took Tiny's hand again as they headed into the foyer. Tiny nodded to Cowboy, who moved to the entrance of the living room and lowered his chin, as if he were giving them privacy and couldn't hear them.

Cowboy might bow to his father, but his presence was just as authoritative as Tiny's, and Sully got the feeling he didn't have to *see* or possibly even *hear* to know what was happening around him.

"We'll miss you, sweetheart, but you're going to have a wonderful life, and we're so proud of you." Carol embraced her. "You are a blessing, Sullivan Tate, and you will always have a place in our home."

Sully forced her voice past the lump in her throat. "Thank you." She looked at Chester, and her heart hurt even more, remembering the night he'd picked her up on the side of the road. He'd said he'd been driving for days, and it had shown in his scruffy cheeks and the bags under his eyes. He'd asked what she was running from, and she'd lied. *I'm not running. My mama is sick.* He hadn't bought the lie, and he said he'd seen stronger girls than her *runnin' from stuff*, and that there *ain't no shame in runnin'.* She'd swallowed her fear and had said, *Yeah, well, I'm not running.* But in her head, she'd added, *I'm leaving.*

After that he'd saved her in more ways than one, but she couldn't think about that when she was on the cusp of leaving the only place she'd ever wanted to stay. "Thank you for picking me up and taking care of me."

"Like I told you that first night we met, I got a granddaughter 'bout your age, and I could no sooner leave you to fend for yourself than I could turn my back on our Theresa." He embraced her and kissed the top of her head. "You just remember what I told you about stealin', ya hear?"

He'd given her an earful when he'd found out she'd stolen the duffel bag and everything in it. "Yes, sir."

Chester scoffed and shook his head. "What'd I tell you about *that?*"

"Sorry." He was always getting on her to call him by his name, but she was too nervous to think straight. At the compound she'd become an expert at not showing her emotions, but after a few weeks with Carol and Chester, it was harder to hold them in, and she struggled to tamp them down.

Cowboy looked at her with a silent *Ready?* in his eyes.

She nodded and reached for her duffel, but he picked it up and motioned for her to walk ahead of him, turning back to Carol and Chester to say, "We'll take good care of her."

Sully followed Tiny and Wynnie out to the double-cab Redemption Ranch truck. Cowboy put her duffel in the back seat and headed for his motorcycle, where he stowed his hat in a compartment and put on a helmet. As they drove away, with the roar of Cowboy's motorcycle behind her and nothing but darkness and the vast unknown in front of her, Sully hoped like hell he'd been telling the truth.

Chapter Three

THE TRUCK PULLED onto the highway, and two motorcycles seemed to come out of nowhere, pulling ahead of the truck. A minute later, two more drove up to their left and another two to their right. Sully's heart raced as she looked from side to side.

"It's okay, honey," Wynnie said reassuringly. "I should have warned you. Those are our friends, fellow Dark Knights. Tiny is the president of the motorcycle club, and they escort us whenever we bring people to the ranch. It's a show of solidarity, to let you, and everyone around us, know that the Dark Knights support the person in our truck."

"But won't that call attention to me or put the Finches in more danger?"

"No. The community is used to the Dark Knights escorting us when we pick up clients, and by now the Finches have been picked up to go to their safe house," she explained. "We've taken extra precautions because of your situation. Club members usually follow us to the home or facility when we pick up clients, but they didn't join us until now, twenty miles away from the Finches. We've also arranged for two decoy vehicles, which are being escorted to the ranch by other club members.

Nobody knows who is in any of the trucks. They just know someone is coming to the ranch."

"Don't worry," Tiny said gruffly. "This isn't our first rodeo. We've been doing this for more than thirty years. We know how to keep you safe."

The way they worked together was a little too reminiscent of how Rebel Joe and his men handled things, which made Sully even more nervous. But she reminded herself that Chester and Carol had protected her and were giving up their lives to stay in a safe house. They had no reason to do anything but help her remain safe. She looked out the back window, feeling a modicum of relief at the sight of Cowboy still leading the pack of motorcycles behind them.

According to the clock in Tiny's truck, it was almost ten o'clock when they pulled onto the ranch property. The main gate had a wooden beam across the top with an iron *RR* in the center. The first *R* was backward. She remembered seeing that same symbol on Cowboy's belt buckle. Two formidable men wearing black leather vests stood in front of motorcycles blocking the gate. Tiny stopped the truck, and they came to his window. Two sets of dark eyes zeroed in on *her*. Both men had short brown hair and scruffy cheeks. One had piercings in his ears, septum, and nostril and tattoos on his neck and arms, making him more intimidating than the other, who looked a little familiar and had no visible ink or piercings.

"Everything good?" Tiny asked.

"All's quiet except this motormouth," the one without the piercings said.

The other guy grinned. "Consider me your built-in entertainment."

"Built-in headache is more like it," the familiar-looking guy said.

Wynnie turned in her seat. "Sully, these jokers are our other sons. Seeley is a veterinarian, and everyone calls him Doc."

"Welcome to the ranch," Doc, the one without any piercings, said.

No wonder he looked familiar. He wasn't as big as Cowboy, but their facial features were similar and their hair was almost the same color and about the same length, while the other guy's hair was darker and shorter.

"And I'm Devlin, but you can call me Dare," the guy with the tattoos and piercings said.

"Hi." Sully was glad they seemed nice.

"Dare is one of our therapists," Wynnie explained. "He specializes in helping teens. You'll meet his fiancée and our daughters and the rest of our staff tomorrow."

"We're going to take Sully to her cabin," Tiny said to the men. "You boys keep things locked down tight."

Dare and Doc nodded and headed back to their motorcycles. They pulled over to the side of the road. After the gate opened, Tiny drove through, and Sully watched Cowboy and only a few other motorcycles follow them in. She was surprised to realize she hadn't even noticed where the other motorcycles had gone and wasn't sure if she was just too nervous or was feeling a little safer. They drove down a long lane, passing pastures, barns, and a number of cabins. The property seemed to go on forever, and she was relieved that it was nothing like the unkempt compound that mostly consisted of broken-down trailers practically on top of one another.

Tiny pulled up in front of a pretty log cabin with a green roof and a screened-in porch on one side. He cut the engine and said, "Home sweet home."

"Is this where you live?" Sully asked.

"No, sweetheart. This is your cabin," Wynnie said.

Astonished, she reached for the door and was surprised to see Cowboy opening it and offering his hand to help her out. Gone was the helmet he'd worn on the ride over, replaced with his cowboy hat.

"Thank you." She climbed out without taking his hand and realized the other motorcyclists hadn't followed them to the cabin. She turned around to get her duffel bag, but Cowboy was already holding it. "I can carry that."

"It's no trouble," he said.

She knew nothing came free in this world and already feared what she'd owe his family for use of the cabin. She didn't need to owe him something, too. "I'd prefer to carry it."

He nodded curtly, that muscle in his jaw bunching again as he handed it to her, and strode up to the screened-in porch, holding the door open for everyone to pass through. The porch was as nice as the cabin, with two green rocking chairs and a small wooden table between them. They looked inviting enough to curl up on with her sketch pad.

Tiny and Wynnie stood off to the side as Cowboy unlocked the cabin door and pushed it open. "It's all yours."

He handed her the key, and she curled her fingers around it, her heart racing. "Who else has keys?"

"Just Tiny and me, honey," Wynnie said. "We keep an extra set to every cabin in our locked safe, in case there's an emergency. But this is your home while you're here, and nobody will go inside unless you invite them."

Sully peered inside and nearly lost her breath at the charming open layout with light wood walls and matching floors. To her left was a beige sofa facing an iron stove atop a stone hearth and a corner cabinet with a television on it. She'd never watched television. To the right of the stove was a bedroom. *Is this really happening?* It was like a dream come true, but the only dream that had ever come true for her was the one she'd fought for and given to herself.

Her escape.

"You can go in and check it out," Cowboy said.

Her heart pounded as she stepped inside and was immediately enveloped by a warm scent so different from the dank smells of the compound, she couldn't place it. On the wall to her left was a row of coat hooks with a flashlight hanging from one of them. She hung the key on a hook and glanced into the bathroom beside it. It was sparkling clean, with a bathtub and a separate shower. Fluffy towels hung on a rack beside a shelf with a box of tissues on it, and the toilet paper looked like it was the kind that probably wouldn't scratch when she used it, like the Finches' had.

She walked farther into the cabin, running her fingers along the back of the couch on her way to the cozy kitchen, taking in the microwave, toaster, and coffeemaker. It felt gluttonous to have so much at her fingertips. The Finches had all those appliances, but they weren't given to her for exclusive use, like this, and she'd been careful not to ask for anything more than they'd offered.

On the small kitchen table were a cell phone and a shiny white folder that had WELCOME TO REDEMPTION RANCH printed above a picture of the property with all its gorgeous fences and barns beneath a clear blue sky. The picture was so pretty, it made her feel hopeful.

"The phone has my number and Cowboy's programmed into it in case you need anything," Wynnie said.

This was *nothing* like the compound. She'd never had her own space, much less access to a phone. She wanted so badly to believe the Whiskeys were *really* there to help her, gratitude overshadowed some of her fear. She went through the living room and looked into the bedroom. The bed had a colorful quilt and a beautiful arched headboard, but it was as big as Rebel Joe's bed, clearly made for more than one person. She swallowed hard and turned back to them. "I know you said you don't expect anything in return, but I also know nothing comes free, and I only have fourteen dollars. I can't pay for all this."

"We wouldn't take your money if you could," Cowboy said.

Worry prickled her skin, and she struggled again not to hold in those worries. She was her *own* protector, and she wouldn't let herself down after she'd come this far. She straightened her spine, meeting their gazes. "I will not pay with my body."

In the space of a few short seconds, she registered empathy in Wynnie's eyes, anger in Cowboy's, and a mix of both in Tiny's. Before she could get a word out, Wynnie said, "Oh, honey, we're not like that."

"When we tell you there are no strings attached, we mean *exactly* that," Tiny said firmly.

"And there will *never* be a time when your body is part of any deal made on this property," Cowboy reassured her. "You've got my word on that."

His vehemence underscored his honest eyes, and that brought a wave of new emotions. "Thank you. I don't have a lot of money, but I want to earn my keep. I can cook and clean, and I can sew, or I can try whatever other jobs you have that I might be qualified for."

"It's late, honey," Wynnie said sweetly. "Why don't we let you get settled in, and we can talk about that tomorrow."

"Okay. Thank you."

"There's food in the fridge if you get hungry tonight," Wynnie said. "We normally try to eat meals as a group with the other residents and staff, who you'll meet tomorrow. Cowboy is going to be helping you get acclimated to the ranch, and he'll come by in the morning to show you around and bring you up to the main house for breakfast."

She glanced at Cowboy, trying to ignore the anxious fluttering in her chest. "What time should I be ready?"

"How does seven thirty sound?"

She'd be up hours before that. "Fine."

"Seven thirty, then," he said with a nod.

After they said goodbye as warmly as they'd greeted her, she locked the door behind them and realized she was truly alone for the first time ever. There was no such thing as privacy at the compound, and Carol hadn't worked outside her home, so they'd spent all day together. She had been alone in her room at the Finches' but never alone in their house.

She'd craved solitude for so long, she couldn't believe she finally had it.

A trickle of fear prickled her skin.

She closed her eyes, reminding herself she was safe. They had people watching the gate and the rest of the property. Rebel Joe couldn't get to her there. Nobody could. The doors were locked, and the Whiskeys seemed like honest people.

With that in mind, she went to unpack her duffel bag. As she put her clothes away, she remembered the panic she'd felt the night she'd escaped.

She closed her eyes for a beat, reminding herself she was safe, and when she opened them and looked around the cozy room, she once again thanked her lucky stars for Chester and

Carol, then went to put away the toiletries they'd given her.

When she was done, she was too anxious to sleep, so she looked through the Redemption Ranch folder on the table. She read the welcome letter and a lot of information about the horse rescue and the therapeutic services they offered. She thumbed through pictures and details about the therapists and ranch staff and found Cowboy's information. Just looking at his picture made her pulse race, so she flipped past the people and withdrew a map of the property.

It had been hard to see the buildings they'd passed in the dark, but there were far more on the map than she recalled seeing. She wanted to take a walk and glanced at the front door, but a flutter of fear held her back. Her fingers curled into fists. How many nights had she spent looking out the window, wishing she could take a walk beneath the stars? *This* was *why* she'd escaped: to have the freedom to be alone. To be in control of her wants and needs.

Refusing to let fear rule her life any longer, she snagged the flashlight from the hook and pocketed the key, but as she reached for the doorknob, panic flared in her chest.

She shook out her hand, trying to shake off the fear, but it clung to her. She took a deep breath, telling herself she'd start slowly and just sit on the porch and get some air. She opened the door and stepped outside, pulling the door closed behind her. As she let go of the knob, the door to the screened porch opened, and Cowboy's face came into focus as he stepped onto the porch.

Shitshitshit. Had he lied about her body not being part of any deal?

"Everything okay, darlin'?"

Her stomach pitched. "I just…Sorry, I thought I could—"

She fumbled for the doorknob, dropping the map.

"*Wait.*" He held his hands up in surrender. "Don't be afraid. I'm not here to hurt you."

"Then why *are* you out here?"

"Just in case you need anything."

"What could I *possibly* need? I have a whole cabin to my-self." She didn't mean to snap at him, but she'd lived at Rebel Joe's beck and call for so long, it was hard to break out of it, despite her gut instincts telling her he was being honest.

He kept his distance, hands still up. "I don't know. I just didn't want you to feel alone or scared. I don't know what you've been through, but the fact that we have to protect you from the people you ran from tells me it couldn't have been good."

"But you said I was *safe*. That no one could get to me." *And I believed you, so why am I being so combative?* She didn't have to look far for the answer. Having faith was new, and that was frightening, too.

"They can't," he reassured her. "I'm not worried about someone getting to you. I'm here because I'm worried about *you*. I want to be sure you feel safe and you have anything you need."

The honesty in his eyes told her who he was, and his actions backed that up. She *believed* him, but she still folded her arms over her chest, steeling herself against the fear of having faith and the other conflicting emotions whipping through her. "But you barely know me."

"I don't have to know you well to be worried about you. That's called compassion."

Her thoughts stumbled, and she felt a little bad for fighting with him when he so obviously wanted to help.

COWBOY MIGHT NOT know Sullivan Tate, but he knew that face, even with her hair hanging in front of one side of it. The chubby cheeks of childhood had given way to high cheekbones, a slightly upturned nose, and lips he wouldn't allow himself to think about. But it was her eyes, with those impossibly long, dark lashes, that gnawed at something deep inside him. They were older and wiser, their indestructible edge buried beneath who the fuck knew what. From the moment he'd seen those eyes looking back at him from across the Finches' living room, he'd known who they belonged to, and that had sparked a visceral desire to take care of her. He had to believe there was a reason this young woman had ended up on his ranch, and he'd damn well do whatever it took to earn her trust and keep her safe.

His parents had filled him in on what they'd learned from the Finches. Sully hadn't revealed much to them about the cult other than that she'd grown up there and had escaped on her own. Cowboy had questions about that and thought about what else the Finches had told his parents. They'd said Sully had been too frightened to leave their house, even to take a walk in the garden, which told him a hell of a lot. He'd like to get his hands on the assholes who had mistreated her, but right now he was more worried about where the young woman who was too afraid of being found to walk in a garden was going all by herself on unfamiliar land.

He had enough experience with improperly-cared-for horses and people to know when to tread lightly and spoke softly. "I'm going to lower my hands, okay?"

She nodded, and he lowered them.

"Can we just talk for a second?" he asked.

She nodded again.

"You're not a prisoner here, Sully, and I'm not hanging around just waiting for an opportunity to do bad things to you. It's my job to be here for you, but hopefully as you get to know me, you'll see that I'm a pretty good guy, and you'll understand why they asked me to be here for you."

"I'm sorry if I came across as rude."

"You should never be sorry for your feelings. They're the one thing you have that is truly yours. You didn't come across as rude. You came across as cautious, and rightly so. It's going to take time for you to trust that we are who we say we are, and that's okay. Is something wrong with the cabin, or were you having trouble settling in?"

"The cabin is great. I was just restless."

"I get that. It's got to be hard settling into a new place when you don't know the people or the lay of the land. Where were you headed?"

"I was going to sit out here and get some fresh air."

"That always helps me take it down a notch, too." He picked up the map she'd dropped and handed it to her, keeping his tone light. "Are you sure you aren't sick of our faces and planning your escape?"

She *almost* smiled and shook her head. "I was thinking about taking a walk, but I wasn't sure where to go. I don't even know where I am."

"Then consider yourself lucky, because I know the ranch like the back of my hand. Let me show you."

She lifted the map, and he held the other side of it, pointing to each landmark as he spoke. "This is the main entrance, where we came in, and we followed this road around to this one, which leads to your cabin. Here. See how the road turns after your cabin?"

She nodded.

"If you follow it up the hill, you'll end up at my place." He pointed to the light beyond the trees. Turning back to the map, he said, "This is the main house, where the therapists work and where we meet for meals. There's a recreation room with books, a television, puzzles, and games. It's a nice place to hang out and talk to other people, and there's a movie room in the main house, too."

"Can anyone use the recreation room?"

"Yes. That's what it's there for. The movie room, too. Our cook and resident manager, Dwight, lives there. If there's something special you want, he can make it for you."

"I don't need anything special."

"We'll see about that." He winked. "And just past the main house, right here, is the paintball field."

"What's paintball?"

"Only the best sport besides anything on horseback." He explained what paintball was and that she was welcome to join in their paintball games.

"I don't think I want to shoot people."

"It's not like that. It's all done in good fun. Even little Gus plays, although we don't hit him with paintballs. But I understand your hesitation." He pointed to the map again. "These are the main barns for the healthy horses, and these are the rehab barns for those horses who aren't so lucky and need more help. This is my parents' house, and Dare and his fiancée, Billie, live here. Doc lives in this cabin, and my sister Sasha is over here. You'll meet her and Billie tomorrow."

"So this is like a compound where everyone lives and works?"

"I guess you could think of it that way, but to us it's a ranch, and not everyone who works here lives here. It's not a requirement that our employees live here or that my family members work for the ranch or live on the property. We each chose to do so, except for my youngest sister, Birdie. She lives in a nearby town called Allure, and she owns a chocolate shop with our aunt Marie and our friend Carly."

"A chocolate shop?"

"Yeah. Do you like chocolate?"

She nodded, eyes lighting up. "We didn't get it often, and I've never been to a chocolate shop."

"I'll take you there one day. But I have to warn you, Birdie will talk your ear off." That earned a genuine smile. "Do you want to try out your navigational skills and go for a walk?"

She looked at him for a long moment before saying, "Okay."

"Want to grab a sweatshirt or a jacket?" It wasn't particularly cold, but Sully was tall and willowy in loose jeans and an oversize cream corduroy shirt. She looked like she might blow away in the slightest breeze, despite her heavy, worn and scuffed leather combat boots.

"No. I like to feel the cool air."

He mentally added that tidbit to the others he'd been gathering, like how determined she was to be strong and how she hadn't shed a tear when she'd left Carol and Chester, though sadness and fear had practically oozed from her pores. He wondered how long she'd been holding back her feelings and what would happen when that dam broke.

Chapter Four

COWBOY LOCKED HER front door and followed Sully off the porch. Since he was just starting to earn her trust, he hung back, walking a few steps behind her so she didn't feel like he was hovering. But she looked over her shoulder at him with an uncomfortable expression. Even in the dark, he could see shadows rising in her eyes.

He held his hands up again. "Pretend I'm not here. I just want to be close by in case you get lost."

"I don't like to be watched. Would you mind walking beside me?"

He tucked away that disturbing information to dissect later. "Sure, but for clarity's sake, I'm not watching you. I'm simply making myself available in case you need anything."

"Don't you have better things to do?" she asked as he fell into step beside her.

"What could be better than taking a moonlight walk with a new friend? Is there anything in particular you'd like to see?"

Her eyes widened with elated curiosity. "*Everything* there is to see."

He laughed. "That's a lot of walking for one night. How

about we head out to a pasture, and I'll introduce you to some of my four-legged friends?" When she nodded in agreement, they walked along the road in comfortable silence. It was hard to believe that just a few hours ago the place had been packed with families and activities for the fundraiser, and now he could practically hear his own heartbeat. He glanced at Sully, looking around, taking it all in. "Have you always gone on late-night walks?"

"Only in my dreams."

The hint of longing in her voice made him want to take back what he'd said about it being a lot of walking for one night and let her walk until she was too tired to take another step. "That's a shame. The night sky has a lot to offer."

She was quiet for a few minutes before saying, "We weren't allowed to leave our rooms at night, but I still got to see the stars. I used to sit at my window at night and look up at the sky. They were like sparkles of hope a million miles away, reminding me that the world was so much bigger than the compound. I'd sit there dreaming about what it would be like to take a walk at night or sleep beneath the stars and feel the air on my skin as I nodded off."

It pissed him off that she hadn't had those freedoms, and he was even more curious about why she hadn't taken walks in the Finches' gardens, but he couldn't ask without making her feel like she was being talked about behind her back. "It must've been difficult living with those types of restraints."

"When I was little, I felt safest inside. Like nothing bad could happen if I was behind four walls. I was always afraid someone would snatch me away from the compound, which is silly, since my uncle Richard and Rebel Joe would never let that happen. But as I got older, I started feeling trapped."

"Rebel Joe?"

"He's the leader of the Free Rebellion."

Cowboy memorized the guy's name, wondering if he'd ever hurt her, and with the mention of her uncle, he wondered if he was wrong about Sully being the girl in the flyer. "You lived with your uncle?"

"Mm-hm. But he got sick and passed away a few years ago."

"I'm sorry to hear that." Where were her parents? Did she have other family? Why wasn't she allowed out at night? He had so many questions, but she was finally talking *to* him instead of *at* him, and he didn't want to accidentally spark any upsetting feelings that might make her clam up.

She shrugged. "Thanks. What about you? Do you spend a lot of time outside at night?"

"I sure do. I prefer to be outside, day or night. This way, darlin'." He motioned for her to turn onto the main road, and they headed toward the pastures. Sully slowed her pace, eyes widening as one of Cowboy's favorite sights came into view. Beyond the barns, pastures, and tall trees, majestic mountain peaks stood out against the starry sky.

"Wow," she said with awe. "It looks like you could climb right up and touch the stars."

He wished she could. He had the strange desire to show her everything beautiful the world had to offer. "There's nothing quite like it. It takes my breath away day and night."

"You're so lucky." She tilted her face up to the sky, and her hair fell away from her face, a smile brightening her entire being. "If I lived here, I'd do nothing but stare at that view." She looked at him, eyes glittering with wonder.

Damn, she blew that mountainous view away. He'd never seen anything so genuine or so beautiful. "Darlin', you live here for now, so you can do just that."

Those glittering eyes brightened even more.

"Do you want to sit in the grass for a while and enjoy the view?"

"I do, very much, but can we see the horses first? I've never seen horses up close, and I don't know why, but I have a feeling if I don't see them now, I might never get a chance."

He didn't need to be a therapist to understand that now-or-never mindset. He'd seen it a million times. Whether it was a person or an animal that had been physically or emotionally abused or neglected, the instincts were often the same. When the fear subsided enough to allow a modicum of trust, a voracious now-or-never appetite for whatever kindness was offered usually followed, fearing it could be taken away at any time.

"We sure can, and you'll have plenty more chances while you're here." He led her to the fence surrounding the pasture.

She squinted into the darkness. "Where are the horses?"

"They're hard to see with an untrained eye." He leaned closer, pointing into the pasture. "See them over there by that tree?"

"Yes! I see them," she said happily. "I love that they're so free."

"You're freer than they are. They're confined to the pasture."

"I'm confined to the ranch."

Man, he hated that. "Only temporarily, until we can be sure nobody from the cult is tracking down Chester's truck or has gotten wind of where you might be. Once we know you're safe, you're free to roam the world, but the horses will still be confined to barns and pastures or to a human holding the reins."

"That's sad."

"Don't be too quick to judge. Most of the horses come to us from abusive or neglectful situations and probably wouldn't have survived if we didn't step in to nurse them back to health and give them the love they deserve. When they're here, they're treated with loving hands and given the promise of a good life. They will never go a day without food, shelter, or kindness."

"But wouldn't they be happier running free?"

"A lot of the horses that we take in have been abandoned and left to run free. They're starving, often injured by their own doing, and they endure all sorts of things you don't want to think about."

"I never thought of all that."

"If I weren't allowed to roam free at night, I'd probably think total freedom would seem like the right and only way to go, too. But there's a big world out there, Sully, and it's always good to know you have options should you want to hide away from it."

She gazed out at the horses again. "Have you ever wanted to hide?"

"I think everyone has at some point in their life."

"Where did you go when you wanted to?"

"I climbed on a horse and rode for hours. That's what freedom is to me. Well, that and riding my motorcycle. There's nothing quite like staring at a stretch of open road. Would you like to see the horses up close?"

She nodded eagerly.

"When I call them over, they'll come running, but don't worry. They're not going to jump the fence or plow through it. They're just excited to see us, okay?"

She nodded. He whistled loud and long, and a sight he'd never tire of emerged from the darkness. Several horses galloped toward them, their powerful bodies driving them forward, manes and tails carried in the wind.

Sully stumbled backward, eyes wide.

"It's okay." He offered her his hand, and their eyes connected for what felt like ten heart-thumping seconds in which she looked like she was trying to figure out if she could trust him but in reality was probably only two seconds before she slid her hand into his and held on tight. He wanted to reassure her that she was safe with him and he wouldn't let anything happen to her, but he'd always been a firm believer that a man's actions spoke for themselves.

The horses slowed as they approached, and when they put their big heads over the fence, hungry for affection, Sully took another step back, holding his hand so tight, her fingernails dug into it.

"It's okay," he reassured her. "They just want love." Sunshine pushed her muzzle into his chest. "Hey, baby girl. Did you miss me?" He petted her with his free hand, pressing a kiss to her forehead, and petted the others as they nosed their way in.

"They're so *big*."

"They're beauties, aren't they?" He reached for Sunshine again, scratching her jaw. "This is Sunshine. She's a sweetheart."

"Did you rescue her?"

"We did, a few years ago. She and two others were in horrible shape when we saved them from being slaughtered. I love all my ladies and gents, but Sunshine has a special place in my heart."

"Why?"

"I don't know exactly. There's something in the way she's always looked at me, like I was supposed to be in her life. Would you like to pet her?"

She tightened her hold on his hand. "I'm afraid."

"I'll help you, unless you'd rather not." She stepped closer, and he unlinked their hands, placing his on her lower back. "See how her ears are up and facing forward? That means she's aware of you, interested in you. If her ears were pinned or flattened, you'd want to keep your distance."

"Okay," she said a little shakily.

He took her right hand in his. "We're going to let her smell your hand, but don't worry. She won't bite. Real easy, just offer her your palm." He turned her hand over, moving it toward the horse. Sunshine sniffed it and pushed her nose into her palm.

Sully's eyes flicked to his.

"She likes you. Come here." He guided her to the fence in front of him so she could pet Sunshine's neck and felt her tense up. He lowered his hand from her back, hoping to ease her discomfort, which he had a feeling was from their close proximity rather than the horse, but stayed close enough to step in if she got scared.

"She's soft," Sully said quietly. "And she feels strong."

"She is strong. Her life is proof of that. It was touch and go for a while when we first brought her home. I used to sit with her at night in the rehab barn and talk to her, try to coax her into fighting to stay alive."

"What did you say?"

He liked how curious she was. "I told her what I've been telling all our horses since I was a little kid and used to sit with them with my old man. I said that I was sorry for how she'd been mistreated and that there was a good life waiting for her, but she needed to fight for it."

The tension around her eyes and mouth eased. "Do you think that helped?" She continued petting Sunshine.

"Yes, I do. Horses need love and comfort just like humans. It's amazing what being around the right people and environment can do for them."

"But how can you promise a good life? The information in the welcome packet said you rehome a lot of horses. How can you be sure they won't be mistreated?"

"We stand behind our promise by thoroughly checking out prospective adopters. We do site visits to make sure their other animals are well cared for and they have ample facilities to care for the horse. We speak to their vets, neighbors, and the local police, and we make sure they have never been convicted of inhumane treatment of animals. Once a horse has been adopted, we not only follow up with scheduled site visits, but we also retain the right for our staff—or our associates if the adopters aren't local—to do drop-in visits."

"You really do care about them."

"These horses are my life. I'd no sooner let anything happen to them than I would to anyone on this ranch."

She seemed to think that over, her brow knitting. "Have any horses come back to the ranch?"

"Not yet," he said proudly.

As they petted the horses, he could feel her defenses coming down. Horses had that effect on some people, and he hoped he had a calming effect on her, too. After a while, they sat in the grass so she could enjoy the view. Neither said a word for a long time. Cowboy had always been comfortable with silence, but he'd found that most people needed to fill that space, as if to avoid listening to their own thoughts. Sully seemed as content with the silence as he was, and he liked that about her.

When they finally headed back to her cabin, he was still curious about those walks she'd missed and couldn't keep from asking a question that could lead to the answer. "Did you take a lot of walks with Carol and Chester?"

She shook her head, causing her hair to fall in front of her face again. He got the feeling that was a practiced and strategic move, like when horses looked away from people whose energy was too intense, so he didn't push for more, allowing silence to settle around them again.

They were turning onto the road that led to her cabin when she said, "I wanted to take walks," catching him off guard. "The Finches offered to go with me, but I didn't feel safe enough."

"I'm glad you felt safe enough to walk with me tonight, but to be honest, I was surprised you agreed to go."

"Me too." She looked up at him, one eye still covered, her small smile barely visible.

"Thank you for trusting me."

"You should thank the Finches. I trust them, and I don't think they'd put me in danger."

"And here I thought I had charmed my way into your good graces."

She laughed softly, and it was such a tender, happy sound, he vowed to earn more of it.

SULLY COULD COUNT on one hand the number of situations when she hadn't felt some level of fear, and she hadn't expected tonight to be one of them. Her guard wasn't completely down, although she had a feeling she could trust Cowboy, because she hadn't been scared at all since her initial jolt on the porch. He was easy to be with, and she liked his gentle humor, but the name Cowboy didn't feel right to her. It felt like it could be anyone's name, like calling a cook, *Cook*, and he didn't seem like just anyone.

"I'm sorry your family had to go to all this trouble for me," she said. "But I sure am grateful to be safe."

"It's no trouble at all."

She wasn't sure she believed that. There had been a lot of men on motorcycles escorting them, and they were taking extra precautions with people watching the ranch. Those men had to have lives and families to tend to, but she was curious about *him*. "What else do you do here besides taking lost girls on walks?"

"You mean you didn't read all about me in the welcome packet?" There was a teasing arc to his voice.

"I must have missed that page."

"Damn. I figured my picture stopped women in their tracks."

She smiled, shaking her head, appreciating the levity.

He nudged her with his elbow. "I'm kidding."

"No, you're not. You're hard to miss. You probably turn a lot of heads."

"I'm not gonna lie. Every time I walk by the barn, the female horses try to get my attention."

She laughed softly. "I bet they don't have to try too hard. You seem to really love them."

"They're my heart and soul, and to answer your question, they're also my job. I take care of the horses and handle the training after they're rescued, and I oversee the maintenance of the property and manage the ranch hands. But taking lost girls on walks has now become my favorite task."

She blushed, not knowing what to make of that. "Have they always called you Cowboy?"

"Pretty much since I was a kid. But once I became a Dark Knight, it was chosen as my road name, which is like a nickname. We all have them. They're like a badge of honor."

"I see. That makes it special. But it feels funny calling you Cowboy. It's a little generic, and Callahan is such a nice name. It's strong and unusual. It suits you. Not that Cowboy is a bad nickname."

"I've never thought about it that way. You can call me Callahan if you'd like."

"Really?" Why did that make her so happy?

"Sure. Why not?"

"Good. *Callahan.* I like that." Her cabin came into view, and she was a little disappointed, hoping they could walk and talk longer. She snuck in one more question. "Have you always lived here?"

"Born and bred."

"You never went away to school or anything?"

"Nope. Learned everything I needed to know right here. I've been working the ranch since I was old enough to put on my own boots, and it's all I've ever wanted to do. Well, that and become a Dark Knight."

"What's that like?"

"Being a Dark Knight is knowing you'd lay down your life to save another. It's having forty brothers who will always have your back and watch over your family no matter what and knowing you'd do the same for them. We have mandatory club meetings every Tuesday night, called church, showing our commitment to each other and the club. I love all of it. It's the best feeling in the world, right up there with being out on a horse with nothing but the wind at my back."

He was so passionate, she hoped one day she'd find something to be that passionate about. But she had a feeling freedom would always soak up her passion. "That sounds too good to be true, but what I meant was, what is it like knowing exactly who you are and what you want to do with your life?"

"Oh. Well, I've never thought much about it," he said as they came to the cabin. He held the screen door open and followed her up the steps.

She pulled the key out of her pocket. "It's okay. I'm sorry I asked."

"Don't be sorry. It's a great question, and I'll get back to you with an answer as soon as I figure it out."

"Don't worry about it. Thank you for walking with me. I really enjoyed it. I was so on edge when I left the Finches, and I feel better now."

"I'm glad you do. I enjoyed our walk, too. I'll be out here tonight in case you need anything."

"Out *here*?"

"Yeah. Right there, to be exact." He pointed to a rocking chair.

She was surprised to feel a little relieved that she wouldn't be alone. "Let me get you a blanket."

"I'll be fine."

"No, that's not right. Just give me a minute." She hurried inside, grateful he didn't follow her in. She felt safe with him, but she knew how being confined could change things. She grabbed the extra blanket she'd seen in the bedroom closet and brought it out to him.

"Thanks." He tossed the blanket on the chair. "Shoot me a text if you need anything."

She fidgeted with the hem of her shirt, hating that she was so far behind the times. "I didn't want to say anything before, but I've never used a cell phone."

"No problem. I'll show you how," he said without a hint of judgment or surprise. "I'll wait out here while you get your phone."

She retrieved the phone, and they stood on the porch as he showed her how to turn it on and off and walked her through finding and adding contacts—as if she had anyone's phone number to add—making a phone call, sending a text, and turning off the ringer.

"Go ahead and give it a try," he said. "Send me a text."

She navigated to a text message. "What should it say?"

"Obviously you should tell me that I'm the best walking guide on the planet and my horses are beautiful. You can throw something in there about my charming wit if you'd like."

She couldn't stop grinning as she hunted for each letter on the tiny keypad. It was taking forever, and she didn't know why anyone would ever text instead of calling, but she finally finished texting the thing that mattered most. *Thank you for making me feel safe. Sully*

His phone chimed, and as he read her text, those muscles in his jaw bunched again, but when he looked up, those all-seeing eyes were thoughtful. "You're welcome."

He held her gaze for so long, the butterflies she'd thought were gone fluttered to life.

"You don't have to sign your name. It's programmed into the phone and comes up on the other person's phone when you send a text or make a call." His lips curved up. "But I'd know it was you even if it didn't."

"Oh." Was that a good thing? It felt like a good thing. Or maybe it was because nobody else worried about being safe, which might not be a good thing. Why was her heart racing? Pushing that nerve-racking thought aside, she said, "Thank you again. I'll just…" She motioned to the door. "Good night."

"Sweet dreams."

She went inside, locked the door, and leaned her back against it, closing her eyes and trying to calm her racing heart. Why was she nervous? She wasn't scared. In fact, she felt safer than she ever had. She didn't know why she felt like her heart might jump out of her chest, but she had a feeling it had something to do with not wanting the night to end, which was crazy *and* exhilarating. They were becoming friends, but she'd never felt like this around Ansel.

Or anyone else, for that matter.

Then again, she'd never known anyone like the gentle giant sitting vigil on her porch.

Chapter Five

COWBOY FINISHED SADDLING Sunshine and ran his hand over her thick coat. "How's my girl? Ready to make someone smile?"

Sunshine nuzzled against his sternum.

He'd never been so anxious to see a woman as he was to see Sully. He'd heard her moving around in the cabin on and off throughout the night and had debated sending a text to make sure she was okay. He'd wanted to help her feel at ease, but he had a feeling it would only make her uncomfortable. The more he thought about the glimpses into her life she'd given him last night, the more the name he'd memorized felt like the start of a hit list. Was fucking Rebel Joe the one who refused to let her walk around at night? Or was it her uncle? Where were her parents? What else had happened that had made her want to escape?

His questions were endless.

Stuffing them down deep, he mounted Sunshine and headed for Sully's cabin. Most of the cabins had two or three bedrooms. His parents had been smart to give her a single unit, rather than a cabin with a roommate, given how much of the night she'd spent awake.

As he neared her cabin, he spotted Sully sitting in a sliver of sunlight streaming through the umbrella of trees with her face tipped up toward the sun. Most of her hair was loose, but a thin braid ran down each side of her head. She looked so peaceful, he was about to pull the reins to keep from going any farther, but she looked over, and her eyes lit up—at him or Sunshine, he couldn't be sure, but it didn't matter. Her smile was heaven on earth. But that light dimmed as unsurety slid into place, and she scrambled to her feet, pushing up the sleeves of her light gray long-sleeve shirt. She was probably five foot seven or eight, and the bottoms of her jeans stopped about three inches shy of her leather boots. She looked great, but he wasn't sure if the too-short jeans were purposeful or not. Given that she'd arrived with only one small duffel bag, he had a feeling she might need some clothes. He didn't want to embarrass her by asking, so he made a mental note to pay attention.

"Mornin', darlin'. Your hair looks nice."

She blushed and touched one of her braids.

"You don't have to stop soaking in the sun on my account." He dismounted and walked Sunshine over to her.

"It's okay. I was just waiting for you." She watched him intently but not with the fear she'd come to them with. Her gaze was softer, as was her tone. "You brought Sunshine."

"I thought you might want to ride her up to the main house."

Her eyes widened. "I've never ridden a horse."

"I kind of assumed that since you said you'd never seen them up close. She's real gentle. Come say hello."

She walked over and stood beside him, holding out her hand, palm up, her eyes darting between him and the horse. He put his hand on her lower back to reassure her, and she looked at him gratefully. "I just want to be sure you feel safe."

"I know." Sunshine touched her nose to Sully's palm. Sully grinned up at him.

"She never forgets a friendly face."

"Can I pet her again?"

"Sure. She likes to be loved. Right, baby girl?"

Sunshine neighed softly and nuzzled against his sternum.

"That's so sweet," Sully said, petting Sunshine's neck.

"That's one of the ways horses give hugs. Sometimes they'll put their head on your shoulder. Want to try riding with me?"

"*Yes*, I'd really like to, but would it be okay if we did it another day? I'm a little nervous."

"It's all okay. We'll walk her up to the house."

"Should I bring anything to breakfast?"

"Just your cabin key and that beautiful smile."

Her cheeks pinked up again.

"Did you sleep okay?"

She nodded. "You?"

"Probably about as good as you did." He winked.

She bit her lower lip. "I've never been a very good sleeper."

"Maybe that'll change now that you're here."

"I hope so. I have my key if you're ready to go."

"A'righty."

As he turned toward the road, she said, "The map shows a trail through the woods that goes to a field by the main house. Can we go that way, or is it too hard for Sunshine?"

"That's a walking path. It's cleared. She'll be fine on it." They crossed the road and headed up the path through the woods. "I guess your navigational skills are solid after all."

"I'm an early riser. I had a lot of time to study the information in the packet and the map. I read about the types of clients that come here for help and that most of them live and work here as part of their therapy."

"That's right. We've found that having a sense of purpose helps with all types of healing, and working on the ranch gives them that. It gives them something to focus on, excel at, and be proud of, and living on-site offers a variety of benefits. They have access to their therapists and can focus on healing instead of worrying about the headaches of daily life." They followed the trail around a boulder. "And the reason we try to eat together is for support. Many of the people who come here have lost touch with their families, and being around other people who have also gone through life-changing circumstances, where they won't be judged or treated differently, helps. We often become the only family our clients have, and when they leave here to build their lives, they know they'll never be alone again. They'll always have us. That way, when hard times hit, like if they're going to be alone on a holiday, they know they can come back and spend it with us, so it doesn't hinder their recovery."

"That's pretty amazing. Your family sounds incredible."

"It's not just our family. It's the other therapists and all the other people who work here and our benefactors who donate to the ranch and allow our programs to exist."

"And do all of them do therapy in the main building and then work with the horses?"

"They work with the horses or around the ranch, and they all have therapy in the main house, with the exception of Dare's clients. He holds therapy sessions outdoors, working side by side with his clients as they talk."

"Do any of the other therapists do that?"

"No. The rest of them work in their offices. Dare is a brilliant therapist. He's helped a lot of people, but he wouldn't do well trapped in an office. He's got too much energy, and he mostly works with teenagers and belligerent clients. From what he says, it's easier to get them to talk when they're focusing on something else."

As they followed the path through a group of trees, she said, "That makes sense. I helped teach some of the little kids on the compound, and it was always easier if they didn't realize they were being taught."

"So, you had a school on the compound?"

"Yes, and my best friend Ansel's mom, Gaia, made sure he and I never missed a day. I don't have a diploma or anything, but Gaia said I could take a test and get one if I ever got off the compound."

"She's right. You can get your GED. It must have been hard to leave your best friend."

"It was," she said softly as they came out of the woods at the field.

"Do you miss him?"

She nodded and blinked rapidly, as if she were trying not to cry.

He bit back the emotions clawing at him. "I'm sure he misses you, too. I'm sorry for upsetting you."

"You didn't. He was like a brother to me. We grew up together and talked about everything. I can still see his face the day I left. He had a seizure when he was born, and I don't really know what happened, but one side of his mouth is paralyzed, and he has a clumsy hand. But he has the cutest crooked smile, and the day I left, his shaggy brown hair *almost* hid the tears in his eyes."

"Aw, man. Poor guy sounds like he was heartbroken."

"It was hard to leave him, but I pretended not to notice his tears. He was always more emotional than me, and he hated that almost as much as his clumsy hand. I'd give anything to see that adorable smile one more time, but I couldn't stay there."

Cowboy clenched his jaw to keep from asking why she couldn't stay on the compound, because he couldn't guarantee he wouldn't lose his shit if the answer was anything like the assumptions going through his mind.

As they came out of the woods, she pointed to the massive stone, wood, and glass building. "Is *that* the main house?"

"Yeah. That's it."

"It's huge. Everything here is so pretty and well kept."

"We take care of things we love. This property has been in my family for generations, and hopefully it'll be here for many more."

"I can help take care of it. I'm stronger than I look, and as I mentioned last night, I want to earn my keep."

Most people who had been through something traumatic would just be thankful for a safe place to stay, but it was clear Sully wasn't like most people. "There's plenty of time to figure that out. I'm going to put Sunshine in a paddock on the other side of the building. I'll be back in one minute."

"Okay."

He walked Sunshine around to the paddock, and when he returned, Sully was standing with her face tilted up to the sun again, like she was starved for it. He had a feeling there were a lot of things the pretty little filly had missed out on. "Was your outdoor time restricted during the day, too?"

"Not really restricted, but we had strict schedules that we followed."

"Were you ever free to do as you wished?"

She shook her head, shrugging one shoulder, and lowered her eyes.

Fucking bastards. His hands curled into fists, readying for a fight he couldn't have. He took her chin between his index finger and thumb, lifting her face so he could see her eyes. "I want you to do me a favor. Make a list of all the things you wanted to do and couldn't."

Her brows knitted. "Why?"

"Because I'm going to make damn sure you get to do every one of them."

She stared at him in disbelief and, if he was reading her right, a little mistrust.

He brushed his thumb over her jaw, wishing he could take that mistrust away. "I'm not *them*, Sully. I'm not going to ask anything of you or take anything from you or pretend to be someone I'm not for my personal gain. I just want you to be happy and have access to all the things you want and deserve."

She swallowed hard. "If that's true, then I've never met anyone like you."

"There are a lot of good people in this world, and I'm about to introduce you to some of the best. It might be a little loud and overwhelming, but I'll be right by your side. And just so you know, only the Dark Knights and my mother know where you came from and how you got out. None of the other residents or staff know. My sisters and Dare's fiancée don't know either. That's your private business, and we aren't taking any chances with word getting out."

Relief washed over her features. "Thank you. What should I say if someone asks?"

"Whatever you'd like. But the people here know not to

poke around in other people's backgrounds, so don't be surprised if nobody asks pointed questions. They're more likely to treat you like they've known you forever, and it's just another day on the ranch."

"Okay."

They headed inside. The foyer led directly into a two-story recreation room with several couches, chairs, game tables, bookshelves, and a stone fireplace. A second story ran around the perimeter of the room, and the din of the breakfast crowd floated in from the dining area to their right. Cowboy spotted his parents and Simone at the buffet. Dare and Billie were sitting with Sasha and Doc at one of the enormous farmhouse-style tables along with Hyde and a few of the other ranch hands and men and women currently going through their programs. Doc's black Lab, Mighty, was meandering through the room.

Cowboy felt Sully tense up beside him, and he put his hand on her back, giving her his full attention. "It's okay. Just breathe." Her eyes seemed to say *I'm trying*. In an effort to distract her from her worries, he said, "This is the recreation room. Staff residences and rooms for our younger clients are on the second level. Down the hall to our left are meeting rooms and offices, and to our right, past the noisy breakfast bunch, is the kitchen, the movie room, and more offices and meeting rooms."

"It's beautiful in here, and something smells delicious," she whispered.

"Dwight's an amazing cook. Are you ready to meet everyone?"

"Not really," she whispered. "But I will."

"We can take a minute if you need it. Do you want to go back outside?"

She shook her head. "I'll be okay."

He leaned closer and lowered his voice. "You single-handedly escaped a bad situation with a powerful enough group that you need protecting. I've got a feeling there's nothing you can't handle."

She blinked those long lashes, squaring her shoulders like she was readying for battle. "You're right. I wanted a normal life, and this is where it starts."

"Attagirl. A few mouthy cowboys should be a walk in the park."

The din quieted as they walked into the dining area, and all eyes turned to Sully. She inched closer to Cowboy. His gaze moved over their curious faces, and hell if Hyde and Taz—a crazy-ass Aussie and the fastest ranch hand he'd ever known—weren't drinking her in. The two had been known to share women, and Cowboy wasn't letting Sully anywhere near their wolf dens.

His hands fisted, as *back off* snarled through his head.

He'd never had such a visceral reaction toward someone he'd only just met. It wasn't right, and it sure as fuck wasn't rational, but he could no sooner shut it down than he could stop himself from casting threatening glares in their direction. That's when he noticed Dare's quizzical expression, causing him to check himself, and *holy hell.* They weren't drinking Sully in. They were looking at her with warmth and concern. What the hell was wrong with him? Those men were his brothers. They'd been at the club meeting. They knew what she'd been through, and they'd never disrespect her any more than he would.

I'm a damn idiot.

He cleared his throat. "Hey, everyone. This is Sully. She's staying with us for a while."

There was a round of *Hello*s and *Nice to meet you*s, and then they fell back into their typical loud morning banter. Sully had inched so close to Cowboy, he decided to skip individual introductions for now. "Why don't we grab some food?"

They headed to the buffet, where his parents were getting breakfast. His mother handed Sully a plate. "Good morning, Sully. How are you, sweetheart?"

"Good, thank you," Sully said as Mighty bounded over to greet them.

"Wonderful. Enjoy your breakfast, and we'll chat afterward," his mother said.

"Okay, thank you." She reached down to pet Mighty, and Mighty put his nose in her crotch.

"*Mighty*," Cowboy snapped, and the dog backed off. "Sorry. He's one of Doc's pets."

"It's okay. I like dogs."

"G'morning, little lady," Tiny said as he loaded up his plate. "Was the cabin okay for you last night?"

"Yes, sir," she said.

"We go by first names here. You can call me Tiny." He eyed Mighty as the dog started to sniff her again, and in a gruffer tone, he said, "Doc, come get your wingman," and headed over to a table.

Doc pushed to his feet. "I don't need a wingman. But you've got to admit, he's got good taste." He nodded at Sully and called his dog. Mighty trotted over to him. "Sorry about that, Sully. Better grab some food before Cowboy eats it all."

"Go ahead, darlin', fill your plate." Cowboy stepped back as she perused the buffet.

His mother sidled up to him, speaking quietly. "You okay, honey? You look a little tense."

"Just worried about her with all these people. Maybe we should've come up later."

"It's helpful for her to be surrounded by good people and see that we're more than just workers."

"But she doesn't *know* anyone."

"She will. Stand down, sweetheart, and trust the process."

"I do, but there's something else that's bugging me." He whispered, "She looks a lot like the age-progression pictures of that missing girl. But she said she lived with her uncle, so she can't be. It's just not sitting right with me."

"I see some similarities, but they're not striking. I know you want her to have something better than she had, a family she can count on, but don't get your hopes up for that kind of miracle."

"I'm not."

"I've been meaning to ask if you've confirmed movie night with the Boy Scouts yet." He hosted events for the Boy Scouts a few times a year.

"Yeah. I sent Maya a text with the date." Maya Martinez was their office manager.

"Good job. I'll let you get your breakfast."

His mother headed over to a table, and he went to the buffet and began piling food on his plate. As Sully stepped away with barely any food on hers, he said, "Hold up, darlin'. That's not enough sustenance for a bird." He took the plate from her and began putting more food on it.

"*Callahan*," Sully complained.

"There's no use fighting him," Simone warned. "Hi, I'm Simone, and I work with Cowboy. He used to do the same thing to me. He obviously ate too many Wheaties as a kid, and now he's stuck feeding all those muscles, and he thinks everyone needs to eat just as much. He's made it his mission to make sure we're stuffed to the gills. At this point I think it's part of his love language."

Sully looked curiously between them, a smile playing on her lips.

"Hey, Cowboy," Hyde said as he walked up to the coffee area. "I ate all my breakfast. Do you love *me* the most?"

Cowboy glowered at him, and laughter rang out. He cocked a brow at Simone. "Love language? Is that what they're teaching you at counseling school? Go eat your breakfast before it gets cold."

"Maybe I like cold food." Simone leaned closer to Sully, speaking conspiratorially. "You can slip the extra biscuit to Mighty under the table."

SULLY LAUGHED SOFTLY as Simone sauntered away. She liked the auburn-haired girl, and she could tell Callahan did, too, by his mildly amused expression, as he handed her a plate with more food on it than she could eat in a day.

"Hi, Sugar! I'm getting a muffin!" a little curly-haired boy shouted as he ran into the dining room, followed by a dark-haired man with deeply tanned skin and a petite brunette wearing skintight exercise shorts and a cropped sweatshirt.

"Good morning, Gusto!" a pretty blonde called out from one of the tables.

"Cowboy!" The little boy bolted toward them, and the adults who'd followed him in headed for Tiny. "You didn't eat all the blueberry muffins again, did you? Last time I had to eat the corn muffin. *Blech.*"

"Not yet, little man," Callahan said. "Do you want one?"

The little boy nodded emphatically, curls bouncing around his face as Callahan handed him one of three muffins he had on his plate.

"Thanks!" The little boy turned twinkling brown eyes up to Sully. "Hi. I'm Gus. What's your name? Do you like muffins?"

His eagerness tugged at her heart. She'd been in such an emotional frenzy since she'd left the compound, she hadn't slowed down enough to realize how much she missed the children that lived there, until now. She crouched to look him in the eyes. "Hi. I'm Sully, and I do like muffins."

"Here." He thrust his muffin in her direction.

"Thank you, but I already have one. See?" She pointed to the muffin on her plate.

"Okay!" Gus darted away, shouting, "Mighty!"

The petite brunette hurried over with the dark-haired guy she'd walked in with. She grabbed Callahan's arm. "Hey. You have to come by the shop. I met the perfect woman for you."

Callahan and the dark-haired man shared a glance Sully couldn't read, and Callahan said, "Birdie—"

"Just *listen*…"

"Hi, Sully, I'm Ezra, the mini-tornado's father," the dark-haired man said, drawing her attention away from Callahan and the brunette, who she realized was his sister.

"Hi. It's nice to meet you. Gus is adorable."

"Thanks. He keeps me on my toes." Ezra grinned. "I'm a therapist here, and Gus and I live on the property, so I'm sure we'll see you around. I'd better go after him before he gets Mighty riled up, but I wanted to introduce myself."

"I'm glad you did."

As he walked away, Callahan said, "Birdie, *stop.*"

"Way to appreciate your own personal matchmaker," Birdie said with an eye roll.

"Birdie, this is Sully. Sully's new here," he explained. "Sully, this is my sister Birdie. The one who I said would talk your ear off."

"Ain't that the truth," Birdie said cheerily. She looked much younger than Callahan, and the difference in their personalities was night and day. "Hi. It's nice to meet you." She eyed Sully's plate. "Let me guess. My brother piled that food on your plate."

"*Birdie,*" he warned.

"What? You gave her enough food for three people. It's no wonder you're single. You can't do that when I set you up. Women like to be in control of their own bodies."

"You're *not* setting me up."

"Watch me!" Birdie plucked a piece of sausage from his plate and took a bite, then pointed the remaining piece at Sully. "I love your hair, and I look forward to getting to know you, but I have to go to a yoga class. I just came in to get food to eat on the way." She snagged a biscuit and another sausage from Callahan's plate and hurried out the door.

Sully touched her hair. She'd been a little self-conscious of it after leaving the cult. She'd always wished she could cut it, but she hadn't been allowed, and now it felt like a chain to her past. But she'd taken a long, hot shower this morning and had used incredible-smelling lavender shampoo that made her hair less frizzy, and not only had Callahan noticed, but Birdie, too? She'd definitely be using that shampoo again. "She's kind of a whirlwind, isn't she?"

"She's something like that," he said with a shake of his head. "Welcome to the mayhem. Let's go find a seat."

There were so many people, and they all seemed to be talking at once. She was nervous about sitting with strangers. Callahan was scanning the tables, and she hoped he was looking for two empty seats near each other, as she was.

"Sully," a pretty girl with long dark hair called out from across the room as she pushed to her feet beside Dare, who was shoveling food into his mouth. "I'm Billie, Dare's better half. I'm done eating, so you can have my seat next to Sasha." The pretty blonde beside her, who had called out to Gus, waved.

Sasha. Callahan's other sister. Sully looked at him, and he nodded. As they headed over to the table, she noticed him staring at Dare.

Dare cocked his head. "Really, dude?"

Callahan's eyes narrowed.

Dare uttered a curse and pushed to his feet. "Guess I'm done, too."

The guys around him laughed as Dare and Billie carried their dishes toward the kitchen. Sully was relieved to know she'd be sitting with Callahan, but she felt bad for Dare.

"Hi. I'm Cowboy's sister Sasha." Sasha smiled up at Sully, as did the men and women sitting around her. "I run the rehab barn and nurse our horses back to health."

"Hi. I'm Sully." Callahan pulled out a chair for her, and as she sat down, she realized no one had ever done that for her before.

He set his plate on the table beside her. "Do you want coffee?"

"No, thank you."

"Water? Juice?"

"Juice would be great, but I can get it." She started to stand, but he placed his hand on her shoulder and said, "I've got it."

She wanted to tell him she'd get it herself, but everyone was watching them. Her stomach sank with disappointment *in* herself as she relented. "Okay, thanks."

As he walked away, Sasha asked quietly, "Are you okay?"

"Yes. I just...I don't need to be waited on." She didn't know exactly why it was so important to her to do things for herself, but it was.

"Then get up and tell him," Sasha said firmly. "He can't read your mind, and he thinks he's helping."

Sully remembered what Callahan had said about women's opinions mattering and hoped he was telling the truth as she got up. She tried to ignore her pinging nerves and the eyes she felt watching her as she went to him. He was filling a glass with orange juice. "Callahan?"

"Oh, hey, darlin'."

"I can get my own juice, thank you."

He cocked a brow. "It's just juice."

"I know to you and probably everyone else in here it's just juice. But to me, it's..." She scrambled for the right word. "It's part of breaking free and being independent. I really appreciate your kindness, but I need to do this, even if you think it's silly."

"I don't think it's silly. I respect the hell out of you for it. Glasses are over there." He nodded toward the tray of clean glasses.

Relief swept through her, and as he walked away with the juice he'd poured, Sasha gave her a thumbs-up. Sully filled with pride. She'd craved respect for as long as she could remember from men she'd known her whole life and had never earned it from any of them other than Ansel, and she'd somehow managed to earn the respect of Callahan Whiskey with one nerve-racking sentence. He couldn't know the magnitude of the gift he'd just given her.

Wait. That wasn't right.

The gift I've just given myself, she corrected. She poured a glass of juice and headed back to the table feeling like there was nothing she couldn't handle.

Chapter Six

AFTER A LOUD and overwhelming, but still enjoyable, breakfast, during which Sully had a nice conversation with Sasha and was introduced to more people than she could possibly remember, Callahan showed her around the rest of the main house and left her to meet with Wynnie in her office. But Wynnie had been called away to speak with another therapist, leaving Sully alone with her thoughts.

Of which she had far too many.

What happens next? What if they decide not to let me stay? and *Where will I go?* were on the top of that list. The Whiskeys had already done more than she could have hoped for. Carol and Chester had said that Wynnie could help her but that she needed to be honest about what she'd been through. That had Sully even more nervous, and on top of that, she didn't know what kind of help she needed. How did a person start a new life with nothing to her name?

She sat on the sofa, worrying with her hands, her heart and mind racing as she looked around the sunny office. Several pictures of Callahan and his siblings decorated the blue-gray walls. There were only a few in which Callahan wasn't wearing a cowboy hat, but he was easy to spot among his siblings. Not only was his hair lighter than his brothers', but even as a little boy, his features and demeanor were all his own. Doc was taller and lankier, and Dare had an unmistakable mischievousness about him, while Callahan's body language and serious expression made him look like he was trying to hold down the fort in every picture, except the ones where he was on a horse. In those he was grinning and looked at ease.

She studied a picture of Callahan and Birdie on a horse. She was sitting in front of him, and he looked to be about fourteen or fifteen, while Birdie couldn't have been more than six or seven. He had one arm wrapped around her, and her face was tilted up, looking at him like he was her hero. Sully thought about his short conversation with Birdie before breakfast and wondered about Callahan's personal life. He was handsome and kind. Surely he had lots of women chasing after him. So why did Birdie feel the need to set him up?

An unfamiliar knot formed in her stomach, and she forced her gaze away from the picture, her attention catching on a photo of Wynnie sitting behind Tiny on a motorcycle. Sully went to take a closer look at the couple behind Redemption Ranch. They were much younger in the photo, around Sully's age. Even back then, Tiny had an imposing appearance in his dark T-shirt and black leather vest. His hair and beard were long, bushy, and dark. He had one hand on the handlebar, the other on Wynnie's leg. Wynnie's blond hair hung well past her shoulders. She wore a denim jacket, jeans, and cowgirl boots. Tiny's expression was as serious as Callahan's was much of the time, as if they carried everyone else's troubles on their shoulders, while Wynnie was smiling brightly. They looked like a cloud and its silver lining.

"Sorry that took so long," Wynnie said as she breezed into the office.

Sully spun around. "Sorry, I was just looking at your pictures."

"Oh, honey, there's no need to apologize. That's what they're there for." She glanced thoughtfully at the picture. "That was taken shortly after Tiny and I met."

"Did you meet here?" Sully asked, noticing Wynnie was dressed similarly to her younger self in the picture, in a pretty blue blouse, jeans, and boots.

"Not on the ranch, but in Hope Valley, at the Roadhouse bar, which Billie's parents own now. I'd just graduated from college, and I was celebrating with my sister and friends, and in walks this big hunk of a man with long dark hair and eyes that hit me like a bolt of lightning. He walked right over to me and said, 'Hey there, darlin'. I'm Tiny Whiskey, and I'm going to be the last man you ever go out with.'"

"That's a little scary," Sully said carefully.

"That's exactly what I said. But then he said that what he meant was if I went on one date with him—*one date*—I'd never want to go out with anyone else. And if I'd agree to go on a date with him, if he was wrong about my feelings, he'd never bother me again."

"Sounds like he was really confident."

"Oh yes, he was, and rightly so, it turned out. I was curious and wildly attracted to him, so I agreed to go out on one date. But he was a big man, and that made me a little nervous, so I told him he had to meet my father, and we had to go someplace public. It was summertime, and he picked me up on his motorcycle. I kid you not, Sully, when I climbed on the back of that bike and put my arms around him, I had two thoughts.

The first was that we felt like a puzzle that fit together perfectly."

"I can't imagine knowing something with such certainty so
fast. What was your second thought?"

"I hoped I wouldn't die." She laughed.

"On the motorcycle or by his hand?"

"Oh, honey, that was a joke, and not a good one. I'm sorry.
I was nervous about riding the motorcycle because I had never
been on one before, but I have never once worried that Tiny
would physically hurt me. I did have a sliver of worry about
what it would be like to be *out* with him. He was much rougher
around the edges than the other young men I'd gone out with,
and as you've seen, he's gruff and tells it like it is. But that night
I learned that he was all heart. I had gone out with plenty of
young men in college, and none of them treated me as well as
Tiny did. With him, I felt like a queen. Not that he had much
money, or bought me presents. He didn't need those things.
His love was more precious than anything money could buy."

Sully had gone her entire adult life without crying. Why did
that story make her choke up? "That's beautiful."

"It is, isn't it? I can't imagine my life without him."

"And you've been together for all these years?"

"That's right. My father owned this ranch at the time. It
was only a horse rescue back then, and when Tiny found out I
was sticking around the area and going to graduate school in the
fall, he got a job on the ranch and put a ring on my finger a few
months later."

"That was fast."

"It was, and I have no regrets. Don't get me wrong. We
argue like any healthy couple, but loving relationships are built
on communication, compromise, and understanding. I don't

want to imagine a day when I don't wake up with that burly tattooed man beside me, and when I think about how much we've accomplished as a team and all the people we've helped, it blows me away."

"I've never known anyone who was in love like that." She thought of the Finches, and she was sure they loved each other, but their love felt different from what Wynnie had described, and she hadn't seen them holding hands or kissing at all.

"You do now. You know us, and you met Dare and Billie. They've been in love since they were kids. It took their stubborn hearts forever to figure that out, but true love always finds a way." She motioned to the sofa. "Would you like to sit down and chat?"

"Sure." Sully sat down, her questions nagging at her. "I really appreciate you letting me stay here, but I'd like to earn my keep in some way."

"I understand how important that is to you, and we will talk about that." She grabbed a notebook and pen and sat in an armchair. "But first I'd like to go over a few things, like what I do here and how I can help you, and see how you feel about it." She went on to explain that she was a licensed psychologist, that everything Sully said would remain confidential, and that she'd been helping people overcome traumatic experiences for thirty years. She explained that therapy was different for everyone and that some people met with her daily, others less often. She suggested they meet daily until they both had a grasp on what she'd been through and how Wynnie could best help her.

"I wasn't sure what kind of help you were offering, but I hadn't realized therapy was part of it."

"Therapy can help you feel like you've escaped quicksand and found dry land, but it is hard work. It can unearth feelings and experiences you might have buried because of how thinking about them made you feel."

"Then why dredge any of it up?"

"Because burying something within ourselves allows it to fester like a wound that never heals. Even if you're unaware of it, subconsciously you're always fighting to keep it at bay and living in fear of it. Those things we bury always rear their ugly heads, and we often don't understand that *that's* what's happening. I've seen past hurts ruin relationships and entire lives. That's why I recommend facing those things head-on with a professional, so you can work through your feelings and learn to move forward without harboring fears or holding on to misplaced emotions. Does that sound like something you're interested in doing?"

Sully pressed her hands into her thighs. "It sounds nerve-racking, but I think about everything I've been through all the time, and finding a way not to would be a blessing."

"A big part of successful therapy is wanting it to work, so I'm sure we'll get there. It won't be easy, and there might be days when you want to crawl into bed and not get out, but you're not alone in this anymore, and we'll figure it out together."

If she only knew that crawling into bed also scared Sully. She'd had a recurring nightmare on and off for as long as she could remember, and it always rattled her.

"Before we get started, how are things going with Cowboy? Are you comfortable around him?"

Warmth spread through her chest. "Yes, I am. Leaving the Finches was scary, and I was leery of where I was going and who everyone was. But he and I talked last night, and I don't feel that way anymore. He seems honest and kind, and he told me all about the work you do here. I hope you can help me find my way, too."

"I'm glad to hear that. If you ever feel uncomfortable with him or anyone else, you let me know, okay? And don't worry. Whatever you tell me will not go any farther than this room."

She nodded. "Okay. I will."

"I'd like to start by getting to know you. I realized that I don't even know how old you are or when your birthday is."

"I'm twenty-five, and my birthday is January thirteenth."

"Great. Did you grow up on the Free Rebellion compound?"

"Yes."

"And what about your family? Did they live there, too?"

"Only my uncle, but he died a few years ago."

"I'm sorry to hear that. What was his name?"

"Richard Tate."

"How about your parents? Where do they live?"

"I've never met them. My uncle didn't know who my father was, and he said my mother couldn't afford to raise me, so she asked him to."

"How old were you when you went to live with your uncle?"

"I don't know. I don't remember ever living with my mother."

"Do you know her name or where she lives?"

"Her name is Allison, and I know she lived out West, but I'm not sure where."

"I see. Well, this is a good start." She jotted something in the notebook. "You got a good dose of our noisy group this morning at breakfast, and I know we can be a lot to take in. How was that for you? Was it overwhelming, or was it similar to how meals were handled at the compound?"

"It was a little overwhelming, but everyone was really nice, and it was nothing like where I grew up. Meals were never like that."

"In what ways were they different?"

Determined to be honest, she said, "In every way, right down to who made breakfast." Callahan had introduced her to Dwight, the cook and residential manager. "Our mealtimes were quieter, and men didn't cook or do dishes, and they didn't joke with women the way people here do."

"How did you feel about that when you lived there?"

"I was okay with it, I guess. I didn't have a lot to talk about anyway."

"I'd love to hear more about what your life was like. Did you have your own room in your house? Did you have friends?"

"I've never lived in a proper house. My uncle and I lived in an old camper, and when I turned ten, I moved into one of the girls' dorms, which were in bigger trailers, and we all slept in one big room."

"How many girls stayed there?"

"All the girls who were ten and older. We had cots and shared dressers."

Wynnie wrote something down. "How did you feel about that?"

"Good and bad. I liked being around other girls, but I never felt like I fit in with them."

"In what way?"

Every way. "I don't know. They were always so *good*, like they were born knowing how to behave."

"What does that mean to you, to behave?"

"To listen and do as you're told. It took me a long time to

learn how to do that, and I got punished a lot. I just couldn't stop myself from acting out, and I didn't understand why the other girls weren't fighting against some of the rules."

"What kind of rules?"

"We weren't supposed to talk back or get dirty or do anything too loud, and we always had schedules to follow. I wasn't good at holding back my opinions."

"It sounds like you were a strong-willed child. There's nothing wrong with that. Did you *want* to be like them and follow the rules?"

Sully swallowed hard, reaching deep to say the truth. "No. But I knew I had to."

"Why?"

"Because I got punished a lot, even before I moved into the dorms, and the only way not to get punished was not to break the rules. But it was a hard lesson for me to learn."

"Strong people are not silenced easily, nor should they be. Do you remember how old you were when you learned to conform?"

She shrugged. "Maybe about a year after I moved into the dorms."

Wynnie wrote something down. "How were you punished?"

Memories pummeled her, and she struggled to answer, mentally picking through the punishments and leaving the worst of them out. "If I refused to do a chore, I might get slapped or yelled at, and if I cried or spoke back, I was spanked or banished from activities and made to do extra chores for hours on end." Anger she'd had to hide all those years burned in her stomach. She pressed her hands into her thighs, trying not to let that anger show.

"I'm sorry, honey. That must have been very difficult. I'm

curious about who did the punishing. Was it your uncle?"

"Not always. We had group leaders for tasks, and they were the ones who punished us."

"I see, and were the group leaders men and women?"

"Yes, but the women punished differently than the men."

"How so?"

"The women would usually just give us extra chores. The men were more physical."

Her brows slanted, but her gaze softened. "Did the men ever touch you sexually as a punishment?"

She could still feel Rebel Joe's rough hands on her, the weight of his body pressing down on her. Bile rose in her throat, and she struggled to swallow against it. "No. Not as a punishment." Her hands curled into fists, and she put them under her thighs, bracing for the conversation she was sure would follow.

"That's good. We'll come back to that," Wynnie said gently.

That brought a hint of relief, but she knew it was only delaying the inevitable.

"Do you think they were right to use physical punishments?"

"*No.* I wanted to hit them back."

A pained smile appeared, and Wynnie reached out and patted her hand. "I hope you realize just how strong you are for not losing your fighting spirit as you suffered through that."

"My fighting spirit is what led to the punishments."

"Your fighting spirit is what allowed you to save yourself and escape, and that same fierceness will help you work through the trauma you've experienced and learn how to cope with it, so you can move forward and build a life that *you* are fully in control of. A life where *you* decide who and what you will let into your inner circle."

"I want that so bad" burst out like it had been trapped for years.

"You're *already* on the right path and making those decisions. Do you realize that?"

As she nodded, the realization brought the burn of tears she refused to let fall. She focused on a spot on the floor, willing the feeling to pass.

"If this is too difficult, we can take a break," Wynnie said compassionately.

"It *is* hard, but I know I have to tell someone so you'll understand why I don't want to go back."

"Honey, you don't have to tell anyone anything you don't want to, and we will still make sure you never go back."

Don't cry don't cry don't cry. "Thank you."

They talked about her schooling and what her days were like, and Sully told her about Ansel and how much she missed him.

"Was he your boyfriend?" Wynnie asked.

"No. It wasn't like that."

"Have you ever had a boyfriend or a girlfriend?"

Sully shook her head. "I wasn't allowed."

"Would you have wanted one if you were allowed? Was there a boy or girl you were interested in in that way?"

"No." *All I wanted was to get out.*

"Did other girls your age have boyfriends or girlfriends?"

"Yes, boyfriends. Being with girls wasn't allowed."

"Why were other girls allowed to have boyfriends if you weren't?"

Sully lowered her eyes, feeling a pang of shame that she knew wasn't warranted, but it was still there. "Because I belonged to Rebel Joe, and some of the other girls didn't."

"Some of them? Does that mean there were others that belonged to him?"

"Yes, several."

"And were they your age?"

"Some were younger, some older." Her chest burned with disgust.

"I see, and what does it mean to belong to him?"

She forced herself to meet Wynnie's gaze. "It meant nobody else could touch me."

"But he could?"

She nodded, sickened by her admission.

"Do you remember how old you were when you became his?"

"He claimed me when I was ten, but he didn't touch me...*that way*...until I was sixteen."

"He waited a long time. Do you know if that was typical for him? Or were there reasons he waited longer to be with you?"

"He waited with all of us. There were rumors that sixteen was the age of consent, but I don't know if that's true."

She noted something in her pad. "How old is Rebel Joe?"

"I'm not sure, maybe in his forties."

Wynnie looked like that bothered her as much as it bothered Sully. "Do you have any children?"

"No. Ansel's mother is a midwife, and she secretly gave me and a couple of other girls birth control shots so we wouldn't get pregnant."

"Ansel's mother sounds like a guardian angel. What is her name?"

Tears threatened again. *Nonono.* "Gaia. She was like a mother to me. My uncle loved me, and he hugged me sometimes and told me bedtime stories when I was little, but Gaia treated me like she treated Ansel and his sister, Emina. She was *always* hugging us and telling us how great we were. She was the one who helped me learn how to stay out of trouble."

"She sounds wonderful. How did Rebel Joe react when you didn't get pregnant?"

"He drank more and said mean things. Sometimes he was rougher when we had sex. But he had a lot of girls, and most of them got pregnant."

"Honey, I need to ask you a difficult question, and you don't have to answer if it makes you too uncomfortable, but it will help me to understand what you've been through. Did you want to be with him, or were you forced?"

Shame engulfed her like a wave of fire. "I didn't want to be with him, but it was expected of me. If he claims you, it's your job to service him, so I went willingly to avoid being punished."

Wynnie put her notebook down and came to sit beside her on the couch. She took Sully's hand, holding it between both of hers. "Sully, when you don't *want* to be with someone and you do it to avoid punishment, that's being forced, and it *is* a form of rape. That man had no right to touch you."

Hearing what she'd always known to be true from someone other than Gaia and Ansel brought a rush of emotions and tears she didn't want to let fall. She looked away, fighting against them with everything she had, but a few broke free. She swiped angrily at them, and Wynnie handed her tissues from a box on the coffee table. "I *know*. I'm so ashamed for being too weak to refuse."

"You are *not* weak, Sully. You are unbelievably strong and incredibly smart to have known at such a young age what you needed to do in order to survive and to get yourself out of there for good."

It took everything Sully had to drag air into her lungs and meet her gaze. "Thank you." She wiped her eyes, trying to regain control.

"What you went through is not your fault, and you can press charges against Rebel Joe and anyone else who hurt you, and they will be punished for what they've done."

"But it would be my word against them, and if they don't go to prison, they'll come after me."

"Based on the things you've just told me, I don't think there's any chance of that happening. Pressing charges would also stop those men from hurting other girls and help get the other girls out of there. That would also give you a level of control, so you don't have to live in fear of them finding you."

They talked about it for a long time, and Sully knew it was the right thing to do, but she never wanted to see them again, and despite Wynnie's assurances, she still worried that going after them could lead them to her, and *that* was terrifying. "Can I think about it?"

"Yes, of course. I think we've covered enough for one day, but I'd like to talk to you about seeing a doctor. Did you have regular medical and dental checkups on the compound?"

"Yes. Gaia did the medical checkups, and one of the members was a dentist."

"Good. I know you didn't want to see a doctor with the Finches because you were worried about the Free Rebellion finding out. Is that right?"

"Yes. Rebel Joe has connections with lots of people, including the police."

"I see. Well, we have a doctor who works for us, and I think it would be a really good idea if you would let her examine you and do some blood work. She's someone we trust, and she'll keep your information confidential. Young women's bodies go through so many changes. We want to be sure you're healthy, and she can speak with you about whether you'd like to continue using birth control and answer any questions you might have. Would that be okay?"

"Yes, if you trust her."

"I do. I also think we should do a DNA test. Do you know what that is?"

"Sort of."

"It's a test that can help determine who your family is. It could lead us to your mother and any other family members you might have."

Fear prickled Sully's skin. "What if Rebel Joe finds out you're looking for her?"

"He won't. The Dark Knights would do the investigating, and they have been working behind the scenes for decades. They're well versed in discretion."

"You don't understand," she said anxiously. "If he finds out where I am, he'll come get me."

"That is *not* going to happen. We'd never jeopardize your safety. There's no way anyone can get on our property without us knowing. We have men covering the perimeter, and we have security cameras as well. We're alerted if anyone crosses onto our land."

She wanted to believe her so badly.

"Would you like to find your mother? To see if you have a family?"

"I don't know. She didn't want me."

"I thought you said she couldn't afford to raise you."

"Yes, that's right."

"Honey, those are two very different things. If she couldn't afford to raise a baby, that's very different from not wanting her child. Her circumstances could have changed over the years, and you might even have brothers and sisters. Wouldn't it be nice to know? Family can be a big source of support."

Her stomach knotted. "How will you know if she's a good or bad person?"

"Let me explain how this would work. We would start with a DNA test, and hopefully that will help us figure out who your family is and where they are. From there, we'll do a complete background investigation and find out everything about your mother and any other family members, including if they have criminal records or a history of abuse or neglect. We also use a private investigator to find out what they do for a living, places they frequent, and who they associate with."

"What if she sends me back?"

"You're an adult, Sully, which means any and all decisions concerning you, including who is notified of the DNA results and your whereabouts, is *yours* to make, and yours alone. Nobody can send you anywhere."

Sully stared at her with disbelief, stunned into silence. Had she really gone from having no control to having it all?

Chapter Seven

COWBOY STRODE INTO the main house to talk with his mother and meet up with Sully late Sunday afternoon and nearly plowed into Doc on his way out. "Sorry, man."

"You okay? Word is you've got a hair up your ass today."

"I'm *fine*." He was far from fine, and yeah, he'd been a bit short-tempered because he couldn't stop thinking about Sully, imagining the worst for what she'd been through. He was worried about how her first therapy session had gone and whether she'd agreed to see a doctor. It didn't help that he was going to have to leave her alone to go to church Tuesday night. He knew she'd be safe with the extra security they'd put in place, but safe and comfortable were two very different things. He needed to find someone to check on her while he was at church, but it had to be the right person. Someone he trusted not to make her uncomfortable or to pry into her background.

"You don't seem fine," Doc said. "Anything I can help with?"

Yeah, help me find the motherfuckers who kept Sully trapped like an animal so I can find out what else they did to her and tear them apart. "No. Just got a lot on my mind."

"A'right. You want to grab a beer with me and Sasha after dinner?"

He thought about how well Sasha and Sully had hit it off over breakfast. Sasha was empathetic and knew better than to ask a lot of questions of the people who came to the ranch. She might be just who Sully needed while he was at church. "Not tonight. I want to stay close to Sully in case she needs anything."

"Another night, then."

Doc walked out, and Cowboy headed for his mother's office. She was just ending a call when he walked in. "Where's Sully?"

"Hi, honey, it's nice to see you, too," his mother said.

"Sorry, Mom. I'm just worried about her. Where is she?"

"Your father drove her down to her cabin."

Damn it. "I thought your text said I was supposed to meet her here."

"I told you to come here so I could speak with you first."

"Is something wrong? What did you find out?"

His mother patted his cheek. "Oh, my sweet protector, you know I can't tell you anything she and I talked about."

He clenched his teeth. "Mom, they wouldn't even let her take a fucking walk at night. I need to know what she's been through, because the awful shit in my head makes me want to kill someone."

"I'm sorry, honey, but if Sully wants to share her past with you or anyone else, that's up to her. Maybe we should sit down and talk about what's going on in *your* head."

"No. I'll be fine, but she *escaped.* You know damn well that means bad shit went down." His mother didn't nod or flinch or change her expression in any way. "At least tell me if she saw the doctor."

She gave him a *you know I can't do that* look. "I'd suggest you take a walk before you see her. She doesn't need to see you all riled up."

"Yeah, I know. Don't worry. I'd never make it harder for her. Do you see any reason not to ask Sasha to be there for her while I'm at church Tuesday night?"

"No. They got along well at breakfast. She might enjoy that."

"Okay. What did you want to talk to me about?"

"I know this duty your father has given you is Dark Knights' business, but you're still my boy, and I know how you carry other people's burdens as your own. I wanted to make sure you were okay with watching over her."

"Yeah, I am. She's a good person, and you know I'll do right by her."

"I know you will, honey."

"A'right, well, I'll head down to her place." He went for the door, then turned back. "Is there anything I can do or say to make things easier for her?"

"Just be a friend, and treat her how you treat your horses and everyone else who comes here."

Lead with admiration, not pity. That was the way they all did things around there.

With a nod, he headed out of her office and down to Sully's cabin. He found her sitting on the steps to the screened porch, hunkered down over a notebook. Her long hair fell over one shoulder, and her face was pinched in concentration.

"Working on that list I asked you for?"

She closed the notebook, and as their gazes met, a smile lifted her cheeks. "I didn't think you were serious about that."

"I was dead serious. Mind if I sit down?"

She shook her head and moved over, making room for him on the step beside her.

He sat down, itching to ask how her day had gone, but he didn't want to risk losing that smile. "Were you journaling?"

"No. Just drawing."

"Really? Can I see?"

"It's not very good."

"How about you let me be the judge of that?"

She looked down at the notebook, as if she were thinking about it. "You promise not to laugh?"

"Cross my heart."

She handed him the notebook, those beautiful blue eyes watching him intently as he opened it and admired an impeccable sketch of a little girl twirling in the grass. The lacy frills of her dress and her long hair lifted with her twirls, and her face was tipped up toward the sky. The level of detail was so fine, he could practically feel the warm breeze lifting her hair and the glee rising off the page.

"This is phenomenal. Where did you learn to draw like this?"

"Just practice, I guess. I've been drawing for as long as I can remember. Do you really think it's good?"

"Are you kidding?" he asked incredulously. "You're really talented, Sully. Is this you when you were little?"

She shook her head.

"Who is it?"

"Just someone I made up in my head."

"Then you've got a great imagination. Did you draw more of her?"

"Uh-huh, but I had to leave my old notebooks behind when

I left the compound. Carol gave me this one. I did draw this, though." She reached over and turned the page, revealing a picture of *him* riding Sunshine.

It was like looking in a mirror, only better, because it was made by her hands. "You drew this from memory?"

She nodded.

"Holy shit, Sully. You even got Sunshine's markings right. Do you have a photographic memory?" He sure as hell hoped not if she'd gone through anything like the awful shit he imagined.

"*No.*" She laughed softly. "They're not that good."

"Yes, they are. I've never known anyone who could draw like this. You could illustrate children's books. Hell, any books."

"No, I couldn't."

"Maybe we'll debate that during our walk tonight."

She looked surprised. "You wouldn't mind walking with me again?"

"It's a hardship, but I think I can handle it." He bumped her with his shoulder, and she smiled. "I'm heading down to talk with Sasha before dinner. Want to come with me and see the rehab horses?"

"I'd like that. Let me just put this inside and get my key."

He got up to open the door for her.

As she walked through, she said, "You're such a gentleman. You don't have to hold doors for me or pull out my chair. I'm not used to that."

"Welcome to the Whiskey world, darlin', where badass ranchers ride motorcycles and treat ladies right."

She blushed and went inside. Damn, he liked that blush. He couldn't remember the last time he'd actually seen a woman blush. It amplified Sully's sweetness, making her even more endearing.

When she came back out, they headed down to the barn. Cowboy waved to a few of the guys on their way down.

"That's Hyde and Taz, right?" she asked.

"Yeah, and the kid with them is Kenny. He's in high school. He went through our program with Dare, and now he works a couple of days a week after school and on the weekends, and he's learning to ride motocross with Billie."

"What's motocross?"

"It's an off-road motorcycle racing sport. The motorcycles are small, like souped-up bicycles. We have a course behind Dare's place, and he's getting ready to build another one so Billie can start teaching other kids how to ride. She used to be a professional racer back in the day."

"That's impressive. Why did she stop?"

"She and Dare and their best friend since childhood, Eddie, were the ultimate daredevils. They lost Eddie to a stunt gone wrong on a motocross bike several years ago, and it really messed Billie and Dare up for a long time."

"Oh my gosh, that's awful. No wonder she stopped. They both seem so confident and unflappable."

"They are, because they have each other now. But it took a long time to get there." He nodded toward the barn. "I should warn you that the rehab horses don't look anything like Sunshine and the other horses you saw last night. Some of them are severely emaciated, and others are working through injuries and surgeries. They can be withdrawn and timid."

"I assumed they'd be in bad shape from what you said last night."

"It can be shocking and hard to look at. I just want you to be prepared, and if it's too much for you, we'll leave."

"It won't be. I've seen bad things before."

Fuck. Of course you have. He stopped just before the entrance to the barn. "I'm sorry. I wasn't thinking. Maybe we shouldn't go in. I don't want to bring up bad memories for you."

"Callahan, I appreciate you trying to protect me, but I can handle seeing bad things. I might not have much to my name, but I have my confidence, and I'm trying hard to hold on to it. So I would appreciate it if you would treat me like you did this morning when you said I could handle anything."

"I'm sure you can. It's just that this is different. Seeing animals suffer is heartbreaking."

"I know it is. We had animals on the compound. Not horses, but we had dogs, and I saw two of them die, and cows and goats and chickens that we'd care for just so they could be slaughtered and used for food. I *get* it. But this place is the polar opposite of where I came from. You're helping animals and people heal, and I like that. I want to see the proof of that, and I need to see them when they're hurting, so I understand how they heal."

"*Shit*, Sully. I'm sorry. I tend to be a little overprotective. I'll try to keep that in check."

"That's all I'm asking. I'm overprotective of my independence right now, because I never want to be seen as the girl who can't fend for herself, so I guess we're both learning."

Yeah, they sure were. He'd probably been told to stop being overprotective hundreds of times, but this was one of the few times he'd actually listened. "I'll try to remember that from now on. And if I slip, you just slap me upside my head."

She grinned.

They went into the barn and were greeted by the familiar

scents of leather, horses, and *hope*. Sasha was working with a black mare they'd rescued about a month ago. Her hair was pinned up in a ponytail, and she wore jeans, a pink T-shirt, and as always, her maroon cowgirl boots. He tipped his chin. "Hey, Sash. How's it going?"

"Hi, you two. I'm just finishing Kelly's massage for her anxiety."

"Does it work?" Sully asked.

"Most definitely," Sasha said. "Just like with people, human touch can heal or hurt."

A shadow of something—*a bad memory?*—passed over Sully's face. "What happened to her?"

"Her owner was a selfish bastard who ate like a king and starved his horses." Sasha ran her hand down the horse's neck. "But Kelly is doing great other than her anxiety, and we're on top of that. She's going to be just fine."

"Did the owner get in trouble?" Sully asked.

"Yeah. Eighteen months in jail and fines that weren't nearly enough," Cowboy said.

"At least he's getting punished," Sully said. "Can I see the other horses?"

"Sure. I need to put Kelly in her stall anyway."

As Sasha walked Kelly back to her stall, Cowboy said, "Some of the horses can be skittish, and the ones with red stall handles can be aggressive, so don't get too close."

Sasha joined them, and they walked through the barn.

"Are all stalls metal?" Sully asked. "I don't know why I thought they'd be wood."

"Most are wood," Sasha said. "The metal slats allow us to see the horse's entire body, and for horses that are used to open spaces, it helps them feel less confined."

As they walked through the barn, Sasha told Sully about each of the horses and what they'd been through. Sully asked questions about how long each horse had been there and what their therapy had been like. Some of them were drawn to her, and as she petted them, the look of peace that came over her was a sight in and of itself.

"This is Thistle," Sasha said as they reached a chestnut mare's stall. "She came to us about two months ago with ligament and tendon damage."

"How do you fix that?" Sully asked, her eyes never leaving the horse.

"It depends on the extent of the damage, but in general it's a long process of rest, icing, and anti-inflammatories. It takes about three months for scar tissue to form and then several more months before the tissue reaches maximum strength." She went on to tell her about Thistle's rehab as they walked to the next stall, where a recent rescue was lying down. "This is Beauty, and in the next stall is her sister, Belle. As you can see by the sad shape they're in, they were severely neglected by their owner."

Pain rose in Sully's eyes. "You can see her ribs. Is she too weak to stand?"

"No, she can stand, but I think she's having a hard time *wanting* to," Sasha said.

"She only knows pain and neglect, and she doesn't trust people," Cowboy said.

Sully crouched to look through the bars. "Poor thing. Is that why she turned away when we walked over?"

"Yes," Cowboy said.

"We can usually connect with a neglected horse fairly quickly, but while her sister has interacted with us, Beauty has yet to voluntarily interact with anyone," Sasha added.

Sully pushed to her feet. "What will happen to her if she never interacts with people?"

"We're not going to let that happen. We won't give up on her," Sasha said. "It's just going to take some time to figure out what or who she'll respond to."

Doc came into the barn through the back doors. "Hey, sorry to interrupt. Sasha, Cowboy. You got a sec?"

Cowboy put his hand on Sully's lower back. "We'll only be a minute, okay?"

"Take your time. I'll be fine."

As they went to speak with Doc, Sasha said, "She's tough, huh? She sure took a stand with that juice this morning. What's her story? Mom said she got out of a bad situation."

Cowboy kept it simple. "Haven't most of the people who come here?"

"Yeah, I guess so."

She let it go at that, and as Doc updated them about a horse who had had surgery that morning, Cowboy glanced back at Sully. She was crouched in front of Beauty's stall, talking to the horse. He returned his attention to Doc, who was now wondering how the training was going with another horse they'd rehabbed.

"She's responding well," Cowboy said. "Hyde is taking over until I have more time during the day, but I think she'll be ready to rehome in a few weeks."

"Cool," Doc said. "I've got to get back, but I'll see you guys at dinner."

After Doc left, Cowboy turned to Sasha. "Think you can do me a favor Tuesday night and make yourself available for Sully while I'm at church? Maybe stop by to check on her or see if she wants to hang out or something?"

"Sure, but why are you watching her so closely? Is she a suicide risk or something?"

"No. She's just new, and you know how it is. Coming out of tough situations affects people differently. I want her to know she's not alone." He glanced at Sully again and couldn't believe his eyes. She was standing in front of Beauty's stall with her forehead touching the bridge of Beauty's nose, stroking the horse's cheek. "Holy hell, would you look at that?"

Sasha followed his gaze. "Holy hell is right. Is she some kind of horse whisperer?"

"I'm wondering the same thing."

They headed for Sully slowly, so as not to scare the horse, and as they neared, they heard her talking to Beauty.

"You're a strong girl, a survivor, and you're doing great. I'm so proud of you. You're going to get healthy and be running around with your sister in no time."

Cowboy and Sasha exchanged incredulous glances, and Sasha whispered, "Did you tell her about horses responding better to admiration than pity?"

"No." *But she's a survivor, too. She knows.* As the thought ran through his mind, he realized his earlier mistake, underscoring Sully's strength to have pointed it out to him in the first place. He vowed never to make that same mistake again.

Chapter Eight

MONDAY EVENING, SULLY sat in her cabin, drawing pictures of the places Callahan had shown her on their walk last night. Like the rope climbing course his father had built for Dare, Billie, and Eddie when they were kids, and the paintball field, which Callahan and his brothers had helped his father build and he and Sasha had recently expanded. She couldn't imagine having a father who went to those lengths for his children. She and Callahan had ended up sitting with Beauty after their walk, and he told her stories about the horses they'd rescued over the years. She loved his passion for the animals, and she liked spending time with him. There were no expectations or pretense. It was like being with Ansel only better, because there was something deep and introspective about Callahan. He didn't just listen to the things she said. She could tell by his facial expressions and body language that he thought about her responses. He was engaging and interesting in a way other men had never been, and then there was that entrancing thrum between them that seemed to get stronger with every conversation.

As she sketched a picture of Callahan sitting in Beauty's stall with her last night, she remembered the instant connection she'd felt with the horse yesterday afternoon. She understood the urge to shut everyone out after being mistreated. If she could've survived alone, she probably would have done the same thing after escaping the Free Rebellion. When she'd told Callahan that, his jaw had ticked, and he'd said he was glad she didn't. She was glad, too.

She was starting to understand more about the ranch, like how working there could give a person a sense of purpose and how eating meals with everyone created a familial bond. She was proud of connecting with Beauty when no one else had been able to, and Sasha had invited her back anytime, as long as she or Callahan was there to supervise. And the dining room had been just as loud today as it was yesterday, but it wasn't overwhelming this time. It was interesting and amusing to watch everyone interacting, and Callahan had coaxed her into playing checkers in the recreation room after dinner. He was nudging her out of her comfort zone, and she appreciated it, because it meant he'd listened to what she'd said yesterday about not mollycoddling her. She wasn't used to having people listen to her and support her needs. It made her less nervous about opening up.

She finished her drawing and started working on the list he'd asked for. She didn't think she had many things to put on it, but once she started writing things down, she thought of all sorts of things she hadn't been able to do on the compound.

Laugh, cry, yell, and talk whenever I want to, as loud as I want to

Sleep under the stars
Dance
Decide where, when, and what to eat

Make friends I fit in with
Earn money
Cut my hair
Go to a library and choose my own books
Buy my own clothes
Walk on a beach
Go swimming at night
Watch television
Watch a movie
Ride a bike
Drive a car
Chew gum
Wear shorts

Thinking of yesterday, she added, *Help a horse heal. Learn to ride a horse. Play more games with Callahan.*

A knock at the door startled her. She set her notebook down and peered out the window. Her stomach flip-flopped at the sight of Callahan standing with his hat in his hand, wearing a flannel shirt over a T-shirt. Why were her hands sweating? She wiped them on her jeans and took a calming breath before opening the door.

A slow grin crawled all the way up to his eyes. "Hey, horse whisperer. Sick of me yet?"

"Not yet." Boy, she liked his voice *and* that look in his eyes. No one had ever looked at her the way he did. It wasn't lecherous, like Rebel Joe, or off-putting, like other men on the compound. It was like he truly saw her, and he found her appealing in a nonthreatening way, which made her a different kind of nervous. She liked that butterfly-inducing nervousness.

"You busy?"

"I was just working on a list for this guy I know."

"About damn time." He winked. "Care to share?"

She couldn't stop grinning. "Not yet."

"A'right. Then how about keeping a lonely cowboy company on a walk?"

"That depends," she teased. "Where are you headed?"

"Wherever you'd like."

He couldn't know how much having options thrilled her, but she was curious about *him* and his life. "Do you have any favorite places you could show me?"

"Only about a dozen or two."

Excited to see what he found special, she said, "Okay. I'll go."

"Do you want to see someplace out in the open, or are you okay with a walk in the woods?"

"You pick."

"The woods it is, then." He tossed his hat on a chair. "Grab your flashlight, darlin'."

She grabbed her key and the flashlight and pulled the door closed behind her. He eyed her long-sleeve shirt.

"Are you going to be warm enough?"

"Uh-huh. I like to be a little cold."

He wiggled the doorknob, checking the lock as he had last night, and she handed him the flashlight. "Why is that?" he asked as they stepped off the porch and headed down the lane that he'd said led to his cabin.

"It makes me feel alive."

He looked at her, his expression serious. "As opposed to…?" The road veered up to the right, but he put a hand on her back, leading her through the grass toward the woods.

His touch had become a welcome comfort. "I don't know. Feeling numb, I guess." She felt a shift in the energy around him, tension rising at her response, but she wasn't afraid. It was like when the temperature dropped and the clouds turned gray, but they were moving so fast, she knew the storm would miss her.

He turned on the flashlight and shined it at the edge of the woods. "We're going to walk between those two trees. There's no trail here, but it'll lead to a trail about fifty feet in." His voice was calm, deep, and soothing. He walked beside her, pointing the flashlight at the ground in front of her. "Careful of that log, darlin'." She stepped over it, and as he held a branch for her to walk under, he said, "Have you always felt numb?"

"For as long as I can remember."

"Guess that makes the smiles I've earned even more precious." He pointed the flashlight at a trail up ahead. "We're going to follow that trail to the left."

He said it matter-of-factly, as if he hadn't just taken her breath away with his comment about her smiles.

"I don't like you feeling numb, darlin'. There are about a billion reasons to feel something and only one reason I can think of that a person would want to stop feeling altogether. I hope I don't make you feel that way."

She wondered what that one reason was but had a feeling it wasn't far off from the truth. "You don't." *I look forward to seeing you.* "Where are we going?"

"You wanted to see one of my favorite places, and it doesn't get more meaningful than this."

They turned onto the trail, and she heard the sound of water before he shined the light on a creek to their right. "We're going to follow that creek down to the lake."

"There's a lake?" She got excited as they headed down the trail.

"Sure is. This was my grandfather's favorite trail. He taught me all about horses and ranching and how to read a compass so I'd always know where I was heading." He stopped and pulled the chain that was attached to his belt loop, withdrawing a silver compass from his pocket and showing it to her. It looked weathered, and there was a cursive *W* engraved on the back. "This was his. I've carried it every day since he gave it to me."

"Your prized possession."

He gave a single curt nod.

"It's beautiful. How does it work?"

"It detects the earth's natural magnetic fields and responds to them. No matter where you are, the needle, which is really a magnet, will always point to the North Pole." He showed her how to read the compass, and after she turned in a circle, trying it out, he put it back in his pocket.

"Thank you for showing me how to use it."

"My pleasure, darlin'. My grandfather got me to join the Scouts when I was a kid, and through them, we did all sorts of things together."

"What are the Scouts?" she asked as they headed down a big hill.

"It's a group that teaches kids survival and leadership skills, sports, arts and crafts, and team building. You do a lot of community service and volunteer work and take an oath to help others." He held up three fingers and waved them.

Her heart stumbled as a memory flashed before her of the day she'd escaped and saying goodbye to Ansel. He'd held up three fingers, their sign for I love you. "Why did you hold up three fingers?"

"That's what you do when you recite the oath."

"Ansel and I used to do that."

Callahan's brows knitted. "Was he ever a Scout?"

"No. He was born on the compound. It was our way of saying I love you, or *Friend love forever.* Tell me more about the Scouts and your grandfather. I like hearing about the things you did."

"Well, through the Scouts, I learned outdoors skills, and my grandfather and I would come out here and practice. We built shelters, camped, tracked animals. He taught me to live off the land. It was pretty great."

"He sounds wonderful."

"Careful." He grabbed her arm, guiding her around a rock. "It gets steep here, so I'm just going to hold on to you so you don't fall."

"Thanks." His hand was big and warm and distracting in a way a man's touch had never been. She forced her thoughts back to their conversation. "Does your grandfather live here, too?"

"Not anymore. He passed away a long time ago. I miss him every damn day. He was a good man, but he was tough. He believed in hard work and straight answers, and he always put animals and family first."

"Sounds like you."

"What do you know about me?" he teased with a low laugh.

"Only what you've shown me. How long were you in the Scouts?"

"I'm still connected with them. I hold events for the kids here at the ranch. In fact, I have a camp-out and movie night coming up in a few weeks."

"Really? I love working with kids. On the compound, I helped the younger kids with homework and taught them all sorts of things. They're like little sponges, the way they soaked up everything from hugs to lessons. I miss them."

"Maybe you can help me out on movie night."

"I would *love* that."

"Great. Hopefully we'll get the all clear by then, and it'll be safe for you to interact with the public."

As he said it, reality came crashing in, stopping her cold.

"What's wrong?" Slivers of moonlight cut a path across his handsome face, illuminating his serious expression.

"I got so caught up in your story, for a second I actually forgot they might be looking for me."

He took her hand, giving it a gentle squeeze. "And how'd that second make you feel?"

"Hopeful. Happy. Definitely *not* numb. I want to live in that second!"

He laughed and pulled her into a hug. It was just a quick, natural embrace, but in those few short seconds, she'd felt good in ways she was afraid to define. Her cheeks heated, and she was thankful for the darkness as they continued walking down the hill.

They came to a steep drop-off, and the sound of water got louder. He jumped down and turned to face her. "I'll help you down."

"Thanks." She put her hand on his shoulder, and he grabbed her by the hips. His touch sent a streak of tingles and heat through her core as he lifted her over the large rocks. She'd been touched hundreds of times by Rebel Joe and had never felt anything like that.

As he set her on her feet, his jaw tightened, and she wondered if he'd felt something, too.

"Check this out," he said, drawing her from her thoughts. He shined the light toward the creek, illuminating where the land dropped off and large rocks formed a waterfall.

"I've never seen a waterfall. How can ugliness exist in a world this beautiful?"

"I don't know, darlin'. It's pretty steep here." He offered his hand, and she took it. His expression turned serious again. "I wish I could erase everything bad you've ever experienced."

"I wish I had a grandfather like yours," she said as they made their way down the hill.

"What was yours like?"

"I only knew my uncle. But I saw the doctor today, and she's running a DNA test. They said it could help find my mom and any other family I might have."

"That's a good thing, Sully."

"I guess. I still wish I'd had someone like your grandfather to teach me how to live off the land and read a compass. Then maybe my first attempt at escaping would have worked."

"How many times did you try to escape?" he asked gruffly, as if the idea upset him.

"Twice before I made it out. The first time was at night. I got lost in the woods, and they found me a couple of hours later. The second time I was hiding in the back of one of their trucks when I thought they were going into town. But I got in the wrong truck, and they stopped to load up the back with wood and found me."

"What happened when they found you?"

"I got punished."

He stopped walking, dark eyes boring into her. *"How?"*

She didn't know why she was telling him any of this, but she couldn't just pretend it hadn't happened. Not with him, anyway. She didn't want to, and she'd held it in for so many years, it was eating away at her. Festering like a wound that never heals. *Wynnie was right.* "The first time I was hit with a belt, and they made me sleep in the box for a few weeks and barely gave me any food. The second time I got the brand."

"What the *fuck* is the box?"

"A metal box with bars on the front."

His chest heaved, and his nostrils flared. "And the *brand?*"

She swallowed hard, remembering the searing pain of the brand as it had touched her skin. "A burn."

His hands curled into fists. "How old were you when you tried to escape?"

"The first time was right before I turned sixteen, and the second was two years later." Her heart was thundering, and she could feel more questions clawing at him, just as she had last night. It was too much tension, like a ghost between them she wanted to slay. "What? Just *ask*."

"What else did they do to you?" he growled.

She didn't want him to look at her differently, but at the same time, her past was part of her. She could escape the grasp of the Free Rebellion, but she couldn't escape the things she'd gone through. Before she could chicken out, she said, "Probably all the things you think they did."

His jaw clenched, his chest swelled, and the veins in his neck bulged, making him appear impossibly larger, but she wasn't afraid of him as he gritted out, "How many men?"

She was shaking, not out of fear but because the truth felt like a noose, making it hard to breathe. "A lot of them hurt me," she said just above a whisper. "Mostly at Rebel Joe's direction. But only Rebel Joe touched me like *that*."

"Did *he* hurt you when he touched you?" The pain in his eyes rivaled the anger tightening his features.

Hot tears flooded her cheeks as she told him what she

hadn't even told Wynnie. "Gaia warned me to just let him do what he wanted and not fight back. But I was sixteen the first time, and it hurt so much, I tried to get away. He held me down, and that was pretty awful. After that he didn't have to, because holding me down hurt more than the act itself, which sometimes left me bruised. As long as I didn't struggle, he just did what he wanted."

Callahan's nostrils flared, his chest rising with his heavy breaths as he drew her into his strong arms, cocooning her with his body, his touch protective, not hurtful. His heart beat strong and fast against her cheek, her tears wetting his shirt as he gritted out, "Never again," and kissed the top of her head. "Never fucking again."

She closed her eyes, breathing in the safest place, the safest *being*, she had ever known.

Chapter Nine

CALLAHAN HELD HER for a long time, surrounded by the scent of damp earth and the sounds of the creek trickling, his body tense, muscles flexed. One hand was pressed protectively to her back, the other gently rubbing the back of her neck. It was the gentlest, kindest touch Sully had ever experienced, and as her tears abated and the tension that had been her constant companion for as long as she could remember started to ease, she didn't want to move from the safety of his arms. But she also didn't want pity, and even though she was afraid he might look at her differently now that he knew the truth, she forced herself to step out of his arms and meet his gaze.

He *was* looking at her differently, but there was no pity, no judgment or shame, only a mix of admiration and empathy. His hand slid down her arm, and he caught her fingers. "Thank God you got out of there. You should press charges against those bastards."

"I'm thinking about it."

"Sully," he said seriously. "You can stop them from hurting other people, and we'll protect you. *I* will protect you."

"I believe you will. I'm talking with your mom about it. It's just scary. I still can't believe I got away. Sometimes I have nightmares of them finding me, and when I wake up, it takes a minute to realize it wasn't real."

He pulled her into another reassuring embrace. "They'll never get near you again. That's a promise."

She believed him. She didn't know whether or not that was naive, but she had a feeling he would protect her with his life. "Thank you for caring."

"Don't thank me. Just put those fuckers away where they belong. Would it be too difficult for you to tell me how you finally got away?"

"No. Escaping is the one thing that *isn't* hard for me to talk about."

"Are you still up to see the lake, or do you want to head back?"

She tried to lighten the air and ease the cloud her confession had left over them. "Let me think about that." She tilted her head and tapped her chin. "Do I want to be outside, where there are natural waterfalls and fresh air and a protective cowboy who will keep me safe, or do I want to be trapped in a cabin alone with my thoughts?"

He sort of smiled, but it was weighed down by all she'd said. "The lake it is, then."

As they followed the creek down the hill, she told him about the night she'd escaped. "Every month Rebel Joe and one of his right-hand men would drive three hours to Graveston for supplies. Sometimes they'd let one of us go with them as a treat if we were good. We weren't allowed to speak to anyone, but it got us off the compound. I hadn't been allowed to go since the last time I tried to escape several years ago."

"*Jesus.* They basically imprisoned you and dangled a restricted field trip like a carrot."

He helped her over another rocky drop-off, and she committed the waterfall to memory so she could draw it later. "I guess, but all I saw was my last chance at freedom."

Callahan stopped cold. "What do you mean your *last* chance?"

"Ansel's mother, Gaia, had secretly been giving me birth control, and she told me that Rebel Joe was going to take me to some kind of doctor to *fix* me so I could get pregnant. I knew if I had a baby with him, I'd never get out of there. A couple of years ago, a girl *died* giving birth, and once you had his baby, he kept even closer tabs on you. I had my escape all planned out. I just had to get to the bathroom of the Mega Mart. I don't even want to think about what Rebel Joe would have done if he'd caught me."

His jaw clenched. "What's that asshole's last name?"

"I don't know. He makes newcomers change their names, so Joe probably isn't his real name." The lake came into view, moonlight rippling off the water like diamonds. It was so beautiful, she wanted to get closer to it. "Can we sit by the water?"

"You bet." They made their way over rocks and dirt and sat by the water's edge. "What happened in Graveston?"

"I got myself so worked up repeating my plan in my head on the way there, when we got out of the truck, I froze. I remember thinking about the *box* and the *brand* and Thursday nights."

"What happened Thursday nights?"

Her chest constricted, and she stared out at the water. "That's the night Rebel Joe went to Nigel's, a bar in Bucksboro. He always came back drunk." Memories of those sweaty nights and the stench of alcohol turned her stomach. "Those nights were the worst."

"*Fucking hell*," he bit out. "I'd like to get my hands on that asshole."

"It was hell," she said, meeting his gaze. "But I'm away from him now, and I have to focus on that. I fought too hard to get here to let him steal anything else from me, including too many of my thoughts."

"You're right. I'm sorry for reacting, but the thought of any man treating you like that infuriates me."

"You don't know how much that means to me, to know you care. But it's a slippery slope for me, and I need to stay strong, like I did that night. I was so worried about what they'd do to Ansel if they found the fourteen dollars he'd given me, I forced myself to snap out of it."

"You weren't allowed to have money?"

She shook her head. "I have no idea how Ansel got it in the first place. Rebel Joe said money created too competitive of an environment and fostered the government's ability to control people. Anyway, I said I had to go to the bathroom, because that's where I was going to escape, but they wanted to get ammunition first, which they got out of the back of a tackle shop a few doors down. I was too nervous to wait, so I acted like I really had to go, and he finally let me, but he sent Hoyt, his right-hand guy, with me."

"Did Hoyt ever hurt you?"

She traced the edge of a rock sticking up through the dirt. "Yes. Rebel Joe made him brand me."

Callahan cursed, turning his face the other way, but his anger showed in his rising shoulders and fisted hands.

"Hoyt didn't want to," she added. "I could tell."

"But he *did*," he snarled, and faced her again. "Any man weak enough to hurt a woman doesn't deserve to walk this earth." He blew out a breath and drew another big one in, like he was trying to calm himself down. "Go on."

"I didn't mean to upset you. Are you sure you want me to tell you the rest?"

"Yes, sorry. I just want to get my hands on those motherfuckers. Please, go on."

"A woman and a child were washing their hands in the bathroom, so I went into a stall and waited for them to leave. I was so nervous, but the second they left, I ran out of the stall and opened the bathroom window so they'd think I went out that way. Then I went into the third stall and climbed on top of the toilet, which I had checked out years before. It was really hard, but I pulled myself up onto the metal divider between two stalls and used one hand to hold myself steady and the other to lift the ceiling tile. I was so afraid someone would walk in and see me. I think I held my breath the whole time. Once the tile was out of the way, I felt around for the metal bar I'd found the last time I was there."

She opened and closed her hand. "I can still feel the cold metal cutting into my hand as I pulled myself up. I had to be careful to step on the metal and not the tiles, and when I tried to put the tile back into place, it landed crooked, and pieces crumbled off and fell into the toilet. A lady and her kid came into the bathroom, and the kid ran into the stall below me but the woman told him it was dirty and flushed the toilet. She took him into another stall, and I managed to shift the tile into place and crawled across the metal bars toward the far end of the building."

"Jesus. How did you know to do that?"

"I had checked it out a few months before I tried to escape the second time. I was going to escape that way, and I should have left that day. But I didn't want to leave without saying goodbye to Ansel, and then I got frustrated waiting to be chosen to go to town again, and I ditched my plan and hid in the truck."

"Jesus, Sully. You must've lived in a constant state of fear."

"I had some good moments with Ansel and his mother and sister. I was scared a lot, but it was more like this constant state of waiting for an opening to get out."

The pain in his eyes was palpable again. "Like a fighter always ready for battle."

"Yeah. I know it sounds unbelievable, and that day, in the attic of the Mega Mart, I was terrified. It was hot and dark, and I was wearing a skirt. My knees got all cut up as I hurried along the metal bars. I had to hold the rough edges with my fingers, which hurt like crazy. At one point a sliver of metal got stuck in my knee, and I had to pull it out and use my skirt to stop the bleeding." She put her hand over her racing heart. "My heart is beating as hard now as it was then."

He covered her hand with his. "Do you want to stop?"

"*No.* This is my victory, and it's the only one I have. I want to finish telling you—unless you'd rather I didn't."

"I want to know. I just didn't want to make it harder for you."

"You make everything better, Callahan, not worse," she said honestly. "I was too far from the bathroom to hear anything, but a little while later I heard my name announced over the loudspeaker. They were telling me to go to the customer service counter. I don't think I've ever been that scared. I kept expecting Rebel Joe to burst through the ceiling. I was balancing on metal bars that were eating into my skin, but I had to get farther away, so I crawled along the bars toward the back of the store, where the tiled ceiling ended and the rafters were exposed to the warehouse. I saw workers down below and moved far away from the edge so I couldn't be seen. I heard my name a few more times, and I knew Rebel Joe was probably telling everyone his daughter was missing. That's how he referred to all the girls on the compound, even though we were his to *use*."

"*Christ*, Sully." His jaw clenched.

"It is what it is. It was expected of me."

"I fucking *hate* that."

"Me too." Their gazes held, and he put his hand over hers, squeezing it reassuringly. It was reassuring, and it made it easier for her to finish telling him about her escape. "I waited there in the attic, afraid to move or breathe, and the time in between hearing my name over the loudspeaker got longer and longer, until it finally stopped. I sat there for hours. Eventually the store closed, and the lights went out. I knew Rebel Joe wouldn't call the police because he didn't want them coming to the compound. But I wasn't sure whether he was hiding in the store, so I kept waiting and listening for any noises. I hoped they'd think I went out the window, but I was so scared. I was starving and shaking, and everything hurt. I don't know how long I waited after the store closed, but it was probably a couple of hours before I finally got up the courage to inch to the edge and peer into the warehouse. I heard cars outside and waited until they were gone. And then I gave myself a heck of a pep talk and made sure the coast was clear one last time before I hung from the edge of the metal and dropped to a stack of boxes below me."

"*Jesus*, Sully. I'm scared for you just listening to your story.

You must've been petrified."

"I was so afraid of being caught, I swear, the silence felt like it breathed around me. But I couldn't afford to be frozen in fear, and I literally told myself that. I ran through the store and grabbed a duffel bag and some clothes and food and changed out of my bloody clothes. Then I went back to the ladies' room to go out the window so I wouldn't set off any alarms. I pushed the duffel through the window and dropped it into a dumpster below. When I climbed out, my hair got caught. I have a bald spot where it was ripped out. It's just starting to grow back." She reached up and touched the short patch of hair.

Callahan reached over, his thick fingers following hers, those compassionate eyes as appealing as the heart he hid inside his broad, muscular chest.

IT TOOK EVERYTHING Cowboy had to keep his rage toward the assholes who put their hands on Sully at bay. As he gazed into her beautiful eyes, his fingers brushing over hers, he knew there was nothing he wouldn't do to protect her. "You're a warrior, and that's your battle wound. It'll grow back."

"I felt more like a chicken than a warrior."

"You're no chicken, darlin'. You're fucking amazing, and so damn brave. You should be proud of taking control of your life."

"I am, but I have a long way to go. I feel bad about lying to Chester when he picked me up the night I escaped. I was so scared that he might know Rebel Joe, I told him my mom was sick and I needed to get to her in the next town over. Thankfully, he saw right through that excuse, because when I fell asleep, he drove as far away from West Virginia as he could. A few hours later, he turned off the highway and stopped by a river so he could rest. I went down by the water, and I was so proud of myself and so happy to have gotten away, I lay back in the grass and looked up at the rising sun. But I was bone tired, and eventually I closed my eyes. A little while later a shadow darkened everything, and when I opened my eyes, there were two guys staring down at me. A tall, gnarly guy and a fat bald man with tattoos. The tall guy said, 'Lookie what we have here.' The bald guy said, 'Ain't she a pretty one?'"

Every muscle in his body tensed up. He clenched his jaw to keep from losing his shit. "What'd you do?"

"I jumped to my feet and apologized. I was walking backward, hoping to get to the truck, but the tall guy said the riverbank was *their* place, and the bald guy grabbed my arm. I kicked him in the groin and ran, screaming for help, but the other guy grabbed my ankle, and I fell face-first into the dirt." She lowered her eyes, her voice shaky. "And then the bald guy was on top of me, ripping open my jeans and calling me names, saying I was going to pay for kicking him." She swallowed hard. "The other just stood there laughing, and then there were gunshots, and that sent the bald guy to his feet."

"*Chester?*" he asked gruffly.

She nodded. "He was at the top of the hill with a gun aimed at them. I sprinted to him, and one of them said they were only having fun. Chester told me to get in the truck, and as I ran to the truck, I heard him say, 'You call that fun? I'll show you what fun is,' and then there was another gunshot."

"*Christ.*" It wasn't fucking fair. "You've been through so much."

She looked down at her lap. "That's why I feel guilty that the Finches had to leave their home. I owe them my life in more ways than one."

"You shouldn't feel guilty. They're just glad you're safe. Hell, I'm glad you're safe. We all are. We can go after those assholes if you can identify them."

"I can't, and I just want to move on." She leaned back on her palms and looked up at the moon, sighing. "It feels good to get all that out of my head. Thank you for listening."

"Sully, you can tell me anything."

She looked at him, and a small smile appeared. "I feel like I *can* tell you anything, which is weird, because I didn't think I'd ever trust another man. But now I need something from you."

"Anything. What do you need?"

"Will you tell me one of your creek stories or a story about this lake? I don't want to think about what I went through anymore. It takes a lot out of me, and I just want to be happy."

Man, that fucking killed him. "Sure, darlin'." He looked out at the water for a moment, trying to think of a story. "When my brothers and I were younger, we used to come out here and dick around. That was always fun. My old man hung a rope from that tree." He pointed to the large tree about twenty feet away. "We'd do flips off it and have chicken fights in the water."

"It's deep enough for that?"

"In the middle it is."

"Have you always gotten along with your brothers and sisters?"

"For the most part, but I'm sure Dare thinks I'm a big old pain in his ass."

"Why?"

"Because he likes pushing limits, and before he and Billie

got together, he didn't always make the best decisions."

"What do you mean?"

"Well, like the summer after high school, he made out with Billie when Eddie was at the same party, and I had to step in and split them up before they all got their hearts broken."

"Yikes."

"Yikes was right. Then he went away to college, and the summer after his freshman year, he was drinking too much, and I stopped him more than once from making foolish mistakes."

"What kind of mistakes?"

"Like hooking up with two women down here by the water when he was too shit-faced to even know their names."

She studied him for a moment. "So, you don't just protect people who come to the ranch? You protect girls you don't even know?"

"As a general rule, yeah. If someone's in trouble or headed for trouble, I'll try to step in. But in that circumstance, I was protecting him *and* them. Dare isn't a bad guy, though, and he's not like that anymore. He's as loyal as they come, and he'd do anything for Billie."

"It sounds like he's really changed."

"Or he finally got what he always wanted. He's always been a great guy. I think he was just so in love with Billie back then, he didn't know what to do with all his feelings when she was dating someone else, so he ended up with creek-side trouble."

She was quiet for a long moment, eyes on her finger trailing over the ground beside her. "What about you? Did you bring girls here, too?"

There was an innocence about her that conflicted with her strength, and it made him want to protect her in many more ways than just physically. He wanted to help her understand how life really worked and show her that all men were not worthless pigs.

"No, and I don't pick up women if I'm drunk. In fact, I can't remember the last time I got drunk. I'm usually watching out for my buddies and my sisters, and honestly, I'm too responsible for that anyway. I don't take those kinds of risks, and I like to be fully present when I'm entertaining a lady."

Her cheeks pinked up, and her eyes remained trained on a tuft of grass she was fiddling with. "What does that mean?"

He didn't want to embarrass her, but he wanted her to understand that he was different and to really hear what he had to say. He reached over and lifted her chin so he could see her eyes. "It means I treat women with respect. They're not playthings to me. They're gifts. And when I'm with a woman, she's the only thing I'm thinking about. I'm solely focused on bringing her pleasure, and the only way to do that is to listen to what she says, feel her reactions, and read her body language. I don't want any woman who's been with me to look back and think it was a mistake. I want them to think, *Damn, he was the best I've ever had.*"

Her lips parted, then closed. She lowered her eyes, and a tentative smile appeared before her gaze flicked up again. "I don't even know what that means, but it sounds nice."

He'd probably go straight to hell for hoping he'd be the one to show her one day, but he sure as fuck didn't want another man touching her.

"You must have loved growing up here," she said. "What was it like growing up *free?*"

He pulled one knee up and leaned his forearm on it. "It seems unfair to tell you that after what you've been through."

"No. It'll help me. I only know what I've been told by Gaia

about life outside the compound. I really want to know what it was like, and it makes me happy to think about a different type of childhood and life."

"In that case, it was damn near perfect. When I was little, I'd get up at the crack of dawn so I could follow my grandfather and my old man around the ranch before school. I'd meet them down in the kitchen before anyone else was awake. They'd have coffee, and I'd have chocolate milk." He laughed at the memory. "Then we'd put on our boots and hats and head out to walk the property as the sun came up. I loved that time with them. There's nothing like watching the sunrise with someone you're close to."

"I've never seen a sunrise. I had to be up prepping breakfast with a couple of other girls before everyone else got up, but we were indoors."

"Then watching a sunrise better be on your list, because I'm definitely going to make that happen."

She smiled. "I'll add it. I want to know more about when you were growing up."

"A'right. Ranch life isn't easy, but it's rewarding. My brothers and sisters and I worked hard even as kids. We did chores before and after school, and then we'd run around with our friends and have fun, and after dinner we'd do more chores and homework. But chores never felt like work to me. I loved doing anything for the horses, even mucking stalls."

"Did your brothers and sisters like it?"

"You met Birdie. Do you think she'd enjoy shoveling horse manure?"

She laughed. "No."

"She's six years younger than me, so when I was fifteen, she was nine, and she'd plead with me to help her with her chores."

"Did you?"

"What do you think? She was this cute little thing, stomping around in cowgirl boots and talking my ear off. Yeah. I did it. Probably shouldn't have, but she turned out okay. My family has always been close, and we'd go to all the town festivals and celebrations, and our parents held events here for the ranch and the motorcycle club. The club also has its own events and rallies that we'd go to. We still do, of course, and we always have big holiday dinners with whoever's at the ranch at the time, the whole nine yards."

"That sounds wonderful."

"Did you celebrate holidays?"

"Not really. Rebel Joe didn't believe in religion or basically anything people outside our compound did as a group. But Ansel and I would give each other a little something on our birthdays."

"When is your birthday?"

"January thirteenth," she said with a smile. "When's yours?"

"April seventeenth. Couldn't Ansel have helped you run away? Gone with you in the middle of the night or something?"

She shook her head. "He has a little sister, Emina. She's eleven, and he'd never leave her."

We need to get that little girl out of there. "And his mother, Gaia, is okay with her daughter ending up in that guy's hands?"

"No. She wants to leave, but she can't. Her husband is one of Rebel Joe's right-hand men, and she's taking care of all the other women. But I don't want to think about the compound right now. Can we not talk about it anymore?" She began unlacing her boots.

"Yeah, of course. Sorry about that." He eyed her tugging off her boots. "What are you doing?"

She pulled off her socks, eyes bright with excitement. "I want to feel the water."

"It's ice cold, darlin'. Trust me, you don't want to go in."

"I just want to put my toes in." She rolled her jeans above her ankles and pushed to her feet.

"You're in for a shock." He pulled off his boots and socks.

"What are *you* doing?"

He rolled up his jeans and rose beside her. "I've got to be ready in case you bolt into the water."

"I'm not a wild animal." She laughed. As soon as she touched her toes to the water, she squealed and jumped back. "Come in with me!" She grabbed his hand, tugging him into the water, and she squealed again, dancing on her tippy-toes, as excited as a foal taking its first run. *"Brr!"*

He chuckled. "I told you it was cold."

"You're not afraid of a little cold water, are you?" She kicked water at him, splattering his jeans, and gasped, eyes wide, like she hadn't meant to do it. A second later, she burst into laughter and did it again.

"You're in for it, Tate!" He reached for her, both of them laughing as she darted out of his reach, dashing through the shallow water, squealing and splashing. He grabbed her hand and spun her around. The joy emanating from her was immeasurable, and he didn't want to squelch it, so he spun her again and drew her into his arms, sliding into a slow dance. Their eyes caught, their amusement silenced by sparks of lust crackling between them. She was breathing hard, her cheeks pink and utterly radiant in the moonlight. He fought the urge to lower his lips to hers and taste the most remarkable woman he'd ever known and focused on how incredibly right she felt in his arms.

She rested her cheek on his chest, swaying with him. "I told you I wasn't a wild animal," she said softly.

"You're far more dangerous than a wild animal, darlin'."

She blinked up at him through those long, thick lashes, and the world seemed to still around them. Then, with a burst of giggles, she pushed away, spread her arms wide, and spun around with her face tipped up to the moon, her long dirty-blond hair flying behind her like a cape, and those adorable bare feet dancing in the icy water.

He was in big trouble.

IT WAS LATE when they finally headed back. Cowboy took off his flannel shirt and put it on her. She looked down at the sleeves, which had swallowed her hands, and they both laughed as he rolled them up. She lifted her shoulder to her nose and sniffed it.

"It's clean, darlin'. I swear."

"It smells good. It smells like you."

"Well, that's good to hear. Birdie gave me some body wash a while back. I like it, but you know how those things can change from person to person." He finished rolling her sleeves and straightened the collar. She looked adorable and beautiful.

"It smells like happiness."

He cocked a brow.

"Seriously. Smell it for yourself." She turned her shoulder toward him.

He leaned down, inhaling the sweet scent of *Sully*. Big mistake. "All I smell is you, darlin'."

"What do I smell like?"

"Trouble waiting to happen. Let's go."

She giggled as they walked, and it was a sound he wanted to hear more of. They talked the whole way back to her cabin, and when he walked her up to the door, she said, "I had a lot of fun tonight."

"Me too. Take a hot bath before bed tonight. It might help you sleep."

"Are you going home?"

"No. I've got to take care of something, and then I'm coming back. I'll be out here if you need anything. But keep that door locked, you hear?"

"I will. I'll leave a blanket and pillow on the chair for you."

"I'll be fine. Now get in there and warm up before you catch a cold."

"Oh, Callahan, you're always worrying about me," she said as she went inside. "Good night."

He waited until he heard the door lock before hightailing it up to his parents' house, every step bringing back Sully's words and the pain in her voice—*I was hit with a belt, and they made me sleep in the box for a few weeks and barely gave me any food. The second time I got the brand.* By the time he got to his parents' house, he was fit to be tied and banged on their door. When they didn't answer, he used his key and stormed inside, his heart slamming against his ribs. He headed for the master bedroom just as Tiny walked out of it, wearing underwear and pulling on a T-shirt.

"Where are your pants?" Cowboy snapped.

"You're lucky I put underwear on."

"We've gotta go to West Virginia and get those cult mother-fuckers." He paced, hands fisted, voice escalating. "They did awful things to her, and I won't let that stand. I want to tear every one of them apart and make them suffer."

"Slow down, Cowboy."

"No, I'm *not* going to slow down. You don't know what she's been through. Jesus, Dad. If you won't get the guys to go, then I'm going by myself. I'll call Biggs and get his chapter on board."

"A'right, son. I hear you. Just take a breath, and let's talk about it."

"I *can't* fucking take a breath! I don't know how that sweet girl"—he pointed in the direction of Sully's cabin—"is still sane after what she's been through, and there are more just like her on that compound. And you know what else? They make newcomers change their fucking names. Who does that? People who have something to hide, that's who. I know she lived with an uncle. But was he really her uncle?" He whipped out his wallet and pulled out the flyer, thrusting it in his father's direction. "*That's* her. That's Sully. Look at that little girl's eyes. I fucking feel it in my gut, and it makes me sick to think she's been there all this time. So, are you with me or not?"

"Absolutely, but we've got to do some recon and come up with a plan. The DNA test results should be in soon, but if they're stealing kids and abusing young girls, then this is much bigger than our club. They need to be put behind bars—"

"After we fuck them up," Cowboy seethed.

"*Son*, use your head. If we go in there ready to take them down, we need to know they're going to stay down, or those girls could be in worse danger."

"Trust me. If I get my hands on them, they're *not* getting back up."

"You can't help anyone from prison," he warned. "I'll talk

121

to Manny and prep him for the meeting, and I'll call Biggs and see if he can get a couple of his boys to do some recon. We'll circle back and strategize at church tomorrow night."

His mother came out of the bedroom in a bathrobe, her hair tousled. "What's got you two all riled up?" She eyed Cowboy. "Why are you all wet?"

"I took Sully to the lake."

Her brows knitted. "Is *she* what's gotten under your skin?"

"It's that fucking cult. Do you *know* what they did to her?" he demanded.

"You know I can't answer that, honey."

"Right. The *fucking* rules. Those assholes on the compound follow their own damn rules, and I want to shut them down."

"Watch your mouth around your mother," his father said.

He bit out, "*Sorry*. Tomorrow night, then?"

"You've got my word. I'll make some calls and get things ready."

With a nod, Cowboy headed for the door.

"Honey," his mother said softly.

"Yeah?" He turned to meet her gaze.

"Be careful, Cowboy. She's in a vulnerable place, and she could misconstrue gratitude for something else."

"Do you *really* think I'd let her make that mistake?"

"No. I know you wouldn't. But you're pretty worked up. Maybe we should appoint someone else to keep an eye on Sully."

"I'll rein my shit in," he hissed. "And if it makes you feel better, you can have ten other guys watch her, but I'll *still* be by her side every night just like I would anybody else that I'm supposed to watch over."

Chapter Ten

"YESTERDAY WHEN WE talked about your relationship with your uncle, you said he told you it was an honor to be with Rebel Joe, and you mentioned that other girls felt that way, too. But you never did," Wynnie said Tuesday afternoon during their session. "I'd like to talk about your relationship with Rebel Joe."

Sully's thoughts skipped back to her walk with Callahan last night. When she'd told him about Rebel Joe, she could tell he'd wanted to ask more questions, but he hadn't, and she'd been surprised that part of her had wanted him to. It had felt so good to run through the water and laugh with him. When he'd pulled her into a slow dance, the rest of the world fell away, and just for those few moments, she felt like a regular girl dancing with a guy she was attracted to, and that was amazing. But she wasn't just a regular girl, and Callahan wasn't just a regular guy. He was special. He was caring and thoughtful and protective in a way she appreciated instead of fearing.

"Sully?"

"*Hm?* Sorry. I was just thinking."

"About Rebel Joe, or is there something else on your mind?"

"About him," she said, not wanting to reveal what felt like private moments with Callahan to his mother.

"What do you think about when you think of Rebel Joe?"

"How glad I am that I'm away from him," she said spitefully.

"Did you always feel that way about him?"

"No. When I was young, all I really knew about him was that he was the leader of the group and that only special girls were allowed in his shack. I hate to admit it, but before I moved into the dorms, I wanted to be one of those girls."

"That's nothing to be ashamed of. You were groomed to be one of his special girls, brainwashed into thinking it was a prized seat, so to speak. What did you think happened in there?"

She thought about that for a minute. "I don't think I ever really thought about it. I just knew I wasn't allowed to go in."

"Sounds like your competitive spirit coming through. Did that change after you moved into the dorms?"

"Yes. When I moved into the dorms, I heard whispers about what went on in there, and from then on, I feared it."

"That must have been scary for you, knowing you'd end up in a grown man's bed."

She nodded, remembering the stomachaches she'd had every day.

"How did you handle that?"

"I didn't. I mean, I tried to say I didn't want to be claimed, but I just got punished and reminded that it was an honor to be chosen, and eventually I learned to keep my mouth shut, which I will *never* do again."

"I'm glad to hear that. Some people who come out of situations where they were forced to suppress their feelings have trouble learning to speak their minds. It's good that you aren't afraid to."

"I had been trying to escape since I was fifteen." She told her about her two failed attempts and how she'd finally gotten out. "If Gaia hadn't been there for me, I probably would have ended up with kids, like the other girls. She supported me getting out and encouraged me to talk privately with her about what I felt and how angry being there, and with him, made me. That's probably why I'm not afraid to speak my mind now."

"It's no wonder you're as far along as you are. It sounds like even at ten you knew something wasn't right."

"I think I knew it before that, and that's why I hated having to follow the rules so much."

"Yes, you mentioned that. How did Rebel Joe treat you when you weren't in his trailer?"

"When I was little, or as an adult?"

"Both."

"When I was younger, he'd give me special attention and act like he was interested in whatever I was doing. And once I'd been in his bed, he treated me like I was his property. He made it clear who I belonged to and what was expected of me, and if he thought I looked at another man for too long, or if I took too long to get to him when he sent for me, he'd scold me."

"What was he like when you were intimate?"

"What do you mean?"

"Was he kind? Did he say nice things to you? Did he touch you gently or rough?"

"He wasn't nice or mean. He did what he wanted, and then he'd roll over and go to sleep, and I'd have to wait for him to tell me I could leave."

"How long would you wait?"

"Sometimes it was right after, and other times it could be

two days later."

Wynnie nodded. "Was it ever enjoyable?"

"*No.* I was doing my duty. I didn't like how he smelled or felt or touched me."

Her gaze softened. "Sully, did Gaia or anyone else ever tell you that sex can be very different than that?"

"Yes, Gaia told me often. She didn't join the Rebellion until she was in her twenties, so she'd had normal relationships and experiences before coming there. If it wasn't for her and Ansel, I'd probably hate all men."

"Do you know why she joined them?"

"She came with her boyfriend, and eventually they got married. She told me she didn't know how bad things were until she'd had Ansel, and by then it was too late to get out. She couldn't go without leaving him behind."

"That's a shame. What did she tell you about intimacy?"

"She said that when you love someone, being close to them can be enjoyable and even exciting and that when a man truly loves you, he won't want to be with someone else. But she also said that even outside the compound, a lot of people had relationships with more than one man or woman, but that it was their *choice*, not something anyone has to do."

"She's right about all of that, and I'm glad she shared that with you. When you're with someone you want to be with, sexual intimacy can be a wonderful experience that brings you closer together."

Sully couldn't imagine what that would be like, but she also couldn't stop thinking about Callahan and what he'd said Sunday night about when he was with a woman. She'd wanted to ask what he'd meant by *the best they'd ever had*. The best *what*? She couldn't remember one pleasurable thing about sex or kissing or any of that. But the way he'd spoken about being solely focused on a woman's pleasure made her want to know what it would be like to be in his arms.

"How do you feel about intimacy?" Wynnie asked, as if she'd read Sully's mind. "Does the thought of kissing, touching, or having sex scare you?"

"The thought of doing those things doesn't scare me. Doing them with Rebel Joe or any other man I don't want to be with makes me sick, but I'll never allow myself to be in that position again."

"That fighting spirit of yours is a wonderful thing."

They talked for a long time, and when Callahan came to get her, his muscles straining against his shirtsleeves and his jeans stretched tight over his thick thighs, those butterflies fluttered to life again. Why was she noticing those things? She'd never noticed so much about men before him.

He put a hand on her lower back as they left the building. "Everything go okay?"

"Mm-hm. I like talking with your mom."

"Good. I'm glad. Listen, I have to run some errands in town, and I thought you might like to spend time with Sasha down at the rehab barn while I'm gone. Does that sound all right to you?"

"It sounds great. I'd like to spend time with Beauty. Do you think Sasha will mind?" She'd gotten to know Sasha better during mealtimes, and she really liked her.

"Having a horse whisperer hanging around for a while?" he teased. "Not at all. I've already asked her. Do you need anything from town? I noticed you only had one duffel bag. We still have some warm days ahead, and the nights will get colder. Do you need shorts, shirts? Do you have a jacket? I can pick you up a few things."

"That's okay. You guys have already done enough."

"Sully, it's not a big deal."

"It is a big deal, but I'm fine, really. I've never had shorts, so it's not like I miss wearing them." Shorts were on her list, but she didn't want him spending his hard-earned money on her. "On the compound all the girls dressed in similar skirts and tops. We weren't allowed to wear shorts or show any individuality."

His jaw tightened, and as they walked past one of the pastures, he said, "I have my club meeting tonight after dinner."

"I remember." She'd been thinking about it since he'd mentioned it when he'd told her about the club. She was going to miss seeing him tonight. She wanted to ask him if he was going to come by after his meeting to walk with her, but she'd heard Dare and Doc talking at breakfast about going to the Roadhouse after the meeting and teasing Hyde about picking up women. She wondered if Callahan would spend the evening solely focused on a woman and tried to ignore the knots forming in her stomach at the thought.

"I asked Sasha to check in with you in case you need anything, and we'll have guys watching your place."

"Thanks. I'll be fine."

Sasha walked out of the barn, looking cute in a cowgirl hat, a long-sleeve shirt, shorts, and maroon boots. "Hey, guys. I think Beauty has been waiting for you, Sully."

"I'm excited to see her," Sully said.

"Great. I'm just going to grab a bucket. I'll be right back."

As Sasha walked around the side of the barn, Callahan said, "You going to be okay?"

"Of course."

He shook his head, grinning. "I shouldn't have asked. Sorry."

"It's okay."

"Still have your phone?"

"Yes." He'd texted after their walk last night, and when the phone had vibrated on the kitchen table, she'd nearly jumped out of her skin. She'd never forget the way seeing his name on the screen had made her giddy or how the two simple words he'd texted—*Sweet dreams*—had made her feel good all over. When he'd picked her up for breakfast, he'd suggested she bring the phone. It felt weird carrying it in her pocket, but he'd said she should have it in case she ever needed to reach him. Now she realized he'd meant while he was gone.

Sasha came around the side of the barn carrying a bucket. "You're still here?"

"I'm taking off." He held Sully's gaze. "Text if you need anything."

"I will." She knew she wouldn't need to reach out, but it made her happy to know she could.

"She's *fine*, Cowboy. Get out of here, and let her have some fun." Sasha looped her arm through Sully's, leading her into the barn. "Too bad you're not a Cowboy whisperer. Maybe you could get him to loosen the reins a little."

Sully glanced over her shoulder at Callahan, catching him as he was turning to leave. He winked, and she sighed inwardly. She didn't know what Sasha was thinking. She liked the big-hearted, responsible cowboy just the way he was.

WHEN COWBOY FINISHED the errands for the ranch, he headed into the arts and crafts store for sketch pads and colored pencils and walked out twenty minutes later with a handmade leather sketchbook cover that had a pocket for colored pencils, several sketch pads, and a deluxe wooden art box with colored pencils, watercolors, pastels, paintbrushes, and all the necessary accoutrements. Sully had gone without long enough. He'd give her the fucking world if he could.

He headed out of Hope Valley and drove to Birdie's chocolate shop in Allure, a nearby town with brick-paved roads, old-fashioned streetlights, and brick storefronts with ornate iron fences. As he drove past Karma's boutique, which was owned by one of Birdie's friends, he thought about stopping to get Sully a few things. But he didn't know her sizes.

His phone rang with a call from his father, and he put him on speakerphone. "What's up?"

"I spoke to Manny and brought him up to date for tonight, and I talked with Biggs. He's got Bullet and Diesel doing recon." Bullet was Cowboy's cousin, and Cowboy had grown up with Diesel Black in Hope Valley. They both lived in Peaceful Harbor, Maryland, now, and they were two of the toughest men Cowboy knew. "Hopefully we'll have a report from them by tonight. I also left a message for Reggie Steele, the PI who put out that flyer about the missing girl."

"Great, thanks. I talked with Doc and Dare earlier and brought them up to speed." He'd been careful not to breach Sully's confidence. "Anything else? I'm just pulling up to Birdie's shop." He parked at the curb in front of Divine Intervention.

"Nah, we're good. Tell Bird to visit her old man sometime." Birdie was always on the move, and their father was endlessly trying to eke out a little more time with her.

"She was just there Saturday for the event and Sunday morning for breakfast."

"That wasn't a visit. That was a blur."

Cowboy chuckled. "I'll let her know. See ya tonight."

He headed into the chocolate shop, causing the bells above the door to chime. There was nothing quite as enticing as the scent of freshly made chocolates. Sully came to mind, and he tried like hell to push thoughts of the off-limits sweetheart away, but it was like trying not to breathe.

"Be right there!" Quinn Finney called out as she came through the kitchen door carrying a tray of chocolates. "If it isn't one of my favorite cowboys."

Quinn was one of Birdie's besties and her employee. She was gorgeous, with an hourglass figure and soft chestnut waves framing her always perfectly-made-up face. She eyed him up and down from behind her black-framed glasses. He was used to that from her and plenty of other women, but she wasn't his type. While he could go for a slice of rich decadence once in a while, he sure wouldn't enjoy it with one of Birdie's besties, and he'd always preferred natural beauty to made-up perfection. A woman who could get dirty in and out of the bedroom without worrying about her hair and nails. Sully tiptoed into his thoughts again, tempting him for the hundredth time. There was no denying he wanted to show her how good everything could be—touching, kissing, sucking, licking, fucking. *Christ, what am I doing?*

He cleared his throat to try to clear his head and said, "How's it going, Quinn?"

"Oh, you know. It's *goin'*. I haven't seen you at the Roadhouse for a few days."

"I've been busy. Where's Birdie?"

"Out lining up beautiful women for you that you won't pay any attention to."

He followed her to the front counter. "Tell me you're lying."

"She is!" Birdie popped up from behind the counter holding a screwdriver. Her hair was piled on top of her head in a messy bun, and a pencil was tucked behind her ear. She wore a long-sleeve black shirt beneath overall shorts that had thick blue and red stripes on one leg, yellow and purple stripes on the other, and a patchwork bib. A leather toolbelt hung around her waist, with a hammer hanging from one side and an enormous heart-shaped lollipop sticking out of the other.

"What's up, Bird the Builder?"

Birdie pointed the screwdriver at him. "I'm fixing the shelves."

"Need some help?"

She planted a hand on her hip. "*No.* I don't need any help. I'm perfectly capable of—" Her words were lost to the sounds of wooden shelves crashing to the floor.

Cowboy arched a brow, and Birdie rolled her eyes.

Quinn giggled and went to put the chocolates she was carrying in the display cabinet.

"Let me take a look." He started to walk around the counter, but Birdie held up her hand.

"Stop right there. I'm part owner now. I can do this."

"Shelves can be tricky. Why don't you let me take care of it?"

"*No.* I've got this," Birdie insisted.

"She's *had it* for almost two hours now," Quinn chimed in.

"Hush up, you pest," Birdie snapped.

He remembered how important his support of Sully's independence was to Sully and said, "Have it your way. I need some chocolates."

"Oh, yay! For who?" Birdie asked.

He wasn't about to give little Miss Matchmaker that information. "Myself."

Birdie's eyes narrowed. "Don't try to play me, big brother."

"What? A guy can't enjoy a little chocolate?"

"Not a guy who has bought chocolate for himself only twice in his entire life."

He cocked a brow. "You want to sell chocolate or not?"

"Fine. Heart-shaped box?" She smirked.

"Nope."

She sighed. "You'd impress more with a heart."

"I don't need to impress myself." And he didn't need to confuse Sully with a heart-shaped box. He was just being a good guy. Giving her something to make her smile.

Birdie grabbed a small rectangular box.

"Bigger."

"Ah, *okay.* Now you're thinkin' straight." She grabbed a larger box.

Cowboy went through the display, picking out chocolates. "A couple of these, and these, and those."

"Don't forget truffles. Women love truffles."

He glowered at her, chose a few other types, then circled back, hoping she wouldn't notice, and pointed to the truffles. "And a couple of each of those."

"Good choices," she said as she closed the box. "Can I put a ribbon on it?"

"Birdie," he warned.

"*Please?* I promise it won't be too much. I won't even do

red. Just a pretty pink one?" She pressed her hands together, giving him puppy-dog eyes.

"Fine."

She wiggled her shoulders. "This is so exciting."

"Don't go making up shit in your head. It's just candy."

"You can't control what happens in my head." As she tied the ribbon in a bow, she said, "Do you know what Sasha's doing tonight?"

"She's going to check on Sully while I'm at church and see if she wants to hang out. As a matter of fact, thanks for the reminder. I wanted to buy Sully a few things to wear, but I don't know her size. I'll have Sasha ask while she's with her." He pulled his phone from his pocket.

"Sully?" Birdie's eyes lit up. "The cute new girl I met?"

"Yeah. She didn't bring many clothes."

"Don't bother Sasha," she said as she rang up his purchase. "I'm great with sizes. I'll pick her up a few things at Karma's and swing by for a girls' night with them." She told him how much the chocolates were, and he handed her his credit card.

"I don't know if Sully will be into a girls' night, but are you sure you don't mind picking up some clothes for her?"

"Did you forget who you're talking to?" Quinn asked as she walked past with the empty tray. "She's the shopping queen."

"That's me." Birdie waved Cowboy's credit card. "I'll just hang on to this for her clothes and drop it off later."

"Thanks. I appreciate your help. She needs shorts, jeans, and a few things to wear as the weather changes. But don't buy her anything too skimpy. I think she'd be uncomfortable showing too much cleavage or ass, and don't get anything too...*that*." He nodded toward her outfit.

She looked down at her overall shorts. "What's wrong with

this?"

"It's perfect for you, but she's low-key. I don't think she wants to be flashy."

"She's not a girl. She's a *woman*. I promise to buy things that are appropriate and that she'll love." She put the box of chocolates in a bag and handed it to him. "Are these for Sully, too?"

"Birdie, don't make me regret letting you help."

She planted her hand on her hip again. "Why is it that guys can talk to each other about everything they do with women, but you can't even tell your sister if you like one?"

"First of all, I don't share that shit with anyone, and second of all, you're my little sister, which is reason enough not to share it with you. But more importantly, there's nothing to share. I'm just looking after her."

"Then *who* are the chocolates for?"

"Me." It wasn't a total lie. It made him happy to see Sully smile. "You should stop by and see Dad soon. He misses you."

"No, thank you. He wants to lecture me because Manny saw me kissing a guy last night at the Roadhouse."

"*What?* Who?" he demanded.

She crossed her arms and lifted her chin. "First of all, I don't share that stuff with anyone, and second of all, you're my brother, which is reason enough not to share it with you."

"My ass it is."

She pretended to zip her lips and throw out the key.

"You know I'll see Manny at the meeting tonight."

"Stupid good-old boys' network," she mumbled.

"Want to fess up?"

"Nope. I have shelves to fix." She turned her back to him.

"Be careful with guys you don't know, Birdie. We'd all lose

our fucking minds if anything happened to you." He saw her shoulders drop a little. "And as far as the shelves go, I admire your effort, but let me know if you want me to stop by before or after church to fix them."

BEFORE HEADING BACK to the ranch, Cowboy stopped by the Roadhouse to talk with Manny. He wasn't there, but Billie was behind the bar.

"Hey, big guy. What's got your briefs in a bunch?" She slid a glass of beer to a customer.

"Who was Birdie kissing last night?"

"You know I can't spill those beans. It'd break the girl code." Billie grabbed a rag and wiped down the bar. "But I'm watching out for her. Don't worry."

"Billie, you know how she is. She's tough, but she trusts too easily."

She draped the rag over her shoulder and leaned both hands on the bar, staring at him. "And you distrust everyone until they prove themselves worthy."

"It's safer that way where my sisters are concerned."

"I get that. But you can't be everywhere she is. At some point you've got to trust her to handle her own shit."

"Right. I'll make sure Doc is running point when I can't."

She laughed. "What is *wrong* with you Whiskeys?"

"Not a damn thing, as proven by the fact that you're going to marry the craziest one of us." He tapped the bar. "I've got to get back. See you later."

He drove to the ranch, caught up with the guys watching

the gate, and headed straight to the rehab barn. As he climbed out of the truck, he spotted Sully and Sasha walking one of the horses toward the barn. The glow from the low-hanging sun gave Sully an ethereal look. Her hair was twisted into a knot on top of her head, revealing her long, slim neck, which he was aching to kiss. She noticed him and waved, a smile brightening her face. Hell if his stupid heart didn't beat a little faster. He lifted his chin and headed over.

"Good timing," Sasha said. "We just finished, and Sully was awesome with the horses. They're really drawn to her."

Sully beamed proudly.

"That's not surprising." He held Sully's gaze. "They can sense good people."

She lowered her eyes a little bashfully but only for a moment before looking up again. "I really enjoyed spending time with the horses, and, Sasha, you taught me so much. If you ever need a hand, I'd love to help."

"I was just about to say you're welcome to come back and help anytime. Not just with Beauty, but like you did today," Sasha said. "Spending time with the horses helps them realize that they're important to us, and every little bit helps. Even if you just bring a book and read near them while they eat, it builds that bond."

"How about tomorrow?"

"Sounds great to me. You can come every day if you'd like," Sasha offered.

"I'd love that." Sully grinned at Cowboy.

"Now you look like a woman with a purpose," Cowboy said, earning an even bigger smile.

"I'm going to put Belle in her stall," Sasha said. "Thanks for a great afternoon, Sully. I'll see you at dinner."

As he and Sully headed to his truck, she said, "Today was incredible."

He opened her door and helped her in. "I want to hear all about it."

As he settled in behind the wheel and drove toward her cabin, she said, "Sasha is amazing. She taught me all about horses, so I'd understand what she meant when she mentioned their muzzles, or poll, or cannons and hooves. There's so much to learn, like the right way to hold the lead and where to stand when you're walking them. I loved learning about how she helps them. She's teaching me how to groom them, which she said is good for their muscle tone and for bonding with them." She went on to tell him about each horse and what she'd done with them. Her excitement was contagious.

"Sasha knew exactly what to do in every situation. If a horse tried to bite or refused to walk, she didn't even flinch. She's so patient, too. I must have asked her a million questions, and she took her time answering each one. And the horses..." She put her hand over her heart. "I *love* them. Now I know why you'd sit in the barn with your dad with the rescues. This is going to sound strange, but I feel a kinship with them. I know what it feels like not to trust the people who want to help. I think they sense that and know they can trust me when I tell them it's going to be okay."

Cowboy parked in front of her cabin. "That's not strange at all. Horses read human emotions. They sense what's in our hearts."

"They must. It feels good to be around them. It's fulfilling. I'm looking forward to working with them tomorrow as much as I look forward to our walks."

"Well, damn, darlin'. You just made my day."

She blushed adorably.

"I look forward to our walks, too. I got you a little something." He reached behind his seat and grabbed one of the bags, setting it on the seat between them.

Her eyes widened. "What's that?"

"Take a look."

"Callahan, you didn't have to get me anything."

"I wanted to, and don't worry. You don't owe me a damn thing."

"I wasn't going to ask if I did. I know you're not like that." She peered into the bag and withdrew the leather sketchbook holder. Her brows knitted as she ran her hand over the soft leather. "This is beautiful."

Like you.

She opened it, revealing the sketch pad and colored pencils he'd put inside and looked up at him with disbelief. "Callahan...?"

"You're too talented to draw in notebooks, and this way you can take it with you in case you want to draw while you're in the field or by the lake or something."

"I've never had anything this nice before."

"You deserve a lot more than that." He moved the empty bag to the floor and reached behind him, grabbing the wooden art supply box and placing it between them.

Her eyes bloomed wide again.

"I thought you might want to try some different things." He opened the box, showing her the contents. "I bet you'd be good with pastels and watercolors."

Her jaw dropped. "I can't accept this. It's too much."

"No, it's not. I want you to have it."

"But it must have been expensive, and you work hard for

your money."

"Yes, and I'll spend it as I see fit." He took her hand and tried to ease her mind. "I know you're not used to being given gifts, and honestly, I'm not used to wanting to buy them. But it makes me happy knowing you have things that make *you* happy. So please accept it."

"Are you *sure*?"

"Darlin', I've never been more certain of anything in my life." He squeezed her hand. "I might've gotten you one more thing."

"*Callahan.*" She laughed. "What has gotten into you?"

"Maybe I just like seeing your smile."

He reached behind the seat for the candy and handed her the Divine Intervention box. She glanced at him a little bashfully as she untied the pink ribbon and opened the box, a smile overtaking her face. "*Chocolate?* There's so much."

"I might have gone a little overboard. I wasn't sure what you liked."

"*I* don't know what I like. Will you try one with me?" She held the box toward him.

"You first."

Her eyes moved over the chocolates. "There are two of these." She handed him a chocolate and picked up its twin.

He winked, and they both ate their chocolates. As the sweet treat melted in his mouth, Sully closed her eyes and tilted her face up, moaning. *Sweet baby Jesus*, this girl just might be the death of him.

"This is *so* good. Let's try another." She set the box between them and found two more matching chocolates, handing him one. She bit into hers. "*Ohmygosh.* This is heavenly. There are pretzels in it. *Pretzels!* How did they think of this?"

He laughed, and as she chose another, he got out of the truck and went around to help her out. He opened her door, and she threw her arms around him.

"Thank you." She held on tight as his arms circled her.

"Totally worth those smiles, darlin'," he said, trying like hell not to think about how good she felt in his arms.

Chapter Eleven

SULLY SAT ON her couch with her beautiful leather sketch-book holder on her lap, sketching Callahan down by the lake. She spent extra time on his eyes, trying to get the honesty and emotions to shine through the way they always did when they were together. Sketching him was easy, as he always seemed to be on her mind. She liked the way his eyes were squinty when he was being serious and the way his laughter made everything about him seem brighter. She drew him smiling, and as she sketched his lips, she got that fluttery feeling in her chest again.

She lifted her pencil and rested her head on the back of the couch, remembering how he'd looked like he hadn't wanted to leave when he'd dropped her at her cabin after dinner and had told her to text if she needed anything. She'd said she would, but she'd known she wouldn't. She eyed her phone on the coffee table, debating texting him. But what would she say? *I miss you?* How was it possible to miss him when she'd only just met him?

A knock at the door drew her from her thoughts. She set her sketchbook on the table beside the chocolates she'd been nibbling on and went to look out the window. Sasha and Birdie were on the porch. She'd forgotten Sasha was stopping by and she hadn't realized Birdie was, too. She opened the door. "Hi."

"Hi," Sasha said. "We thought we'd see if you want to hang out with us."

"I have clothes for you!" Birdie held up several shopping bags. "And we're going to watch a rom-com."

"Clothes?" *What's a rom-com?*

"Yup! Cowboy wanted to get you a few things, but he didn't know your sizes, and since I can guess a girl's size from across the *state*, I offered," Birdie said. "Besides, I have better taste than he does. Is it okay if we come in?"

"Um, sure."

As Birdie walked in, she eyed Sully's outfit. "Oh no. It's worse than I thought. You're borrowing clothes from Cowboy?"

Sully looked down at his flannel shirt, having forgotten she was wearing it. "No. He lent it to me when we went to the lake last night." She closed the door behind them.

"He showed you the lake?" Birdie asked.

Sasha gave Birdie a look Sully couldn't read and said, "That was sweet of him."

"*Yes, it was,*" Birdie said in a singsong voice. "I got you really cute things. Why don't I lay them out on your bed and then you can try them on?" She marched into the bedroom without waiting for an answer.

"Sorry. I know she's a lot," Sasha said quietly. "You can tell her no."

"It's okay. I like that she doesn't pretend to be someone she's not."

Sasha glanced at the sketchbook. "Holy cow, Sully. Did you draw that?"

"Yeah. It's not finished."

"It's fantastic," Sasha said. "Birdie, you have to see this picture of Cowboy she's drawing."

Birdie came out of the bedroom to check it out. "Wow, you drew that?"

"Uh-huh."

"I can barely draw a stick figure," Birdie said. "You almost nailed it, but you drew him smiling, and that's a rarity. Cowboy is more like this." She scowled, brows pinched, and Sasha laughed.

"He is like that a lot," Sully admitted. "But I've seen him smile a number of times."

"Then consider yourself lucky." Birdie's gaze landed on the chocolates. "Oh, you *are* a lucky girl. Did he give you those?"

"Yes." She noticed Birdie and Sasha exchanging glances again. "Why? Is he not allowed to? Will he get in trouble?"

"*No*," Sasha reassured her. "He's definitely allowed to. We've just never known him to give a woman chocolates before."

"But we *love* that he did!" Birdie chimed in. "It's about time Cowboy got his head out of the barn."

"He loves the barn," Sully said.

"A little too much, if you ask me," Birdie said.

"Birdie can't understand our love of horses," Sasha said. "But we're both glad he gave you chocolates. It means he likes you, and that's nice for both of you."

Sully held the box out toward them. "Do you want some? They're delicious."

"I know. I made them." Birdie grinned. "Why don't you try on the clothes. I'm dying to see what you think of them, and then we can get to know each other better."

"Don't be so pushy," Sasha chided.

"That's like asking a dog not to bark." Birdie motioned toward the bedroom. "Go try them on so we can see how they fit."

She liked their lighthearted banter. "That was nice of you, but I really don't need more clothes."

"Don't be silly. Every woman needs more clothes, even when she has a closetful." Birdie turned her by the shoulders and nudged her toward the bedroom, following her in. "Cowboy said you were more natural than flashy, so I went with batik and boho tops, a cozy cardigan, tank tops, a few tees, some basic long-sleeve shirts, and a few pairs of denim shorts and jeans." She held up a gorgeous long-sleeved, flowy white minidress with red and tan flowers. "But I couldn't resist getting you this boho minidress. It's so feminine, and with your hair color, you'll rock the heck out of it." She put it down and picked up a thin, colorful robe. "And you *need* this kimono. It'll look great over a tank top or T-shirt, and you can wear it with shorts or jeans. Last but not least, I wasn't sure if you had a purse, so I got you this adorable canvas crossbody bag."

"I love that kimono. I should let you shop for *me*," Sasha said.

Sully stared incredulously at all the cute outfits and accessories. She must've bought out the store. "It's all beautiful, but—"

"No buts," Birdie said. "Just try them on."

"Let's give her privacy." Sasha pulled Birdie out of the bedroom. "Take your time, Sully."

"Come out and show us each one!" Birdie called out just before Sasha pulled the door closed.

Sully picked up one of the tops and sat on the edge of the bed, clutching it to her chest, as overwhelmed as she was touched that Cowboy had thought of her *again* and that Birdie had gone to the trouble of picking out so many beautiful things for her. She loved the easy styles Birdie had chosen, and she hadn't seen anyone else wearing boho dresses or batik tops. She liked the idea of being different so much, it made her feel a little guilty *and* greedy, which made her feel even guiltier.

"Come on, girlie!" Birdie called out, snapping Sully from her thoughts.

Pushing her guilt away, she stripped off her clothes and tried on a pair of denim shorts with flowers on the back pockets. It felt strange having bare legs, but it was freeing and felt a little rebellious, and she liked that a lot. She put on a purple, pink, and tan V-neck batik top with baggy sleeves gathered at the wrist and turned toward the mirror. Her breath caught in her throat. She looked so different.

She looked *pretty*.

She laughed a little, then quickly covered her mouth.

"I'm eating all your chocolates!" Birdie called out.

What if she thought she looked pretty, but *they* didn't? There was only one way to find out. Steeling herself, she walked out of the bedroom, feeling a little self-conscious.

"Whoa, mama," Birdie exclaimed. "I've still got it. You look *hot*."

"With legs like that, you'll be getting chocolates every week," Sasha said.

Sully blushed and looked down at her legs, wondering if Callahan would think they were nice, too. "I'm not used to wearing shorts."

"Did you move from Alaska?" Birdie teased.

"No. West Virginia. But we weren't allowed to wear shorts."

"Oh." Birdie wrinkled her nose. "Why not? Was it a religious thing?"

"No. We just weren't allowed."

"Well, you are allowed to here, and you look great," Sasha said. "How do they feel?"

Sully touched the hem of the shorts. "They're really comfortable, and I love this shirt."

"*Yay.* Two winners! Try on another outfit," Birdie urged.

She went into the bedroom and tried on a tank top, jeans, and the kimono. The jeans made her look curvier than the ones she'd snagged from the Mega Mart, and the kimono was super cute and comfortable. When she walked out, Birdie whistled, and they gushed over her, making her feel giddy again.

They raved about how cute she looked in every outfit she tried on, bolstering her confidence more with each one. By the time she was down to the last outfit, the dress, she was walking on air. The dress hung loosely around her and reached only to the middle of her thighs, which felt weird, but it was so comfortable, she wanted to live in it.

As she opened the door, Birdie said, "Let's go! Runway time."

Feeling bold, Sully stepped out of the bedroom and twirled. "What do you think?"

"I think I could make a killing as a personal shopper," Birdie said.

"Is that a thing? Personal shopper? If so, you'd be really good at it," Sully said.

"She is, and you look like you walked out of a boho-chic catalog," Sasha said. "You're going to turn a *lot* of heads in that."

There was only one head she was interested in turning. "I don't need to turn heads, but I like how it makes me feel."

"How's that?" Sasha asked.

"*Pretty*," she said honestly.

"Try *gorgeous*, and like it or not, you'll be turning heads," Birdie said. "Cowboy is going to lose his mind."

"In a bad way?" she asked carefully.

"No," they said in unison.

"In the very *best* way," Sasha said.

Sully couldn't stop grinning as she went back into the bedroom and changed into her regular clothes, with Cowboy's flannel over them, loving the feel of being wrapped up in his scent. She looked over the outfits. She loved them all, and she'd be lying to herself if she said she didn't *want* them all, but she didn't *need* them. She would pick one, and then she'd ask Wynnie if she could work in the kitchen to earn money to pay Birdie back. As she tried to choose an outfit, the shorts called out to her because she loved the way she felt in them, but then there was the dress, which felt a whole different type of good. *Cowboy is going to lose his mind.*

She snagged the dress and hung it in the closet. Then she carefully folded the rest of the clothes and carried them out to the living room. "That was a lot of fun. Thank you for buying everything. I'm going to keep the dress, but I'll pay you back for it." She handed Birdie the other clothes.

Birdie popped to her feet. "You didn't like any of these?"

"Are you kidding? I loved them all, but I don't need that many clothes, and I don't have the money to pay for them."

"Cowboy paid for them. They're a gift, and trust me, our brother is *not* short on money." Birdie carried the clothes back into the bedroom.

"But he's already given me too much."

"Cowboy has a big heart, Sully," Sasha said. "I don't know what things were like where you used to live, but here it's a nice gesture to give someone you like a gift. It means you're special to him, and he values your friendship."

"I know he does, but he already gave me the chocolates and drawing supplies."

"He gave you drawing supplies?" Birdie asked, wide-eyed.

"He's so thoughtful," Sasha said, giving Birdie a stern look.

"He is. He's quickly, and unexpectedly, become a good friend."

"Good, because I'm sure he'll want you to keep all the outfits, so you can hash it out with him," Birdie said. "The night is young, and we have a movie to watch. How do you feel about microwave popcorn?"

"I've never had it."

"Seriously? No shorts and no popcorn? That's a tragedy." Birdie whipped a box of microwave popcorn from her bag.

"Birdie." Sasha glowered at her.

"I'm just saying I couldn't live without shorts and popcorn." Birdie put the package of popcorn into the microwave. "Do you like rom-coms?"

Sully looked between them. "What's a rom-com?"

"A romantic comedy." Birdie must have seen her confusion, because she said, "A funny romantic movie?"

"I've never seen a movie."

Birdie's brows slanted. "Did you grow up off the grid or something?"

Sully liked being around them. They were confident and different from the girls at the compound, and from each other, and she didn't want to lie to them about where she'd grown up, but she wasn't ready to share the whole truth, either. "I guess you'd call it that. I lived on a compound. We didn't have microwaves or televisions, and we rarely left our site. I know my life was very different from yours, but I hope you'll still want to hang out tonight."

"Who cares if our lives are different? I like you," Birdie said. "And I've never known anyone who grew up off the grid. Did you have electricity? Water? Internet? Phones?"

Rebel Joe had the internet and all the men had phones, but she didn't need to go into all that. "We had electricity and water, and certain people had internet and phones, but I never did."

"I would have lost my mind," Birdie said.

"That's because you have the attention span of a gnat," Sasha teased. "I think it's cool to live off the grid. Did you live off the land, grow your own food, and make homeopathic remedies?"

"Yes."

"Awesome. Did you like living there?" Sasha asked.

"Not really. I'm glad I'm here."

"We're glad you're here, too," Sasha said.

"Why *are* you at the ranch?" Birdie asked. "Did you have a drug problem?"

"*Birdie*," Sasha scolded.

"Sorry," Birdie said. "I didn't mean to pry. It's just that most of the people who come here have come from rehab or jail, and I didn't think you came from jail."

"It's okay. I'm here because there might be some people from the compound looking for me, and I don't want to go back."

"I don't blame you," Birdie said. "If you ever want to go out and see the town, Sasha and I can show you all the cool places."

"Thanks. I appreciate that. For now I think I'll stick around the ranch, but I'd really like to eat popcorn and watch a rom-com with you."

THE DARK KNIGHTS' clubhouse, an old firehouse at the edge of town, had always been a sanctuary for Cowboy, much like the ranch. It was the place where he could shoot the shit with the men he'd known most of his life and trusted explicitly. Cowboy sat with his brothers and buddies, too keyed up to talk to the guys about taking down the cult to sit still. He was biding his time as his father and Manny sat at the head table giving a wrap-up of the Ride Clean fundraising event. How could that have been just last weekend? It felt like Sully had been at the ranch for a month.

Doc nudged him, speaking quietly. "If your leg bounces any harder, you're going to start an earthquake. Chill out. He'll get to it."

Cowboy stilled his leg and pulled out his phone, texting Sasha. *Did you check on Sully?*

Her response rolled in a minute later. *Yes! We're at the Roadhouse having drinks with Birdie.*

What the fuck? He thumbed out, *Get her out of there NOW. She's not supposed to leave the ranch.* He should have clued Sasha in to what was going on so Sully wouldn't be in danger. He knew the guys watching the ranch and, more specifically her cabin, would've followed them to the bar, but they weren't *him*, and even the thought of Sully getting leered at and uncomfortable made his blood boil.

Sasha's response was immediate. *Ha ha! Gotcha! We're watching a movie at her cabin. Why can't she leave, and since when do you buy chocolates for girls at the ranch?* She added a heart-eyed emoji.

Relief swept through him, and on its heels came a hot streak of jealousy. He wanted to be watching a movie with Sully. Never in his life would he give up church for anything, but he wanted to be with her more than he'd ever wanted anything. Well, almost anything. He wanted to get his hands on the fuckers who hurt her just as badly. He sent a response to Sasha. *It's part of her program.*

His phone vibrated a minute later. *And the clothes and chocolates? Are they part of her program, too?*

Uttering a curse, he typed, *Just being nice.*

His phone vibrated again, and he read Sasha's text. *Liar.* He pocketed his phone, grinding his back teeth against that reality.

"Our next order of business is about Sullivan Tate, the young lady we brought to the ranch Saturday night," his father announced. "It has come to our attention that the Free Rebellion cult she escaped from is abusing young girls—"

Cowboy shot to his feet. "Not only that. I think they kidnapped Sully. I think she's Casey Lawler, the girl who went missing twenty years ago, and I know others don't agree based on the age-progression photo, but I feel it in my gut, and I want to take those fuckers down."

"Hell yeah!" someone called out, and murmurs from the other men followed.

"Let's get those assholes!" Hyde hollered.

"Hold on." His father held his hands up, quieting the room. "That's speculation about kidnapping. I spoke to the PI who was hired over the summer to try to find that missing girl—"

"Casey Lawler," Cowboy growled angrily. "Her name is Cassandra 'Casey' Lawler, and her sister is looking for her."

"*Right*," his father bit out. "Reggie said when Casey first went missing, the detectives on the case checked out the cult and there was no sign of her, but he also said something smelled dirty about that whole investigation. He went back a couple of months ago and questioned members of the cult, and there was no sign of Casey."

Cowboy's hands fisted. "Then they fucking *hid* her."

"Maybe so. If you'd hold your damn tongue and let me finish, you'd hear there's more to this," his father barked. "Reggie has a hotline set up for calls about Casey, and a few days after Sully escaped, they got an anonymous tip from someone who thought they spotted someone who looked like Casey with a trucker. Reggie said they've gotten hundreds of bogus sightings, but this one plays out in the way Sully got here."

"See? I fucking knew it." Cowboy sneered. Had that person noticed her eyes, too? Hell, it didn't matter. At least he wasn't alone in his assumption.

"I see a likeness, too," Doc called out, meeting Cowboy's confused gaze. "I didn't at first, but I didn't spend much time looking at that flyer before she got here."

Cowboy nodded, glad his brother had taken a closer look.

"I *hear* you, but we can't just accuse them of kidnapping without proof. Sully's DNA results should be back this week, and hopefully that will give us the answers we need. But if the test proves that Sully *is* Casey, kidnapping is a matter for the FBI, not our club."

"So, what are we supposed to do? Sit on our asses and do nothing while other girls are being abused?" Cowboy shouted.

"Cowboy is right." Doc pushed to his feet. "Take out the kidnapping and you still have abuse."

Dare stood. "I'm *in* to take those fuckers down."

"We're in, too." Rebel, Hyde, and Taz rose to their feet, followed by every other man in the room, all standing and calling out the same.

His father pushed to his feet, and the murmurs died down. "We're *all* in to take down child abusers," he said vehemently. "Manny and I would head up that charge. But the Dark Knights don't go in half-cocked to any situation, so sit your asses down and listen to what we're up against."

Everyone sat down, except Cowboy.

His father held his gaze, speaking gruffly. "Bullet and Diesel are watching the comings and goings and doing recon on the compound. This is what we know right now. The Free Rebellion has an arsenal of weapons."

"We've got plenty of guns," Cowboy fumed.

"Yes," his father agreed. "But there are dozens of women and children on that compound. Do you want to be responsible for them getting caught in the crossfire?"

"Fuck."

"Fuck is right, son. We *all* want to do the right thing, but we've got to be smart about it. Reggie said the FBI handles a number of crimes against children, including physical and sexual assault. We're going to help them take down the Free Rebellion, but we're not doing it in a way that could end the lives of innocent women and children. Wynnie is speaking to Sully about pressing charges, and when the DNA results are in, we'll know if we're dealing with kidnapping and abuse, or just the latter."

"This is bullshit," Cowboy fumed. "They deserve to have their asses handed to them."

A rumble of agreement rose around him.

"They *will*. We've got ex-cons among us," Manny said. "They'll tell you what happens to child abusers in prison."

"They'll get beaten within an inch of their lives, over and over again, but never killed," Hyde said. "Because dead bodies don't feel pain."

"If it's not done by my hands, it's not fucking enough." Cowboy sat down, feeling like a chained tiger. He pulled out his phone and texted Diesel. *Hey, man. I need a favor.*

SULLY SAT BETWEEN Birdie and Sasha on the couch in her cabin watching the end of *Never Been Kissed*, a movie about Josie Geller, a reporter who goes back to high school impersonating a high schooler and falls for her English teacher, Sam Coulson. Sully had thought the movie might make her laugh, but it was a tumultuous ride that had her laughing, crying, and getting all twisted up inside, the way she did around Callahan more often than not. She clutched a handful of tissues, watching Josie lay her heart on the line in the middle of a baseball field in front of the whole town, hoping Sam would hear her confession and return her affection. But Sam was nowhere in sight, and Sully's heart was breaking.

"Where *is* he?" she pleaded angrily. "He *can't* just leave her there."

"He won't," Sasha said.

"But he *is*." Commotion erupted in the movie, and Sully sat up straighter, scooting to the edge of the couch as Sam appeared in the bleachers. "There he is!" Tears spilled from her eyes as he ran down to the field with the crowd cheering him on. He apologized to Josie for being late and kissed the hell out of her.

Birdie and Sasha cheered. Sully was laughing and crying, unable to look away from Josie and Sam kissing, as mesmerized by the emotions coursing through her as she was by the ones emanating from Josie and Sam. The townspeople applauded and whistled, as the never-ending kiss bound Josie and Sam together in a way that felt magical, irritating the heck out of Sully.

She sank back against the cushions, conflicting emotions whipping through her. "Why do people watch movies like that? The whole thing was torture. The kids were mean to Josie, and she felt so bad about herself. It was so up and down. My heart broke several times for her, and *then* they made kissing look magical and wonderful, and it's not like that at *all*."

"The roller coaster of emotions is the whole point," Sasha said. "It makes the happily ever after that much sweeter."

"And with the right guy, kissing is *exactly* like that." Birdie flopped back beside her. "Don't you love the anticipation of a first kiss? When the chemistry is so strong, you get butterflies, and every time you think of the guy, your heart races, and you can't wait to see him again?"

"And the moments right before you kiss," Sasha added. "When he puts his hands on your face or around your waist, and you hold your breath, just waiting for that special moment."

"The face grab! *Yes.* I *love* that," Birdie exclaimed. "And when your lips finally touch, you get so swept up in the other person, nothing else matters."

Sully listened with rapt attention. She had only *ever* felt those things with Callahan, and she hadn't even kissed him. "I've never felt that way during a kiss."

Sasha and Birdie looked confused.

"Never?" Sasha asked.

"You've never felt butterflies or your heart racing?" Birdie asked.

"I have felt those things, but never when I was kissing."

"So you felt that way about a guy, but you didn't feel it when you kissed him?" Birdie asked. "That's disappointing, but some guys are just bad kissers."

Sully shook her head. "No. I mean, there's only been one guy who makes me feel like that, and I haven't kissed him."

"Do you want to?" Sasha asked.

Something about the look in her eyes made Sully feel like she was asking if she wanted to kiss Callahan, which made her nervous. She shrugged noncommittally, but her body was saying *yes!* And those overanxious butterflies in her chest made it hard to think straight. She'd been trying really hard not to mentally go there with Callahan, but now she wondered if Gaia and Wynnie had been right. Was there more to intimacy than just servicing someone? She couldn't imagine it being pleasurable, but that on-screen kiss and what the girls had said brought Callahan's words rushing back to her again. *I'm solely focused on bringing her pleasure, and the only way to do that is to listen to what she says, feel her reactions, and read her body language.* He was such an intense listener when she spoke, she could only imagine the way he read a woman's body.

"Wait, you didn't leave the guy you feel that way about on the compound, did you?" Birdie asked.

"No. I didn't know him then," Sully said.

Birdie and Sasha exchanged another curious glance. "Well, when the time is right, I'm sure it'll happen," Sasha said. "It's hard to fight chemistry."

Sully reached for a piece of chocolate as Sasha and Birdie talked about the *heat* of chemistry, and kissing, and the feel of a man's hands, while she couldn't stop thinking about that kiss and Callahan. Would he kiss like Sam kissed Josie? Would the world slip away like it had when they'd danced?

The sound of a motorcycle sent Birdie to the window. "It's Cowboy."

Sully's pulse skyrocketed, and her cheeks burned, as if she'd been caught thinking about kissing him. She knew that was crazy, but that didn't stop her from feeling like it was written all over her face.

"Does he come over every night?" Birdie asked.

"I have trouble sleeping, so sometimes we take a late walk together." Was that why he was there? Had he skipped going to the bar with the guys to see her? Oh boy, that made her even more nervous.

"*Really?* I love that." Birdie hurried to the door before Sully could get there and yanked it open. "Hey, big brother. Unfortunately, you have the wrong equipment for girls' night."

"What's up, Bird?" His gaze drifted over Birdie's shoulder to Sully. He winked, despite his serious expression, and her butterflies turned to bees.

Birdie's eyes lit with mischief. "Sully looks hot in the clothes you bought her."

"She's a gorgeous woman. She'd look good in anything. Got my credit card?" He held out his hand, those serious dark eyes drifting back to Sully.

The fire in her cheeks spread to her chest with his compliment. She couldn't stop looking at his lips. What was wrong with her? That movie must have really messed with her mind. She tore her eyes away as Birdie handed him his credit card.

"Take her someplace where she can wear a dress," Birdie said. "But not tonight. We're having a girls' night, and I have some unanswered questions for our new friend."

"Birdie, don't do that," he warned.

"I won't let her," Sasha said from the couch.

"Give me a second with Sully, will ya?" he said.

He looked so serious, it rattled her. Had he noticed something different in the way she was looking at him? If he did, maybe he was mad about it. She remembered that he was supposed to be making sure she was okay. It was his *job* to be nice to her. She swallowed hard against that reality as Birdie stepped aside, waving her through the door.

As she stepped onto the porch, he looked bigger than life in his black leather vest, carrying his helmet in one hand, his tree-trunk legs anchored to her porch with black biker boots. His gaze swept down the length of her, and his brows knitted. She remembered she was wearing his shirt and started taking it off. "Sorry. I meant to give it back."

His hand covered hers, stopping her, and a sexy grin slid into place. "It looks cute on you, darlin'. Keep it."

She felt the world tilting on its axis and didn't know what to say.

"Are you having a good time?"

"Yeah," she managed. "Your sisters are great."

"They'll probably keep you busy pretty late, so I guess we'll skip our walk."

Her stomach sank, but she tried to hide her disappointment. "Okay."

"Want to catch the sunrise in the morning? I can pick you up around six fifteen. Sun's up at seven."

Her heart skipped. "I'd love that."

"See you then." He turned to leave, and as he reached for the screen door, he looked over his shoulder and said, "For the record, I'll miss our walk tonight."

She watched him descend the steps and climb onto his motorcycle, and as he drove away, she whispered, "Me too."

Chapter Twelve

SULLY WAS UP and ready by five thirty the next morning, anxious to spend time with Callahan and to see her first sunrise. The girls had stayed over until midnight, and she'd heard Callahan on her porch shortly after. She'd woken up at three in the morning from a dream that had turned into a nightmare. In it, she and Callahan were standing in a field with the horses, and he'd cradled her face between his hands the way his sisters had described, lowering his lips toward hers. Her heart had raced, and her body had heated, but before their lips touched, Rebel Joe's face appeared out of nowhere, startling her awake. She'd *never* dreamed about kissing a man, and she hated that Rebel Joe still had a hold on her, but when she'd peeked out the window and seen Callahan sleeping on a chair on the porch, she'd known Rebel Joe could never touch her again.

It had taken a while for her to get back to sleep, and Callahan had been gone when she'd woken up again, but she'd known he'd be back. She'd showered and dressed and added a number of items to her things-she-wanted-to-do list, including *Get a job*, and *Be kissed like Josie Geller*, leaving off *by Callahan*. She wanted to do something special for him this morning, but she didn't have the right ingredients for baking, so she'd made him coffee instead and put it in a thermos she found in a cabinet. It was piping hot when she answered the door at six fifteen sharp. He looked just as strikingly handsome as he had last night, only today he was wearing another flannel over a black T-shirt.

"Aren't you a sight for tired eyes? You look awfully pretty, darlin'."

Her cheeks warmed, and she looked down at the bootleg jeans, olive-green tank top, and tan cardigan with pale green around the edges that Birdie had given her. "Thank you. These are some of the clothes you had Birdie buy for me, which was beyond nice of you, and I'm going to pay you back."

"Seeing you in them is payment enough."

She shook her head, unable to help her smile, because she knew he meant it, and she also knew he expected nothing in return. She wanted to wrap up his kindness and stow it away for those harder moments when she needed a reason to feel good. As the thought hit her, she realized she hadn't had many of those harder moments lately. She'd been happier this week than ever before.

"We'll see about that," she said, and held up the thermos. "I made you coffee. I wanted to make you biscuits or muffins, but I didn't have the ingredients." That sexy grin appeared again, and her mind tiptoed back to thoughts of kissing him. *No more rom-coms!*

"You didn't have to do that. The coffee is much appreciated, darlin', but we're both going to need two hands for this. I'll drink it when we get back." He wrapped his hand around the thermos, his fingers covering hers for a few heart-stopping beats, before taking the thermos and setting it on the table by the chair. "We'd better get going. The sun waits for no one."

As she grabbed her key, he said, "Listen, I'm leaving tomorrow after breakfast to take care of some business. I've arranged for Doc to be with you, and you'll spend time with Sasha and the horses, too. I'll be back Friday morning and will come get you for breakfast."

Disappointment weighed heavily on her, but she tried not to let it show. "Okay." As they walked off the porch, she saw a big black horse. "We're taking a horse?"

"He's taking us. This is Thunder."

"But I don't know how to ride."

"We're going to work on that soon, but for now I've got you. You'll sit in front of me."

Her nerves pinged as he led her to the horse and gave her a moment to offer her hand and make friends with Thunder. The horse was much thicker than Sunshine. He reminded her of Callahan, immensely powerful but sweet when she offered her hand.

"Ready, darlin'? When I lift you up, swing your leg over his back and hold on to his mane."

"Won't that hurt him?"

"Not even a little," he said with a low laugh.

He clutched her waist, lifting her like she was light as a feather, and set her down on the horse's back. She let out a surprised squeak. "It's so high!"

"Are you afraid of heights?"

"*No.* I jumped from the attic of Mega Mart, remember? It was just surprising."

He climbed on behind her and grabbed the reins. She could feel his heart beating against her back, his body heat making her tingle in places she didn't realize she could. He made a clicking sound and guided Thunder up the road and onto the long grassy expanse that led up to the main house. It was strangely provocative feeling the massive animal moving beneath her, with Callahan's strong body pressed against her back.

He leaned in, his scruff brushing her cheek, sending more tingles to those surprising places as he spoke huskily into her ear. "You a'right?"

"*Yes.* Can we go faster?"

"Sure can. How much faster are you thinking?"

"As fast as he can go."

His breath warmed her ear as a low laugh tumbled out. "Okay, darlin', but you've got to trust me so you don't get hurt."

"I wouldn't be on this horse if I didn't." She was hit again by how foreign it was to trust a man other than Ansel, especially since she'd grown up with Ansel. She didn't know how old Callahan was, but she guessed he was several years older.

He took the reins in one hand, wrapping his other securely around her middle. "This is going to be bumpy and your instinct will be to tense up, but try to relax and give yourself over to me. Let *my* body guide *your* movement. Do you think you can do that?"

Why did that make her think of kissing him...and more? She managed a nod.

"Okay, here we go."

She clung to the horse's mane as he leaned forward, holding her tight, lifting her so her bottom rose off the horse, and growled out, "*Hya!*" Thunder bolted forward, and Sully instantly tensed up. But Callahan was holding her so tight, she felt completely safe, like nothing bad could happen, and she didn't have to fight too hard against her instincts to relax into his movements, because her instinct to trust him overpowered everything else. They charged across the grass, the crisp air kissing her skin as the world sped by. It was exhilarating and spectacular, like she was flying without a care in the world. She felt freer than she ever had. She had a fleeting thought about how she could possibly feel free when she was relying on Callahan to make sure she didn't fall, but somehow she knew it was *because* of him that she felt so free. Thunder galloped up the hill, passing the main house and flying across the field behind it. He sprinted up another hill. As they neared the crest, Callahan slowed him down, bringing him to a stop with a "*Whoa*," and tightened his hold around Sully's middle. "You still with me, sweetheart?"

The way he said it felt intimate and protective. "*Yeah*," she said breathlessly, her heart racing. "That was amazing! I want to do it again." She laughed. "I want to do it all day long!"

He laughed, too, giving her a squeeze around her middle. "We'll make a cowgirl out of you yet."

He dismounted and helped her off the horse, setting her on her feet. He was *right there*, so close, she wanted to touch his face, just to see how it felt. She ached to run her fingers over his tight jaw and feel the tension he held there. To feel the scratch of his whiskers, the ruggedness of his cheekbones, and—as if she'd ever have the courage to do it—to trace his lips. But he was looking at her with so much admiration and something tangibly deeper, she wondered if he sensed her thoughts, and it was all she could do to remember how to breathe.

He reached up and tucked a lock of her hair behind her ear, and that felt special, too. Maybe riding that fast had jostled her brains. *And my heart?*

"Second-guessing trusting me, darlin'?" he asked.

She shook her head. "No. That was incredible."

"*You* were incredible." He tied the horse to a tree and took her hand, leading her to the top of the hill. Her heart nearly stopped at the sight of a thick plaid blanket spread out on the grass, with a picnic basket and another blanket beside it. She looked at the man who was opening so many doors for her, showing her things she'd only dreamed of, and proving that all men weren't arrogant abusers and was at a loss for words.

"Your first sunrise should be memorable."

"I can't believe you did all this. Do you always do all this when you watch a sunrise?"

"All what? This?" He gestured to the blanket and picnic basket. "Or bring company?"

"Both, I guess," she said awkwardly.

"You're the first, darlin', for both."

The *first*? Her pulse quickened. She'd assumed a man like him, who loved the outdoors and sunrises, would have shared his love of them with many girlfriends. She wanted to ask why he hadn't, but as they sat on the blanket and she drank in the glorious ribbons of orange and yellow peeking over the mountaintops, her question was lost in the beauty of the moment. She stole a glance at Callahan, who was leaning back on his palms, his long legs crossed at the ankles. He was as relaxed as could be, enjoying the sunrise, while she was mesmerized by the man who was giving her yet another of the most special experiences of her life.

"You're looking the wrong way, darlin'. The sunrise is over there." He grinned, nodding toward the view.

"I'm just trying to figure you out."

"I'm not going anywhere. Figure me out after you watch the morning come to life."

She liked that idea and leaned back as he was, crossing her ankles.

"There you go. Isn't that better?"

As gorgeous as the sunrise was, it didn't make her feel as good as seeing him did. "The world seems so big from here. Full of possibilities and so much beauty."

"What was the compound like?"

"Not like this. It was all overgrown grass with worn foot-paths snaking through it, with broken-down trailers and shacks in various stages of deterioration. There was one big building with bathrooms and a kitchen. That's where we ate and bathed, went to school, and had group meetings. Ivy was *everywhere*. It found its way into pop-up campers and tents and snaked up the corners and sides of the big building and all the shacks, which made them look like they'd sprouted from the earth. There were firepits, but not stone like the one at the cabin where I'm staying. Just big pits in the center of dirt clearings with upturned stumps surrounding them. We had weathered wooden tables beneath vinyl awnings and tarps. The whole place was surrounded by trees, but they didn't feel beautiful. They felt like bars, trapping me in."

"You were trapped, darlin'."

"I know I was. I still wake up every morning expecting to be back there, like it was all a dream, and then you show up and I know it's real. I always knew there was a lot more to life than what I had. Our walks, getting to know everyone over meals, and last night with your sisters all make me so happy."

"I'm glad. My sisters stayed pretty late. Was that okay? I hope they didn't try to get into your business."

She didn't want to tell him that Birdie had asked a lot of questions about the two of them after he'd stopped by. She hadn't told his sisters that he was the butterfly-inducing man she wanted to kiss, of course. She'd simply told them the truth, that she and Callahan were becoming good friends.

"They didn't. It was nice. We watched a movie and talked. I'd never seen a movie before. It was kind of weird watching someone else's relationship on television." As gorgeous rays of color crept higher into the sky, she said, "This is a million times better than the movie, but I had a good time last night, and I liked getting to know your sisters."

"I'm glad. Birdie can be nosy *and* noisy, but she and Sasha are good people."

"I like Birdie just as she is. She's unapologetically herself, like you."

"I like who you are, too, darlin'."

How could such simple words make her feel so special? He held her gaze, inducing more butterflies. He must have sensed her nervousness, because he looked out at the sunrise again and said, "What movie did you watch?"

"*Never Been Kissed.*"

"*Christ.* What's that?"

"A rom-com." She smiled. "I didn't even know what a rom-com was until last night. It was so up and down. Some parts were hard to watch. Is that how relationships are in real life?"

"I've never seen the movie."

"But you've had relationships, right?"

"Short term. I don't do drama, and those movies usually have a lot of it."

"I'm with you. I don't think I can do drama either. Why don't they write love stories without all the ups and downs? I lived on pins and needles my whole life. It just seems unnecessarily stressful to put all those anxious moments in a romance."

"Most of the girls I know love the roller coaster of romantic comedies, but I understand why you didn't enjoy it."

"I liked parts of it. The happy parts." She was quiet for a minute, wanting to share more but worrying and hesitating only because she didn't want to bore him with her troubles. But he'd told her she could tell him anything, and she trusted that. "This might sound weird, but sometimes when we're eating at the main house with everyone and I hear other girls talking, and last night when your sisters and I were hanging out, I get the feeling I'll never catch up with them. Like I lived in an alternate society for too long, and I'll never be that carefree or understand all the things other girls do."

"That's not strange at all. I understand why you feel that way. But I think some of us have lived too much life and seen and experienced too many things to ever be truly carefree. And the people you think are carefree rarely are. Everyone has their trials and tribulations. Some a lot worse than others. But the bottom line is, this life we've got is different for everyone. You don't have to catch up with anyone. You just have to be happy with who you are."

"I *am*. I mean, I have things I want to learn and do so I don't feel so out of touch with the modern world, but I think I'm a good person."

"You are a good person, and speaking of things you want to learn and do, when are you going to show me that list of yours?"

"I'm not done with it."

"It'll never be finished, because we're always learning and growing. That's the point of a list like that. Ten years from now you'll have different things you want to do, but you'll look back and see how much you've accomplished. We should start working on it before it gets too long."

"We already are. I'm watching a sunrise, and you said you'd teach me to ride a horse. Those are on my list. Do you have a list of things you want to do?"

"Sure."

"Like what?"

"Like watching more sunrises with you and teaching you to ride a horse."

She laughed softly. "We need to talk about this generous soul you're harboring."

"No, we don't."

"Yes, we do. You bought me way too much stuff. I'm going to talk to Wynnie about getting a job so I can pay you back."

"I'm all for you working if that's what you want to do, but I won't take a penny of your money."

"Callahan."

"You can argue all you want, but you're wasting your breath. You came here with one duffel bag, and everyone needs clothes. That *isn't* up for debate."

"And the art supplies? And the chocolates?"

"We already had that discussion. Is it so bad that I like to see you smile?"

"No. I just wish I could do something for you."

"Trust me, darlin'. You're already doing more than you know."

Chapter Thirteen

COWBOY SPED THROUGH the winding roads of Bucksbo-ro, West Virginia, Thursday night on the motorcycle Diesel had arranged to have waiting for him at the airport. Thoughts of Sully trampled through his mind. *I don't want to pay with my body...It was expected of me...The box and the brand and Thursday nights.* He gripped the handlebars tighter, jaw so tight he thought his teeth might crack, and he didn't give a fuck if they did. Rebel Joe was going to pay for what he'd done.

He opened the throttle and didn't slow down until he rolled into town, which looked more neglected than lived in. He cruised down the main drag and spotted the run-down bar at the end of the block. The *G* in the red neon NIGEL'S sign above the door blinked on and off. As he turned onto the side road across the street from the bar, he spotted Diesel's motorcycle and pulled over. He climbed off his bike, and Diesel, a mountain of a man at six foot six with cold dark eyes and absolutely no people skills, walked out from the shadows with three of Cowboy's cousins. *Fucking Diesel.*

Cowboy tore off his helmet. "What the fuck, Diesel? These guys have babies and wives. I told you *I'd* handle this."

"Good to see you, too, asshole," Diesel said. "I'm not bringing a body back to Tiny. That motherfucker would tear me apart."

"He wouldn't have had to. I said *I've got this*," Cowboy seethed, hoping it was true. He couldn't die. Not before he had a chance to give Sully all the things she deserved.

Bullet set a serious stare on him. "What the hell, Cowboy? Our babies didn't take our balls." He was ex–Special Forces, as big as Diesel, bearded, and tatted from neck to ankle.

"Our wives did," Bear, the youngest of his Maryland cousins, and the biggest jokester, said with a laugh.

Bones clapped Bear on the shoulder. "Speak for yourself, little brother. I've still got mine." Bones was a clean-cut physician, and like Doc, he looked low-key and harmless but could flick like a switch to lethal as poison in the blink of an eye.

Cowboy eyed his cousins. "I appreciate the backup, but please tell me you did *not* tell Biggs, because my old man would kick my ass if he knew I was here."

"No shit," Bullet growled.

"There are quite a few things Biggs doesn't know about," Diesel said.

"And we sure as hell wouldn't tell him the Boy Scout is out for blood when the president of the club told him to stand down," Bear added.

Thank God. Cowboy looked at the bar, and fire blazed in his gut. "Is the asshole in there?" He rolled his shoulders back, wanting to charge in there and tear the fucker apart.

"Yup. This is your target." Diesel handed him his phone with a picture of two guys walking into the bar. "He's the one on the left. Brown hair, looks to be in his late forties. He's a big guy, but he's soft. He's got nothing on you."

Not many do. Cowboy studied the picture of the man who had assaulted Sully for years and saw red. Blood red.

"They came in that truck. Your guy was driving." Diesel motioned to a truck parked beside the bar. "But the bar's filled with people he knows. So don't get any ideas. We're sticking to the plan and taking him down twelve miles out."

"Banker Road." Cowboy had memorized the map Diesel had sent.

"It's desolate as fuck," Diesel said. "Nobody's going to see this go down."

Cowboy eyed his cousins. "You guys should head home to your wives. You know these guys are probably packin' heat, and I don't need your bodies on my conscience."

"How about you stop daydreaming and we get to our places before this fucker comes out?" Bullet motioned to Bones and Bear, and the three of them headed across the street.

"You good?" Diesel asked Cowboy.

"I will be. Did you bring what I asked for?"

Diesel nodded. "You know this isn't going to take away that sick feeling you get every time you think of what he did to your girl. It's a part of her, and now it's a part of you."

My girl. Don't I wish. "No shit. This isn't about that. It's about vengeance and justice. I'm doing what she and those other innocent girls couldn't't."

"We got this, brother." Diesel tugged him into a hug and clapped him on the back.

They climbed on their motorcycles, and Diesel drove down the road, getting into position. Cowboy turned his bike around and parked at the corner, facing the bar, as Bullet's truck headed out of town, followed by Bear and Bones on their motorcycles.

COWBOY WAS RUNNING on sheer adrenaline, his heart rate spiking every time the door to the bar opened. He didn't know how long they waited, but when Rebel Joe finally came out of that bar with some other asshole, it took everything he had not to forgo the plan and charge forward.

He watched them climb into their old Ford truck and pulled onto the road behind them as they drove away. He drove past Diesel and saw him texting the other guys. A few minutes later, Diesel's headlight shone in his rearview mirror. A mile later Bear took up the rear. Cowboy thought of Sully, safe at the ranch with Doc watching over her. He'd do whatever it took to make sure she could move forward without fear of ever being hurt again. He tightened his grip on the handlebars as they turned off the main road and drove down a few back roads. They finally turned onto Banker, a mile from where Bullet was waiting in his truck on the side of the road.

A mile from retribution.

Cowboy drove around Rebel Joe's truck, as if he were going to pass them on the narrow road, just as Bones's headlight appeared barreling toward them in the opposite direction, and Bullet's truck pulled out, blocking the road in front of them. Rebel Joe slammed on the brakes. Cowboy and the others were already on their feet, storming forward. Cowboy threw Rebel Joe's door open, hauling the hollering man out of the driver's seat, and slammed him against the side of the truck at the same time Diesel dragged the other guy's ass out of the passenger seat.

"Who the fuck are you?" Rebel Joe fumed.

"Your worst fucking nightmare." Cowboy's fist connected

with his jaw, and Rebel Joe's head snapped back. He hit him again and again, blood pouring from the prick's mouth and nose. Cowboy released him, letting him step away from the truck. The guy stumbled and swung, but Cowboy easily dodged it, hulking over him, gritting, "This is for Sully." He punched him in the gut. Rebel Joe doubled over, and an uppercut sent the asshole reeling backward. He landed on the pavement with a *thud*. Cowboy was on him in seconds. "And this is for every other girl you've ever touched." His fists flew. Blinded by rage, he landed punch after punch, until he was dragged off the prick's bloody, limp body. Seething, he fought to get back to him, to do more damage.

"Cowboy!" Bullet hollered. "You're gonna kill him, man. He's not worth it."

"I *want* him dead," Cowboy barked, trying to break free from Bullet's and Bear's grasps.

"He's *done*, man. He ain't moving," Bear said.

Bones was leaning over Rebel Joe. He looked at Bullet and nodded.

"I left you a piece of this fucker," Diesel said from the other side of the truck. "His name's Hoyt."

Cowboy ripped his arms away from his cousins and strode around the truck. The guy's nose was broken, his mouth bleeding, eyes nearly swollen shut. "You fucking *branded* her." The first punch sent Hoyt to the ground, the second knocked him out, and the third was to ensure he stayed there. Cowboy pushed to his feet, standing over the piece of shit, and held out his hand. Diesel handed him one of the two branding irons he'd had made, and Bullet was behind him, holding the blowtorch.

When the deed was done, Hoyt had CHILD ABUSER branded on his neck, and Cowboy stalked back to Rebel Joe, lying on the pavement. He smacked him until he opened his eyes. "I want you awake for this, motherfucker. There'll be no hiding from the boys in prison." They heated the second iron, and Rebel Joe screamed until he passed out as Cowboy branded CHILD RAPIST on his neck.

Chapter Fourteen

IT WAS CLOSING in on six o'clock Friday morning when Cowboy arrived back at the ranch. He stopped in front of Sully's cabin and rolled down his window as Doc came off the porch to talk to him. "Thanks for watching over her. Everything good?"

"Yup. She's in her cabin, and I covered for you with Dad. He thinks you went to help wrangle some injured wild horses." He glanced at Cowboy's cut-up knuckles and the blood splattered on his shirt. "You okay? Anything broken?"

"I'm fine."

"How about your head? Need to talk?"

"Nah. I'm good." He'd done nothing but pick apart what he'd done on the flight back. There was no pride in it, but there was a definite sense of satisfaction and at least a modicum of justice for Sully. "You can take off. I'm just going to shower. Do you want a ride home?"

"No thanks. I'll walk. Glad you made it back alive."

"That makes two of us."

As Doc headed home, Cowboy drove up the hill to his place. He climbed out of his truck and saw his father rising from a chair on the porch. His father crossed his arms, nailing him with a harsh stare. *Fuck.* Cowboy drew his shoulders back and went to face his due.

As he climbed the porch steps, he said, "How'd you find out?"

"There was no *finding out*," his father hissed. "I knew you were taking things into your own hands the second you sat down in the meeting."

"How?"

"Because I *raised* you. I know every damn look in your eyes, and that one said, *Fuck the FBI. Fuck my old man. I'm handling this.*"

Cowboy lifted his chin. "Then why didn't you stop me?"

His father closed the distance between them, fury and worry warring in his eyes. "Because you're a man, son, and it ain't my place to stop you. You're just lucky you came back in one piece because I don't lie to your mother, and if something had happened to you and she'd asked if I knew you were going, I'd have to tell her I did, and *that* might've cost me the love of my life."

"I know I should apologize for going against you and the club, but I *can't.* I *had* to go." He couldn't keep his voice from escalating. "And if I had the choice, even knowing I'm going to carry the weight of what I did with me until the day I die, I'd do it again."

His father's eyes narrowed.

"You raised me to do the right thing, and I did it. Now you can kick me out of the club or give me hell. But just do it, because I want to shower and get back to Sully."

His father's jaw clenched tight. "How'd you get there and back so fast?"

"I called Treat. Told him I had to get to Maryland for an emergency." Treat Braden was a real estate mogul and owned a private jet. He was also the son of one of their father's oldest friends and lived a couple of towns away from the ranch in Weston, Colorado.

"Jesus, Cowboy. You know what that costs him?"

"I do, and I offered to pay."

"And he didn't take your money, did he?"

"No, sir." Cowboy felt a dose of shame for that, but he rolled his shoulders back, holding his father's gaze. "It was worth it, and you can't tell me you wouldn't have done the same thing for Mom."

"You're damn right I would have. But I wouldn't have been dumb enough to trust that big of a secret to brothers who can't lie worth shit."

"What're you talking about?"

"None of y'all can lie to save your life. You're all just like you were when you were four, six, and eight, when you set the damn hay barn on fire."

Cowboy remembered that all too clearly. They'd heard about starting fires without matches, and they'd gone for it—in the fucking hay barn. Idiots.

"I could've gotten Doc to fold like a deck of cards yesterday, but I didn't need to. I asked where you were, and he got that look like he was already caught, just as he did back then. And you know Dare's lyin' grin hasn't changed. And then there's you." His father scoffed. "You've never even tried to lie. You climbed those steps staring me down just like you did as a kid, ready to take whatever punishment I doled out. My fucking Boy Scout."

Cowboy clenched his teeth.

"You know that's why your grandfather got you into Scouts, don't you? Because you're the one who got them to try to light a fire without matches. You've always had a thing about survival. It's no wonder that little lady caught your eye. She's made of the same grit you are. But just learning about survival was never good enough for you. You wanted to know you could do it and master it. Hell, Cowboy, the summer after you turned nine, you packed a bag and went out to the woods and told us you'd be back in a couple of days. Do you know how hard it was for me to watch your every step without you seeing me? You were a spry little thing, climbing trees and running through the woods like a wild banshee."

Cowboy's chest constricted. "You did that? I thought I was out there all alone."

"You're never alone, son. Now get your ass over here." His father hauled him into a hug. "Don't you ever scare me like that again."

"I can't make any promises."

"No, I guess you can't. By the way, if you think Biggs wasn't watching all that go down last night with more of his guys at the ready, then you don't have enough respect for your uncle."

"*Shit.* He knew?"

"Fathers always know. You did some pretty heavy shit. You might want to talk to your mother or Dare about how to handle all that."

Maybe one day.

COWBOY GOT DOWN to Sully's cabin at seven and found a note on the door. *Callahan, I went to the lake. I'll be back in time for breakfast. Sully*

They had enough guys watching the grounds that he knew she was safe, and as he set out for the lake, he felt himself smiling, glad his nature girl felt comfortable enough to explore.

It didn't take him long to reach the lake, and as he came off the trail, he saw Sully standing in waist-deep water. Her hair was piled up on her head, her face tipped up to the sun, fingers trailing the surface, and her gorgeous breasts on display. She was the single-most beautiful creature he'd ever seen. As she started walking out of the water in languid, graceful movements, their eyes connected with the heat of an inferno and the thrum of his racing heart. Just as he realized he was staring, she crossed her arms over her chest.

He turned around, uttering a curse. *"Sorry."* He felt like a heel, but that didn't stop her beautiful image from being etched into his mind. He heard splashes as she hurried out of the water.

"I didn't know I was down here that long," she said nervously.

Fuck. "It's my fault," he said with his back to her. "I didn't know you were going *in* the lake. I'm sorry, Sully."

She didn't respond, but he heard her putting on her clothes. "It's okay. You can turn around. I'm dressed."

When he turned, she was pink-cheeked, sitting on the ground, pulling on her socks. He had to find a way to get past this so she wasn't embarrassed. He sat beside her and started taking off his boots.

"What are you doing?"

"Getting naked so we're even."

Her eyes widened. "No, you are *not!*"

"Why not? Then I can be embarrassed, too."

"*You* wouldn't be."

"Yeah, you're right, and you shouldn't be either," he said gently. "We're adults, darlin'. So I saw your beautiful body. That doesn't mean things have to get weird between us."

"Every time you look at me, you'll picture me *naked*." She whispered *naked*.

He cocked a teasing grin. "Don't be silly. I was picturing you naked when you were fully clothed."

She gasped, but she was smiling. "Callahan!"

He leaned against her side. "It was a joke, darlin'. We can get past this, can't we?"

"I hope so. Just don't talk about it."

"Okay. Was the water freezing?"

She glowered at him.

"Sorry. That wasn't about you being...the way we're not talking about. I just can't believe you went in."

"It was on my list."

"If getting naked in the woods was on your list, I'm going to need to take a look at the rest of that list right away."

She smiled, shaking her head, and he helped her to her feet. As he picked up her towel, her brows furrowed. "What happened to your hands?"

"Nothing. Just got a little cut up yesterday wrangling horses."

"Let me see."

"Nah. I'm good." He put his hand on her lower back as they headed for the trail. "What time is your session today?"

"Two. Sasha said I could work with her this morning."

"Great, then we have time for a horseback riding lesson after lunch."

Her eyes lit up. "Really?"

"I told you we would make a cowgirl out of you. It's damn near time to start. You've been loafing long enough."

She looked at him curiously. "I'm so glad you're going to teach me to ride. I guess you're right. We can move past *you know what*."

"I don't know." He feigned a dramatic sigh. "I might picture you *naked* on that horse." He whispered *naked*.

She swatted his arm, laughing, and that was music to his ears.

THOSE BUTTERFLIES SULLY had been living with were nothing compared to the way her body had caught fire when Callahan saw her naked. She'd seen a hunger in his eyes that was so different from anything she'd ever seen before, it had brought more than just tingling between her legs. Her nipples had pebbled, and she'd gotten hot all over. He'd said she was *beautiful*. She didn't feel beautiful, but around him she felt different, prettier. Special. It hadn't helped that *he* was the reason she'd gone to take a dip in the freezing lake in the first place. She'd had a sexy dream about him, and in it she'd felt his big, rough hands all over her body. She'd woken up wet between her legs, with the urge to touch herself, which had *never* happened before. In all the years she was with Rebel Joe, she'd never felt that way. The cold lake and brisk morning air were supposed to get rid of those feelings, and they *almost* had, until their eyes had met and her body had reignited.

They'd sat next to each other at breakfast like they usually did, but everything felt different. When their legs brushed under the table or he leaned closer to talk to her, it stirred all those feelings again. She'd managed to keep herself in check while helping Sasha, but then she'd seen Callahan loading hay bales onto a trailer, and seeing him hard at work, doing the things he loved for the horses he adored, had sent her body into overdrive. Lunch had been no easier than breakfast. Every glance and every graze of their limbs had caused sparks to fly.

Now it was early afternoon, and she was still reeling as he taught her to ride Sunshine. When he touched her hands to show her how to hold the reins or moved her legs and feet into position, she warmed all over and swore she saw a flicker of heat in his eyes, too, and when he teased her, it sounded flirtier. There was something new and deeper in his encouragement, too. Or maybe her mind was playing tricks on her, and that was what she wanted to see.

Or maybe he really *was* picturing her naked on the horse.

She swallowed hard against the *whoosh* of warm tingly feelings that brought and the embarrassment for liking it so much. Thank goodness riding the horse felt as natural as breathing, because her brain was too muddled to concentrate.

"Are you sure you haven't done this before?" he asked as she rode around the ring.

"Yes, but I think I might have been born to ride horses."

"My kind of gal." He winked.

Hello, tingles. Maybe they should just practice all day, so she could enjoy those enticing sensations.

"Why don't you bring her to a stop, and we'll work on posting so you can learn to trot." She pulled back on the reins, and Sunshine stopped.

Callahan's phone rang. "Excuse me for a sec." He put the

phone to his ear. "Yeah. She's right here. I'm giving her a riding lesson." He was quiet for a moment, brows slanting, jaw tight. "And?" He cursed under his breath. "Yeah. Be right there." He pocketed his phone. "We need to cut our lesson short, darlin'. Why don't you come on down?"

"Is everything okay?" She started to dismount the way he'd taught her, but he caught her around the waist and lowered her to her feet as he had when they'd watched the sunrise.

"Yeah." Tension riddled his features. "That was my mother. She has some things to go over with you and wants to meet now instead of later."

"Okay. Why do you look worried?"

"I'm not worried, darlin'. Just bummed about cutting your lesson short."

Me too.

A little while later they walked into Wynnie's office and found her talking with Tiny. Tiny and Callahan locked eyes, and Sully felt Callahan's hand on her back tense up. Something was happening that she couldn't read, and it rattled her.

"Hi, honey. Come in and sit down," Wynnie said warmly, but there was a hint of tension there, too.

Sully looked at Callahan, wishing she could ask him what was going on, but he was studying his parents.

"Let's go, Cowboy," his father said gruffly, and headed for the door.

Callahan's hand pressed more firmly to her back, drawing her eyes to his. "I'll come get you when you're done."

With the tension in his voice, it was all she could do to nod. Was Rebel Joe looking for her? Or had someone noticed her reaction to Callahan at lunch? Was she in trouble? She sat on the couch as Callahan and Tiny left, closing the door behind them. Wynnie didn't sit in the chair like she usually did. She sat on the couch beside Sully, which made her even more nervous, and she blurted out, "What's wrong?"

"Nothing is wrong, honey. I have some good news for you. Your DNA results came back. You know how we talked about the possibility of you having more family?"

"Yes."

"You do have more family, but you're not the person you were led to believe you were."

"I...I don't understand."

"Let me explain. Your DNA results showed that your real name is Cassandra, or *Casey*, Lawler, and Casey went missing a little more than twenty years ago. Does that name ring a bell?"

Goose bumps chased up her arms as she shook her head. *My real name?* "No. But what do you mean went missing?"

"When you were four years old, you were going with your parents, Craig and Sarah Lawler, to pick up your older sister, Jordan, from a camp in West Virginia, and there was a car accident. I'm sorry, honey, but your parents didn't survive, and when the authorities got there, you were gone."

Sully tried to make sense of what she said. *I have a sister? My parents were killed?* "That doesn't make sense. My mother lives on the West Coast. She's not dead. What do you mean *gone*? Did my uncle come get me?"

"No, honey. This is a lot to process, but the man who raised you wasn't your real uncle, and the story he told you about your mother wasn't true. I spoke with a private investigator who your older sister, Jordan, hired to help find you. He believes the man who claimed to be your uncle either caused the accident or happened upon it and abducted you. He took you to the Free Rebellion compound, where he told everyone you were his niece. Now, the investigator has no way of knowing if he did that right away, or if he was holding you someplace else for some amount of time before he took you to the compound. But the investigator believes that man is the one who abducted you."

Sully was trembling with anger and confusion. "*Why?* Why would he do that?"

"He might have done it to please Rebel Joe, but we'll never know for sure since he's passed away." Wynnie took her hand. "I know this is a lot to take in all at once, and we're going to talk about all of it, but, honey, do you remember anything? Do you remember your sister, Jordan?"

"*No.*" Tears welled in her eyes. "What does this mean?"

"Most importantly, it means you have a family. You have an older sister and an aunt and uncle who love you and have been searching for you for a very long time. But it also means that you were abducted as a child, and that's a federal offense. The FBI is putting together a team to take down the cult and arrest Rebel Joe and the other men who hurt you. They're sending a field agent out to speak with you, and I'll stay with you the whole time. But I need to know if you've decided about pressing charges."

Her hands fisted as she tried to drag air into her lungs. "They *stole* me from my family." Tears spilled from her eyes. "They *hurt* me and *raped* me and lied to me about who I was. I'll do whatever it takes to put them behind bars."

Chapter Fifteen

COWBOY PACED THE halls of the main house, his every muscle knotted up. Sully had been with his mother all afternoon. His father had explained that the DNA results had proven that she was Casey Lawler. The FBI had sent a field agent to speak with her, and once things progressed further, the prosecuting attorney would be in touch. He wished like hell he could have been with her when she met with the FBI agent, but at least his mother had been there for her. He knew she'd make sure Sully was okay. Or rather, as okay as she could be. He couldn't imagine how hard this was going to be for her.

His father was calling an emergency meeting of the Dark Knights to keep them in the loop, but Cowboy wouldn't be there. He needed to be with Sully. *Casey.*

He fucking knew it.

His phone vibrated, and his mother's name flashed on the screen. He opened and read her text. *Sully didn't bring her phone with her, but she'd like you to walk her to her cabin. She's just had her life upended again, so go easy.*

As if he'd do anything else?

He knocked once and opened his mother's office door. Sully

pushed to her feet as he walked in, looking sad and angry and so fucking vulnerable, it slayed him. He didn't think as he opened his arms, and she walked into them. He held her, stroking her back, wishing he could go back in time and save her from everything she'd gone through. "It's okay, darlin'. Everything's going to be okay." He sure as hell hoped he was right.

He felt his mother watching them and met her gaze. Worry, love, heartache, and hope stared back at him, all too overwhelming to pick through. "I'm going to take her home."

His mother nodded.

Sully was quiet on the way to her cabin. He wished he knew what was going through her mind. Was she scared? Confused? Angry? What could he do to help? He wanted to wrap her in his arms and keep the rest of the world at bay, but this wasn't about what he wanted. "Do you want to be alone?" he asked as he walked her to the door.

She shook her head. "Will you stay?"

"Of course." He followed her inside, trying to figure out how to comfort her. "I can make you some tea or get you a glass of juice."

"No thanks. Would you mind just sitting with me?" They sat on the couch, and she worried with her hands. "Wynnie said Tiny told you about the DNA results."

"He did, and I can only imagine how difficult this is for you."

"I'm just...I think I'm in shock. Nothing is what I thought. I'm not even twenty-five. I'm twenty-four, and my birthday isn't in January. It's in April. April seventeenth, just like you." She tried to smile but failed. "A bright spot in the darkness." Tears welled in her eyes.

He drew her into his arms. "It's okay, darlin'."

"No, it's *not*. Everything I know about myself is a lie." She buried her face in his neck, shaking and crying.

He stroked her back, his heart breaking for her. "I'm sure it feels that way, but that's not true. What you believed about your family and where you thought you came from was a lie, but what's in your heart and the person you are hasn't changed. Those things might change as you learn and grow and put the pieces of your life back together, but a name doesn't change the fabric of your being." He drew back and cradled her face between his hands. "I know this is scary and confusing and hurts like hell. Your entire life has been turned upside down. But even if you don't feel like it right now, make no mistake, you are a strong, capable woman, and nothing can take that away from you." She nodded as he wiped her tears with his thumbs.

"I know you're right, but it's all so scary. I'm supposed to be someone I don't know. Your mom showed me a flyer with a picture of Casey—of *me*—on it, and it was like looking at a stranger."

"You just have to look a little closer." He pulled out his wallet and withdrew the flyer.

"How long have you had that?"

"A while. Your sister hired a PI over the summer, and an alert went out to all the Dark Knights chapters. I've been carrying it with me ever since, staring at that picture. I felt a connection to it and had no idea why. There was something in your eyes that I couldn't get out of my head. When I first saw you at the Finches, I thought for sure you were Casey. But then you mentioned your uncle, and since the few people I spoke to about the age-progression photo in the flyer didn't think the resemblance was that strong, I didn't push it. Then the other night when we were talking, everything started to hit me all at once. The way newcomers had to change their names, what you'd been through, the fact that you never felt like you fit in, and I don't know why, but I knew in my gut you were Casey."

"Why didn't you say something or show it to me?" she pleaded.

"Because you'd been through enough, and what if I was wrong? I'm not a therapist. I wasn't sure if showing you would hurt you in some way."

"You're *always* worrying about me," she said softly, but a little sharp, too.

"I'm not going to apologize for that, darlin'."

"I don't want you to. It was a fact, not a complaint." Her brows knitted as she studied the flyer. "I wish I knew this little girl. She looks like she can take on the world."

"So does the woman holding it."

Her eyes flicked up to his, full of disbelief, and she shook her head.

"You might not feel that way right now, but you're a survivor, Sully. You've seen and experienced a hell of a lot more than that innocent little girl did, and you were forced to hide that take-on-the-world edge. But you didn't lose your will to take it on, and when I look in your eyes, I see that beautiful quiet strength and so much more."

She sighed heavily, but it was a sound of relief as she sank into the couch cushions and leaned against him. He put an arm around her, pulling her closer.

"I felt *alone* my entire life. I knew I didn't belong on the compound, but I had no place else to go. Only I *did*. I had a sister that whole time, and they stole that from both of us." Tears streamed down her cheeks. "It's so unfair."

He held her tighter, his throat thickening. "I know, sweetheart. I'm so sorry."

"I'm *so* angry I want to scream or kick something, but I'm too emotionally exhausted to do either."

He kissed her temple, wishing he knew what to say, but he had a feeling she just needed to get it out.

She wiped her eyes and took a few breaths, sinking deeper into his side. "I'm so grateful for you and your family. I never feel alone here."

"And you'll never be alone again. You've got us, and now you've got family, too." He held her a little closer at that bittersweet reality. Finding her family most likely meant she'd be leaving the ranch.

"I had parents who loved me, and I don't even remember them," she said shakily.

"I know, baby, and I wish I could change that. But at least now you have a few answers. This explains why you never felt like you fit in and why when you were little, you felt safest inside and worried you might be snatched off the compound. This is why you always knew something was wrong with what went on there. You might not remember the time you had with your family, but somewhere in your head and in your heart are all the things your parents taught you. The love they showed you and the values they impressed upon you about right and wrong and what a family should be. It's all in there somewhere, and you'll always have those things."

"But I don't *remember* them." She teared up again. "I can't see their faces or hear their voices. I can't remember their arms around me. I just wish…"

He put his other arm around her, embracing her as she cried. "I wish I could bring them back for you," he whispered, her tears cutting him to his core. "At least now you know you have a sister who loves you, and that's a blessing."

"It should be. But *is* it?" She drew back, swiping at her tears. "They're going to let Jordan know I'm here, and your mom asked if I'd be willing to meet her."

"How do you feel about that?"

"I told her I would, but I'm afraid it's going to be like meeting a stranger. Your mother said Jordan is five years older than me and remembers everything about me. What if she's disappointed that I don't remember anything?"

"Nobody who meets you could *ever* be disappointed. She's been looking for you for so long, she's going to be thrilled that you're safe and well. I'm sure she'll be just as overwhelmed and nervous as you are, and you never know. Meeting her might jog your memories."

She settled in against his side again. "That's what your mom said."

"That would be good, wouldn't it?"

"Who knows," she said frustratedly. "I'm afraid to hope or believe in *anything*. Nothing feels real right now."

He covered her hand with his, lacing their fingers together. "That's understandable."

"But I believe in you," she said softly, moving her index finger around the cuts and bruises on the back of his hand.

His chest constricted. "I believe in you, too, darlin', and I know it's going to be a long, hard road, but I'm not going anywhere. I'll help you through as best I can."

"Thank you," she said just above a whisper. "The FBI agent said when they take down the cult, it'll be all over the news, and eventually I'll have to talk to whatever lawyer handles the case, but it might be on a video conference. Will you stay in the room with me if they let you?"

He held her hand a little tighter. "I'll do whatever you need, whenever you need it."

"I asked him what will happen to Ansel and his family, and all he said was that they'd be safe and taken care of."

"This isn't the FBI's first rodeo. They'll protect the innocent, and I'll try to find out as much as I can about Ansel and his family after the dust clears. Did they tell you they're keeping your name and the Finches and all of your whereabouts out of the reports, so the media won't come here looking for you? There'll be no public link between Sullivan Tate and Casey Lawler."

"Yes. I'm glad they're doing that."

"You know, those flyers have been all over social media since summer. If people ever find out you're Casey, the public will rally on your behalf. Your story will give millions of people hope because a lot of missing kids are never found."

"That's so sad. If I hadn't escaped, I'd probably be one of them. I'm glad it will give people hope, but all I want is a normal life, and now I don't know who I am, and everyone will always think of me as the girl who escaped from the cult. I'll never have a normal life."

"Yes, you will." One way or another, he'd make damn sure of it.

"Not if people find out I'm Casey. You said yourself those flyers were all over the media. If someone recognizes me, like you did, or if somehow word gets out, everyone, everywhere will know what I've been through. Once word gets out about the cult, everyone will know I was raped and branded, and…" She buried her face in his side, crying.

He held her tighter, forcing his anger to remain at bay.

"What they'll know is that you were the victim of a sick man and the cowardly assholes who followed him. You have nothing to be ashamed of. Your actions are saving all those other girls from going through what you went through, and that makes you a fucking hero." He lifted her chin, gazing into her tortured eyes, and his heart split open. "*That's* what they'll see, Sully, just like I do. But if it's too much for you, or you don't want to deal with it, you can always change your name. This is your life to live on your terms."

She blinked up at him, a small smile on her beautiful lips. "There must've been an angel on my shoulder to have brought me here."

"I've been thinking the same thing." He wanted to kiss her so badly, to let her know he'd always be there to protect her. But she wasn't his girl, and with this new information, she could be gone tomorrow, so he kissed her forehead instead of her lips and said, "Do you want to lie down and rest for a bit?"

She nodded and leaned forward to take off her boots. She set them aside and pushed to her feet. "You don't have to stay if you have work to do."

"I'm not going anywhere, darlin', unless you want me to leave."

"Then will you lie down with me and just hold me? I feel safest when I'm with you, and I don't want to be alone."

His fucking heart nearly burst. "There's nothing I'd rather do."

COWBOY AWOKE TO the vibration of his phone in his

pocket and the feel of Sully fast asleep in his arms. It was dark, and he glanced at the clock on the nightstand—*8:25*. They'd slept through dinner. He carefully pulled out his phone and saw the incoming call was from his mother, and he had missed several texts from his siblings. He moved off the bed and headed out of the bedroom, closing the door softly behind him as he answered the call. "Hey, Mom."

"Hi, honey. We missed you guys at dinner. How's Sully doing?"

"She's overwhelmed, but she's napping."

"Good. The poor girl probably feels like she's been put through the wringer. Reggie called. Sully's sister and her aunt and uncle are coming to see her tomorrow morning. If she wants to talk with me when she wakes up from her nap, just bring her over to the house. It doesn't matter what time it is."

"Okay."

"If she'd rather not talk tonight, we can meet in the morning before they arrive."

"I'll let her know. Did you guys check out these people? I know the woman is her sister, but do you know if she's a good person?"

"*Yes*, honey. Reggie had already checked out Jordan and her aunt and uncle, and your father and I spoke to her on the phone a little while ago. She's a sweetheart, and you'll never believe who she's engaged to. Zev's brother, Jax Braden." Zev was Carly's husband. They split their time between Colorado and the East Coast.

That made him feel better. Treat had about a million cousins, and although Cowboy had a hard time keeping them all straight, he'd been hearing about them for years, and there wasn't a bad one in the bunch. "Which one is he?"

"Jax is the bridal gown designer. He and Jillian are twins."

"Right, he's the fancy one. Nice guy. I remember now. I met him briefly at Carly's wedding."

"There's one more thing. I don't know if you've seen the news, but the cult has been disbanded. The leader and several of his underlings were arrested, and many others are being held for questioning. They found an arsenal of weapons, and the members who were searching for Sully never left West Virginia. They've got them in custody, too, so she's safe. No one is coming after her."

About fucking time.

"It's all over the internet. Your father has spoken with your sisters, and the staff was curious about the FBI showing up, so we held a meeting to answer their questions and make sure Sully's name and whereabouts are kept confidential. It might be a good idea to keep her away from the television tonight."

"Wouldn't it be good for her to see that to get closure?"

"Yes, but given all she's dealing with tonight, it might be best if she sees it after a good night's sleep. There's been no mention of Sullivan Tate. Hopefully that won't change. How are you holding up?"

"I'm fine, just worried about Sully. Can you do me a favor? Ask Dad to find out where Sully's friend Ansel and his family are. She's worried about them."

"Sure, but that might take a few days."

"That's what I figured. I'll talk to Sully and give you a heads-up if she wants to come by tonight."

"Great. Do you want me to bring some dinner over for you two?"

"No. I'll get us something when she's ready. Thanks."

After he ended the call, he scrolled through the missed texts from his siblings.

Dare: *Hey, man. How's Sully holding up? Billie and I are here if she needs anything.*

Doc: *Glad you got to those fuckers first. Here if you need me.*

Sasha: *I heard about Sully. Can I do anything to help? Is she okay?*

Birdie: *Holy shit. How is Sully? Her story is all over the news. Why didn't you tell me? We could have gone out there and beat the crap out of those assholes!*

He smiled at Birdie's text, and the crazy thing was, he knew she meant it. He thumbed out a group text. *Sully's resting. We're good for now. I appreciate your support, and I know she will, too.*

He pocketed his phone and headed back into the bedroom. She was still fast asleep. His heart ached for his sweet, willowy girl. He wanted to protect her from everyone and everything, but he knew she was right about what would happen if word got out. Too many people would see her as *the girl from the cult.* He made a mental note to speak with his mother about that gigantic what-if and see if she had any suggestions. But that could wait.

Everything could wait.

He climbed onto the bed behind Sully and wrapped an arm around her. She snuggled into him, and he buried his face in her hair, breathing in the scents of lavender and sweet, frightened Sully. Her hand moved down his forearm, coming to rest over the back of his hand, and she pressed it to her breast. It was an innocent move. She was *asleep*, for Pete's sake, but he was too damn into her, and his body reacted. Feeling guilty, he put space between her ass and his erection. But she pressed his hand tighter against her chest as she wiggled her hips, inching back until she was tight against him again. He had a fleeting thought that maybe she wasn't really asleep, but he felt her heart beating steadily.

He sent a silent message to his dick—*That's not what we're here for. Calm the fuck down*—closed his eyes, and focused on the trust she had in him rather than the feelings she evoked.

WAKEFULNESS TIPTOED IN, dragging Sully out of a delicious dream involving Callahan's lips on hers, bringing into focus his enticingly rugged scent, the warmth of his big body wrapped around her, and his hand cupping her breast. Her pulse quickened, and her eyes flew open, slowly adjusting to the darkness, registering 10:38 on the clock. She didn't move a muscle, reveling in the feeling of waking up in a man's arms not only free from trepidation but consumed with desire. How could she feel so much goodness with all the worries hanging over her?

"You awake, darlin'?" he whispered against her neck.

Her nerves prickled, and she turned in his arms. "Did I wake you?"

"No. I got up to take a call two hours ago, and when I came back, you put my hand *where you put my hand.*" He said the last part in a playful voice, flashing a heart-stopping grin. "And you put your ass *where you put your ass*, and...yeah. I couldn't sleep, but I didn't want to move, because you were snuggled in tight and needed your sleep."

"Oh my gosh, are you *kidding?*" Her cheeks burned. "First you see me naked, then *I* put *your* hand on my...?" She buried her face in his chest. "Sorry."

"You don't hear me complaining." He lifted her face. "Besides, I get it. You were dreaming about me." He waggled his brows.

"I was *not*." She wasn't about to admit the embarrassing truth.

He lowered his voice. "I wouldn't blame you if you were."

"Would you *stop*?"

They both laughed, and he hiked himself up on his elbow, bringing them face-to-face. "Are you done being embarrassed?"

"I hope so." He had a knack for making the most embarrassing situations laughable, and she really liked that about him.

"Good." His expression turned serious. "That call I took was from my mother. I have some news."

She wasn't sure she could take any more news. "Good news or bad news?"

"Great news. The men who hurt you have been arrested."

Her eyes widened. "Really?"

"Yes. It's over, darlin'. The cult has been disbanded, and you don't have to worry about them coming after you anymore."

She threw her arms around him, her heart racing, laughter and tears breaking free. "Thank you."

"This was all you, darlin'."

"No. It was all of you, too. You and the Dark Knights kept me safe, and Wynnie convinced me to take the DNA test, and you both gave me the courage to do something about it and not just pretend it didn't happen." She propped herself on her elbow, so they were lying face-to-face again, her heart and mind racing. "I can't believe it's over. I know I'll have to testify and everything, but...I'm really *free*."

"You're really free, darlin', and I have more news. Your

family is coming to see you tomorrow."

Anxiety spread through her like wildfire. "Already? That was fast."

"They've been looking for you for a long time. I'd imagine they're excited to see you. Your sister and your aunt and uncle will be here tomorrow morning."

Her nerves got the better of her, and her worries tumbled out. "What's going to happen? What if they don't like me? What if I don't like them? What if they want me to go back to Maryland with them? I don't want to leave here. Wynnie is helping me a lot, and…" *I don't want to leave you.* "Am I even allowed to stay if they claim me?"

"Slow down, Sully." He cradled her face in his hand, brushing his thumb over her cheek, his comforting tone as soothing as his touch. "First of all, nobody's *claiming* anyone. The real world isn't like the compound. You're part of their family— that's a given—but that's just a blood relation, darlin'. Being part of a family doesn't mean they own you or can tell you what to do or where to go. *Nobody*—not us, them, or anyone else— has the right to make those decisions for you."

She exhaled with relief. "I know you're right, but knowing it and really believing it is harder than it seems. What if we don't like each other? Can I stay here? Is that even an option?"

"Yes. You can stay as long as you'd like, but they are your family, and that's important. And if you decide to go with them, you can come back anytime. You will *always* have a safe place here, and you'll always have one with me."

"Do you mean that?" she asked carefully.

"Yes."

His expression was so serious, the honesty in his eyes wrapped around her like an embrace, bringing another wave of relief. She burrowed closer. *He'd* become her safe place, her anchor, her calm in the face of a storm, and as her heartbeat settled, she wished she could stay right there in his arms forever. His hand rested firmly on her back, keeping their bodies close. She was acutely aware of every hard inch of him, as she hadn't allowed herself to be before, sending desire slithering through her, hot and needy.

"I mean everything I say to you." He pressed a tender kiss to her forehead, keeping her close.

His lips were so warm and soft, she desperately wanted to know how they'd feel on hers. She felt his heartbeat quicken. Did he want her the way she wanted him? She leaned back just far enough to see his face, and their eyes connected, those dark pools of emotion calling out to her, making her want him even more.

"What is it, darlin'? What do you need?"

What if her family convinced her to leave tomorrow, and tonight was all they'd ever have? She didn't want to think about leaving, but even more than that, she didn't want to go her whole life without ever kissing him. Before she could think too much about it, she said, "*You*," and touched her lips to his.

He didn't kiss her back.

She drew away with a sinking feeling. "I'm sorry if you didn't want that."

He held her tighter, his penetrating gaze *still* calling out to her, but his face was a mask of pure restraint. "You have no idea how much I want that, Sully. That and so much more. But we don't know how long you'll be here, and with everything you're going through, I don't want you to confuse your feelings for me with everything else and then regret it."

"How I feel about you is the *only* thing I'm *not* confused about." Her words came fast and vehement, straight from her heart. "I've spent my whole life doing what everyone else wanted me to do. I *know* my future is uncertain, but I also know what I feel *right now*, and that's what matters. There's no way I'll regret doing anything with you, because being with you is what *I* want. Please don't try to take that decision away from me."

"I won't, and I'm sorry it came across like that." He brushed his lips over hers, whispering, "*Sully.*" The heat in his voice and the taunting way his lips brushed over hers again had her breathing harder, craving more. He slid his tongue along her lower lip, alighting tingles in her core. "So sweet." His words were drenched with desire, heightening her anticipation as he kissed the corner of her mouth and his hand slid up her back and into her hair. Their hearts pounded out the same frantic rhythm, an inferno blazing between them as he gazed deeply into her eyes, but he didn't say a word. He didn't have to. She felt his desire as powerfully as his restraint and knew he was giving her a chance to back out, but no part of her wanted to.

"*Kiss me,*" she pleaded.

"One kiss will never be enough," he said gruffly.

She lost her breath at the words that could have come straight from her heart as his mouth came down over hers in a luxuriously sensual kiss, intensifying her desire with every stroke of his tongue. He tasted sweet and hot and kissed her, *held* her, like he'd been waiting a lifetime to do it. How was it possible to make her feel so special with just a kiss?

But this wasn't just a kiss. It was soft and sweet and dark and erotic, freedom and connection intertwined with white-hot gratification. It was *everything*.

She clung to him as he intensified their kiss and lowered her to her back. She couldn't get enough of his mouth and returned his efforts ravenously, taking as much as he would give, and *oh*, how he gave! His tongue delved deeper, exploring the hills and valleys of her mouth. She'd never been kissed so thoroughly, so deliciously, and it made her want so much more. She arched beneath him, grasping at his back, his muscles flexing with restraint against her hands. As their lips parted, his eyes bored into her, hazy with lust and something much bigger.

"*More*" fell urgently from her lips, and she pulled his mouth back to hers. Then he was kissing her like he couldn't get enough either. His tongue plunged and swept, taking, claiming, *possessing*, and for the first time in her life, she wanted to be claimed. His hot hand roamed over her hip and up her ribs, his thumb lightly brushing her breast. She moaned into their kisses, bowing beneath him, and he made the sexiest guttural sound she'd ever heard. He palmed her breast, sending shivers of heat through her core, pooling low in her belly. "I love kissing you," he murmured against her mouth, and kissed her so sensually, heat spread between her thighs. His warm, hot lips trailed over her jaw and down her neck, his hand sliding down her ribs to the edge of her shirt, teasing along an exposed sliver of skin.

"Touch me," she panted out.

His mouth came down over hers in a toe-curling kiss as his hand pushed under her shirt, teasing her nipple through her bra. She bowed beneath him, wanting to feel his hand on her skin. He sealed his mouth over her neck, sucking hard enough that her sex clenched with desire. "Oh *God*," she said in one long breath. What was this magic he was doling out, making her *feel* and *want* and *lust*? His mouth found hers again, his tongue tracing her lips. She heard herself whimper, and he continued teasing her lips with his and her nipple with those long fingers until she was panting and rocking. He trailed kisses down her neck, his hand pushing behind her, taking hold of the clasp of her bra. Anticipation stacked up inside her.

"Stop me if you want to, baby. You're in control of what happens between us."

"I don't want you to stop," she said breathlessly.

He unhooked her bra and lowered his mouth to hers, kissed her slowly, emotions radiating between them. His hand snaked around her, palming her bare breast. She moaned, long and low at the feel of his rough hand caressing her so gently. When he rolled her nipple between his finger and thumb, shivers of heat slithered south. He deepened their kisses and squeezed her nipple just hard enough to send bolts of desire between her legs. Her hips shot off the mattress, and he did it again, drawing a needy moan from her lungs. He drew back with fire in his eyes, holding her gaze as he stripped off her shirt and bra. His eyes smoldered as he drank her in, his desire turning her on even more. She'd never *wanted* like this before, and she had no desire to hold back.

"You're gorgeous, baby," he said huskily.

"I want to feel your skin against mine." She tugged at his shirt.

He reached over his shoulder, tugging off his shirt. Her heart nearly stopped at the sight of his sculpted, broad chest with just a dusting of hair and his thickly muscled torso, so beautiful she wanted to touch and lick and kiss all of him. His head dipped, and he lavished her breasts with kisses and caresses. Every touch of his lips caused a rush of heat. When his tongue slid around and over her nipple, "*Ah, yes,*" slipped out. He did it again, causing her breathing to hitch, and lowered his hot mouth over her nipple, teasing and sucking. She arched off the mattress, pushing her hands into his hair, holding him there as he drove her out of her mind. He shifted his body, using one hand on each breast as his mouth moved from one to the other, licking, sucking, and grazing his teeth over her sensitive skin. His every touch earned a sharp inhalation. His hands remained on her breasts, teasing, as he kissed, nipped, and sucked his way down her stomach, until she was dizzy with desire, breathless for more. But *more* had never felt good. He kissed just above the waist of her jeans and touched the button, his approval-seeking eyes finding hers.

Gathering all her courage, she said, "I want you to touch me, but nothing has ever felt good…down there."

"There's no rush. We can wait." He pressed a kiss just below her belly button.

"*No*," she said urgently. "Everything is different with you. I want to try, but I may not react how you hope."

"My only hope is to make you feel so good, you forget anyone who touched you before tonight."

Her heart turned over in her chest. "I want that, too."

He didn't tear off her jeans or rush to touch her the way she was used to. He continued tenderly loving her stomach, ribs, and breasts, until she was moaning and writhing, every inch of her begging for more. Only then did he take off her jeans, but even that wasn't rushed. He drew them down slowly, kissing the skin he revealed. "Just breathe, darlin'. Enjoy the way it feels to be cherished." He left her panties on, kissing and caressing his way up from ankles to knees and along her thighs, as if he was healing every inch of her. And that's how it felt. His tender touches and sweet kisses were balms to her mishandled heart. His scruff tickled, and his touch was as loving as it was intoxicating. When he pressed a kiss just above her sex, she could barely breathe for the need coursing through her.

"You okay, beautiful?"

"*Uh-huh*" came out dreamy and breathy.

"You hold the reins, baby." He kissed her stomach again. "We can stop at any time."

"I don't want to stop."

His hands slid up her outer thighs as he trailed kisses lower. Through her panties, she felt the warm, insistent press of his lips and the slide of his tongue, sending heat radiating outward. He did it again and again, so tantalizing and different from anything she'd ever felt, she closed her eyes, reveling in the sensations overtaking her. Her hips rose in time to his efforts, his every stroke taking her higher, until she was shaking with desire. His mouth moved higher, and his tongue pressed down on her panties at the apex of her sex, massaging nerves that sent tingling sensations racing down her limbs. She rocked and writhed, lost in the pleasures coursing through her, and then he was kissing his way up her body, bringing them chest to chest and lip to lip.

The feel of his warm skin on hers was as alluring as his touch, and the emotions in his eyes halted her heart. "Still with me, darlin'?"

"*Yes.*"

He took her in a passionate kiss that she felt all the way down to her toes. He shifted beside her, and she missed the heat of him, the weight of his body. But his hand skimmed down her body, over her underwear, teasing her as he'd done with his mouth, slowly, sensually, and *intently*. "Love touching you," he said against her lips, and reclaimed them, kissing and touching her with such care, such talent, it was as if he'd known her body his whole life. He brushed his lips over hers. "Feel good, baby?"

"So good."

"Ready for more?" He dipped his head, teasing her nipple with his tongue, those dark eyes trained on her.

It was all she could do to nod.

"That's my girl. Want to come for me?"

"I can't. I've never…"

"You will, baby. By my hand, and when you're ready, by my mouth and my cock."

Oh God, yes. He took her in another panty-melting kiss, and his hand pushed into her underwear, his thick fingers sliding between her legs. "So wet for me," he said against her lips. His mouth slanted over hers as his thumb found those oversensitive nerves, moving in slow, precise circles. Her breathing hitched, and she felt him smiling as they kissed. He continued rubbing and stroking. Heat prickled her limbs as his fingers pushed slowly into her. She sucked in a breath, and he kissed her slower, deeper, his fingers moving in and out in the same mesmerizing rhythm as his tongue sweeping over hers. He crooked his fingers, and pleasure sparked hot and sharp inside her. She tried to concentrate on their kisses, his touches, the heat gathering low in her belly, but her senses whirled and skidded, and she couldn't hold on to any one thought. She clung to him, riding his hand, chasing the highs he brought.

"That's it, darlin'. Feel it, own it, *demand* it."

"Faster." The sound that earned, something between an appreciative growl and a moan, had her demanding more, and it felt amazing to be in charge. *"Don't stop. Kiss me."*

"That's my girl." He captured her mouth, quickening his efforts so perfectly, she couldn't think, could only give herself over to the pleasure stacking up inside her. His thick fingers moved in and out of her, his thumb expertly taking her higher.

Heat raced up her legs and through her core, consuming her entire being like wildfire, so all-consuming, she could do little more than dig her heels into the mattress as he took her right up to the edge of madness, as he continued touching and devouring until her head fell back, and he sealed his mouth over her neck, sucking *hard*. Pleasure exploded from every part of her, and she shattered into a million fiery pieces, crying out as the world spun away. And then she was soaring, light as a feather, free as a bird, wrapped in a cloud of pleasure, and the most incredible man she'd ever known was kissing her, whispering against her skin—"So sexy...so sweet...so trusting"—loving her through the very last ripple of ecstasy.

She collapsed beneath him, feeling like a tigress freed from its tethers, and as Callahan's handsome face came into focus, all she could think about was how much she wanted to do even more.

Chapter Sixteen

IN ALL THE years Cowboy had worked the ranch, he'd never missed a day of rising with the sun. But it would take an act of God to drag him away from the sleeping beauty in his arms. Sully had slept in a T-shirt and underwear, and he'd shed his jeans before they'd turned in for the night. The feel of her bare legs against his was the sweetest kind of torture, but the thoughts going through his head were the worst kind of torture. He had to wonder if he'd fucked up and put her in a difficult position with all she was going through.

She jerked in her sleep, making a pained sound. He held her tighter, feeling her heart race. She jerked again, startling herself awake.

"You're okay, darlin'," he said. "You must've had a bad dream, but I've got you."

She turned in his arms, nuzzling against his chest. "Sorry."

"No need to apologize." He kissed her forehead. "Are you okay? Do you want to talk about it?"

"It's just a nightmare. I used to have it a lot, and then it stopped for a long time, but it keeps coming back."

"What happens in it?" He stroked her hair.

"I don't know. It's dark, and there's a bloodcurdling scream, but that's it. I don't know where I am or who it is."

His chest constricted. "Maybe it's a memory from the accident."

"I didn't think of that. You might be right. I just want it to stop."

"Have you talked to my mom about it?"

She shook her head.

"She might be able to help you figure out what it means, or at least give you some ideas about how to make it stop."

"I will. I'm glad you're here with me." She reached up and touched his cheek with a dreamy look in her eyes.

Damn that was a good look on her. "What?"

"I like your face. I've been wanting to touch it."

"I like your face, too, darlin'." He pressed his lips to hers. "And you can touch any part of me whenever you want." He ran his hand down her back, holding her close. "I was going to ask how you felt this morning—about us and what we did last night. Since you're not kicking me out of your bed, I guess you're okay with it? No regrets?"

Her cheeks pinked up. "I like that there's an us. I never knew a kiss could feel so magical or that my body was capable of feeling the way you made me feel. That was…I don't even know the right words."

"We're just getting started." He brushed his lips over hers and kissed her softly. "But I'm going to have to come clean to my mother and let her know there's something between us. Are you okay with that?"

"Yes, but will you get in trouble?"

"Don't worry about me. I can handle anything that comes my way, but I'm worried about you with all that you have going on. You're not in danger anymore, and you don't need to hide from the public. You might want to lie low while you figure things out with your family, but this is huge, baby. You're finally free, and I want to be with you more than I want my next breath, but I don't want to make things harder for you. I don't want you to feel pressure about being with me as you figure out who you are and how you want to live your life." He didn't want to lose her, but this wasn't about him. He knew who he was, and he *had* his life. If she needed space to figure those things out for herself, he needed to give it to her, no matter how much it killed him.

"You make things better, and when I'm ready to go out, I want it to be with you, unless…" Her brows knitted. "Are you trying to say that you don't want—"

"Do *not* finish that sentence." He knew if she truly wanted to be with him, he had to take it slow, but he held her tight, letting her feel what her beautiful body, her beautiful *being*, had done to him. "You're *all* I want, darlin', but I want you to be happy, and no matter what that means, I'll never hold you back."

"Oh, *good*," she said with a sweet smile.

She was so damn cute, he had to kiss her. "You have a big day today. How're you feeling about meeting your family?"

"Nervous. When Wynnie asked if I'd be willing to meet them, she said I could start with just meeting Jordan. Will you stay in the room with me when I meet her?"

"If that's what you want."

"I do. I'd feel better with you there."

"Then I'll be there. I'm sure everything's going to be fine. Do you want to talk about it?"

She shook her head. "I want to stay right here with you and

pretend we have all day together even though we don't."

"I can definitely give you something else to think about." He lowered his lips to hers, taking her in a passionate kiss. She pressed her hips forward, grinding against him. A growl slipped out before he could stop it, and he rolled her onto her back, trying to distract himself from taking things too far. He continued kissing her, lost in her taste, the feel of her softness beneath him, and those sweet, needful sounds she made. "I'm dying to get my mouth on the rest of you."

Her brows knitted. "The rest of me?"

"That's right, baby." He rocked his hips against her center. "I want to make you feel even better than last night."

She blushed, whispering, "Well, that sounds *fun.*"

He dipped his head to her shoulder. "You're going to be the death of me."

"Hopefully not before you fulfill that promise."

He kissed her, both of them laughing, and then he took it deeper, turning her laughter into a hungry moan. Her mouth was made for him, hot and sweet and so fucking delicious, he could lose his mind kissing her for hours. But they didn't have hours, and she was arching beneath him, rubbing against his cock, making him want so much more. He drew back, gazing into her lustful eyes as he lifted her shirt. "This needs to come off, baby."

She grinned as he stripped off her shirt and tossed it aside, taking a good long look at her. "You're so damn gorgeous." He teased and tasted his way down her body, slowing to love her breasts the way he'd learned she liked. He grazed his teeth over her nipple, earning more enticing sounds. "Baby, those sexy sounds you make drive me wild."

"*Good,*" she said breathily, writhing beneath him.

As he loved his way down her body, lavishing her silky skin with openmouthed kisses, she spread her legs wider to accommodate his breadth. He ran his tongue around her belly button, earning a sweet sound between a giggle and a sigh. When he dipped his tongue into her belly button, a sinfully sexy sound fell from her lips and her hips rose off the mattress. "*Mm.* My beautiful girl likes my tongue." He skimmed her panties down her legs and tossed them to the floor, then dusted kisses along her thighs and around the tuft of curls between her legs. "Your scent is intoxicating. I can't wait to taste you."

Her cheeks flamed. "*God*, the things you say."

"Sorry, baby." He was holding back the things he really wanted to say, but he wasn't sure how that other fucker had spoken to her, and he didn't want to stir bad memories.

"No. I'm used to silence or grunts, like I could be anyone. I like when you talk to me. I want to know what you feel."

"Careful what you ask for, darlin'. I've got a dirty mouth, and I don't want to offend you."

She met his gaze with flames in her eyes. "I don't want to be careful with you. I know I'll like everything you do and say, and if I don't, I'll tell you."

"*Damn*, baby. Do you know how hot that is?" He pressed a kiss to those soft curls. "I loved touching your pussy last night, feeling you come and knowing you'll come even harder on my mouth." He paused to gauge her reaction, and her wanton moan told him everything he needed to know. He brushed his thumb over her wetness, earning another sexy sound. "Beautifully wet for me." He slicked his tongue along her glistening sex, taking his first taste of her and earning more needy sounds. "*Christ*, you're sweeter than honey." She lifted her hips. "Want my mouth on you, baby?"

"*Yes*," she said breathily.

He slicked his tongue along her pussy and over her clit, slowing to add pressure where she needed it most. She whimpered and writhed as he teased, taunted, and feasted, soaking in the greedy sounds falling from her lips and the way her back bowed and she clawed at the mattress. "So fucking sweet." He licked her swollen clit and slowly pushed two fingers into her tight pussy.

"*Callahan—*"

"Too much, baby?"

"*No.* It's just...with you, everything feels so good."

He fucking loved that. He flicked his tongue over those greedy nerves as he loved her with his fingers, stroking over that secret spot that made her whimper and moan. He found a pace that had her gasping, emitting needy sounds and desperate pleas that had his cock raging to get into the action. Her legs trembled, and he quickened his efforts, sucking her clit between his teeth. Her breathing shallowed, her hands fisting in the sheets, eyes closed. He held her there, wanting her climax to be explosive. "*Please*," she begged. "*Oh...Cal...I can't take it.*"

"I've got you, baby." He swapped his mouth for his fingers, working her clit as he devoured her sex. Her legs flexed, her hips rose, and he pushed his tongue into her slick heat as she cried out his name. Her pussy pulsed, her essence spreading over his tongue, as she bucked and writhed. A stream of indiscernible sounds tumbled from her lips as she rode out her climax. He stayed with her, enjoying every hot pulse, and as she sank to the mattress, panting for air, he pushed his fingers inside her again, covering her clit with his mouth, sending her right back into another magnificent orgasm, and held her trembling and begging at the peak.

As she finally came down from her high, her skin flushed, her body shaking, she was so fucking gorgeous, so incredibly trusting, he couldn't resist thanking her in the best way possible. He lavished her swollen sex with kisses, his every touch earning a sharp gasp. Knowing she'd be overly sensitive after two orgasms, he gently dipped his fingers inside her again, finding that hidden spot with laser precision.

"*Ah...Cal*, I'm—" She closed her eyes, digging her heels into the mattress.

"I know, baby. But this one's going to be twice as good." He loved her slowly with his mouth and hands, and it didn't take long before her hips bucked, and his name flew from her lips like a prayer. It was the best damn sound he'd ever heard.

When she collapsed to the mattress, he took his time, kissing his way up her to her belly button, murmuring against her heated flesh, "So sexy...so sweet." He held her just below her hips, his hands trailing higher as he kissed her lower belly. His fingers brushed something rough along the top of her left ass cheek, and her body went rigid. His gut seized, knowing it was the brand, and he choked out, "Let me see, baby."

"*Callahan*," she whispered sadly.

"It's okay, darlin'."

She rolled onto her side, revealing *RJ* seared into her pale skin. Tears stung his eyes, bone-deep sadness battling with all-consuming anger. But Sully didn't need to feel that anger, so he stuffed it down deep and pressed a kiss to her scarred flesh. He wrapped his arms around her and closed his eyes as she lay on her side, holding her until he was sure his anger wouldn't rear its ugly head. Only then did he move beside her and gather her in his arms. "I'm so sorry that happened to you."

"I hate that you saw it."

She looked so vulnerable, it tore him up inside. "Darlin', you're beautiful to me, inside and out, and nothing can change that. You're a survivor, and that scar proves your strength."

"I'm not strong. I passed out when they did it."

He was torn between feeling gutted and relieved she'd passed out so she didn't have to feel all that pain. "You *are* strong. You got out of there, and you saved a lot of other people from suffering."

"But I'll never be rid of him or that place. It's on my body forever."

His heart broke for her, and he knew it didn't matter how many times he, or anyone else, told her the brand wouldn't change his feelings for her. She was right. That fucker had found a way to put her through hell every time she saw her own body in the mirror or changed her clothes and touched that brand, and *that* made Cowboy's blood boil. Even knowing he'd done it right back to the asshole didn't temper his wrath.

He gazed into her sad eyes, wanting to make her feel better, but he didn't have a good answer. "I wish I could make it go away."

"Me too."

"I'd suggest a tattoo to cover it, but it's difficult and often impossible to tattoo over a brand. I don't know anything about cosmetic surgery, but brands might burn too deep for that, too."

"I'm stuck with it forever. I just hate it so much."

He was *this close* to telling her what he'd done, but she didn't need to see him in that light. "I know, baby. I'm sorry. But he made a big mistake, because knowing what you went through just makes me admire you even more."

Tears dampened her eyes, and he kissed her softly. She was quiet for a long time, and when she spoke, it was just above a whisper. "He stole our moment."

"What do you mean?"

"You and I were so close, and then you saw the brand, and he was in the room with us. He stole our moment."

He looked into her teary eyes and held her tighter. "He can *never* steal our moments. Not that one or any of the others we've had or will ever have. They're ours and ours alone, and talking about this stuff only brings us closer together, not farther apart."

"But I didn't get to tell you how much I loved your mouth or how good you made me feel or anything like that."

"Don't worry, darlin'. I felt it, and I loved being close to you, too." He pressed his lips to hers and tried to ease her worries with playfulness. "But if you want to tell me how much you like my mouth, I'm all ears."

She giggled. "It's *very* sweet and *surprisingly* dirty, which I *like*...I mean..." Her cheeks flamed. "Okay, *yeah*, I like it. It's kind of my new favorite thing."

"Better be careful, or you'll get me going again."

Her eyes lit up. "Want me to tell you what I liked most?"

"Jesus..." His cock twitched. "What do you think?"

"I liked the way you talked dirty." She ran her fingers down his chest. "And that thing you did when you used your tongue—"

Her words were silenced with the hard press of his lips, and he proceeded to give her more of all the things she liked...and then some.

A LONG WHILE later, locked and loaded for further pleasure that wasn't going to happen, Cowboy dragged his ass out of Sully's bed before his restraint snapped and went home to take an ice-cold shower. But even that didn't take the edge off. He had to take things into his own hands to relieve the pressure, and he came to the sound of Sully's sweet voice in his ear and the lingering taste of her on his tongue.

After his shower, he grabbed his hat and headed over to his parents' house to break the news that would probably piss off his mother. He knocked on the door but was too anxious to wait for them to answer and walked in. His mother was sitting on his father's lap in the living room. His father's hand was up her shirt, and they were making out. *"Jesus Christ."* He turned around. "Aren't you too old for that?"

"You'd better hope not since you're my kin," his father said.

His mother laughed, and he heard her climbing off his father's lap. "Oh, Cowboy. You've seen us kiss before."

"I didn't need to see Dad's hand up your shirt." He turned around and found both his parents standing by the couch.

"If you'd've given me ten more minutes, I'd've been going *downtown.*" Tiny laughed at his own joke.

"Jesus." Cowboy glowered at him. "I can't unhear that."

That only made his father laugh harder.

"*Tiny*, you're awful," his mother teased. "Ignore your frisky father, honey. How's Sully?"

"Nervous about meeting her family."

"It's going to be a trying day," his mother said. "But hopefully it will be the start of a new beginning for her. How are you holding up?"

"I'm worried about her, but good otherwise. Although you and Dad might not be in a minute."

His father's brow furrowed. "Why is that?"

"Because I've got to tell you something." He paced for a second, then met his parents' eyes. "Sully and I got together last night."

Anger rose in his mother's eyes. "*Cowboy.* What were you thinking? You've just made this a hundred times harder for her."

"*She* made a move on *me.* I told her she was going through a lot and I didn't want her to confuse her feelings about me, and she said I was the *only* thing she *wasn't* confused about."

"Don't act like you didn't have a choice," his mother fumed. "I can't believe this. You should know better."

"What do you want me to say? You're damn right I had a choice. I tried to keep my feelings to myself, and I *couldn't.* They run too deep." He straightened his spine. "Go ahead and give me hell or call me a selfish prick, but it won't keep me from being with her. *This* is where we are, and now that it's on the table, just tell me where we go from here."

"For starters, I can't be Sully's therapist anymore," his mother said sharply. "That's a conflict of interest."

Cowboy's stomach sank. *Fuck.* "I didn't think about that."

"Clearly," she snapped. "But you should have."

He gritted his teeth, meeting her steely gaze. "It wasn't my intent to put her in that position and screw up her therapy. I don't want to mess that up for her."

"It's too late. She's *in* that position," his mother pointed out. "I have to transition her to someone else."

He felt sick. "Wait, *no.* We didn't even have sex."

"That doesn't matter. You have feelings for her, and you're my son. End of story," his mother said.

"*Wait.* I want to do what's best for her, and you're the best therapist we have."

"You know we have excellent therapists, but this isn't up to you, and I can't discuss it any further. I'll take it up with Sully," his mother said firmly.

His hands fisted at his sides. "You can't just drop her with all she's going through. Can you at least let me talk with her before you dump that on her? I'll do it tonight, after she meets with her family, and you can tell her at your session tomorrow."

His mother looked conflicted. *"Fine."*

"Thank you."

"I've never known you to cross lines like this," his father said, but his eyes told Cowboy he was referring to what he'd done in Maryland, too. "She must be important to you."

"She is." Cowboy took off his hat and scrubbed a hand down his face, hoping switching to a new therapist wouldn't mess up Sully's healing. "I am sorry, Mom. I know how hard you've been working to help her."

His mother exhaled a long breath, and her expression softened. "Honey, as your mother, *not* as Sully's therapist, I get it. The heart has a mind of its own, and I respect that. But be careful. I don't want either of you to get hurt."

"You think I do?" he said. It came out sharper than he meant it to. "I care about her, and I want to help her heal and make sense of her life and find happiness. That's the *most* important thing to me. I forgot about the conflict-of-interest thing, and that's on me, but I'm not some dumb kid rushing in with my eyes closed. I know it's not ideal for us to get involved with all she's been through. I've worked with enough people who have come out of horrific situations to know there are about a million layers of shit to go through at all times, and even when things get better, they can get worse when the wind changes directions. I get all that, and I'm *still* all in with Sully."

"You've never put your heart on the line like this, son," his father said. "How're you going to feel if she walks out that door this afternoon with her family and never comes back?"

Cowboy's chest constricted. "Don't worry about me. There's nothing I can't handle." He wasn't sure that was true where Sully's leaving was concerned, but he'd deal with that if and when the time came. Turning to his mother, he said, "What do I need to know to make sure I'm helping her as much as I can?"

"You know what to do," his mother said kindly. "Treat her like you treat everyone you care about. Be honest to a fault. Even when you think it might hurt, make the tough choice and do the right thing. Make sure you listen to her and *hear* what she's saying and what she isn't, and remember, even people who grew up under the best conditions can have a hard time differentiating protective feelings from affection, gratitude, or a dozen other emotions. Like I said, I don't want to see either of you get hurt."

Her comment about misconstruing his emotions wasn't lost on him, but he wasn't going to argue a misguided point. "What about the ranch's no fraternizing rule?"

"That rule was put into place for employees," his father said. "Sully isn't employed by us."

"But she *is* going through therapy, and she *has* asked about eventually taking on a paying position," his mother pointed out. "And, Cowboy, you were in a position of protecting her, so there is a line that was crossed, although it's separate from the ranch. That's on the Dark Knights."

"No, there wasn't. The Dark Knights' protection ended when the cult was disbanded and those assholes were arrested.

We didn't get together until late last night, so we haven't crossed that line."

"I guess that's technically correct, although now I have a feeling that outburst Sunday night was driven by your feelings for Sully, not just anger over the cult, and that could get me in trouble," his mother said.

Cowboy closed his eyes for a beat, trying to rein in his emotions. When he met her gaze, guilt tightened like a noose. "It was both. But I never acted on it with her, and I never said a word to her about my feelings. No lines were crossed, so there's no way you could've known."

His parents exchanged a troubled glance.

"I'm sorry," Cowboy relented. "I hope this doesn't blow back on you, but I'm not sorry about being with Sully."

"That's clear," his mother said matter-of-factly. "This is going to be a very difficult time for both of you, but I hope you know that even though this complicates things, and I'm worried about *both* of you, she couldn't have chosen a better man."

His father nodded in agreement, which Cowboy appreciated, but as he headed out the door, chastising himself for screwing up Sully's therapy, he wondered how life could be so fucking unfair as to bring him the one woman who made him see past the ranch, the woman he wanted to hold on to with everything he had, when her future was so unclear.

Chapter Seventeen

AFTER BREAKFAST AND a meeting with Wynnie, Sully rewatched one of the dozens of videos showcasing the arrests of Rebel Joe and several other cult members on Callahan's phone as she waited in Wynnie's office for Jordan to arrive. She and Callahan had watched several of the videos before breakfast and had seen the reports stating Casey Lawler had been found. The name Casey Lawler had been linked to statements like *it's a miracle* and *by the grace of God*. But in Sully's mind, if God were full of grace, he wouldn't have allowed her to be abducted in the first place. But if there *was* a higher power, did it have a hand in her ending up at the ranch as a way of making up for its egregious mistake?

Or had that been sheer luck?

Either way, she was thankful she was there, and she was glad the FBI had kept her current name and whereabouts out of the reports, although Callahan had been right about complete strangers rallying in support. There were videos of crowds carrying signs calling for the death penalty outside the building where Rebel Joe and other cult members were being held. It had been a hot topic at breakfast. Everyone had heard the news, although since Sully's name wasn't in it, most didn't know she was Casey. But Birdie, Sasha, Dare, Doc, and Ezra were in the know, and they'd sought her out privately to offer their support. She had worried the girls might look at her differently once they knew where she'd come from, but she'd seen only warmth, comfort, and kindness in their eyes.

They'd rallied behind her, just as Callahan had suspected people would. But they were his family. Even Ezra was his brother through the club. They were some of the kindest humans Sully had ever known, but because of their affiliation with the ranch, they were also adept at seeing past people's troubles to the very heart of who they were. While she knew some strangers might see her for the person she was becoming, she knew that to many others she'd always be just *the girl from the cult.*

As she stared at the face of the man who had stolen two decades of her life, had lied to her, raped her, had her branded, and forced her to endure other harsh punishments, she was flooded with relief that he'd finally pay for what he'd done. But that relief didn't overshadow her hatred for him, and she was pretty sure nothing ever would.

"Are you sure you want to keep watching that, darlin'?"

She glanced at her big-hearted protector, his thick arms crossed, chin low, jaw tight, and those serious, caring eyes trained on her. Even her torment wasn't enough to chase away the butterflies inhabiting her chest. He'd been stressed all morning, probably because *she* was so nervous about meeting Jordan. Callahan had calmed her down, and now, as her tension eased a little more by the mere sound of his voice, she wished she had the same effect on him. But she knew nothing would ease his worries until *she* found solid ground, and who knew how long that would take. She felt a pang of guilt for bringing confusion into his life, but she couldn't have turned away from him if she'd wanted to.

She realized he was waiting for a response and said, "I still can't believe it. But it becomes more real every time I see him being dragged off in cuffs." A mug shot of Rebel Joe appeared on the screen, and she paused the video, studying it. "How did I miss this before? Did you see this?"

"What?" He leaned closer.

"Look at his neck." She pointed to the words CHILD RAPIST seared into his skin. "Who would do that? How did they get to him?"

"Why does it matter? The fucker deserves a lot worse than that."

"I know he does, but he's untouchable. His men would never do that to him." Callahan's phone vibrated in her hand, and a text bubble popped up from Dare. She handed him the phone. "Where was the person who did it to him when he was doing all those horrible things to me?"

"Maybe they didn't know you at the time," Callahan said as he read Dare's text. He met her gaze. "Baby, you have more important things to think about. Jordan's here. My mom is bringing her back now."

Sully's nerves spiked, the mug shot forgotten. "This is it." She paced, her heart racing. "I'm going to meet my sister. I hope she likes me. What if I don't like her?"

"She's going to love you, darlin', and chances are you'll love her, too. But if it gets too overwhelming, we can cut it short. You just give me the signal."

"What's the signal?" she asked anxiously.

"I'll see it in your eyes. Don't worry," he said, and she knew he would, because he'd known exactly what she'd needed since the very moment they'd met.

The door opened, and Sully froze. Her heart lodged in her throat, and she looked at Callahan. He nodded reassuringly. With a long inhalation, she gathered her courage and turned around, taking in the tall, slim, incredibly beautiful blonde standing in the doorway with Wynnie. She had an air of elegance about her, with high cheekbones and wise blue eyes. She wore a beige cardigan over a white blouse, skinny jeans, and high heels. Sully had been so nervous, she'd changed her clothes several times and had finally decided to wear the outfit that made her feel the least confined and the most confident. The loose-fitting purple and pink batik shirt and denim shorts she'd chosen had caught Callahan's attention when he'd come back after his shower. He must've told her how gorgeous she looked ten times, and she'd felt good in it. *Great*, even. But now her confidence dwindled. She paled in comparison to the stunning, refined woman before her, and she wondered how they'd ever find common ground.

"Sully, this is Jordan." Wynnie stepped aside, allowing Jordan to walk into the room. "Jordan, this is Sully, and my son Cowboy."

Sully's voice was caught in her throat, and Callahan must've noticed, because he nodded to Jordan and said, "Nice to meet you."

"Hi." Jordan's voice trembled, as if she was trying not to cry.

Sully had thought seeing her, or hearing her voice, might trigger a memory, but it didn't, and she felt bad for *not* getting teary-eyed, which made their differences feel magnified. She finally managed, "Hi, Jordan."

Tears slid down Jordan's cheeks. "I'm sorry." She dug tissues out of her sweater pocket and dabbed at her eyes.

"It's okay to cry." Sully stepped closer as Wynnie discreetly left the room and closed the door. "They said you're five years older than me. You must remember everything." She'd racked her brain this morning, trying to remember something— *anything*—about her life before the compound, but she'd come up blank.

"I do. Every second." Jordan inhaled a ragged breath.

Sully ached for both of them. "I don't remember you. But I'd like to."

She opened her mouth to speak, then closed it. "I'm sorry, but I've missed you so much." She swiped at her tears. "I thought I'd never see you again."

Sully drew her into an awkward embrace, but that only made Jordan cry harder. She felt Callahan watching them and remembered his soothing words from when she'd broken down. "You should never be sorry for your feelings. It's the one thing we have that's truly ours."

"You sound like the older sister." Jordan wiped her eyes as she stepped out of her arms.

"I've had a lot of practice taking care of younger kids." Sully glanced at Callahan, and he winked.

Jordan dabbed at her eyes. "I'd like to hear about that one day, and maybe I could tell you about our family, too."

"I think I'd like to hear about your family. Do you have time to talk now?"

Jordan's brows knitted, as if she'd said something troubling. "Yes."

Sully realized she'd said *your family*. But she couldn't help it. They didn't feel like hers. Callahan pulled out a chair for her, and after Sully sat down, he gave her shoulder a reassuring squeeze, then stood a few feet away, her ever-present comfort.

"What would you like to know first?" Jordan asked.

Sully studied her face, trying to remember her. She noticed a scar above Jordan's right eyebrow, but no memories came. "I don't know. Wynnie thinks details might help jog my memory. Can you tell me about our parents?"

Jordan's eyes lit up like it was a favorite subject. "They were amazing, and they loved us so much. They'd been in love with each other since high school, and believe it or not, they were born on the same day."

"They died on the same day, too," Sully said more to herself than to Jordan.

Jordan got teary-eyed again. "Yeah."

"Sorry. I shouldn't have said that."

"No, it's okay. I'm just emotional today." She wiped her eyes. "We share Mom's blue eyes, although yours are much brighter than mine, and she had light blond hair like me. She was soft-spoken, but she was a beacon of happiness, always telling us we could do or be anything. She called us her little doves, because doves symbolize hope, and she used to sing us to sleep. She had the prettiest voice."

"What would she sing?"

"'My Girl' by the Temptations was her favorite song."

She remembered Callahan calling her *my girl* last night. Sadness welled up inside her at the thought of being so loved by a mother she couldn't remember. How many nights had she cried into her pillow, wishing someone would hold her, while a dozen other girls slept around her?

"I wish I remembered that."

"You used to like it, and you loved when she painted stars

on our toenails. I still paint them on mine." Jordan slipped off a high heel and wiggled her toes, which were painted red with white stars.

"Maybe that's why I love looking at the stars so much." She glanced at Callahan, and the edges of his lips tipped up. "What else can you tell me about her?"

"She never raised her voice," Jordan said. "Even when she was mad."

Sully thought about how often she'd gotten in trouble for yelling and talking back at the compound when she was young and how they'd punished that out of her.

"She loved looking at fashion magazines and sketching her own designs."

"Did she dress fancy?" *Like you?*

"No. That wasn't Mom's thing. She liked pretty clothes but not fancy. I have all her old sketch pads. I can show them to you sometime. She's the reason I love fashion. When we were young, I used to sketch dresses all the time."

"I sketch, too," Sully said, feeling a thread of…she didn't know what. Hope? Proof that she had a link to the mother and sister she didn't remember?

"You do?"

"Mm-hm. Not clothes, though. Mostly people, animals, and nature."

"She's really talented," Callahan boasted, and Sully's heart warmed.

"I bet she is," Jordan said. "I'd love to see your sketches sometime."

Mulling over her use of *sometime* and hoping she would see Jordan again, she said, "Sure. What was our father like?"

Jordan got a dreamy look in her eyes. "He was a big, burly

construction worker. He loved to laugh, and his hands were so big, they swallowed ours."

Like Callahan's hands.

"You loved riding on his shoulders. You were most like him. He always stood up for the things he believed in and for the things we wanted, and you did the same thing. You'd argue for whatever you thought was right."

My fighting spirit. "Like what?"

"Well, you were little, so you argued about little-kid things, like if you should be able to go outside in the rain when you wanted to play carwash with your trucks." Jordan smiled, and it made her even prettier. "You were always feistier and stronger-willed than me. You wanted to be just like Dad."

"I did?"

"*Yes.* You even dressed like him, in flannels and T-shirts and sweats or leggings, and you always wore construction boots like his." She glanced at Sully's worn leather boots. "They were a lot like those."

"Really?" Sully felt herself smiling. She thought about Callahan's flannel shirt and how much she loved wearing it.

"He loved that about you. You were always running through puddles or digging in the dirt."

"With you?"

"No. I've always been more like Mom. You and I were total opposites. I loved fancy dresses, but you hated them, and you had no trouble telling me how *yucky* you thought they were."

Sully winced. "Sorry."

"No, I liked that you were your own person. I'd be twirling in the grass in my princess dress, and you'd be making mud castles, filthy from head to toe."

Sully thought about the drawings she'd made over the years

of the little girl twirling in the grass, and her chest constricted. She felt Callahan watching her and knew he was thinking the same thing. But she didn't remember seeing Jordan dancing in the grass, and she didn't want to give her false hope, so she kept it to herself. "Did I get in trouble for getting dirty?"

"No. Our parents believed kids should be kids. They didn't get mad when I'd wear my fancy dresses out to play or when you dug up the garden to make a construction pit." Jordan told her stories about their father scouring yard sales for secondhand dresses for her and buying himself and Sully matching flannels.

Jordan showed her pictures of their family and told her about their lives before the accident and about their aunt Sheila, their father's sister, and her husband, Gary, whom she'd gone to live with in Massachusetts after the accident, but nothing rang a bell.

"You can keep the pictures," Jordan said. "Maybe they'll help you remember something."

"Thank you. I hope they do. What is your life like now?"

Jordan told her she lived in Pleasant Hill, Maryland, not far from Prairie View, the town where they'd lived with their parents, and that she'd just gotten engaged to Jax Braden, a renowned wedding-gown designer. She told her how wonderful he and his family were and that she hoped Sully would get to know them one day.

By the time they came to a natural lull in their conversation, Sully was full of questions and feelings she didn't know what to do with. But she knew one thing for sure. She wanted to see Jordan again. "Can you come back tomorrow? Maybe we can take a walk and talk?"

"Yes. I'd like that very much. Would it be okay if I hugged you goodbye?"

Sully nodded, and as they hugged, she said, "You felt like a stranger when you first walked in, but you don't now."

Jordan started crying again.

"You must have gotten all the emotional genes in the family."

"I was always the crier, and you were the tough one." Jordan wiped her eyes. "I guess some things never change."

As Jordan left the room and Callahan came to Sully's side, her world felt a little fuller. Maybe she and Jordan could find some common ground after all.

"How do you feel, darlin'?"

She felt so many conflicting emotions, she said, "A little lost and a little found. Does that make any sense?"

"It makes perfect sense." He gathered her in his arms, and as he kissed her, that feeling of being found got a little stronger.

Chapter Eighteen

SULLY SAT ON her porch steps after dinner, sketching a picture of Jordan. As she drew her blue eyes, she thought about what Jordan had said. *We share Mom's blue eyes, although yours are much brighter than mine, and she had light blond hair like me. She was soft-spoken, but she was a beacon of happiness, always telling us we could do or be anything.* A wave of sadness moved through her for the woman whose eyes she shared but would never see smiling at her.

She looked up as Callahan came around the side of the cabin, and that confident, sexy grin lit her up from the inside out. After meeting Jordan, she'd needed the day to process everything she was feeling, and he'd given her the space she'd asked for. She'd seen him working with a horse in one of the riding rings when she was down at the rehab barn helping Sasha, and they'd had lunch and dinner together, but he hadn't pushed her to talk about her feelings. She'd wanted to see him after dinner, but he'd said he had to take care of a few things first.

"Hey, gorgeous. Got room for a big ol' cowboy on that step?"

"I think I can manage that." She'd added more items to the list he'd asked her to make, and she tucked it into her sketchbook as she scooted over.

"Miss me yet?"

She nodded, grinning as he kissed her. "Thanks for giving me time to sort through my thoughts today. Helping Sasha with the horses was just what I needed."

"No worries. I've got plenty to do around here, and you don't need me hovering twenty-four-seven. I know you'll talk to me when you're ready. But I've got something I need to talk to you about."

"Okay."

"I screwed up, darlin', and I am truly sorry. Healing from what you've been through and finding your footing so you can move forward are the most important things to me. But I got so caught up in being with you, I didn't slow down to think about how it would affect your relationship with my mom, and our being together creates a conflict of interest for her as your therapist."

"What do you mean?"

"She has to have your best interest at heart, and knowing I have feelings for you could cloud her judgment, which means she can't be your therapist anymore. I asked her if it would make a difference if I backed off, but it won't. Just knowing how I feel creates the issues. I didn't mean to screw that up for you, and I feel horrible about it."

"But I want to be with you, so you didn't screw it up. We both did." Guilt tiptoed in. "I hope I didn't cause trouble between you and your mom."

"You didn't do anything wrong. That's not what this is about. It has to do with what's ethical in her profession."

"I guess that makes sense, but why didn't she say anything about it in our session this morning?"

"I asked her not to until I had a chance to tell you myself. I'm sure she'll talk with you about it tomorrow. She'll have to transition you to another therapist."

"Okay. I really like working with your mom, but maybe this is for the best. There were a couple of times when I was thinking about you during our sessions and I felt like I had to keep my feelings to myself because she's your mother."

He leaned his elbows on his knees, rubbing one hand with the other. "I don't like you feeling like you have to hide your feelings. I get why you did, but hopefully now you won't feel like that. I was really worried that this was going to upset you."

"I'm not thrilled about starting over with someone new, but it makes sense. I liked Colleen when I met her. Maybe she'll let me work with her."

"Colleen's a great therapist."

She thought about their conversation, and as always, she had questions. "Can I ask you something?"

"Anything."

"Why did you tell your mom if you didn't think about it being a conflict of interest?"

He met her gaze, his lips tipped up in a boyish smile, so different from what she was used to seeing on him, it tweaked her heart. "Mostly because I thought it was important that she know, since she was working with you, and I didn't know how a relationship might impact your progress. But also because I'm proud to be with you." He shrugged. "To be honest, I'd like everyone to know."

That made her all kinds of happy, and she felt herself grinning. "If you'd thought about the conflict of interest, would you have kept your distance from me?"

"I would have tried." He shook his head. "But I don't think I could have stayed away from you. I like you a hell of a lot, Sully. I like everything about you, from your sweet nature and beautiful smile to your determination and quiet strength, and I really like the way you connect with me and the horses. I know your future is unclear and you've got a lot to deal with. But I'm not a kid, darlin'. I'm thirty-one and I've lived a lot of life, so none of that scares me. I want to be there to help you through it. You can lean on me or use me as a sounding board, and more importantly, if your life takes a turn and this is all we get, I wouldn't trade it for the world."

She was rendered speechless. There was no comparison between him and Rebel Joe, but she couldn't help thinking that Rebel Joe had wanted her because she was a rebellious teenage virgin he could claim and thought he could tame. *The ultimate power trip.* While Callahan got to know her, tried to help her, and wanted to be with her for *her*, baggage, scars, and all.

He leaned in and kissed her softly on the lips. "Any other questions?"

"How did I get so lucky?" she whispered.

"I've been asking myself how I got so lucky since the day I met you." He put his arm around her, hugging her against his side. "Are you up for a walk? I'd like to show you something."

"I'd love that. I missed our walk last night." As they pushed to their feet, she said, "Although I very much enjoyed our other *activities.*"

"Me too, darlin'." He drew her into his arms. "I like doing everything with you, but hearing you say my name when I'm making you feel good is right up there at the top of the list."

Her cheeks burned, but he kissed her deeply, turning her

embarrassment into spine-tingling lust.

"Now, how about we take that walk before we end up in your bedroom and you miss seeing the stars."

Skipping the walk for more of those delicious kisses sounded good to her, but she didn't want to come across as too needy. "Let me put my drawing stuff inside."

"Bring it with you. You'll be able to finish when we get where we're going."

He slung an arm over her shoulder, and they headed back the way he'd come and turned up the road that led to his place. She reveled in their closeness and the comfortable silence that always seemed to find them on their walks. Callahan's truck came into view parked next to a motorcycle in front of a log cabin with a wide front porch that was much larger than the one she was staying in. Pretty flowers sprouted up through the grass, as if seeds had been dropped like raindrops from the sky. Just beyond the driveway to the right was a large patio with a firepit and several chairs around it.

"Is this yours?"

"Home sweet home."

"It's beautiful. I feel bad that you stayed on my porch all those nights when you could've been *here*."

"That wouldn't have been as good."

"Why? This place is gorgeous."

"Because you weren't there, darlin'." He leaned down for a kiss and took her hand, leading her along a walkway toward the left side of the house, as if he hadn't just stolen another piece of her heart with that comment.

They followed the walkway around to his home, which was built on a hill, giving way to breathtaking views of rolling mountains and lush pines. The back of the cabin was almost all glass, with another gorgeous patio and a second-story deck that ran the full length of the house. Twinkling white lights decorated the deck railings, and more were strung along another walkway leading down the hill. "Wow, what a view."

"It sure is." He squeezed her hand, drawing her attention, and she realized he'd been looking at her and not the mountains when he'd said it, turning her insides to mush.

He led her down the other illuminated walkway, toward a massive deck overlooking a wide creek. She felt like she'd walked into a fairy tale. A fire blazed in a raised stone firepit with a domed grate overtop and two comfy-looking cushioned chairs beside it. On the other side of the deck was a bed of thick, fluffy blankets and pillows surrounded by candles in pretty glass jars. Her heart swelled as she gazed up at him, too choked up to speak.

"I wanted to give you a night beneath the stars. But don't worry, I don't expect anything. We can sleep fully clothed, or I can sleep on a chair, or walk you back to your cabin if you want to sleep alone tonight."

Tears welled in her eyes. "This is a dream come true. Do you really think I want to spend the night alone in my cabin instead of right here with you?"

"I didn't want to assume."

She wound her arms around his waist and kissed the center of his chest. "I don't know what I did to deserve you, or any of this, but I sure am glad we found each other. You can't imagine how much this means to me. How much you mean to me. Thank you."

He cradled her face between his hands, gazing at her affectionately. "I told you I'm going to make sure you get to enjoy all the things you missed out on."

She went up on her toes as he met her halfway in a sweet kiss. Her heart was so full of him, she couldn't imagine how there would be room for anything else.

"I've got some goodies for you by the fire." He took her hand, leading her toward the deck. "I thought you might want to try your hand at checkers again, and I brought a few other games in case you want to broaden your horizons."

"I *do*. I've been wanting to play more games with you," she said excitedly.

"Great, and if you're going to stargaze, you have to have s'mores."

"I'll take your word for that." As they stepped onto the deck, she saw a cooler on the other side, packed with several different types of drinks and a tray with marshmallows, chocolate bars, and a box of graham crackers. "That's a lot of snacks and drinks. Are other people meeting us here?"

"No. The snacks are for s'mores, and I wasn't sure what you liked to drink besides orange juice and water, so I brought some of everything. Do you like soda?"

She shook her head. "I've had Coke, and I didn't like the bubbles."

"Okay, well, I also brought iced tea, lemonade, and a few other things. I wasn't sure if I should bring alcohol," he said carefully. "I didn't want to bring up bad memories with sights or smells, but I also wasn't sure if you wanted some. So I brought a few alcoholic drinks and hid them under the ice in the cooler."

"You *hid* them?" He'd thought of *everything*. Maybe that shouldn't surprise her given the way he was always looking after her, but it did.

"Yeah, pretty stupid, huh?"

"More like incredibly thoughtful. Thank you for thinking of that. It doesn't bother me to see alcohol, and I don't know if it will bother me to smell it." It might bother her, but she felt like that was giving Rebel Joe the power to stand between her and a regular life, so she said, "Maybe we'll try it later and see."

"No pressure from me."

Taking in the games and romantic candles and blankets, she said, "Did you peek at my list when I was sleeping or something?"

"You mean the list that had 'swim naked in the lake' on it? No, but I'd like to see it. Why?"

"Because all of this is on it, except the somemores."

He grinned. "*S'mores*, darlin'. Replace the O-M-E with an apostrophe."

"Oops." She laughed softly. "Still, all of this is on my list."

"I'd like to say I read your mind, but you told me you used to look out your window and wonder what it would be like to sleep under the stars. Remember?" A tease sparked in his eyes. "And as for the rest, maybe I'm just thinking about sidetracking you with games while I get you high on chocolate and lick it off your body."

"You don't have to get me high for that." She didn't know where her boldness was coming from, but it felt so natural to tease like that with him, she had a feeling it had been in her all the time, locked down tight, like so many other parts of her personality.

He arched a brow. "We're never going to make it to stargazing if you keep talking like that."

"*You* started it." She laughed.

He leaned in, rasping against her lips, "I'm going to enjoy finishing it, too."

Thrills darted through her as he kissed her.

"Set your sketch pad down and have a seat, darlin'." He flashed a devilish grin. "It's time to get sticky."

She put her sketch pad by the bed and sat in the chair beside him as he placed graham crackers, chocolate bars, and marshmallows on a plate. "How do we do this?"

"Basically, we're making chocolate marshmallow sandwiches, with graham crackers as the bread. I think people put a piece of chocolate on top of the graham cracker, add a roasted marshmallow, and top it off with another graham cracker. But seeing how you're a chocolate fiend, I have a feeling you'll want to eat it my way, with an extra piece of chocolate on top of the marshmallow. It gets a little messy." His voice turned low and seductive. "But it's nothing a few licks can't clean up."

"I think I'm going to like these messy s'mores."

As they made the sticky treats, she told him about her afternoon with Sasha, and he told her about the horses he was training and shared tidbits about the rest of his day. He told her how Birdie used to get him to make her extra s'mores while she was eating the ones she'd made, and they joked about that. He stole kisses as he told her more stories about his sisters trying to follow him and his brothers around when they were younger and how he and Sasha were the reigning champs of paintball, and Birdie was the best mechanical bull rider around. They talked about many things, but they didn't talk about her time with Jordan, and she was glad, because that, and the sexy things she and Callahan had done last night, were all she'd thought about all day. How had he known that learning more about his family, laughing, and sharing chocolate kisses would be the perfect way to spend the evening after such an emotional day?

The s'mores were ridiculously delicious, and so thick, she

had to squish them to fit them into her mouth. She was a sticky mess, and she felt so close to Callahan, every time he licked his lips or his fingertips, she imagined him licking *her*.

"I think I could exist on s'mores." She took another bite and tried to wipe a smear of chocolate from her thigh, but her fingers had chocolate on them, too, making it worse.

Callahan laughed and shook his head as he pushed to his feet. He tossed his hat onto the deck and planted his hands on the arms of her chair, leaning in so close, she could practically taste the chocolate on his breath. "What am I going to do with my sticky girl?" He slid his tongue along her lower lip and kissed her.

"Now you're messy, too." She reached up and wiped chocolate from the edge of his lips with her fingertip. He guided that finger into his mouth and sucked it clean, sending her body into a wild flurry of desire.

"I'm about to get even messier." His eyes smoldered as his mouth came down over hers hungrily in a deep, passionate kiss that went on and on, igniting flames beneath her skin. He consumed more of her with every stroke of his tongue, taking them from hot to *scorching*, making her entire body ache for his touch. Just when she thought she might combust, he drew back, leaving her breathless and dizzy with desire as he lowered himself to his knees.

His eyes turned volcanic, and his fingertips trailed up her thighs, sending rivers of heat between her legs. His eyes never left hers as he slanted his mouth over her inner thigh, kissing, licking, and sucking so exquisitely, she felt herself go damp. The feel of him and the mix of pleasure and hunger in his eyes were all too much. She couldn't keep from rocking her hips, pleading, "*Please don't stop.*" He intensified his efforts, sucking harder. *"God—"*

He slid his tongue along the pink spot he'd left on her flesh and lavished her other thigh with the same attention, driving her out of her mind. His fingers snuck beneath her shorts, tracing the edge of her underwear, so close to where she needed it, she lifted her hips, desperate for more. She'd never been happier about loose clothing than she was at that very moment, as his fingers glided along her skin. But in the next breath, he pushed to his feet, and the air rushed from her lungs.

He didn't say a word as he took her by the wrist, lifted her to her feet, and sat down in the other chair, guiding her onto his lap. She straddled his thick waist, feeling his hard heat beneath her. He threaded one hand into her hair, bringing her face closer to his. "I missed you today, baby." His voice was thick with emotion.

She heard, *Me too*, in her head, but "Kiss me," came out, and he reclaimed her mouth, rougher and somehow also more sensually, as his fingers climbed up her thigh again, teasing along the edge of her underwear. Being on top made her feel bold and in control. "Touch me," she demanded, rather than asking, earning another hungry growl that turned her on even more.

His hand tightened in her hair. "You're so damn sexy." A devilish glimmer flashed in his eyes, and he took her in another toe-curling kiss, pushing his fingers into her underwear. She gasped with pleasure as he deepened their kiss and teased her wetness, drawing a needy moan from her lungs. With the heat of the fire at her back and his big body burning beneath her, she ate at his mouth, rising up to give him better access. He pushed his thick fingers inside her, sending intense pleasure rolling through her. Her head fell back. "That's it, baby, ride my fingers. You're so sexy in the moonlight. I want to see more of you."

She started to take off her shirt and realized she was still holding the last piece of her s'more. He took the sticky treat, flames burning in his eyes as she stripped off her shirt and bra.

"You're so beautiful." He kissed one breast, then the other, sending white-hot tingles through her. Holding her gaze, he dragged his finger through the chocolate he was holding and painted it around and on her nipples. He tossed the last of the sticky treat off the deck and said, "Open your mouth, baby girl." When she did, he put his chocolate-covered finger in it. "Suck it clean for me."

Everything he said sent shivers of desire racing through her, making her want more of his words, his mouth, *him*. As she sucked his finger, he lowered his mouth to her breast, his other hand moving up her thigh again, pushing beneath her underwear and sliding inside her. She moaned around the finger she was sucking. He lavished her breasts with openmouthed kisses and slow strokes of his tongue, growling, "*So fucking sweet,*" against her skin. *God*, his words made her wetter. When he pulled his finger from her mouth, she longed for its return, but that hand found her breast, and *boy* did it feel good. She had a hard time holding on to her thoughts for the greedy desires consuming her as he stroked that spot inside her, making her tremble with need. He sealed his mouth over one nipple, sucking hard as she rode his fingers. Prickling heat stacked up inside her, pulsing beneath her skin. She rocked her hips faster and clung to his head, keeping his mouth on her breast.

"Suck *harder*," she demanded, and she gasped as he sucked so hard, she could feel his teeth. "*Ohmy...So good. Cal...*"

He tore open her shorts, using his other hand on that bundle of nerves that stole her ability to think. She felt him *everywhere*—in the air, beneath her skin, inside her—and she surrendered to his possession as waves of pleasure crashed over her. *"Callahan—"* She grabbed his shoulders, arching against his mouth, her body quivering and quaking, desperate moans falling from her lips. She was lost in pleasure, lost in *him*. This was heaven. This man, his touch, his *heart*. When she finally floated down from the peak, he drew her into a long, slow kiss, and as their lips parted, her heart tumbled out. "I want more. I want *you*."

"There's no rush, baby."

She gazed into his caring eyes and *felt* his thoughts. "I know you're worried about me, and yes, I was in a terrible situation, and I had to give my body to someone I didn't want to for a very long time. But I'm not going to let that part of my life keep me from doing what I want. You told me to own my feelings, and I want to do that with you. I don't know where my life is heading next week or next month, but I know what I want *right now*, and I'm *choosing* to be with you." She paused, letting that sink in. "Do you want to be with me?"

"Yes, darlin', more than life itself. You and only you."

He kissed her and stood with her in his arms, carrying her to the bed. When he laid her down, she realized there was an air mattress beneath all those fluffy blankets, and her heart filled to near bursting. He rid them of their boots and socks and was gentle and loving as he took off her shorts and underwear and covered her with a blanket. She watched him strip off his shirt and jeans, his erection straining against his black boxer briefs, and swallowed hard. Even though she'd slept beside him last night without an ounce of nervousness and he'd worn nothing but similar briefs, her nerves flamed.

THE HESITATION IN Sully's eyes stopped Cowboy from removing his boxer briefs and took him to his knees beside her. "We don't have to do more, Sully. There's no pressure. I'm not a teenager who can't keep it in his pants, and I'm not going anywhere."

Her brows knitted. "I want to be with you, but I just got really nervous."

"It's okay, darlin'. Do you want to put your clothes back on?"

She shook her head. "Will you lie with me?"

He lay beside her, resting on his elbow so they were eye to eye, but he didn't reach for her, giving her full control. When she scooted closer, he put his arm around her and kissed her softly. "Is this okay?"

She nodded, and he ran his hand down her back, wanting to soothe her but not to coax her into going further. He'd wait months if that's what she needed. But tonight, above all else, he wanted her to feel safe and adored.

"Kiss me," she whispered.

"I love kissing you and holding you." He kissed her tenderly. "This is enough for me, baby. *You're* enough for me." He kissed her more sensually, and as they kissed, she ran her hand up his chest and along his shoulder. "Feels good," he said between kisses. Her hand moved lower, teasing over his nipple, and his cock twitched against her. Her hand stilled, and when she did it again, his fucking dick jerked again. "Sorry."

He felt her heart beating faster, and she drew back, gazing curiously at him with the most beautiful doe eyes he'd ever seen.

She lifted her hand, running her fingers over his lips, along his jaw, and down his neck, and then she leaned up to kiss each of those places. "Is this okay?" she asked tentatively.

"Baby, everything is okay. I'm yours." He lay back, allowing her to explore.

Her delicate hand moved over his chest and nipples. Her gaze trailed lower, watching his body react to her touch. Her mouth followed her hand, and she kissed his chest and slid her tongue over his nipple, smiling at the appreciative sounds he made. She continued kissing and touching his chest, ribs, and stomach, testing his restraint as her soft fingers traced his abs, and her hand coasted over his boxer briefs, grazing his cock, making it twitch. Her curious baby blues flicked to his face as she did it again. The trust she was putting in him was the best gift he'd ever received. He clenched his jaw, fighting the urge to lift his hips as she continued touching, watching, *discovering*. When she pushed her hand into his boxer briefs and palmed his hard length, a growling moan escaped before he could stop it, and she tightened her fist around him.

"*Fuck*. That feels good, darlin'."

She pressed those sexy lips to his stomach as she stroked him, and fucking hell, he was going to lose his mind. She continued the tantalizing torture, kissing and stroking, stilling her hand to feel his cock jerk in time to every press of her lips. When she peeled down his boxer briefs, he took them off and lay back down, giving her full rein over his body. Her eyes were dark and lustful as she knelt beside him in the moonlight, the flames from the fire dancing in her eyes as she visually drank him in from head to toe.

He ran his hand down her back. "You don't have to keep going."

"I've never *wanted* to touch a man before," she said softly, but then her voice grew stronger. "I feel so much for you, I want to touch all of you."

That was the sexiest thing he'd ever heard. "I'm yours, Sully. You can touch every inch of me, and you don't have to worry. I won't expect *anything* more. That's a promise. You control every aspect of what happens, or doesn't happen, between us tonight."

She swallowed hard, nodding, and took her time exploring his body, running her hands along his shoulders, arms, chest, torso, and legs, every touch followed by a kiss, lick, or nip. It was so erotic, forcing himself to remain still as she touched him everywhere other than his cock and balls. His body was on fire, muscles corded tight, cock aching. Her curiosity, intrigue, and trust were as enticing as if she had touched him there, driving his feelings for her deeper. He'd never done anything like this, had never relinquished control in this way, but he'd do anything for Sully, and man, pleasure radiated off her as she took stock of his reactions, biting her lower lip to trap her smile and repeating certain touches or nipping at his skin to earn a louder response. She sucked his nipples and grazed her teeth over his flesh, earning groans and growls.

She straddled his stomach, her arousal wetting his skin, seriously testing his restraint. She leaned down to kiss him, whispering, "Is this okay? I've never been on top."

"Baby, it's more than okay. Your touch is the most powerful thing I've ever felt." He buried his hands in her hair and kissed her. She returned his efforts feverishly, grinding against him. He knew she needed more, and he was aching to pleasure her, but he didn't want her to feel like she had to have sex if she wasn't ready. "Darlin'," he said against her lips. "Straddle my face. Let me make you feel good."

Her eyes widened in disbelief, and he had the feeling she'd never done that before.

"You're in total control," he reminded her. "You can say no."

"I don't want to say no. I just don't want to hurt you...or *smother* you."

She was so fucking cute and innocent. "You won't, baby. Trust me, I'll enjoy every second of it as much as you will."

She moved tentatively into position. "All the way down, sweetheart." He guided her onto his mouth and proceeded to lick and tease, gradually taking more until she was writhing and moaning as he feasted on her.

"*Ohgod...Cal...*" She gyrated against his mouth, and when he used his fingers on her clit, thrusting his tongue deep inside her, she pumped her hips faster, panting out, "*Yes, oh*—" He devoured her, quickening his ministrations on her clit as she pumped and ground, then cried out, "*Yesss*—" A stream of sensual sounds filled the air as she shattered against his mouth and rode out her pleasure.

Her body trembled and shook as she moved off his face, her arousal wetting his chest and abs. He wiped his mouth with his forearm and reached up to cup her cheek. "Come down here and kiss me, darlin'."

She lowered her mouth to his, kissing him slowly at first, like she was getting used to the taste of herself. He threaded his hands into her hair, angling her mouth over his, still letting her set their pace. She deepened the kiss, exploring his mouth the way she'd explored his body, sweeping her tongue over his teeth and along the roof, gradually increasing in intensity, until she was kissing him ravenously, and he was right there with her.

She tore her mouth away, panting out, "I can't get enough of you," and kissed him again, *harder*. She scooted lower, resting her pussy on his cock, slick and hot and so fucking tempting, it took everything he had not to try to shift and angle himself into her. She started moving along his length, slowly and purposefully, and drew back, gazing into his eyes with as much hunger as affection.

Steeling himself against his mounting desire for the amazing woman opening herself up to him, he ran his hands up her thighs. "Feel good, baby?"

"Yes, but I still want more. I want you inside me."

Just hearing her say that made his cock jerk beneath her. "I've got a condom in my wallet."

"We don't need it. I'm protected, and the doctor said I'm clean. Are you?"

"Yes, but are you sure, baby? I don't want you to worry."

"I don't want anything between us." Her brows knitted again. "But I want to be on top."

He cocked a grin. "A front-row seat to my gorgeous girl riding me sounds perfect."

She bit her lower lip bashfully and dipped her head to kiss him. Her hair tumbled around their faces as they aligned their bodies. He was blessed with a formidable cock, and as she sank down on it, he fought the urge to thrust up, allowing her to take her time, until he was buried to the hilt. The air rushed from his *and* her lungs, and *holy hell*, she was tight and hot and he'd never felt anything so perfect.

"Christ, baby, you're tight. Is it too much?"

"No. It feels good," she panted out.

He remained still, his body vibrating with restraint as he gave her body time to acclimate, giving her a chance to make the next move. It was excruciating, but he didn't care. Nothing was more important than the beautiful woman finding herself as they found each other. When she finally started to move, it felt incredible. He grabbed her hips, and it took everything he had not to take control. But this was about her needs, her discoveries. She tried to kiss him while she rocked, but he could tell the rhythm was hard for her.

"Take your time, sexy girl." He tucked her hair behind her ear, gazing into those curious, lust-filled eyes. "You can put your hands on my chest and use me for leverage, or if you want to stay in this position, lace your fingers with mine."

He put his hands, palms up, on either side of his head, and her brows knitted, like she was thinking about it. She laced their fingers together, pinning his hands beside his head, and rocked forward and back. Her head dipped again, her hair tumbling out from behind her ear, curtaining their faces.

"Feel good, baby?"

"*Uh-huh.* I want to do it faster."

"Then do it, baby."

She quickened her pace, tightening around him. "I like that," she panted out, riding him hard and fast.

He ground his back teeth together, trying to stave off the pressure building inside him. When she released his hands, pressing her palms to his chest, he realized she wanted to try it all.

"That's my gorgeous girl. Take what you want."

She rode him faster, *rougher*, and he fondled her breasts, rolling her nipples between his fingers and thumbs. "*Yes.* That feels good."

She arched her back, moaning as she rode him. He knew he could make her come by touching her clit, but she was so damn stunning, learning what her own body could do, taking control of her sexuality, he wanted to open more doors for her. To show her what else *she* could do and what they could do together. "Touch yourself, darlin'." He guided her hand between her legs and was surprised that she held his gaze as she did it, which was hot as hell. "That's it. Good girl." He squeezed her nipple, and she gasped. "Too hard?"

She shook her head. "I like it. Do it again."

He did, earning more appreciative sounds as he pumped his hips. "Find that spot that drives you wild with your fingers. Let's make you come."

"I've never done this to myself," she panted out.

Christ. His heart was so full of her, he wanted to hold her as much as he wanted to make love to her. "That's okay, darlin'. We'll do it together." He covered her hand with his, showing her how to pleasure herself.

"*Oh…Oh my…Wow.*" Her breaths came fast and clipped.

"That's it, baby, keep going." He used one hand to help her, his other on her nipple, as she rode his cock, earning one sharp inhalation after another. They found their rhythm, their energy twining together, binding them as one. She cried out, and her hand stilled as her head fell back, her mouth open. He continued moving her fingers for her, sending her over the edge. Her pussy clenched tight and hot around his cock as sounds of rapture flew from her lips. He struggled against the need to come. "That's my girl," he gritted out. "Keep it going." She was gorgeous, clawing at his chest, back arched, breasts pink from his hands, as she rode out her climax.

When she finally collapsed over him, he gathered her in his arms, kissing her cheeks and lips, fighting his own need for release.

"*More*," she pleaded.

He covered her mouth with his, holding her ass with both hands, loving her slowly. He rolled her onto her back, gazing into her trusting eyes. "Is this okay if I'm careful?"

"Yes."

He lowered his lips to hers, loving her with all the tenderness she deserved and the heat she craved, whispering between kisses. *"You feel so good…So sexy…"* Nothing had ever felt so right as he took her deeper, the tension of their orgasms building, hampering their breathing, pulsing in the air around them.

"Don't be so careful," she pleaded. "I want to feel what *you* feel for me."

"Jesus, darlin'. I feel so much for you. I'm not sure you realize what you're asking for."

"I do. I trust you, so please trust me."

Fuck. She was his kryptonite. "Can you take more of me?"

"I hope so."

He pushed his hands beneath her hips, lifting and angling them, pushing in slowly as deep as he could go.

"Oh *gosh*, that's…*wow*."

He kissed her passionately, reading her body, her sounds, and the way her hips fell into sync with his as he increased their pace. She clung to him, her nails digging into his skin, pleasure-filled sounds moving from her lungs to his as their tongues tangled, and their hearts hammered out a frantic beat. Their skin slickened, and he struggled to stave off his orgasm. His emotions reeled as they lost themselves in each other, and their bodies took over. Their kisses grew messy and wild, their sounds animalistic, and when she came, his restraint snapped, and he surrendered to a release so powerful, it felt like it was dredged from his soul.

When the world started to come back into focus, he touched his forehead to hers, trying to catch his breath. "Still with me, darlin'?"

Her eyes fluttered open. "Uh-huh."

He gathered her in his arms, kissing her lips, cheeks, and forehead. "I hope I wasn't too rough. I got carried away."

"You weren't." She snuggled into him. "My entire body is humming. I never knew it could be like that."

He brushed his nose along her cheek. "Neither did I."

"That wasn't your first rodeo, *cowboy*." A teasing smile curved her lips with his parroted words.

"I've never felt as much as I feel for you for anyone, and that makes everything more intense." He kissed her again, slower and deeper, and brushed his lips over hers, whispering, "Thank you for trusting me."

"I could say the same to you, the way you let me touch you."

"I love when you touch me." He held her as their breathing calmed, her warm, sweet body cuddled safely against him, and gazed up at the stars, wondering how he'd gone his whole life without ever feeling like this. He didn't want to move, didn't want to miss a second of being close, and he allowed himself a few more minutes of that immense pleasure before brushing a kiss to her forehead and saying, "If I'd known we'd end up like this, I'd've brought out a towel to clean you up. I've got napkins, but they're too rough." He grabbed his shirt. "I'll use this."

Her cheeks pinked up. "You're going to clean *me* up?"

"You're my girl. Of course I'm going to take care of you." He realized that might embarrass her and said, "Unless you don't want me to."

Tears welled in her eyes, and she buried her face in his chest.

Fuck. He kissed her forehead and tipped her face up. "I'm sorry. I didn't mean to upset you."

"You didn't. I'm happily overwhelmed. I've just never been treated like I mattered after…"

His throat thickened with emotions. "Those days are over, sweetheart. It's time to get used to being cherished."

CHERISHED.

That wasn't a word Sully would have ever imagined being linked to herself in any way, but as she lay in Callahan's arms long after they'd made love, stargazing and talking as he played with her hair and stroked her back, it was exactly how she felt. Treasured and special. Feelings of guilt crept in, so ingrained from the cult, she had to remind herself that it was okay to be happy, to *want* and *need* and *take* as well as give.

On the heels of all those emotions came something akin to relief. She hadn't realized her worries about fitting in had bled into every aspect of her life. She'd wondered if she'd ever be capable of having a normal, healthy relationship. As she lay basking in the aftermath of all they'd done, thinking about the control Callahan had allowed her to enjoy and the way he'd gently helped her get there, so different from the coldness of Rebel Joe's uncaring hands, she remembered what Callahan had said when she'd admitted to feeling a step behind other girls her age. *You don't have to catch up with anyone. You just have to be happy with who you are.* That made her feel less like an outsider to the rest of the world—and so very grateful for Callahan.

Chapter Nineteen

THEY LAY TOGETHER for a long time and eventually headed into Callahan's cabin to use the bathroom. He put on a clean shirt and gave her a sweatshirt to wear. It hung nearly to her knees, but she loved wearing his clothes. They made her feel even closer to him. They were both hungry, so they raided his kitchen and headed outside with chips and guacamole.

Callahan added wood to the fire and brought the cooler closer to the blankets, where she sat nibbling on chips. "What would you like to drink, darlin'?"

She eyed the drinks. "What do you think I'd like?"

"Me." He leaned in for a kiss.

"Someone could get rich bottling you up."

"There's only one problem with that idea. Yours are the only lips I want on mine."

She sighed inwardly. How could this be her life? She peered into the cooler. "Do you have anything fruity? *Wait.*" She was on a high, reclaiming parts of herself that Rebel Joe had stolen for far too long, and she wanted to continue doing that. "I want to know if alcohol is going to trigger me."

His brows slanted. "Are you sure?"

"*Yes.* I feel safe with you. If something is going to trigger me, I'd rather find out with you. Is that okay?"

"Sure. How do you want to do this?"

"Well, do you have a beer and some liquor? I could smell them first and see if they bother me."

"The only liquor I have out here is fruity, for you."

"That's fine."

He grabbed a beer and a spiked lemonade and sat beside her. "Are you sure you want to do this?"

She nodded.

He opened the beer bottle and handed it to her. He put his arm around her as she looked it over. "I don't like this, Sully. You're shaking."

"Because I'm worried it *might* trigger me."

"Then don't do it," he said firmly.

"*Callahan,* I love that you worry about me, but there's nothing I can't handle, *remember?*"

He nodded, the muscles in his jaw bunching.

She lifted the bottle to her nose and sniffed. "It smells gross." He held her tighter, reaching for it, but she pulled it away. "I said gross, not triggering."

"*Sully,*" he warned.

"Just give me a second." She smelled it again, and her stomach knotted.

"Anything?" he asked urgently.

"It's uncomfortable, but it's not like it throws me back there. I just remembered that other guys drank on the compound, and they didn't trigger me, so I might be fine." She handed him the beer. "Will you take a sip?"

"Not if there's a chance it'll drive you away from me."

"There's not. I know it's you, and I trust you. But I heard

the guys talking about the Roadhouse. I know you drink beer."

"But I don't *have* to. I don't need to drink."

"Let's just do it so I know, okay? Please?"

He huffed out a breath and took a sip, but he didn't look happy about it.

She leaned in and kissed him, but he kept his lips tightly closed.

"Well?"

She crawled into his lap and put her arm around him, feeling the tension in every part of his body. "Kiss me like you mean it, not like you're holding your breath."

"You're killing me, darlin'."

"Please? You didn't taste anything like he did, and I want to be sure it's not just because of how you kissed me."

He set the beer down and kissed the living daylights out of her. "Well?"

She blinked several times, trying to get her brain to function. "No triggers, but just in case, maybe we should do it again."

He laughed, and then he kissed her again, with all the emotions he'd been kissing her with all night, and as their lips parted, he arched a brow.

"Beer doesn't taste sickening on you. I don't think anything could."

"Thank God." He exhaled loudly and hugged her. "But you might feel different if we're intimate and I've got beer on my breath, so I think I'll stay away from beer for a while."

"That's probably a good idea. Thank you for testing it with me. Let me try the other one."

He opened the spiked lemonade and handed it to her.

She took a sip and raised her brows. "This is good. It's

sweet, like candy, and it doesn't give me any gross feelings."

"Let me have some of that." He filled his cheeks and moved it around his mouth before swallowing, then leaned in for a kiss.

"Now you taste like candy. I like that." She grabbed the bottle from him and took a drink.

"Slow down, darlin'. I wouldn't want you to lose your inhibitions and take advantage of me."

She laughed. "I think I already did that."

"And it was the highlight of my life." He winked.

She ate a chip and leaned against him. "Are you this wonderful with every woman you're close to?"

"No. You've gotten more of me than anyone ever has. Emotionally and physically. I've never let a woman take control like I let you."

"Why not?"

"Because that takes a great deal of trust, and before you, I wasn't looking for a connection. I was all about the ranch and the club."

"Is that what you were doing with me? Looking for a connection?"

"No, darlin'. For the first time in my life, my heart is leading the way. I didn't have to look for a connection. It's been there since the day we met." He took a sip of her lemonade and handed it back. "Actually, it's been there since I first saw your picture on that flyer. Even though the age-progression picture didn't look very much like you, there was something in your eyes that got under my skin. I had this feeling that you were out there waiting to be found, and I couldn't stop thinking about you. It's like my heart was locked and you held the key. I assumed you felt it, too."

There it was. The answer behind her butterflies, the reason

she'd been so drawn to him, she'd been unable to look away. "I did. It's always there, like the air we breathe."

"That's exactly what you feel like to me. The very air I breathe." He wrapped his arms around her, touching his forehead to hers.

"I feel like I'm in a dream that I don't want to wake up from."

"It's not a dream, darlin'. This is reality, and only a small piece of it."

He kissed her again, and a few minutes later she climbed off his lap to reach for the chips and guacamole.

"You had quite a morning. Now that you've had some time to digest it all, how are you feeling about meeting Jordan?"

"It was strange but good. It's still a little scary to think she remembers me and I don't remember her."

"Is that why you didn't tell her about the drawing you made of the little girl in the fancy dress dancing in the grass? It sounded like you'd drawn her when she was young."

She traced the label on the bottle they were sharing. "I thought about telling her, but she was so happy and full of hope, I didn't want her to think I remember more than I do and be disappointed. I have that picture of her dancing in the grass in my head, but I don't actually remember being there or seeing her do it. I kept waiting for something she said to bring all my memories back, but nothing did."

"That makes sense, but you never know. It might have given her a little peace, knowing you'd drawn that moment. Just something to think about. You mentioned feeling a little lost. Have the pictures she gave you helped with that at all?"

"I haven't looked at them again. I wanted to look at them with you."

"That means a lot to me. I liked hearing about your family. It sounded like your parents loved you very much."

"I wish I could remember them."

"Do you think any of the drawings you left behind could have been of your family?"

"I've been thinking about that. The thing is, my uncl—*Richard*—was always telling me stories. I remember drawing pictures of people, but when I'd show him, he'd say they were from this story or that story, and then he'd tell me the story. So I have no way of knowing what might have been a memory and what came from his stories."

"The son of a bitch brainwashed you." He took a drink and shook his head, his jaw clenching. "I'd like to get my hands on that bastard. He's lucky he's already dead."

"You and me both. I wish I could remember the memories he erased."

"He didn't erase them. He rewrote them. They're probably still there, locked inside his stories."

"What if I never remember anything?"

"The way I see it, you were so young when you were taken, you and Jordan are starting over anyway. Getting to know the people you are now, as adults. You can make new memories and develop a new relationship. I'm not saying give up hope of recovering your memories, but I wouldn't let that interfere with building a new relationship with her."

"That's what I'm hoping for. I brought the pictures. They're in my sketchbook. Would you mind if we looked at them?"

"Not at all. I'd like to see them." He handed her the sketchbook.

She unzipped the leather holder and took out the pictures. They looked through them together. "Jordan wrote the dates and names on the backs." There were pictures of Sully as a baby, with whisper-fine blond hair, and as a toddler, with hair as wild and frizzy as it was now. Her eyes screamed of joyful possibilities. Seeing pictures of herself playing with Jordan, and with her parents, made her wish even harder that she could remember them.

"Jordan was right about you dressing like your dad."

In nearly all the pictures of her as a toddler, she was dressed in T-shirts or flannels and the tiny work boots Jordan mentioned. She studied a family photo. She was on her father's shoulders, her chin resting on his dark hair with a sweet smile on her lips and one skinny arm wrapped around his neck like he was *hers*. He was a big man. Not muscular like Callahan or heavy like Tiny, but tall and thick all over, and his love for his family showed in his protective hold on them and the adoration in his eyes. He was holding one of Sully's hands. His other arm was around her mother's shoulder. He was holding her hand, too. Jordan stood in front of their mother, and she looked like a younger version of her, with shiny blond hair, high cheekbones, and big blue eyes. Their mother's arm was draped protectively over Jordan's shoulder, her hand resting on Jordan's stomach.

"Look at you, darlin'. You were so stinkin' cute with those bright blue eyes, hanging on to your daddy like he was your everything." He put his arm around her and kissed her temple. "I'm so sorry."

Tears burned her eyes. "Jordan said this was taken the summer before the accident. I wish I could time travel and spend one day in Casey's shoes, with this family who loved me, so I could feel the connection we had."

"I wish you could, too," he said as tears slid down her cheeks. He hugged her against his side. "It's okay, darlin'. Let it out."

"I *belonged* with them in these pictures, but how am I supposed to ever feel like I belong again if I don't remember belonging in the first place?"

"I don't have the answer, baby, but you didn't know me, and we formed a connection. I think you need to give it time, and you might be surprised by how things go. You haven't even met your aunt and uncle yet."

"I will, but I think Jordan expects me to be Casey, and I'm not her anymore. I'm not even Sully. That's just a name they made up. I don't know who I am."

He took her by the chin, bringing her teary eyes to his. "That's what you're here to figure out, sweetheart. Therapy will help, but it's not just about where you came from. That's important, but maybe what's more important is who you want to be, separate from everything and everyone else."

"I like who I am. I just wish I knew my place."

His expression turned serious. "You just got out of a situation where they tried to put you in your *place*. You're free now, Sully. Free to be anyone you want to be, go anywhere you want to go, and be with whoever *you* feel deserves your presence. Your *place* is wherever *you* want it to be, and it can change as often as you like. I understand wanting to feel like you belong with a family and know and feel all the things you did when you were little, and I hope you get that back. *God*, baby, I'd give everything I have if it would get those memories back for you, and I'll help every way I can to try to make that happen."

"I know you would," she choked out.

"But even if you never remember that time in your life and you feel a step behind Jordan, you've *got* to know that she loves you, and she wants you in her life. That sounded unconditional to me, regardless of what name you use or whether you remember hating frilly dresses. So while you're working on remembering your past with the sister who *finally* found you, instead of assuming she wants you to be the same person you were all those years ago, try talking to her about how you feel and who you are now. I think you'll find that she can't help but adore you as much as I do."

Tears poured down her cheeks, and he drew her into his arms. "I'm sorry. I don't want to upset you."

"You didn't. I know you're right."

"I usually am," he teased.

She smiled, thankful for his humor, and wiped her eyes. "I just feel like there was Casey and then there was Sully, but neither feels right now."

He cradled her tear-stained cheeks between his hands and kissed her salty lips. As he wiped her tears with his thumbs, he said, "I'm sure in time the answer will come to you."

"I guess I have nothing *but* time right now."

"That's not all you have, darlin'. You also have me and my family, the friends you're making here, Beauty, and the freedom to make your future anything you want it to be." He gathered her in his arms again, his heart beating sure and steady against hers. "You can choose any name you'd like, but whatever you decide to call yourself, I hope you'll always let me call you darlin'."

After years of hoping and praying for a better life, longing to *matter* and be cared about wholly and completely, his words broke the dam, and her emotions flooded out.

Chapter Twenty

THE NEXT MORNING, they watched the sunrise from within their cozy nest on the deck tangled up in each other's arms. They took a walk along the creek and cooked breakfast together in Callahan's enormous kitchen. They talked and kissed, teased and laughed, and played Scrabble while they ate breakfast. Sully finally showed him her list of things she'd like to do and crossed off *wear shorts, play more games with Callahan,* and *sleep under the stars.* When he walked her back to her cabin so she could shower and get ready to see Wynnie, he kissed her at the door and told her to shoot him a text if she wanted to talk afterward. It was incredible being with someone who wanted to know how she felt about everything and didn't shy away from difficult subjects. She relished those feelings, because they were another type of freedom she hadn't anticipated.

She'd had the absolute *best* night and morning of her entire life. But it was also eye-opening. When she'd been in Callahan's house, she'd noticed everything felt like *him,* from the substantial furniture, rugged wood floors, and gorgeous stone fireplace to the warm decorations and treasured family pictures. He told her the stories behind some of the pictures, sharing names of special horses he'd worked with, things he and his family had done, and places they'd gone, and she loved hearing all of them. They underscored so many of the things she admired about him, like his loyalty to his family, how he'd always known who he was, where he belonged, and who he wanted to be. But as she sat in Wynnie's office, she felt a bone-deep longing for something of her own to hold on to. Something to work toward, to *know*. On top of that, as good as she felt about being with Callahan, she also felt guilty about messing things up with Wynnie—and it all came tumbling out in an anxious ramble as Wynnie took her seat.

"I'm sorry about me and Callahan. I didn't mean to do anything wrong, and I really want to figure out who I am and who I want to be, what I want to do, and what I'm *capable* of doing to have a real life, and I don't want to hurt anyone's feelings or do the wrong thing."

Wynnie smiled and sat back. "Okay. Well, there's a lot to unpack there."

"I'm sorry. I guess I have a lot on my mind. I didn't expect to blurt it all out at once. My brain is just going in too many directions."

"No need to apologize, honey. This is good, and it's not all that unexpected. You've had a lot of changes all at once, and we'll talk about all of them, but let's start with Cowboy. As far as the two of you are concerned, you didn't do anything wrong. You're a grown woman. You can be with whomever you'd like. But there are certain things I can't do as a therapist, and treating someone who is involved with a family member is one of them."

"I understand, but you went out of your way to help me. I like Callahan a lot. I know my life is up in the air right now, and who knows how long we'll be together, but I'm happy we found each other. I just feel bad for messing things up with you."

"You didn't mess anything up, sweetheart. You took a step forward and followed your heart, which means you're taking control of your life. That's a good thing, although you two did come together *very* fast, and I worry about you taking on too much all at once."

"I know I have a lot going on, but he's the only part of my life that *isn't* overwhelming. He centers me, and he's helping me find parts of myself that I thought were too broken to fix and some that I didn't even know existed."

"I'm glad to hear that. As much as I want to talk with you about that, I don't want to cross any lines that shouldn't be crossed and get into an intricate conversation about you and Cowboy. I have spoken with Colleen, and she'd be happy to start working with you. How would you feel about that?"

"I'm okay with it. She seemed nice when I met her, and if you trust her to help me, then I trust her, too. I'm thankful she's willing to help. I still can't believe how much your family is doing for me. I'm going to find a way to pay you back one day."

"Finding your way to a stable, happy life is our payback. I thought we'd have our normal session today, and if you're comfortable with the idea, you can transition to Colleen tomorrow. But if you need more time to get used to the idea of working with someone new, we can wait a few days."

"Tomorrow sounds good, and I would really like to talk with you today."

"Then let's get to it. We can talk about anything except Cowboy. You can save that discussion for Colleen. You said you'd like to figure out who you are. Would you like to start there?"

"Yes. I was born Casey Lawler, and now I'm Sullivan Tate, and I know that's part of who I am. I want to talk about that and meeting Jordan, but that's not the part I want to talk about first. This morning I remembered something Gaia used to say to me when I was younger and getting in trouble a lot. She'd say that every day I had a choice to make. I could choose to be the person I was yesterday or the person I wanted to be that day, and in doing so, I was making a decision that could make my life easier or harder and that only I could control that."

"She's a wise woman."

"I know, and she was right in so many ways. I can't change my past, but I *can* change my goals moving forward. I like the person I'm becoming, and I'm grateful for the opportunity you're giving me here. But I feel like I need to have bigger goals than just figuring out where I fit with my family."

"Can you tell me what you mean by that?"

"I don't like living in limbo. I didn't love life on the compound, but I had a purpose every day, and I liked that. And I know everyone here understands how important having a purpose is. I love helping Sasha, and if she'll let me, I'd like to continue doing that. I feel connected to the horses and helping them helps me. But I need to do something to earn money, so eventually I won't have to rely on the generosity of others for things, and so I can do normal things like buy groceries and clothes, and...I don't know, pay rent so you're not supporting me."

"Those are wonderful goals, and you can certainly continue helping Sasha. I think that would be good for you. But you're going through a major transition, and I think it's important for you to work through some of that before taking on too much."

"I know I have things to work on, and it'll take time. I just need to feel like I'm moving in the right direction. Knowing Sasha can count on me every day will help. But at some point I'd like to be able to support myself, even if it takes me months to get there."

"That's perfectly understandable, and I'm glad to hear you're not rushing into anything. What types of things are you interested in?"

Sully shrugged. "I don't know what my options are. I can cook and clean and sew and draw, and I like working with kids and doing just about anything outside. But maybe there are other things I can do."

"There is a world of choices out there, and I'm sure you are capable of many things. And now that you're not confined to the ranch, there are a lot more options. We have great resources for figuring out career paths. But that's a much bigger discussion than one session. Colleen can work through those resources with you, and together you can come up with some ideas for the future. Unfortunately, since you're involved with Cowboy, you can't become a paid employee of the ranch. We've had issues in the past with employees dating, and now we have a policy against it. But while you're figuring things out, you can volunteer in just about any area on the ranch."

"That sounds great. I wasn't asking for you to pay me. I just wanted help figuring out a direction."

"I understand. One thing you can do is start making a list of all the things you enjoy, the things you're good at, and the things you want to learn. Sometimes getting it down on paper spurs ideas."

"Okay. I'll do that." She exhaled with relief. "I feel better already. Thank you."

"This is all you, Sully. I'm proud of the steps you're taking. Just be sure to give yourself time to get to know your family and yourself."

"I will."

"I know we talked about the media coverage before you met with Jordan, but now that you've had time to process it, do you want to talk about that at all?"

"Not really. I'm just thankful they kept my name out of the reports."

"Have you given any thought to your name? Do you have any interest in using Casey?"

"I've thought a lot about it. I'm not Casey anymore. I'm trying to figure out if I'm Sully."

"There's no rush, and I'd suggest taking your time with this one. How you feel might change as you figure out the other areas of your life."

"Maybe, but I doubt it. I just don't feel a connection to that little girl in the flyer."

"Let's talk about that. Yesterday was a big day. How are you feeling about meeting your sister?"

"I feel so many things. Where should I start?"

SULLY LEFT WYNNIE'S office armed with encouragement and ready to see Jordan again. She arrived shortly thereafter, looking sharp in skinny jeans, a pretty gray sweater, and ankle boots. Her hair was pulled back in a low ponytail, her makeup was understated, and she carried a big, fancy bag. After a slightly awkward embrace, Sully said, "I thought we'd take a walk around the property and talk."

"That sounds good to me. I love your top. The boho style really suits you."

"Thanks. I didn't have much when I got here, and Callahan and his sister got me a few things."

"Oh, Sully. I should've asked if you needed anything. I'm sorry. I was overwhelmed yesterday, and I don't know much about your situation. I was hoping we could talk about it today. Do you need anything?"

"No. I have more than enough, but thank you." She took a few big breaths as they walked away from the main house, trying to ease her nerves. "I know you must have questions. What would you like to know?"

"Everything, but I don't want you to feel like you have to tell me anything you don't want to talk about, so I guess I'd just like to know about your life."

"You mean about my life on the compound?"

"No. I mean, *yes*, at some point, but we knew each other as kids, and now we're grown-ups. I was hoping you could tell me about yourself. You know, your likes and dislikes. That kind of thing."

"I'm finally in the process of figuring all those things out," she said as they headed down the grass toward one of the pastures where horses were grazing. "I think I have to tell you about life on the compound for you to understand what I mean."

"Only if you're comfortable doing so," Jordan said empathetically.

"It's the only way you can get a sense of how I grew up and how things have changed since you knew me. When you told me that I had our father's spirit, some of who I was made sense.

The people who abducted me tried to silence that for a long time, and I paid the price for being strong-willed." She told her about Richard and his stories and how her fighting spirit had earned her punishments. They talked about the girls' dorms, her regimented schedule, and the restrictions put upon her. Jordan asked a lot of questions, but Sully could tell she was being careful.

They sat in the grass beside the pasture, and she told her about Gaia and how she was the closest thing to a mother she remembered having and about her friendship with Ansel and how much she missed him. She hadn't planned on telling her everything, but once she started, it was like she'd cut a vein and the past bled out. She shared her failed attempts at escaping and the punishments that had followed, and told her about being *chosen* by Rebel Joe, all of which made Jordan cry. Sully's emotions had clawed their way to the surface, just as they had last night, and there in the field, clinging to the sister she barely knew, she cried years' worth of tears.

As Sully described her escape and how frightened she'd been, Jordan held her hand. She told her about Chester and Carol and everything else that had led to where she was now.

With puffy, teary eyes, Jordan said, "You're the bravest person I know. But you always were. Even as a little girl."

That drew more tears from Sully. Clutching the tissues Jordan had given her, she wiped her eyes. "I haven't cried in years, and lately I'm like a waterfall."

"Maybe that's because you were forced to hide your emotions for so long. Now that you're safe, they're all coming out."

"That's what Wynnie said, too."

"Well, I'm always like this when it comes to you. I lost my mind the night of the accident. See this scar?" Jordan touched the scar over her eyebrow. "Jax and I call it my Casey scar."

Her heart squeezed. "Did I give it to you?"

"No. I was a mess the night of the accident. I felt lost without you or Mom and Dad. They told me that Mom and Dad were killed in the crash, but all they said about you was that they were trying to find you. But I heard them speculating about someone taking you, and I lost it. I ran outside screaming and crying, 'Take me! Bring her back and take me!' and I tripped and hit my head on a rock. The scar is from the stitches."

Tears welled in Sully's eyes again. "Oh, Jordan. I'm so sorry. Everyone worries about what it was like for me, but it must have been awful for you, too. You lost all of us at once."

"It was awful, and I had to hide my feelings for a long time, too, which made it even harder. So I understand what that was like for you, although I didn't get many punishments, because I'm more of a pleaser than a rebel."

"I wish I had some of that in me. Why did you have to hide your feelings?"

"Because I was looking for you in every face of every girl I saw, and when I moved to Massachusetts to live with Aunt Sheila and Uncle Gary, I learned real fast that other kids didn't get it. It scared them. I think it made the idea of someone disappearing real, so I couldn't talk about my missing sister at school or with friends without alienating myself. My therapist and Aunt Sheila and Uncle Gary thought I should move on, and I just *couldn't*. I believed in my heart that you were out there somewhere, so I kept my feelings to myself. Eventually I went to college in Maryland, thinking I might find you, and I moved back to our hometown as soon as I graduated in case you found your way home."

Sully got choked up. "You never gave up on me?" Just like Callahan after he saw that flyer.

"Not even for a second. My boyfriend at the time wanted me to move to New York and act like you never existed. He'd been there for me in college, and I stayed with him for way too long and for all the wrong reasons. But it wasn't just him. Everyone thought I was crazy for insisting that you were still alive after so many years. It wasn't until I met Jax that I felt like I could speak your name. From the moment I told him about the accident, he supported my belief that you were alive. He's the one who hired Reggie Steele, the private investigator who helped get your case back in the public's eye."

"I'm so glad you have Jax. I need to thank him."

"Trust me, I have a million times over."

"I hate that you had to hide your feelings." She realized she wasn't the only survivor. Jordan was a survivor, too. Maybe they weren't that different after all.

"Mom and Dad would have hated that we had to hide our feelings. They were all about expressing yourself." Tears slid down Jordan's cheeks.

Sully tried to blink her own tears away. "Well, we don't have to hide them anymore. Jax sounds wonderful. How did you meet him?"

"You're going to think I'm an awful person if I tell you."

"Look at the type of people I lived with," she reminded her. "Nothing could make me think bad of you."

"It's a different type of awful. Jax is a wedding-gown designer and at the time, my friend Trixie was engaged to his brother Nick. They're married now, but she referred me to Jax to design my gown for my wedding to that other guy I told you about."

"Oh. *Wow.* That's..." She stared at her in disbelief, and

they both laughed.

"I told you it would sound bad. But I had already post-poned my wedding three times. I *knew* I shouldn't marry him, and when I met Jax, I felt such a strong connection to him, I basically ran out of his office and postponed my wedding again."

"It doesn't sound bad. It just makes me wonder about something Gaia used to say."

"What?"

"She said to believe in good things, and eventually the universe would step in to right the wrongs we were going through." Sully motioned around them. "Look where I ended up, with more support than I ever could have imagined. And look who you ended up with."

"I think she was right. I just wish I hadn't waited so long."

"So, what happened? Did you end things with the other guy when you met Jax?"

"No. I was afraid to. I stayed away from Jax for months, trying to get over him, and then I saw him at Nick and Trixie's wedding. We danced, and I swear, Sully, the second I saw him again, I was a goner. I tried to fight our connection, but he was relentless in the sweetest ways. I never cheated, and he never tried to get me to, but I fell hard and fast and *completely* in love with him, and *then* I finally ended the other relationship. Jax is the second-best thing that has ever happened to me."

"What's the best?"

"Finding you." Her smile reached her eyes, but they both got teary again.

SULLY OFFERED TO show Jordan her sketches, and as they walked down to her cabin, Jordan said, "It's really beautiful here. You loved being outdoors when you were little. Do you still?"

"Yes. I would *live* outside if I could, and I love being around the horses. Callahan's teaching me to ride, and his sister Sasha is a horse rehab specialist. She's teaching me to help with the rescued horses." She told her about all the things she was learning. "I have trouble sleeping, so Callahan and I go for long walks at night, and sometimes we watch the sunrise together."

"Does that mean there's more than friendship between you and that handsome cowboy?"

Sully fidgeted with the edge of her shirt, wanting to gush over him, but something in Jordan's voice told her to hold back. "Yes."

"I thought he was a bodyguard. He looked like he'd face a charging bull for you."

"I think he would." She told her about how he'd slept on her porch when they'd thought she was in danger. "He's really helped me get comfortable here, and I like him a lot."

"That's good." Her brows knitted. "I want to be supportive, but the older sister in me worries. After all you've been through, are you sure it's smart to jump into a relationship so quickly?"

Sully understood Jordan's concern, but it had been such an emotional morning, her words came out more passionately than she intended. "I *know* it's fast, and you're not the only one who's concerned. But I've been on my own on that godforsaken compound, biting my tongue and making *smart* decisions every day of my life just to survive. I felt alone and unhappy for so long, I honestly don't care if it's the *smart* thing to do. He makes me happy, and I *want* to be with him."

"I didn't mean...I'm sorry, Case—*Sully*," Jordan pleaded. "Of course you make smart decisions, and I want you to be happy. It's just so fast. I don't want you to get hurt."

"I'm sorry, too. I don't know where that outburst came from, but I have to trust my instincts. Callahan is kind and caring and careful, and he respects my need to do things for myself. I don't think he'd ever hurt me, especially not in the ways I've already been hurt."

"I'm sorry I said anything. I really have no room to talk. I fell for Jax the first time I met him, and I had so much emotional baggage."

"It's okay. I get it. You had baggage, but you also had experience with normal relationships and I don't. It's just one more thing I'm learning. But being with him feels right, and I think you'd like him if you got to know him."

"I'd like to get to know him. Maybe we can all have dinner one night, and you can meet Jax. I know Aunt Sheila and Uncle Gary would love to spend time with you."

"I'd like that. How long are you here?"

"We planned on staying until next Sunday. I was hoping to see you for at least some time each day, but if you don't want to spend that much time with me, I understand. I thought that would give us time to get to know each other, and then we can figure out where to go from there. Obviously I want you to come back to Maryland so we can be together and rebuild our relationship, but we don't have to make that decision right now."

Relieved Jordan wasn't pushing her, she said, "I want to spend time with you, and I'd like to meet the others, but can it be just you and me for another day or two? I like getting to know you, and it'll make it less nerve-racking when I meet everyone else. Maybe we can all have dinner Wednesday night. I can cook."

"You don't have to cook. We can take you out to a restaurant."

"I'd rather meet them here for the first time, where I'm comfortable, and I love cooking, so I don't mind. Is that okay?"

"Absolutely. Wednesday night it is."

SULLY FELT A sense of pride as she showed Jordan her cabin. It might not be hers, but she was proud of how far she'd come and that the Whiskeys felt she was worthy of staying there.

"This is beautiful. The Whiskeys really know how to make a person feel at home."

"I'm grateful they took me in, and while I wasn't sure about everyone eating meals together at first, it's turned out to be really helpful in getting to know everyone and seeing how regular people interact."

"That must have been a culture shock."

"It was, but everyone here made it easier by not treating me like the new girl. Do you want something to drink?"

"No, thanks, but I'm excited to see your work."

Sully tried to hide her trepidation as she got her sketchbook and sat on the couch with Jordan. "I probably should have told you about this when we first met." She opened to the drawing of the little girl twirling in the grass and handed it to her.

Jordan studied it with knitted brows, then looked up with wondrous eyes. "You remembered? That was my favorite dress. You hated the frills and lace, and I loved them so much."

"No. I don't remember. That's why I didn't say anything about it before. I was afraid of giving you false hope. I drew that before I even knew I was Casey. I actually drew a lot of pictures similar to that one over the years, but I had to leave everything behind when I escaped. I thought I made up that little girl in my head because of Richard's stories."

"Oh, *Sully*," Jordan said sadly. "They took everything you knew and turned it into make-believe."

"That's kind of what everyone did to you, too, isn't it? You had a gut feeling that I was alive, but nobody would let you believe it."

They were both quiet for a moment as that harsh commonality sank in.

"I don't know if I'll ever remember when we were young, but I'll keep trying. I was hoping we could get to know each other for who we are now, and if the past comes back to me, then that's great, but I'd rather not focus on it."

Jordan put her hand on her chest with a relieved exhalation. "I'd prefer that, too. I was worried that you felt pressure to try to remember, and the last thing you need is more pressure. I've finally got you back in my life. I'll take time with you any way I can get it."

Sully got teary again and looked up at the ceiling, trying to blink her eyes dry. "I think I liked it better when I never cried."

"I've never had that luxury. I've always gotten emotional at the drop of a hat." Jordan laughed softly. "Can I look at more of your drawings?"

Sully got out the notebook Carol had given her and showed Jordan everything she'd drawn since she'd left the compound. There were pictures of Carol and Chester and Ansel and Gaia, and all the pictures she'd drawn since coming to the ranch.

"These are incredible. You're much more talented than Mom or I could ever be. I can only draw clothes, and Mom was the same. But you draw animals and faces and *look* at Callahan. He looks like he could ride that horse off the page."

"It's not *that* good."

"Yes, it is."

"Thanks, but I don't think so." Feeling self-conscious, she shifted the attention off herself. "You said you work in fashion, which makes sense since you're always so well put together. Do you design clothes?"

"Yes, but that's a recent addition to my life. Jax's twin sister, Jillian, is a designer too, but for women's fashion, not wedding gowns. She owns a boutique in Pleasant Hill, and I work part time with her. But my full-time job is as the director of volunteer programs at an assisted living facility for the elderly. It's a great place, and I love the people there as much as I love designing."

"You're so lucky to do what you love. I want to work and earn money, but I have no idea what I can do."

"*Hello...?*" Jordan pointed at the sketchbook with raised brows. "I bet if you got on one of the dozens of artist-for-hire websites, you'd have more commissions than you'd know what to do with."

"You think people will pay *me* to draw?"

"Yes. Definitely. Let me show you a few of the artists I follow on social media." She took out her phone and poked around on it, showing her several gorgeous drawings. "This girl is still in high school, and she illustrates for all sorts of companies in her free time. She's even done illustrations for a children's book." She navigated to other profiles, showing her several other types of illustrations. "This guy just started his artist page three months ago, and his drawings are rudimentary compared to yours. He wrote an article about how he joined three artists-for-hire sites, and he's already earning almost four thousand dollars a month in commissions. I saved the article for the granddaughter of one of the women at the assisted living center. I'll get you a copy."

"That's amazing. I can't imagine earning four dollars, much less four thousand. We weren't allowed to have money, so I've never earned a penny."

"*Oh.* I didn't realize that. Do you know how money works?"

"Yes. Gaia taught me."

"Okay, well, that's a start, and if drawing is what you love, then it would be worth looking into. I mean, if you want to and when you're ready."

"I wouldn't even know where to begin doing something like that. How would I get drawings to people? In the mail?"

"It's all electronic, using digital drawing tools. I'll show you." She navigated to another website. "This is a drawing tablet. That's what I use. You draw right on the tablet, and it transfers your drawings directly to the computer."

"That's amazing. Are they hard to use?"

"No. I'll show you how to do it and how to use email and whatever else you want to learn. That's what big sisters are for."

A real big sister. Emotions swamped Sully, but she'd seen the price on the drawing pad. It was way out of reach. "Thank you, but I think it'll be a long time before I can afford those drawing tools."

"I can give you money to get you started. I used some of Mom and Dad's life insurance money for my college tuition, but I have some saved, and that's all yours."

"I can't take your money."

"Sully, that money is your birthright." Jordan's eyes implored her. "Mom and Dad would want you to have it. *I* want you to have it, even if it's not for this. The money is yours to use any way you want."

Sully was torn. What she said made sense, but it warred with her need to not owe anyone anything. "Can I think about it?"

"Of course, but...I know you don't remember me or our parents, but you are their daughter. I don't want to make this about me, but I had no way to help you for all those years, and now I can *finally* do something. It would mean a great deal to me if you'd accept the money."

A lump lodged in Sully's throat. "I guess we both have things to get over."

"We sure do, but at least we have each other now, right?"

Their words hung between them, weaving a bond Sully wanted but didn't quite know what to do with, so she tried to jump back into their previous conversation. "Being paid to draw would be a dream come true. But I don't know where to start or even what to charge. And I'm still not sure I'm good enough."

"You *are* good enough. But you don't have to decide today. I'll show you how it works, and we can check out the competition to see what they're charging, so you know."

"I can't believe any of this. It sounds unreal."

"Prepare to be amazed, little sister. Do you have a laptop?"

"No, just a phone."

"No problem. I brought my iPad." Jordan pulled the iPad out of her purse.

"I've never used one of those, but I've seen Sasha's. She uses it to keep track of the horses' treatment plans."

"I'll show you how to use it. This little device is going to be your new best friend."

Sully wondered if eventually Jordan might become one, too.

COWBOY PACED OUTSIDE Dare's cabin, thinking about Sully as he waited to talk with his brothers about Dare's plans for the new motocross track and clubhouse for Billie. It was midafternoon, and he hadn't seen Sully since he'd dropped her at her cabin after breakfast. He couldn't stop thinking about last night and how natural it had felt this morning when they'd woken up together in his yard and had breakfast at his place. She'd texted before lunch to say she and Jordan were going to eat together at her cabin. She'd added a selfie of her and Jordan with the caption, *Look what Jordan taught me to do!*

He pulled up the picture now, smiling to himself as he drank in her gorgeous face and happy baby blues, which had gutted him with her worries and drawn him deeper into her with her affection.

Dare came out the front door, papers in his hand. "What's that shit-eating grin for?"

"Sully just learned to take a selfie." He pocketed his phone. Once he'd told their mother about him and Sully, he'd done little to hide his feelings from others. When his brothers had asked about Sully at lunch, they'd picked up on how he felt about her, and he'd told them that they were together. He had a feeling everyone at the table had heard it, and that was just fine with him.

"Man, can you imagine going through what she is? Finding out your whole life was a lie and having to learn about the world like that?"

"Yes, I *can* imagine it," Cowboy bit out, nodding to Doc as he drove up on a UTV. "I'm in it with her as much as she'll let me be. I should've taught her to take a selfie. I didn't think about it."

"That's because you hate technology. Unlike me, who gets as many naked pictures of my girl as possible."

Cowboy gave him a deadpan look. "Remind me never to borrow your phone."

"I'm kidding. Do you really think Billie would trust me not to lose my phone?"

"Not if she's smart," Doc said as he climbed off the vehicle.

Dare chuckled and set a serious gaze on Cowboy. "Don't beat yourself up for not thinking about selfies. You were worried about bigger things, like Sully's overall emotional health, as you should be."

"Yeah, I know. But, shit, it's just a reminder that there are a million little things I should be helping her with, like using the internet so she doesn't feel a step behind and figuring out what she wants to do with her life. She said as much over breakfast. Not about the internet but about feeling a step behind everyone else."

"That's a lot for someone in her situation," Dare pointed out. "She just got here last weekend."

"I know, but she was with the Finches for a few weeks. She's been off the compound for more than a month, and she doesn't want to dwell on the past. She wants to figure out who she is and how to move on."

"That's what therapy is for," Dare pointed out. "I know you want to fix everything for her, but that's not what she needs from you, so don't put that pressure on yourself. How are you holding up? You jumped into this with her pretty quick."

"I'm fine."

His brothers exchanged a knowing glance, which pissed him off. He was used to being on the other side of those worried looks.

"I said I'm *fine*. I'm worried about Sully, but who wouldn't be?"

"Well, we're worried about you," Doc said.

"Don't be. I'm a big boy. I can handle myself."

Doc cocked his head, squinting. "But can you really? I mean you can whip anyone's ass around the ranch, but you've got to admit you've got a wee bit of a white-knight complex."

"What are you, an armchair psychologist?" Cowboy shook his head. "Just because I rescue horses doesn't mean I feel a need to rescue women. Look where we work. If that were my MO, I'd have a long line of those women behind me."

"He's got a point," Dare said.

"Of course I have a fucking point."

"So he's selective," Doc said. "Think about it, Cowboy. Who was your last crush?"

"What the hell are you talking about? I haven't had a crush in a hundred years."

"He's talking about Carly," Dare said. "She was pretty broken when she was here, and you crushed hard on her."

Cowboy scoffed. "Carly's an awesome person, and if you couldn't see that back then, then shame on you. And Sully isn't *broken*. She's been fucked over. She had her life *stolen* from her. She might not have memories of the family she was taken from, and she's endured more shit than either of you could ever imagine, but it didn't break her the way Zev broke Carly. Carly could barely get out of bed most days, and yes, I wanted to be there for her. I liked who she was despite the condition she was in at the time, but I realized pretty quickly that I wasn't the guy for her, and that was more than a decade ago. It was a fucking *kid crush* compared to what I feel for Sully." He couldn't keep from raising his voice. "And I don't want to *save* Sully. She saved herself, and I admire the hell out of her for what she did to get free from that hellhole. She's one of the strongest women I've ever met. Is she starting from ground zero? *Yes.* Is it holding her back? *No.* Do I want to give her the fucking world? *Absolutely.* Jesus Christ. If *anyone* can understand how rare feelings like this are and that they don't have to be tied to words or traits but to your fucking heart, I would think it would be you two." He stared them down. "So you tell me. When was the last time I gave my heart to *any* woman?"

His brothers exchanged shrugs and head shakes.

"You never have, as far as I know," Doc said.

"That's right. But my heart was Sully's before we even met, so back the fuck off."

"Dude, relax," Dare said. "We get it."

"Yeah, we get it, but I'm still worried," Doc admitted. "I'm not knocking Sully. From the little I know about her, she's everything you said, and she clearly has a good heart because the horses sense it. But, Cowboy, you're our brother, and you're *all in* with a girl who's just getting started. This has heartache written all over it."

"You think I haven't thought of that?" he snapped. "Do you think I'm not holding my breath while she's with her sister? I'd be a fool not to be. But the thing you don't get, and maybe you never will, is that all that matters to me is that the woman I'm crazy about is able to put her life together in a way that makes her happy and whole. If that means she takes off to be with her sister and builds a life that I'm not part of, then that's my cross to bear. But I'll be damned if I'll walk away from the only woman who I've ever felt this way about because I *might* get hurt. I don't walk away from horses that I know aren't going to pull through. I sit with them while they take their last breath, and you know damn well I'm gutted every time we lose one. I think I can nurse a broken heart if it comes to that."

"Don't fool yourself into thinking you're stronger than you are," Doc said stoically. "Some broken hearts don't ever heal."

"That's your cross to bear, not mine." Cowboy felt like an ass for saying it, but he could handle his own emotional shit.

The front door flew open, and Billie strutted out in a low-cut leather vest, hip-hugger jeans, and cowgirl boots. She planted her hands on her hips, glowering at them. "What are you all arguing about?"

"Nothing," Cowboy snarled.

"Sure as hell didn't sound like nothing to me." She came off the porch, eyeing Doc and Cowboy, and turned a smile on Dare. "I'm off to serve drinks to handsy men. Are you coming by later?"

Dare chuckled. "You know just how to get me there."

"I'm no fool. Love you." She kissed him, then glanced at Doc and Cowboy. "If y'all get the knots out of your britches, you can swing by, too."

She strode over to her truck, and as she drove off, Dare said, "Are we going to review these plans or what?"

Cowboy was too worked up to focus on that. "Just make sure you get an environmental and agricultural specialist out here before you start putting in roads and moving dirt."

"Always the Boy Scout," Dare joked.

"Someone has to look out for the animals." Cowboy took

off his hat and raked a hand through his hair just as Sully came running down the road, waving her arms.

"*Callahan!*"

"Shit." His heart lodged in his throat, and he bolted toward her. "What's wrong?"

She launched herself into his arms.

"What happened? Are you okay?" He drew back to look for injuries.

"I'm *great!*"

"Jesus, Sull. You scared the piss out of me."

"I'm *sorry*. Oh gosh, I'm really sorry. I'm just so happy! I had a great day with Jordan. I told her everything. I didn't think I was going to, but I did, and it was such a relief not to feel like I had to hide it, and then we focused on *now*. She told me more about her and Jax, and we talked about you. She showed me how to use the iPad and the internet, and she loved my drawings as much as you do. She thinks I'm good enough to get paid to do it, too. She had all sorts of ideas. I know you said I could illustrate, but she showed me websites where people all over the world can hire you. It's all done electronically, and you never even meet them face-to-face." She was talking too fast for him to get a word in. "She also offered to give me some of our parents' insurance money, but I don't know how I feel about that. I want to talk with Colleen about it. And I want Jordan to get to know you, and I want to meet Jax and my aunt and uncle, so I offered to cook dinner for everyone Wednesday night because I know you can't do it Tuesday night, and I want you to be there when I meet them. Is that okay? Will you join us? Do you mind?"

She finally paused, and he couldn't help but laugh as he hugged her. "I wouldn't miss it for the world. But that's a lot of people. Do you want to do it at my place, where there's a bigger table and more room?"

"That would be great if you're sure you don't mind." She beamed up at him, but then she wrinkled her nose. "I just have one problem. I was so excited, I forgot that I don't have money to buy groceries. I hate borrowing money, but do you think I could borrow some from you if I pay you back? I have fourteen dollars, and I know it'll be a lot more than that, but I'll be careful with prices, and I really want to go to the grocery store with you. I've never had a chance to pick out the food I cook. Is that okay? Do you have time? I should've asked that first. I'm sorry. If you don't have time, I can figure something else out."

Her happiness was contagious. "I've always got time for you, and I'd love to get to know your family. But your first dinner with them is special, so groceries are on me, and please don't argue about it."

"I want to...but I'm too excited to argue. Thank you!" She threw her arms around him again, and he spun her around and kissed her.

As he set her on her feet, she began talking a mile a minute again, telling him more about her day with Jordan. He glanced at his brothers. Dare had a big-ass grin, and Doc was nodding approvingly, although worry hovered in his eyes.

Cowboy couldn't blame him, but spending time with his darlin' was worth the risk.

Chapter Twenty-One

AFTER A LONG transitional meeting with Colleen Monday morning and a nice visit with Jordan, during which she showed her the rehab barn and introduced her to Sasha and the horses, Sully got to spend the afternoon with Sasha, helping out in the barn. Afterward, Sasha showed her a few basic massage techniques for the horses.

"Is this right?" Sully asked, using the flat part of her fingers between her knuckles to massage along the crest of Sunshine's neck.

"It's perfect, just keep going in a circular motion down to her withers."

Working her way along Sunshine's coarse coat, she said, "I didn't know you worked with the horses that weren't going through rehab."

"I try to massage each of the horses at least once a month. It's hard work being a horse, and massages increase circulation, flexibility, and mobility and aid in muscle recovery. Getting my hands on them also helps me identify any sore spots they might have before it gets too bad."

Sully continued massaging. "How will I know if this is helping her?"

"Sometimes the horses will yawn or bow their heads. It all helps, even just having human touch helps to show them they're loved."

"These horses have a good life. It must feel amazing to get a massage every month."

Sasha took off her hat and shook her hair out. "You've never had one?"

"No. There wasn't much self-care on the compound. I wasn't even allowed to cut my hair."

"That stinks. Listen, I meant what I said yesterday. If you ever want to talk about what you went through, I'm a pretty good listener."

"Thanks. I appreciate that."

"You mentioned your hair, which I think is beautiful, but do you still want to cut it?"

"I'm thinking about it."

"My friend is a hairdresser in town. Let me know if you want me to make you an appointment. I'd be happy to go with you, and you should come with me and Birdie the next time we have a spa day."

"What do you do at a spa day?"

"Whatever Birdie wants." Sasha laughed softly. "I go for the massage, because this line of work makes my body ache, but Birdie *loves* being pampered. She makes me get facials and pedicures, and sometimes she talks me into a manicure, which is a total waste of money for me."

Sully thought about Jordan. She'd probably had spa days, too. "Do you mind doing those things with her?" She reached the horse's withers and began massaging her way back up toward Sunshine's head.

"Not really. We always have fun. Plus, you've met her. Do you really think she'd let me off the hook? She's a *needy bird*. She'd nag me until I gave in."

"It's nice that you're so close." She wondered if she and Jordan would ever have the type of sisterly bond Sasha and Birdie had.

"It is, but she wears me out sometimes. She's always on the go, and I'm a little more of a homebody. She drags me shopping and makes me do yoga and go out for drinks." She shrugged one shoulder. "I can't complain too much. She's a great sister. How is it going with Jordan? I enjoyed meeting her this morning. She's really nice."

"Thanks for letting me show her around. I wanted her to meet the horses and see where I spend my time." She'd also shown her around the rest of the ranch and had introduced her to Simone and some of the other people who worked there.

"It must be strange meeting her after all this time?"

"It is. I like getting to know her, but I don't know if we'll ever be as close as you and Birdie are."

"I'm sure you'll get closer as time goes by. It must have been awful for her to lose you and your parents all at once. I would have lost my mind."

"She was devastated." Sully couldn't help but feel a pang of guilt about that, even though it wasn't her fault she was taken. "But she's engaged now, and she seems happy. I'm meeting her fiancé and the rest of my family Wednesday evening. I'm a little nervous about it."

"I can only imagine. Do you want to talk about it?"

"Not really. I'm kind of talked out. I talked with Colleen about it this morning, and it'll just make me more nervous."

"I totally get that. I could show you some breathing exercises that you can try doing before you see your family. It might help calm your nerves. I do them with anxious horses, and sometimes I do them myself before I go out on dates."

As she continued working her way up Sunshine's neck, she said, "Callahan will be there with me, so that will help. But I'm willing to try anything. I'm going to cook dinner for everyone."

"I didn't know you liked to cook."

"I love cooking. That's the one thing that'll probably go well. I've been cooking forever, which is probably why I'm loving all the new things you're teaching me. Not to mention, horses are great listeners."

"I know what you mean. I'd be in trouble if these horses could talk. I tell them all my secrets." Sunshine yawned, and Sasha said, "Look at that. You've got the magic touch. Let me show you another technique. This one works with compression, and it's done with a flat hand, like this." Sasha placed her palm on the horse's neck. "You apply medium pressure in one spot for a few seconds and then release. Move your hand over and do it again." She showed her how. "Then you just continue working your way along her neck and body. Here, you try."

Sully mimicked her motions, pressing her hand flat against the horse's neck, holding it a few seconds, then releasing. "Like this?"

"That's perfect." Sasha's phone chimed, and she pulled it from her pocket, reading a text. "Do you have plans tomorrow night while Cowboy is at church?"

"Not really. I was just going to draw."

"Birdie and Simone are coming over to my place to bake cookies for Gus's class. The last time Ezra did it, he burned them, and Gus begged me to make them. Want to join us?"

She'd had so much fun with Sasha and Birdie last week, she

jumped at the chance to be included. "Are you sure they won't mind?"

"I'm positive. I already asked them." She waved her phone. "They want you there."

"In that case, I'd love to." She remembered that Simone didn't know her true identity. She'd have to be careful about what she said, and she felt compelled to remind Sasha to do the same. "But Simone doesn't know my real identity. Is that a problem?"

"Not at all. Birdie and I have been keeping people's secrets forever. Your secret is safe with us."

That made her feel better.

A little while later, as she finished the massage, the rumble of a motorcycle engine cut through the air, and Sasha said, "Sounds like one of the guys is here."

"Probably Callahan. I swear he has a sixth sense when it comes to me. He ran into town and said he was going to pick me up here when I was done for the afternoon. Do you think you can show me some of those breathing exercises tomorrow?"

"Sure," she said as Callahan came through the back door carrying a motorcycle helmet. He lifted his chin to his sister, and when his eyes found Sully's, a sexy grin slid into place. "How's it going, darlin'?"

Sully's nerves caught fire as he leaned down to kiss her, and memories of last night tiptoed in. When he'd walked her back to her cabin after they'd taken a long starlight stroll, she hadn't been ready to say goodbye and had asked him to stay. She'd had the luxury of exploring his body again and falling asleep in his arms. Callahan Whiskey was the perfect remedy for insomnia. She'd slept right through until morning, without any nightmares.

"I'll take Sunshine out to the pasture. I need to run, anyway," Sasha said as she untied Sunshine's tether.

Callahan arched a brow. "Where are you rushing off to?"

"I'm meeting Flame for a drink after dinner, and I want to wash my hair before we eat."

Callahan scowled. "Be careful with him. You know his reputation."

Sasha gave him a deadpan look. "The male is hardwired to talk a big game. I can handle myself. I'll catch up with you guys at dinner."

"Not tonight you won't," he called after her as she led Sunshine out of the barn.

"Breakfast, then," Sasha hollered.

"Why won't we see her at dinner?"

He draped an arm over Sully's shoulder, leading her out of the barn. "We have other plans."

"We do? Should I shower and change?"

"Nope. You're as gorgeous as ever. But you do need to wear this." He handed her the helmet.

Her pulse quickened. "Are we going somewhere on your motorcycle?"

He gathered her in his arms and kissed her. "Since you're nervous about meeting your family, I thought you could use something other than our usual walk to help get you out of your head tonight."

Her heart squeezed at his thoughtfulness. The only people who had ever paid any *real* attention to her feelings were Gaia and Ansel, but that was totally different. Gaia and Ansel worried about her disregarding the rules or saying something that would get her in trouble. They were trying to keep her safe, but Callahan kept her safe *and* had the freedom to think about what *she* might want or need, and he encouraged her not to hold anything back, good or bad.

"What did you have in mind?" she asked.

"Remember how much you liked riding Thunder when he bolted across the field?"

"*Yes,*" she said, intrigued.

"Wait until you feel what it's like to ride on the back of my bike. Wind therapy is another type of freedom I want to share with you. I promise I won't go too fast. That is, if you trust me enough to take you out on it."

She should probably be a lot more nervous than she was, but she finally understood the faith Wynnie had put in Tiny when she'd agreed to that first date. "I trust you."

"Then let's do this." He gave her a lesson in motorcycle safety and told her to pat his stomach if she got scared, and he'd pull over. Then he opened a storage compartment on the bike, withdrew a Dark Knights' sweatshirt, and helped her put it on.

It fit perfectly. "This can't be yours."

"I had it made for you."

"*Made* for me?" That made it even more special. She couldn't argue with him on this gift. "I love it, thank you."

He kissed her and helped her put on the helmet. She felt a little giddy as they climbed onto the bike and she wound her arms around him. He reached behind her, spreading his big hand over her butt as he hauled her tighter against him. He took her hands, pulling her upper body flush with his back, and pressed her hands over his ribs.

"Hang on tight, darlin'."

This is even better than riding Thunder.

The bike roared to life, and as they cruised away from the barn with the engine vibrating beneath her and Callahan's muscles flexing against her chest and hands, her body heated despite the cool evening air. He drove out of the ranch, accelerating as he turned onto the main road. Cool air seeped through her clothes as the world sped by. Adrenaline coursed through her veins, and she had the urge to throw her arms out to the sides and turn her face up to the sky, but she clung to the man who was opening doors to things she'd never imagined possible.

He drove down deserted roads, passing pastures and gorgeous farmhouses, eventually turning onto a tree-lined road that wound up a mountain. She reveled in the feel of Callahan's powerful body guiding them and the freedom of being out in the open, the thrum of blood rushing through her ears competing with the roar of the engine. When Callahan pulled over on the side of the road by a well-worn trail through the brush, she didn't want to let go.

Her body continued vibrating even after he helped her remove her helmet and climb off the bike. "That was amazing! You weren't kidding about how freeing it was. I wanted to let go of you and put my arms out like wings—"

"Don't ever do that," he said seriously.

She laughed and put her hand on his chest. "I *wouldn't* do it. It just felt *that* good, like it was just you and me flying down the road, and nothing could touch us."

"That's the beauty of the open road, and sharing it with someone you care about makes it that much better. But motorcycles are dangerous, darlin'. Don't ever lose sight of that."

She gazed up at him, touched by the way he never lost sight of keeping her safe. "I promise I won't. It just felt like my past didn't exist for a little while. I know that's a fantasy, but it was nice to feel like I didn't have to worry about who I was or where I came from and just be a regular girl holding on to a great guy as the world sped by."

"That's what I was hoping for." He drew her into his arms and kissed her.

"What other tricks do you have up your sleeve?"

"I guess we'll find out." He pulled a brown paper bag out of the storage compartment and held it up. "I brought sandwiches and drinks for dinner." He withdrew one of the extra sketchbooks he'd given her and held it up. "I snagged this before we left your cabin this morning. In case you get inspired while we're here."

"You sneaky thing. You always think of everything."

"That's easy when it comes to you."

He took her hand, and they headed up the trail. The scent of pine and fresh air surrounded them as they stepped over rocks and broken branches and made their way to a rocky knoll with breathtaking views of Redemption Ranch. "*Wow.* The ranch looks like it goes on forever from up here. I don't think I could ever tire of these views."

"That makes two of us, darlin'."

They sat on a boulder, gazing out at the beauty of the ranch, and Sully filled with gratitude. She thought about how exhilarating the motorcycle ride was and how incredible it felt to be able to just climb on and go, without anyone holding her back. "How did you know I'd love riding your bike?"

"Because you crave freedom, and I want you to experience it every way you can."

She tucked that sweet sentiment away for safekeeping. "Wind therapy is the perfect name for it. A ride like that can totally distract you from your worries and clear your head. It's so different from regular therapy."

He put his arm around her, kissing her temple. "Speaking of therapy, how was your first session with Colleen?"

"Good. I really like her. She has a different way of approaching things than your mom. But unlike wind therapy, talking therapy makes me think. This morning we talked about trust and fear, and I've been thinking about it all day. Let me ask you something. I know I felt safe on Thunder and on your bike, because I know you'll keep me safe, but do you think another reason I wasn't more afraid is because of what I went through on the compound?"

"I'm not sure what you mean."

"Colleen thinks going through so much might have made me less scared of other scenarios, and I was just thinking that it kind of makes sense. I knew I could fall off the horse, and just now I knew we could get into an accident on your bike, but I still took those chances. Maybe she's right, and it's because neither is as scary as having food withheld, spending time in a metal box, or being branded."

He pulled her closer, and she felt his muscles tense up. "I hate that you went through that, and I'm glad you trust me, but do you think any part of your not being afraid to try new things is because they're *your* choices? That ability was taken away from you for so long, it seems like that could have something to do with it."

"I didn't think about that. It definitely could. I feel good about the choices I've made since coming here. Nobody said I *had* to get on that horse. I weighed the consequences and decided to do it. Just like getting on your bike and being close to you."

"It sounds to me like you're not negating your fears but

confronting them. Is Colleen worried about you taking too many chances?"

"I don't think that's what she was getting at. She said it's not uncommon for people who have been in situations like the one I was in to suppress their feelings or see everything in terms of black and white, and I think that's partially true for me. I mean, I feel comfortable telling you my feelings and standing up for myself, but maybe I am suppressing my fears and not seeing gray areas. Thinking in black or white, *scared or brave*, when there are probably dozens of levels in between."

"I don't think you're giving yourself enough credit. If you weighed the consequences of the horse and the bike, you weren't thinking in terms of black and white, and our whole relationship has been about gray areas. You express a wide range of emotions, baby, and not just when we're physically close." His gaze softened. "You show me your fears and hesitations, your curiosity, excitement, desire, and a hundred emotions in between. And from what you've told me about your time with Jordan, it sounds like you're experiencing a full range of emotions with her, too. But if you're worried, then how can we work on it?"

She leaned against him, thinking about all he'd said. "We?"

"Yes, *we*. I want to help you in whatever way I can."

"You help me every day." Why did something so wonderful have to be accompanied by a pang of guilt?

"Then why don't you sound happy about it?"

She sighed. "Because the cult messed me up, and feeling good brings guilt. I feel guilty about so many things, like the fact that I'm here, getting help, and meeting my family, and being with you, and I wonder about the other girls who were on the compound. How many of them had been kidnapped as children? Are they getting help? Will they be reunited with their families?"

"Baby, that's a lot of worrying about unknowns. There haven't been any news reports about other members having been abducted."

"I'm not sure I want to know anyway. It's hard enough dealing with my own past. I don't want to carry the weight of everyone else's troubles. But *that* makes me feel guilty, too. How can I just turn my back on them?"

"Look at me, darlin'." He waited until she met his serious gaze. "You're not turning your back on anyone. You helped every girl in that place get *out*, and that gave them a chance at a better life. You can't be all things to everyone, Sully. It's okay to focus on yourself. I think that's what you should be talking with Colleen about."

"I am. She said guilt is normal, and she's going to help me work through it. She said I need to practice giving myself permission to heal without adding extra burdens."

"I'm sure it's hard to do that when guilt has been drilled into your head for so long, but I think she's right."

"Wouldn't it be great if I could just flick a switch and let it all go so I can move forward?"

"You're too thoughtful of a person to ever just flick a switch and be okay with it. I think that's why you're so conflicted about your family, too."

She rested her head on his shoulder, watching the sun dip from the sky. "How do you know me so well after so little time?"

He kissed her head, hugging her against his side. "Because you let me see the real you."

"I think you see more than what I show you. You see things

I don't even know I'm feeling, and you help me see them, too, which I love."

"Do I hear a *but* coming?"

She leaned into him. "See how well you know me? I know I'm the one who keeps bringing up my therapy and the past, but I loved that feeling of freedom I had when I was on the back of your bike, and I want more of it. Just for tonight, I want to try to set everything else aside and pretend it doesn't exist, and just enjoy each other, and the sunset, and whatever else the evening brings."

"That sounds great, as long as you know that talking about those things doesn't lessen the specialness of our time together. If anything, it strengthens it."

As the sun dipped behind the mountains, her heart filled, and she fell a little harder for him.

Chapter Twenty-Two

SULLY HAD BEEN as excited as she was nervous about joining Sasha and the girls to bake cookies and hang out, and she was glad she'd come. The girls were chatty and fun to be around, and Sasha's cabin was homey and beautiful, with whitewashed walls, pretty scalloped trim, and picture windows overlooking a small grassy yard. A floral area rug covered bleached hardwood floors in front of a white brick fireplace, and an elegant chandelier hung from the two-story ceiling, giving the living room an airy feel. Off-white couches boasted pink, white, and mint-green pillows, which matched the distressed mint-green coffee and end tables and the white cabinets in the open kitchen, where they'd spent the evening baking several dozen cookies.

Birdie and Simone were dancing around the living room to country music as Sasha and Sully pulled the last two trays of cookies from the oven.

"Hey, Sully, how do you like living on the ranch?" Simone asked, her curly hair bouncing around her shoulders as she danced.

"I love it here, and I really like working with the horses."

"You should have seen her massaging Sunshine yesterday. She picked up the techniques like she'd been doing it forever," Sasha said.

Sully smiled proudly.

"Maybe she can give Cowboy a massage and loosen him up a little," Simone said as she sauntered into the kitchen.

"I know you think he's uptight, but I don't see him that way." Sully set the oven mitts aside, secretly wondering how it would feel to massage all those hard muscles instead of just exploring them.

"If Sully gave him a massage, it would have the opposite effect and get him all riled up." Birdie waggled her brows. The girls laughed, and Sully blushed. "He's gaga over you, Sully, and I *like* it."

"He definitely is," Sasha said.

Simone plucked a cookie off the tray and pointed it at Sully. "Okay, I'll admit the man gets hearts in his eyes every time he sees you, so he's definitely not *as* uptight as he used to be. But he's still a self-appointed watchman over anyone who enters his circle. You should have heard him with Kenny the other day. The poor kid said something about going out with friends, and Cowboy gave him a full-on lecture about not falling prey to peer pressure and being a responsible friend."

"I like that he cares about people and takes things seriously," Sully said in his defense. "I would have given anything to have someone like him watching out for my well-being when I was growing up. I swear I hardly slept before I came here, and with Callahan around, I sleep like a baby."

"He's a lot of man to keep up with. I'm sure he wears you out," Simone teased.

"I didn't mean it like *that*." She was still getting used to how openly people joked about things like sex and kissing, and she knew her burning cheeks gave away her embarrassment, so she went for a change in subject. "Besides, Doc seems pretty serious, too. Why don't you get someone to give him a massage?"

"I'm working on it," Birdie said as she twirled into the kitchen, her minidress floating around her thighs. "Doc lost his fun side when he had his heart broken. But I've got him on my matchmaking list, and I'm going to help him find his happy place."

"Don't tell him that," Sasha said.

Birdie rolled her eyes. "He needs my help. He just doesn't know it yet."

"One day I'm going to put myself on your matchmaking list," Simone said.

"I'm ready when you are," Birdie said.

"It'll be a while," Simone said. "In any case, I'm glad you like it here, Sully. This place was my saving grace after I got out of rehab and my asshole drug-dealing ex came after me."

"That sounds scary," Sully said.

"It was," Simone said. "I was in bad shape back then, but thanks to rehab and everyone here, I'm loving life and working toward a counseling degree. It feels good to have my sights set on a solid career path."

"If I'm not mistaken, Cowboy had a lot to do with that," Sasha pointed out, eating another cookie.

"He did? How?" Sully asked.

"I worked with his ranch-hand crew, and he was always pushing me to work harder," Simone explained. "I kid around about him, but I have nothing but respect for the stubborn mule. It took me a while to realize it, but he knew what I was capable of, and he forced me to better myself. I needed that after all the drugs and crap I got myself into in Maryland."

"You were in Maryland?" Sully asked.

"Mm-hm. Peaceful Harbor. Why?"

She reminded herself to be careful about what she said. "I was born in Prairie View, but I left when I was so young, I don't remember anything about it, and now my sister lives in Pleasant Hill, and I think she wants me to go there."

"That's not far from the harbor," Simone said.

"Really? What's it like?" Sully asked.

"Can we move this convo into the living room so we can start our mud masks?" Birdie picked up her tote bag and flitted into the living room, motioning for them to follow.

"What's a mud mask?" Sully followed the others into the living room.

"You've never used one?" Birdie asked.

Sully shook her head.

"I hadn't, either, before Birdie wrangled me into doing them with her on these girls' nights," Simone said.

"Sully hasn't had a massage either," Sasha said.

"Now, that I *have* had," Simone said. "Whatever you do, don't let Cowboy give you a massage unless you want to end up naked. All men think *massage* is code for sex."

Sasha and Birdie nodded in agreement.

Slightly embarrassed, Sully tried to lead the conversation away from sex. "Can we get back to the mud mask? I still don't know what they are."

"It's this crud you put on your face, and it makes your skin soft," Simone explained.

"You're such an over-simplifier," Birdie said as she set out her supplies on the coffee table. "They unclog your pores and remove impurities from your skin. *Shoot*, you need to wash your faces first. I've got headbands to keep your hair out of your faces."

She gave them each a cloth headband, and Sully followed the girls into the bathroom. When they returned to the living room, Birdie pointed to the couch. "Sit your sexy butts down, and then Simone can go back to telling Sully about Maryland while I make you crazy bitches even more beautiful."

Sully sat between Sasha and Simone, and as Birdie began applying a mud mask on Sasha's face, Simone said, "Trying to keep up with conversations with Birdie is like chasing rabbits."

Birdie flashed a grin. "You know you love me. Now, go on, tell Sully about Maryland." She lowered her voice. "I'm not as scatterbrained as she thinks. I just think of lots of things at once."

Simone rolled her eyes. "Anyway, Sully, Maryland is pretty cool. The towns you mentioned aren't that far apart, but they're pretty different from each other. Peaceful Harbor has beaches on one side and mountains on the other, but the mountains aren't huge, like they are here. They're more like big hills, and if you like to hike, that's the place to do it."

"That sounds nice." Walking on a beach was on Sully's to-do list.

"It is, and the Dark Knights have a Peaceful Harbor chapter that keeps that area safe, like the Hope Valley chapter does here," Simone said. "Pleasant Hill is more like a small city in a rural setting. It's more upscale than the harbor, and it's surrounded by rolling hills and sprawling pastures instead of beaches and mountains, and Prairie View is just a charming small town, not as upscale as Pleasant Hill but not beachy like the harbor."

Birdie applied mud to Sully's face next. "We went to my

business partner Carly's wedding in Pleasant Hill. The reception was at her husband Zev's family's winery."

"Jordan said she's engaged to Jax Braden," Sasha said.

"She is."

"Jax is Zev's brother," Sasha said.

Jax's family owns a winery? Sully was once again hit by how different their lives had turned out. She didn't long for fancy things or rich friends, but as Birdie and Sasha told them about the reception and the fun they'd had, she felt a pang of longing for the years she'd missed out on with Jordan.

As Birdie finished applying the mud mask to Simone's face and her own, Sully's dried.

"Are you sure it's supposed to feel like this?" Sully asked. "My skin feels too tight."

"Yes," the three of them answered.

"They're supposed to feel like that. As it dries, it draws the toxins and impurities to the surface of your skin so you can wash them off. Yours looks just like ours." Birdie handed Sully a mirror. "See?"

Her hair was pulled back with a red headband, and the gray mask covered her face, leaving flesh-colored rings around her eyes and mouth. "I look like a raccoon." She looked at them. "We *all* look like raccoons."

They laughed, and the other girls began waving their hands, shushing each other, trying to keep their faces still so they didn't ruin their masks. "Now we look like neurotic raccoons," Simone said, making them laugh harder.

"Or aliens," Birdie said. "We should go to the Roadhouse like this." She popped to her feet and strutted across the room, keeping her mouth as still as possible while she spoke. "Hey, big boy, want to get down and *dirty*?"

They cracked up, and Sasha leaned against Sully. "If Cowboy could see you now!"

"Hyde and Taz would be like, 'Mud wrestling!'" Simone thrust her fist in the air and said, "*Yeehaw!*" sending them into hysterics.

The rumble of motorcycles had them going still, eyes wide. The rumble grew louder, then farther away, and they breathed a sigh of relief, but a rap on the door sent them doubling over with laughter again. Birdie ran to the window and peeked out. "It's Cowboy!"

Sully's heart leapt, then instantly skidded. "The meeting's over already? He can't see me like this!" She ran behind Sasha as another rap sounded and the door flew open, and Callahan stepped into the cabin in all his serious-faced, gorgeous glory, the girls huddled around Sully, whispering and giggling.

"Look away!" Sasha demanded, making them laugh even harder.

He strode across the room, his expression rigid, and he reached between Sasha and Simone and hauled Sully into his arms. He met her gaze, a flash of affection shimmering in his eyes. "A man would have to be crazy to look away from this beautiful woman." He leaned down and *kissed* her, bringing a rush of embarrassment.

Birdie hollered, "Her *mask!*" but that only spurred him on to take the kiss deeper, making the girls laugh and making Sully melt, her embarrassment obliterated by the heat of his kiss. When their lips finally parted, she was breathless, and he was grinning arrogantly, with mud all over his handsome face.

"Damn. I take back what I said about you being uptight," Simone said, and the girls giggled.

Callahan shook his head. "Billie got off early, and she and

Dare are having a bonfire. Are you ladies almost done?"

Birdie squealed. "Yes! A bonfire! Give us five minutes." She grabbed Sully's arm, dragging her toward the bathroom, with Sasha and Simone on their heels.

THE DIN OF conversation was white noise to Cowboy's thoughts as he watched Sully talking with his family and their friends. There was something subtle and seismic in the changes taking place in her. He felt them in her body language, heard them in her laughter, and saw the shadows in her eyes giving way to glimmers of light. He was playing a dangerous game of emotional roulette, falling for a girl who had so much to figure out and so much of life to experience. He tried to imagine her years from now, settled in her relationship with her family, sitting around a bonfire thousands of miles away with people he wouldn't know, eyes clear from the pain she'd endured, heart open to someone else.

But he couldn't see it.

All he could see was those beautiful eyes calling out to *him* as they held hands around a fire, just as they were now.

Dare nudged him, startling him from his thoughts. "Your marshmallow is toast, man." He lifted his chin toward the burnt marshmallow on the end of Cowboy's stick.

"Shit." Cowboy tossed the stick in the fire, and Doc laughed.

Sully glanced over, her sweet smile hitting Cowboy in the center of his chest. "Want mine?"

Damn right I do. Your heart, mind, body, and soul, darlin'.

"No thanks, babe. You enjoy it."

"Sully was just telling us about her first motorcycle ride." Doc arched a brow.

"You took her out on your bike?" Birdie's eyes widened. "Did you tell her what that means to a biker?"

All eyes turned to Cowboy. *Thanks a lot, Birdie.* He wanted everyone to know Sully was his girl, but he didn't need to embarrass her along the way.

Sully's brows knitted. "What does it mean?"

"Everything," Birdie said overenthusiastically. "Especially since he's never let any female who isn't family ride on the back of his bike."

He met Sully's confused gaze. "It means you're my girl."

"*Oh,*" she said softly, her cheeks pinking up. Her gaze shifted nervously around them.

He squeezed her hand, drawing her eyes back to his, and felt that thrum of their connection, stronger than ever.

"How did you like riding?" his father asked.

Sully's eyes lit up. "I *loved* it. I wanted to put my arms out like I was flying."

"Now we're talkin'," Dare said. "We'll have you riding the handlebars in no time."

Cowboy glowered at him. "No, you won't."

"*Dare,* you keep those ideas to yourself," their mother warned.

"What?" Dare splayed his hands. "I've seen Sully riding horses with Cowboy every afternoon. She picked it up like a pro. This isn't that different."

Cowboy glared at him, and Dare held his hands up in surrender.

"Do you really ride on the handlebars?" Sully asked.

"Hell yeah. Check this out." Dare whipped out his phone, poked around on it, and handed it to Cowboy. "Give this to her, will you?"

Cowboy glanced at the screen. Dare had queued up one of the many videos of his radical stunts. "You're the worst influence." He handed Sully the phone. "Don't get any ideas, darlin'. That's dangerous shit."

"I wouldn't say Dare's the *worst* influence," Billie said with a smirk.

"Yeah, have you met Hyde?" Ezra joked as he helped Gus roast a marshmallow.

"I wear that badge proudly, thank you very much," Hyde said from across the fire. He was sitting between Sasha and Simone, and he stretched his arms across the backs of their chairs with a shit-eating grin on his face.

Sully studied the video, shaking her head. "I can't believe you do this. Billie, doesn't it scare you when he rides like that?"

"Yes, but he's careful, and at least he's not jumping over buses anymore." Billie leaned closer to Dare, and he kissed her.

"Buses?" Sully said with disbelief.

"You don't want to know," Cowboy said. "He scared the bejesus out of all of us."

"Everything he does on his motorcycle scares *me*," their mother said. "But if I've learned one thing, it's that if you try to tie down stallions, they just buck harder."

"Unless Cowboy is training him," Doc said.

"Cowboy's a good horse trainer," Gus said from Ezra's lap. "He's gonna teach me how when I'm bigger."

Cowboy nodded. "That's right, buddy." Sully was looking at him and Gus affectionately, and Cowboy fought against his overactive imagination, which wanted to traipse into a future he might never get with her and picture their own children. Hell, he didn't even know if she'd want kids after all she'd been through, and he realized that as much as he wanted a family, when it came to his feelings for Sully, even that wouldn't be a deal breaker.

"Cowboy has been keeping people and horses in line since he was yay high." His father held his hand about two feet above the ground, giving Cowboy an approving nod. "Lord knows we needed it once Dare came along."

"But Cowboy *did* need a little redirecting at times," his mother said. "Don't you remember the first few months after Dare was born? He kept insisting that Dare needed to sleep in a stall in the barn, because that's where foals slept."

Everyone laughed.

"That's so cute," Sully said, gazing at Cowboy.

"It was mighty cute," his father said. "He's a born protector. After Sasha was born, he slept on the floor in her room every night with his plastic rifle in his arms."

"Show-off," Dare said.

"I love that he did that," Sully said, warming his heart.

"By the time Birdie was born, he'd gotten smart and dragged a sleeping bag into her room," his mother boasted. "But when our precocious little girl was about a year old, she learned how to climb out of her crib, and we'd find her curled up on the floor with him every morning. When Sasha realized they were having slumber parties, she insisted on joining them."

"I had a bad case of FOMO," Sasha said, earning chuckles.

"What's FOMO?" Sully asked.

"Fear of missing out," Cowboy explained.

"Yes, well, your slumber parties didn't go unnoticed by your brothers," her mother said. "Doc and Dare had to get in on the fun. They emptied our linen closet and raided Tiny's workbench, arming themselves with sheets, rope, and tools. Cowboy helped them build a sheet fort big enough for all of them, only Dare had other ideas."

"*Better* ideas," Dare corrected her.

"Birdie's walls have never been the same," his mother said. "Dare talked his older brothers into making a hammock for him to sleep in. Suddenly all five kids were sleeping in Birdie's room. Three in the sheet fort, one swinging in his hammock, and Cowboy, sleeping across the threshold of the room with that plastic rifle."

Sully gazed dreamily at Cowboy for a beat before she looked around the fire at the others. "You guys are lucky to have each other."

"What was it like when you were growing up?" Simone asked.

Shadows rose in Sully's eyes. Cowboy held her hand tighter, knowing she couldn't answer in any detail without exposing who she really was and fucking hating that for her. How was she going to navigate *that* for a lifetime?

"I don't really remember, but I don't think it was like that, and this"—Sully held up Dare's phone—"terrifies me." She handed Cowboy the phone to give back to Dare. "I can't even ride a regular bike, and Dare's out there doing stunts as he speeds down the highway."

"Are you kidding about riding a bike?" Billie asked.

"No. I never had a chance to learn, but I want to," Sully said.

"I saw that on your list. I was planning on teaching you this weekend," Cowboy said.

"Why don't we teach her now?" Billie asked.

"Yeah," Dare agreed. "We've got bikes in the garage, and we can turn on the lights in the parking lot by the main house."

"Now? *Really?*" Sully asked excitedly.

"There's no time like the present," Simone urged.

"But there's no pressure," his mother added. "Don't do anything you're not comfortable with."

"The boys taught their sisters to ride. They're awfully good teachers," his father said.

"Correction," Sasha said loudly. "Doc and Cowboy are good teachers. Dare took me to the top of a hill and said, 'Get on and let gravity take you to the bottom.'"

Dare scoffed, "You could've done it."

"And cracked my head open." Sasha looked at Sully and said, "Stick with Cowboy and Doc, and you'll do great."

Everyone started talking at once about teaching Sully to ride. Cowboy leaned closer to her, lowering his voice. "Sorry. I didn't mean to start anything. You don't have to do it tonight."

"I'm excited to try. Will you stay with me in case I get nervous?" she asked.

"Always, darlin'."

Her eyes brightened, and her shoulders rose in an adorably happy shrug. "Okay, let's give it a try."

There was a collective cheer, and everyone pushed to their feet. His father put a grate over the fire, and Dare said, "We'll get the bike and meet you up by the main house."

"Grab a helmet, pads, and gloves, will you?" Cowboy said.

"Want to wrap her in Bubble Wrap, too?" Simone teased.

He shot her a narrow-eyed stare.

Simone laughed, heading up the grass toward the main house with the others. Cowboy draped an arm around Sully's shoulders, speaking into her ear. "How do you feel about

Bubble Wrap?"

TWENTY MINUTES LATER Sully was straddling a purple bicycle, outfitted in knee and elbow pads, gloves, and a helmet. It might be overkill, but she'd been hurt enough for one lifetime.

Cowboy gave her a lesson on using the brakes, and he and Doc stood on either side of the bike, while everyone else gathered around the parking lot to watch. Dare was filming them on his phone, and their mother was holding their father's hand, eyes wide with hope and worry. It was a look Cowboy had seen aimed at him and his siblings many times.

"Are you nervous?" Cowboy asked after teaching her how to use the hand brakes.

Sully's eyes dazzled with excitement. "A little because everyone is watching, but I'm okay."

"Want me to get rid of them?" Cowboy offered.

"*No.* I'll be fine, and they're so excited for me, I'm glad for the support," she said.

"Don't think about them," Doc said. "You need to keep your focus so you can balance."

"Why don't we start with a few running strides?" Cowboy suggested.

"What's that?" she asked.

"You'll stay seated with your feet on the ground and start walking, but let yourself coast a little between steps," Cowboy explained. "That'll get you used to balancing."

"Don't try to use the pedals or the brakes. If you want to

stop, just put your feet down," Doc added.

"You've got this, baby." Cowboy put a hand on her back. "We'll be right beside you."

She nodded, and then she started taking running strides, and everyone clapped and cheered her on.

"Attagirl!" their father said.

"You've got this, Sully!" Dare hollered.

"Purple is a great color for you!" Birdie cheered, making everyone laugh.

Sully's grin lit up the night as she coasted around the parking lot with Cowboy and Doc jogging beside her.

"That's it, darlin'. How does it feel?" Cowboy asked.

"Great! What's next? Now can I pedal?"

Doc laughed. "How about you learn to brake first? Try coasting and then braking so you get the feel of it, but don't brake too hard."

She coasted and braked several times. "Okay. I'm ready!"

"Good job, Sully," his mother shouted.

"You've got to stop the bike, so you know how to start," Cowboy said. She stopped the bike. "There are a few ways you can get going. I think it's easiest to use one foot on the pedal and push off with your other foot. It gives you momentum. But you can also start with both feet on the pedals or scoot forward with both feet and then find the pedals while you're moving, but that can be hard when you're learning."

"Okay. I've got it," she said confidently. "I'm going to try your way with one foot on the pedal."

"You've got this, Sully," Doc said.

Cowboy leaned closer. "Master your balance on the bike, and pretty soon you'll be able to put your arms out while you're pedaling, and you'll feel like you're flying up and down these roads."

"Do I need Bubble Wrap?" she teased.

Doc laughed.

"A'right, smart-ass," Cowboy teased. "Let's show this crowd what you can do."

As Sully pushed off with one foot and then found the pedal with the other, her front tire wobbled. She quickly gained control, and then she was off, pedaling around the parking lot as his family and their friends cheered her on.

"Keep it going," Doc said as he jogged over to join the others.

"That's it, darlin'!" Cowboy ran beside the bike. "There's nothing you can't do!"

"Except ride a motorcycle with no hands!" Dare shouted.

"Look! I'm doing it!" Sully hollered gleefully.

More cheers rang out, and Hyde yelled, "Check it out! She's exercising Cowboy!"

Everyone cracked up, and Cowboy flicked him the bird, earning more laughter, but he didn't care. Nothing could dampen the joy of seeing happiness radiating off his girl.

Chapter Twenty-Three

COWBOY POKED HIS head into Ezra's office Wednesday after lunch and found him working on his computer. "Hey, man, have you got a minute?"

Ezra looked up from the computer. "Sure. What's up?"

Cowboy shut the door behind him. "I just want to bounce something off you about Sully."

"She looked like she had a great time last night." Ezra came around the desk and sat on the edge of it.

"She had a blast. I don't know if I'm overthinking and worrying too much, but I don't want to overlook anything where she's concerned. Ever since Sunday, when she was with her sister, she's been really focused on moving forward and figuring out who she is and who she wants to be, which I think is great. But when I mentioned that to Dare and talked about showing her how to use the internet, he was concerned that it was a lot for someone coming from where she did. And that got me wondering if I'm hurting her by not slowing her down."

"I don't know exactly what Sully's been through, but given the media, it's fairly easy to draw conclusions. It sounds like Dare was just being cautious, or maybe he was surprised at how fast she was moving. But I would let Sully set her own pace. I'm sure she and Colleen are working those things out, and as she gets used to life outside the compound, it's natural for her to want to take on more and find her way to a new life."

"So I shouldn't slow her down?"

"It's not your job to slow her down," Ezra said. "But you *can* help her understand the dangers of the real world as she moves forward."

Cowboy breathed a sigh of relief. "Thanks, man. I am doing that." He noticed a sketch hanging on the side of Ezra's file cabinet of Gus sitting on a fence with Sasha standing beside him. "Did Sully draw that?"

"Yeah. She gave it to me after her meeting with Colleen this morning. She's really talented."

"She sure is. Jordan talked with her about working as an artist for hire when she's ready, and she's been drawing a variety of pictures with hopes of being paid to do it one day." She'd drawn several pictures of the horses and people on the ranch, including Cowboy sleeping, training horses, and standing with his arms crossed in the room with her and Jordan. That was his favorite, because she'd drawn herself and her sister looking as emotional as they had that morning.

"That sounds promising."

"I think so, too, although it worries me. I don't want her to get mixed up with assholes. I showed her how to use the computers in the rec room, and I warned her of the dangers of reaching out to people online. But she's not doing anything like that right now. She's just checking out those websites, seeing how her drawings compare to others and what other people are charging. That kind of thing."

"She sounds determined."

MELISSA FOSTER

"She is. You know, we see people rebuilding their lives here all the time, but it's different watching someone you have feelings for do it. I swear, Ez, it's fucking beautiful, like watching a butterfly break free from her cocoon. You've seen her at mealtimes. She's made friends and seems genuinely happy. That's not to say she isn't wrestling with demons, but she isn't holding them in or pretending they don't exist. She's dealing with them."

"That's good," Ezra said. "How are things between you two?"

"We're closer than I ever thought possible. And I guess that worries me a little, too. I was holding back emotionally, but she didn't want to hold back, so I handed her the reins." He thought about the last two nights, when he'd gone to leave and she'd asked him to stay. Each time they'd made love, he'd continued to let her find her way, and it was like their bodies just knew how and when to fall into sync. "Do you think our being intimate can hurt her in any way?"

"I'm not treating her, so I can't know for sure. Everyone handles trauma differently, and everyone's timeline is different. But it sounds like she's taking control of the parts of her life she couldn't before, and as long as you're listening if she tells you no, then like I said, I'd let her set the pace."

"That's what I'm doing. She has perspective that seems impossible coming out of that situation. Except it *is* possible for her, because there was a woman on that compound who took her under her wing from the time she was a little girl. I think she saved Sully a lot of emotional and physical damage. That's not to say she hasn't suffered more than anyone ever should. I feel her pain when she talks about it, but I also feel her hope and determination to move past it. My question is, am I seeing only what I want to see?"

Ezra smiled. "I wish all my clients had partners like you. I don't know if you're seeing only what you want to see, but I doubt it. I know you, Cowboy, and you're careful. You think through ramifications, and you protect everyone around you. It sounds like you and Sully are building a relationship based on open communication, which is good. If you're worried, I'd advise you to talk to her about it. But keep in mind two things: The first is that traumatic situations can mess with a person's perspective on many levels. Regardless of what kind of perspective she has, her feelings are likely to change, possibly several times over."

"I know that. I think about it all the time. What's the second thing?"

"That just because you know it here." He pointed to his head. "Doesn't mean you believe it here." He patted his hand over his heart.

Cowboy gritted his teeth. "I'll keep that in mind. Thanks, man."

"My door is always open."

COWBOY DROVE DOWN to the rehab barn, and as he climbed out of his truck, he spotted Sully walking into the barn with Beauty, and man, she was gorgeous in a blue T-shirt and jeans that showed off her subtle curves. Her hair was pinned up, and she wore a blue bandanna for a headband. He wondered where she'd gotten it, and on the heels of that thought, he wondered if she needed more hair supplies. As she disappeared into the barn, he looked out at the pasture, thinking about how much things had changed since their first walk.

How much *he'd* changed.

The ranch had always been his sanctuary, and he'd never let anything distract him from his work. But now, the first thing he thought of in the morning was the woman in his arms, and as soon as his workday was over, there was only one place he wanted to be, and that was by Sully's side.

He headed into the barn, and as he made his way to the stall where Sully was talking with Beauty, she looked up, eyes warming affectionately.

"Hey, darlin'. How's she doing?"

"She's getting stronger every day." Beauty pressed her muzzle into Sully's chest. "I love when she does that." She petted the horse's jaw. "I'll be back to see you tomorrow."

He'd seen dozens of women around their horses, but there was something about seeing Sully with them that got under his skin. Maybe it was that every time he saw her loving up a horse, he got the feeling she treated them like she'd always wished she had been treated. She stepped out of the stall, and as she closed it, he wrapped his arms around her from behind and kissed her neck, inhaling the scent of her lavender shampoo. "I like your hair pinned up."

"Me too, if it means I get more neck kisses."

He nipped at her neck, and she giggled, turning in his arms and beaming up at him. "That bandanna is cute."

"Your dad gave it to me. He was here when I pinned my hair up, and he left and came back with it a little while later. He said he thought it would look *mighty cute*. His words, not mine."

"Sounds like my old man. He probably has a hundred of

them in a drawer, and he still wears his old ones. That one looks brand-new. Do you need more hair stuff?"

"No. I'm actually thinking about cutting my hair."

"I noticed that on your list the other night."

"I always wanted to cut it, but we weren't allowed. Now it feels like a chain to my past, and it's a pain when I'm with the horses."

"If you want to cut it, then let's make that happen. Sasha and Birdie go to a friend of Sasha's in town. I'm sure they can hook you up with an appointment."

"Sasha mentioned that, but it sounds expensive. I was hoping your sisters could cut it for me."

"I love my sisters, but *please* don't trust them with scissors around your gorgeous hair. This one's on me."

"You've already done *enough*."

"This is the first time you're getting your hair cut. That's a special event. Please let me do this for you."

"Fine, but I'll—"

"I know. You'll pay me back when you're a big-time illustrator. Are you ready for our date?"

She bounced on her toes. "Yes. I've got my grocery list, and I'm excited."

"You're too cute." He leaned in and kissed her as Sasha walked into the barn.

"*Hey now*," Sasha teased.

"I finished with Beauty. She did great on her walk," Sully said, nervously stepping back from Cowboy.

He reached for her hand, pulling her closer. "How's it going, Sasha?"

"Not as well as it is for you two." Sasha gave him an approving glance, and then she arched a brow. "I hear you're heading to the grocery store. You really know how to woo a girl."

"I'm excited to go," Sully said eagerly.

He cocked a grin. "See ya, sis."

As they drove through the quaint small town where Cowboy had grown up, Sully gazed out the window, chatting excitedly. "The brick shops are so cute. I love the flags by the doors, and look at all the flowers in front of that one." When they neared the fountain in the center of town, she said, "I've never seen a fountain, and look at that diner."

She was too excited to cut this trip short. He pulled over and parked at the curb.

She looked around. "Where's the grocery store?"

"We'll get there." He climbed out of the truck and went to help her out.

She took his hand and stepped out of the truck. "Where are we going?"

"I figured you'd like to get to know the town you're living in."

Hesitation washed over her, but as she looked up and down the street, it was pushed aside by enthusiasm. "There are so many shops, and is that a park at the end of the road?"

"It sure is."

"Where do we start?"

"Anywhere your little heart desires, darlin'."

They started at the park, where they turned into kids again, laughing and running around, swinging on the swing set, climbing monkey bars, and riding down a slide together. They were out of breath as they headed up the street holding hands and made their way through the shops. Sully was as enamored with their tiny post office as she was with the gift shop and all its pretty offerings. Cowboy had seen *chew gum* on her list, so he bought five different flavors, and she opened the first with the joy of a kid opening a holiday present and chewed it with glee in her eyes. She was her sweet self as he introduced her to shop owners and answered all her questions, of which there were many, about the people *and* the shops. They shared a muffin at the coffee shop, and he told her all about the town festivals and other community events.

"I want to go to all of them," she said as they left the coffee shop and headed into the leather shop.

He hoped she'd still be around for them.

"I love how it smells in here," she said. "It reminds me of you."

Damn, he liked hearing that, and drew her in for a kiss. As they walked around the store, she *ooh*ed and *aah*ed over the boots. There were dozens of different colors and styles, but she gravitated toward a pair of low-heeled, square-toed brown boots with distressed leather uppers and just a hint of contrasting embroidery. They were perfectly *Sully*.

"Those would look great on you."

"Maybe one day," she said softly.

A blond salesgirl who couldn't have been more than twenty years old sauntered over to them. "Can I help you find something?"

"Yes." He eyed Sully. "What size are you, darlin'?"

Sully backed away from the boots. "Oh, *no*. I don't want to—"

"Yes, you do. What size are your boots?"

Her eyes widened. "Callahan, you're already buying groceries."

He took her hand, pulling her closer, and spoke quietly. "You're working with horses and riding every afternoon with me. You need a good pair of boots." Before she could argue, he looked at the salesgirl and said, "Why don't you bring out a seven and a half through nine, and we'll start there."

When the saleswoman went to get the boots, Sully turned on him, trying to scowl and failing miserably. "You can't just buy me everything you think I need."

"I'm not. I'm buying the things I *know* you need." He drew her into his arms and kissed her.

"You're *spoiling* me."

"The way I see it, you've got twenty years' worth of spoiling to catch up on, and I'm the right guy to do it. Now, let me have my fun, and then we can knock another thing off your list."

"Boots are *not* on my list," she said with a soft laugh.

"No, but going to the library is."

Her eyes lit up again, and man, he'd never get used to the thrill of seeing that look on her.

Forty minutes later, with new boots on her feet, several borrowed books in a Hope Valley Library bag, and her fourth piece of gum in her mouth, they stood in front of the fountain in the center of town. He'd had to get the library card under his name, because Sully didn't have any identification, which was just one more thing in a long list of things they had to figure out.

He dug a coin out of his pocket and handed it to her. "Make a wish, darlin', and don't waste your wish on being able to see Ansel again. I've already got that covered."

"What do you mean?"

"My old man was in touch with the FBI, and they're going to set up a video call for you two."

"Are you kidding? Really?" Tears dampened her eyes.

"Yes. I don't know when yet. They said it would take a few

days, so maybe next week. But it's being arranged."

"Oh, Callahan!" Tears slid down her cheeks as she threw her arms around him. "Thank you!"

"You're welcome, darlin'. Your wishes have gone unanswered for far too long. It's time to make *big* wishes and dream of wonderful things to come."

She stepped back, wiping her eyes and grinning. "I like that idea. Don't you want to make a wish?"

I've got everything I want standing right here by my side. But wishing couldn't hurt. "Yeah. I do." He pulled another coin from his pocket.

"Let's wish at the same time," she suggested.

He put down the bag of books and took her hand, holding the coin in his other hand. "Do you know what you want to wish for?"

"Yes. *You?*"

"No need to wish for me, darlin'. You already have me," he teased, and kissed her smiling lips. "On the count of three?"

She nodded, and together they counted, "One. Two. *Three.*" As they tossed their coins into the fountain, Cowboy silently sent his wish up to the powers that be. *Please let Sully find everything she could ever hope for and more.* Selfishly, he added, *And, for the love of God, please let me be part of that.*

They sealed their wishes with kisses and headed back to Cowboy's truck.

HALF AN HOUR later they were in the grocery store and had made it down only the first two aisles. Sully meticulously checked prices on every item, forgoing some altogether and opting for generic brands of others. As she compared the prices of two bags of flour, Cowboy snagged them both and tossed them into the cart.

"*Hey!*" She looked at him incredulously.

"I know you're trying to be careful, but this is your big night, darlin'. I love your sense of independence, and I know you're a proud woman who doesn't like being given things. But you've had a lifetime of living minimally and worrying, and tonight I don't want you to worry about anything. Please get what you *want* and don't think about prices. If you want a certain kind of cheese and crackers, *get them*. If a recipe calls for a particular type of *anything*, get it. I don't care if you fill the cart with champagne and caviar, for Pete's sake. Buy whatever your gorgeous heart desires." He took her face between his hands and said, "You've been excited to go grocery shopping for days. Please just let yourself enjoy the experience. Okay? If you won't do it for yourself, then do it for me, because nothing makes me happier than seeing that light in your eyes."

She looked like she might cry, and he wondered if he'd gone too far for his independent girl's comfort. But she placed her hands on the backs of his and whispered, "Okay."

"Yeah?"

She nodded.

"*Yes.* Thank you." He pressed his lips to hers. "Let the grocery shopping commence."

"Wait! Stay here." She ran out of the aisle and came back a minute later with her hands full of avocados and tomatoes and a big, beautiful grin on her face. "I want to make guacamole."

He laughed. "Now, *that's* what I'm talking about."

Chapter Twenty-Four

SULLY HAD BEEN a little nervous about her first in-town outing, but she'd had such a good time exploring with Callahan, she'd been on cloud nine all afternoon. At least until she'd started getting ready for tonight's visit with her family. She'd been cooking for two hours and had made fresh guacamole, chopped salad, baked ginger and lemon chicken, mashed potatoes with chives, and cheddar biscuits from scratch. She hadn't made that type of chicken before, but she'd followed the recipe to a T and hoped it came out okay.

She tossed the chopped salad for the umpteenth time, put more chips on the tray with the guacamole, and was second-guessing her outfit for the tenth time in as many minutes when Callahan strode into the kitchen. He was handsome as could be in jeans and a black Henley, his hair still damp from the shower. She saw him so rarely without his cowboy hat, she felt like one of the girls she'd seen gawking at him in town and tried to ignore the flutters in her chest.

"It smells incredible." His dark eyes slid appreciatively from her face all the way down the length of her, leaving a trail of heat in their wake. "Damn, darlin', you look gorgeous. I love seeing you in my kitchen, and I don't mean because you're cooking."

Her heart flip-flopped. She'd worn her hair down and tucked it behind her ear as she looked at her bootleg jeans, one of the cute blousy, lace-up boho tops Birdie had gotten her, and the new boots Callahan had spoiled her with. The boots were much more comfortable than the ones she'd worn forever.

"Are you sure I look okay? Jordan dresses fancier than I do. What if the others do, too? I have a dress. Should I go change?" She'd been saving the dress for a special occasion, but she'd been too nervous to wear it tonight.

He put his arms around her waist, a sexy smile curving his lips. "Would you be more comfortable in a dress?"

"No."

"Then why change? You're beautiful in everything you wear, and don't forget, your aunt and uncle knew and loved you when you wore flannels and leggings."

She felt herself smiling. "You're right. Clothes don't matter."

"Exactly. But if it'll make you more comfortable, I'll get you one of my flannels."

She wrapped her arms around him. "I have three of your flannel shirts at my cabin. I doubt you have many more." She was loving spending nights in his arms. Sometimes she woke up in the middle of the night and it was as if he slept with one eye open just to be sure she was okay, because he'd hold her tighter, kiss her cheek or her neck, and whisper, *What do you need, baby? I'm right here.* And as for his flannels, she loved wearing them in the mornings when he'd head home to shower and she was left to bask in memories of his sweet words and sensual kisses.

"I've got about ten more upstairs with your name on them."

"And I look forward to claiming them."

He kissed the tip of her nose. "Come take a look at the table."

He took her hand as they went into the dining room, and she realized how much she loved that he was always reaching for her hand or putting an arm around her.

The large farmhouse-style table was set with wineglasses and regular glasses, tan woven placemats, white fabric napkins, beautiful olive-green plates, and shiny silverware. Three petite vases overflowing with pretty fall flowers were lined up along the middle of the table. She couldn't believe how beautiful it looked.

"Let me know what you'd like changed."

"Are you kidding? I've never seen anything so pretty. When did you have time to do all this?"

"While you were cooking. I borrowed the vases from Sasha and picked the flowers from around the yard."

She wound her arms around him, her heart full to the brim. "I can't believe you went to all that trouble. Thank you."

"I'd do anything for you, darlin'."

The doorbell chimed, and her nerves caught fire. She grabbed his hand, her stomach knotting up. "They're here! I hope they like me, and the food. What if they don't? What if I don't like them?"

"Breathe, baby." He took her by the shoulders, gazing reassuringly into her eyes. "They're your family, and they love you sight unseen. It's going to be a great night. But if it gets overwhelming, tug on your earlobe, and I'll pretend I'm sick and get everyone to leave."

She giggled. "My earlobe. Got it." She went up on her toes and kissed him. "Thank you for being with me tonight."

"There's no place I'd rather be."

CALLAHAN ANSWERED THE door with one hand on Sully's back, which she was thankful for. She and Callahan and her aunt and Jordan all said "Hi," at the same time.

"*Sorry.* I'm really nervous," Sully admitted.

"So are we," her aunt Sheila said, already teary-eyed. She looked just like her picture, petite with fair skin, honey-blond hair, and a nervous smile. "Case—*Sully*." She put a hand over her heart. "I'm sorry. I'm still getting used to your new name. I'm your aunt Sheila, your father's sister, and I am *so* happy to see you again."

Tears spilled down Sheila's cheeks, and Sully got choked up. She leaned closer to Callahan, and his hand curled around her waist. "I'm happy to see you, too." She glanced at her uncle Gary, who was holding a bottle of wine. He was several inches shorter than Callahan, with salt-and-pepper hair and kind eyes. He looked as if he were holding back his emotions, too, just as Jordan did. She was holding hands with Jax, who was even more handsome than his pictures, with hair the color of Callahan's and a warm smile. "Hi."

"Hi, sweetheart," Gary said gently. "It's wonderful to see you again." He extended a hand to Callahan. "Hi, I'm Gary Matheson, and this is my wife, Sheila."

"It's a pleasure to meet you. Sully calls me Callahan, but most folks call me Cowboy."

Sully liked the way he hugged her to his side as he said it, making it sound like Callahan was hers and hers alone.

"Cowboy it is, then," Gary said.

"Sully, Cowboy," Jordan said. "This is my fiancé, Jax."

"I've heard a lot about you," Sully said. "Thank you for being supportive of Jordan and believing her about me."

Jax shared a loving glance with Jordan. "You're one of the most important parts of Jordan's life, and she was so certain about you, I'd have done anything to help bring you two back together. I couldn't be happier for all of you."

"Thank you," Sully said, feeling the knots in her stomach loosening.

"Come in, please." Callahan stepped aside as they walked in and offered his hand to Jax. "Good to see you again. We met briefly at Carly's wedding."

"That's right. I remember now. That was a big night, and a blurry one for me. I was pining after a woman I thought I'd never see again." Jax gazed at Jordan as she hugged Sully. "But fate was on my side."

They made their way into the living room, and Sheila said, "This is a beautiful home."

"It's Callahan's. I'm staying in a cabin down the road, but there isn't much space for guests." Sully wrung her hands together. "Can I get anyone a drink? I made guacamole. Not to drink, obviously." She laughed nervously. "Sorry. I'm better at cooking than hosting."

"It's okay, darlin'." Callahan kissed her temple. "Why don't you relax? I'll grab the guacamole and chips, and then I'll get everyone's drink order. We've got wine, beer, mixed drinks, and nonalcoholic iced tea and juice."

"I'll get the drinks," Jax offered. "What can I get everyone?"

Sheila and Jordan asked for wine, while Sully opted for iced tea, and Gary offered to give Jax a hand.

As the guys left the room, Sheila reached for Sully's hand. "You have grown into such a beautiful young lady. I see my brother in your smile and your mother in your eyes. I'm just going to make a suggestion, since we're all nervous. Let's do what we can to make it less overwhelming."

"How?" Sully asked, glancing at Jordan, who looked like she was at a loss, too.

"I'll tell you what's on my mind, and you can tell me what's on yours," her aunt said. "I think that would help."

"Okay. I like that idea."

"Great. Most importantly, I want you to know that Gary and I love you so much, and we want to be there for you in any way we can. I'd like to know about your life, but I'm not going to pump you for information about your past. You can share what you'd like, or we can leave that for another day. I'm just so happy to see you, I'd be thrilled if I could get one hug." Sheila teared up again. "Your turn."

She was as straightforward as Sully, and Sully liked that about her. "Why don't we start with that hug?" She embraced Sheila as Callahan put the tray of guacamole and chips on the coffee table. Their eyes connected, and she answered his silent *Are you okay?* with a nod. When she stepped out of Sheila's arms, she said, "The biggest thing on my mind is that I don't remember anything, and I worry that you might expect me to."

"Then you can rest easy, because I don't expect anything from you," Sheila said. "I just want to get to know you."

Sully exhaled a breath she hadn't realized she was holding.

"It smells amazing in here. Do you like to cook?" her aunt asked.

"Yes. That was one of my jobs at the compound." Sully told her a little about what her life had been like on the compound as they snacked on chips and guacamole. She didn't go into too much detail or mention the punishments or her relationship with Rebel Joe, all of which would overshadow the good feelings she had.

By the time they sat down for dinner, Sully was breathing easier.

Everyone complimented her cooking, and they made small talk, keeping conversations light. Callahan was as attentive and protective as ever. Sully knew he was taking note of every glance, every smile, and every awkward silence. In those awkward moments, he held her hand or put an arm around her, making them a little less difficult.

"I didn't even know a place like this ranch existed," her aunt said as they finished eating. "Sully, I'd love to hear about how you're spending your days."

"My days have gotten pretty full. Everyone usually eats meals together in the main house, which was overwhelming at first, but now it's fun to catch up and listen to everyone's teasing banter."

"Are they a rowdy bunch?" Gary asked.

"*Yes*," Callahan answered. "But Sully holds her own."

"Everyone's really nice, and usually after breakfast I have a session with Colleen, my therapist."

"How is that going?" her uncle asked.

"I thought you were seeing Wynnie," her aunt added.

"I was, but since Callahan and I got together, his mother couldn't be my therapist anymore, so I had to switch to Colleen. But I really like her, and she's helping me a lot."

"That's good," her aunt said. "How do you spend the rest of your day?"

"Well, I've been helping Callahan's sister Sasha, who runs

the rehab programs for the horses. I feed and groom them, walk the ones who need it, and help wherever she needs an extra hand. I'm learning a lot from her. I even gave a horse a massage this week. I really like being around the horses and spending time with Sasha."

"I met her," Jordan chimed in. "She's wonderful, and she thinks the world of Sully."

"We all do," Callahan added, giving Sully's hand a squeeze beneath the table.

"Do you have many friends here?" her uncle asked.

"I have a few," she said, thinking of Callahan's sisters and Simone and how much fun she'd had with them and with everyone around the bonfire and when she'd learned to ride a bike. She wasn't sure if getting to know people over mealtime and bike riding made them friends or not, but she felt like they were getting there.

"Do you ride the horses?" Jax asked.

"Yes. Callahan has been teaching me to ride in the afternoons, and we're going to try a trail ride Friday."

"My brother Nick and his wife, Trixie, own a ranch near us, and Jordan and I join them for trail rides when we can," Jax said.

"If y'all ride, and if Sully's up for it, you can join us on the trails," Callahan offered.

"I'd love that," Sully said.

Jordan looked at Jax, who nodded and said, "We would, too."

Sully looked at her aunt and uncle, hoping they'd want to join them, too. "What about you? Do you ride?"

"We do, and we'd love to come along," her aunt said. "We're leaving early Saturday morning, so that'll be a nice way to end our visit."

"Absolutely," her uncle said. "We look forward to it."

Flutters of anticipation bloomed inside Sully. It was a nice feeling after all her trepidation, but she also felt a pang of sadness that they were leaving so soon.

"It sounds like you're enjoying your time here," her aunt said.

"I am. Callahan likes the outdoors as much as I do, so we take a lot of walks, and I spend a lot of time sitting outside sketching."

"That's wonderful. I'd love to see your sketches sometime," her aunt said. "Jordan said you're incredibly talented."

Sully glanced at Jordan. "I'm not that talented, but I'd be happy to show them to you."

"She's being modest," Callahan said. "Her drawings are so lifelike, they'll blow you away. Jordan suggested Sully look into working as an artist for hire through some websites, and Sully has been drawing up a storm ever since."

"You have?" Jordan asked.

"Kind of," Sully said. "When I looked at those sites, there were all sorts of opportunities, but most of them wanted samples of previous work. Since I don't have any samples of paid work, I wanted to have as diverse a portfolio as possible."

"You're looking for a job already?" her aunt asked with concern.

"No, not right away," Sully reassured her. "But I want to know I'm moving in the right direction, so one day I won't have to rely on other people for everything."

"That makes sense, but don't rush it, honey," her aunt said. "Don't you need time to deal with what you've been through?"

"Yes, and I'm doing that. I'm just trying to get my ducks in

---

a row. There's a lot to deal with and figure out in order for me to move forward. Things I never thought about. I can't even get a library card because I don't have any identification."

"*Oh gosh*," Jordan said. "I should have brought your birth certificate. We left Maryland in such a rush, I didn't even think about it. I'll make arrangements to have it sent right away."

"Text Jilly and tell her where it is. She has a key to our place," Jax said. "She won't mind taking care of sending it."

"Thank you," Sully said. "That will help."

"It must be difficult not remembering who you were and starting over," Jax said.

"It is, but I'm determined not to let my past hold me back."

"You always were fiercely determined," her aunt said. "Even as a little girl, nothing could deter you from what you wanted. You got that from your father."

"That's what Jordan said." Sully glanced at her. "I like knowing that."

"Remember Sully with the sled?" Her uncle chuckled. "I've never seen a toddler so focused on conquering anything as she was when she wanted to learn to sled ride on her own."

"That sounds like a story I'd like to hear." Callahan leaned closer to Sully. "If it's okay with you."

"I'd like to hear it, too," Sully answered.

"It's a good one," her aunt said. "It was the February before the accident, so you were almost four, and your family was visiting us in Massachusetts. We had gotten about six inches of snow overnight, and you and Jordan wanted to go sledding, so your father and Gary packed down a path in the yard. Jordan was sledding on her own, but you were so little, your dad wanted to ride with you, and you wanted *no* part of that. You said you weren't a baby and refused to ride with him."

"That sounds like you, darlin'." Callahan pulled her closer and kissed her temple.

"You dragged the sled over and plunked yourself down on it," her aunt said. "And you told your daddy to give you a push. Well, he barely gave you a nudge, but you rocked forward and back, trying to go faster, and you got about a third of the way down the hill and fell off."

"She left out the part about your dad running next to you as you went down the hill," her uncle said.

"I was getting there," her aunt said sweetly. "When you fell off, your dad scooped you up, but you fought to be put down. You were determined to be like Jordan, and you dragged that sled back up the hill and went down again...and fell."

Everyone laughed, and Callahan said, "Sounds like Sully."

Sully's pulse quickened, flashes of that day or pictures she'd drawn—she wasn't sure which—ran through her mind. Callahan must have noticed, because he put his arm around her, holding her closer.

"You spent the afternoon trying to learn to ride, and finally, after about a dozen falls, you figured it out," her aunt said compassionately. "You were this tiny thing, bundled up in a snowsuit, with the biggest smile I'd ever seen, and Jordan, who has always been your biggest cheerleader, said—"

"I knew you could do it," Sully said at the same time her aunt did. Tears dampened Jordan's eyes, which made Sully tear up, too. Everyone else looked astonished.

"You remember?" Jordan asked shakily.

"Only bits and pieces." Sully blinked away her tears. "Did your hat have a pom-pom?"

Jordan nodded. "A pink hat with a white pom-pom."

"I used to draw two girls sledding a lot. One with a pom-

pom on her hat. But I thought it was just a page out of one of Richard's stories."

"Richard?" her aunt asked.

"He was the man who abducted me and brought me to the cult. He raised me as his niece," Sully explained. "I'm pretty sure he turned every memory I had into a story, so it all blurred together."

Worry washed over her aunt's and uncle's faces.

"Was he good to you?" her aunt asked.

"I used to think he was, but he took me from my family, so does it really matter what *else* he did to me?" She pressed her hands into her thighs. "He's dead now anyway, so it doesn't matter."

Callahan covered her hand with his. "Of course it matters. Everything that affected your life matters."

"I'm sorry, honey. I didn't mean to upset you," her aunt said.

"It's okay. I just don't want to talk about him right now," she said uncomfortably. "I'm still really angry about having my life stolen from me, and we're having a good time. I don't want to ruin it."

"Then he's off the table," her uncle said. "But the fact that you remembered that day is huge, isn't it?"

"I don't know," Sully said honestly, a little frustrated. "Colleen and Wynnie both said my memories could come back, but they also said there's a bigger chance they won't. It's not like I can reach into a bucket of memories and pull them out. I just have flashes of memories that are tied to the things I drew after I was taken. I think I'm remembering the drawings more than the actual events, and it's stressful knowing everyone remembers the person I was except me."

Callahan moved their joined hands onto his leg, as if to say, *I'm here. I've got you.*

"I know that's hard, honey," her aunt said. "But what matters most is that we're all reconnecting. Maybe when you come home, you'll start to remember more, and even if you don't remember, at least you and Jordan can get to know each other better."

"When I come home?" Sully looked between Jordan and her aunt, her heart racing again.

"The ranch was just a stopover, wasn't it? A safe place to land?" her aunt asked. "You were brought here to be protected, and now that the threat is gone, I assumed you'd go back to Maryland with Jordan."

Sully didn't want to leave Callahan, but these people were her family, and it would be selfish to stay away. She swallowed hard against the conflicting emotions. "I'm trying to figure that out. I still need Colleen's help."

"Yes, but how long can you stay here without insurance to cover the costs?" her aunt asked. "That's something we'll have to deal with either way, but there are plenty of good therapists in Maryland you can work with, and it might help you remember your family if you're with your sister, living in the area where you grew up."

Sully was too torn to speak. She couldn't imagine working with another new therapist, and even though she doubted she'd ever remember anything from so many years ago, she couldn't help but wonder if being with Jordan or near her hometown *might* stir a memory. *Do I even want to remember?* Some part of her did, but another part of her was afraid she'd try to become the person everyone expected her to be, and she might never find herself.

"I agree, that might be helpful," Callahan said tightly. "But to answer your question, Sully doesn't need insurance to stay here and use our services. We have benefactors who help in situations such as this. She's welcome to stay as long as she needs to, whether or not she's involved with me."

"Oh, gosh, I'm sorry," her aunt said regretfully. "I was so caught up in having Sully back in our lives, I didn't slow down enough to take your relationship into consideration."

"There's no need to apologize," Callahan said. "I know you want what's best for Sully, just like I do. And Sully knows I fully support her, wherever and however she thinks is best."

Sully's heart ached at the prospect of leaving, but as she looked around the table at the family she'd lost and thought about how much they'd lost, she hurt in an entirely different way. "I haven't made a decision yet. I'm just starting to get my arms around who I am and figure out how to live outside the cult. I feel safe and comfortable here. I'm not sure if I'm ready to start over somewhere else yet, but I'm not ruling it out."

"There's no rush to come to Maryland," Jordan said, coming to her defense. "You're getting the support and guidance you need to move forward from people you trust, and that's the most important thing. You'll always have a home with me and Jax, and you can come whenever you're ready."

That would be their home, not hers.

But the cabin wasn't hers either.

Callahan's thigh flexed under her hand, and when she met his gaze, feeling some of her tension ease, she wondered if it was possible for a person to feel more like a home than any structure ever could.

AFTER A BIT of rocky dinner conversation, they turned to lighter topics and made their way into the living room. Sully showed everyone her drawings, and they were rightfully impressed, especially Sheila, a successful painter, who couldn't say enough about Sully's innate talent.

While Sully talked with Jordan and Sheila about the art world and how difficult commissioned clients could be, Cowboy got to know her uncle and Jax.

They were both great guys who clearly wanted the best for Sully. Gary explained how difficult it had been for all of them when they'd lost Jordan's parents and Casey/Sully had disappeared. He said that Sheila had been very close to her brother and sister-in-law and that he and Sheila had lost a baby a few years earlier, which made losing Sully and her parents even harder to deal with. It was no wonder Sheila was pushing for Sully to get back home to Jordan sooner rather than later. Jax inquired about donating money to the ranch, and Cowboy told him it wasn't necessary. Jax's local relatives were major supporters of the ranch, but he insisted it was important to him and Jordan. There wasn't much else for Cowboy to do but thank him and direct him to their donations page on the website.

By the time Sully's family left, Sully looked like she'd been put through the wringer. She stood on the front porch with a V etched between her brows, watching them drive away.

Cowboy drew her into his arms and pressed a kiss to that V. "I think that went well."

"Me too. It was just a lot."

"What do you say we get out of here and take a walk to

clear our heads?"

"I have a sink full of dishes to wash."

"Keep your hands out of my sink, woman, and that is *not* a metaphor."

That earned a genuine smile.

He took her hand and sat down on one of the chairs, guiding her onto his lap. "You cooked an amazing meal and had a full night of getting to know your family. The only thing you're doing tonight is relaxing. I'll do the dishes, but they can wait." He tucked her hair behind her ear so he could see her eyes. The trouble in them worried him. "Talk to me, baby. What's going on in that beautiful head of yours?"

"I'm just a little overwhelmed. What my aunt said made sense about being near Jordan. I'm not the only one who lost all those years, and I know it's not fair of me to stay here when Jordan has been looking for me for so long. But Colleen is helping me take charge of my life and figure out what all that crap I lived through *really* did to me. I trust her with my secrets, and we *just* started working together. I can't imagine starting with someone new, and working with the horses helps me to heal, too, and I like hanging out with your sisters and getting to know everyone here."

The fact that he wasn't included in the people and things she didn't want to leave was a blow to his gut and his heart, but this wasn't about him, no matter how much it hurt. "I'm sure Jordan will help you find a good therapist and make friends, and you can volunteer at a rescue in Maryland."

She put her arms around him and whispered, "But I just found you."

His chest constricted. "Baby, you know I always want you by my side, but we went into this with our eyes open. We knew every day we had together was a gift, but that goes for every day you get with your sister, too, so if there's even a chance it's going to help you move forward to be with Jordan, then you need to do what's best for yourself and take that step." *Fuck.* This conversation just might kill him.

"That's the problem. I don't know what's best." She exhaled loudly. "Actually, that's not true. I *know* that you're the best part of my healing. You give me strength and encourage me to believe in myself and try new things. You help me see that it's okay to be *me*, whoever that is as I grow and change and figure things out."

He held her tighter, her words burrowing deep inside him, just as his words sliced him open. "I'm glad. I always want you to have that confidence, but that can't hold you back from being with your family, darlin'."

"But I'm not sure going to Maryland would be better for me, and I worry it might be worse. I've been thinking a lot about the past and who I am now. I don't even know if I *want* to remember a life that ended and will never be continued. What if I remember and then Jordan wants me to be that person?"

"Then you'll explain how you feel to her. You're just scared, baby, and that's understandable. But you *are* Jordan's sister, and that's important whether you remember or not. She's your blood, and *she* remembers." He felt like he was tearing his own heart out. "Being with Jordan will add something to your life that no one else can ever give you. Siblings help you grow and figure out who you are in ways partners can't, and, sweetheart, I don't want you to miss out on that." He forced the words past the excruciating pain in his chest. "I know this is hard, but I've seen new light in your eyes every time you get together with

Jordan. You're searching for a connection, and you're making one, just as you should be."

Tears slid down her cheeks. "I'm so confused. I want a relationship with Jordan, but for the first time in my life, I'm really, truly happy. I go to bed feeling safe, and I wake up looking forward to every part of my day. Spending time with you and seeing everyone at breakfast, working with Colleen, and helping Sasha. I can't remember ever having that, even though it sounds like I did before I was abducted. I just don't know if I'm ready to give all that up—to give *us* up—for what *might* be."

Every ounce of him wanted to tell her to stay, to build a life with him, but he had to stand by his promise. "I know it's scary, but I think this is one of those gray areas you were talking about the other night. You can't know how it will be until you give it a chance. You might get out there and find a whole new world of things you love doing. You don't have to make a decision tonight, but you should think about it."

"I am." She rested her head on his shoulder and was quiet for a long time. "I talked with Jordan about the life insurance money, and I told her I'd take it."

He knew that wasn't easy for her to do, given how independent she was. "That's good, darlin'. That will take some stress off your shoulders."

"And add a layer of guilt, because if I don't want to chase those memories of my parents, do I really deserve that money?"

He held her tighter, wishing he could take away her doubts. "Yes, baby, you do. Your parents loved you, and they made sure you would be taken care of after they were gone. That wasn't done with stipulations. If they were here now, they'd just want you to be happy. You did the right thing, and you shouldn't feel guilty about it."

She lifted her head from his shoulder and stroked his cheek. "You really are the best part of my life. You know just what to say to make me stop thinking like I'm still living on the compound, where we were given so little and made to feel guilty for even wanting more."

"If it were up to me, baby, I'd give you the world." *And never let you feel an ounce of guilt.*

"You already have," she whispered, and leaned forward, pressing her lips to his.

Her kiss was slow and sweet, awakening the longing that was always lingering just beneath the surface with them. He threaded his fingers into her hair, taking the kiss deeper, wanting to memorize everything about her. Her taste, her scent, her eagerness as her tongue slid over his. He wanted to carry her inside and love away her worries—and his own. To obliterate the reality he knew was coming and didn't want to face. But she'd had such an emotional evening, he wasn't sure he should, so he drew back, gazing into her moonlit eyes, which were brimming with desire. *Fuuck.* He'd give his life for this woman and couldn't resist kissing her again. She was right there with him, desperately returning his kisses, moaning as he kissed her jaw and the edges of her mouth, the uncertainty of their situation drowned out by the surety of their feelings.

"You've had a big night," he whispered between kisses. "I should walk you home." He dusted kisses over her lips. "But all I want to do is carry you inside and make love to you."

"I want that, too."

Their mouths came together feverishly as he pushed to his feet and carried her inside, stopping every few steps with the ferocity of their kisses. When they finally made it to his bedroom, they were both breathing hard. Their boots *clunk*ed on the hardwood floors as he stripped them both bare and laid her on the bed. He raked his eyes down her beautiful body, his heart aching. She reached for him as he came down over her, meeting him in another passionate kiss. The feel of her beneath him, the taste of her salty tears, and the longing that had already begun to settle in were all too much. *I love you* clawed for release, but he bit it back, not wanting to make her choice any harder, and dipped his head, licking the shell of her ear. "You're the best thing that has ever happened to me." She moaned, clinging to him tighter. He dragged his tongue around the rim again and nipped at her earlobe, causing a sharp inhalation. Her fingers pressed into his back, and he sucked her earlobe into his mouth.

Her hips rose, grinding against him. *"God..."*

The lust in her voice spurred him on, and he tasted his way down to her breasts, teasing and taunting with his teeth and tongue as his hand slid down her belly to the tuft of curls between her legs. He sucked one nipple to the roof of his mouth as he drove her wild with his hand. She arched and writhed, pleading, *"Cal."* He continued teasing and sucking as she bowed off the mattress. He slid his fingers inside her, earning seductive sounds that slithered through him like asps of fire as he rubbed her swollen clit with his thumb. She fisted her hands in the blanket, pleading and panting, *"More."*

"We'll get there. Ride my fingers like you rode my cock the other night."

She mewled and rocked as his fingers moved in and out of her tight heat. He trailed openmouthed kisses lower, loving the underside of each breast, lingering there with slow strokes of his tongue and long sucks of her sensitive skin, taking her right up to the edge of release and holding her there. She was trembling, pleading, and panting, so fucking gorgeous, he wanted to draw out her pleasure even more.

"I can't...take it..."

"Enjoy it, baby." He wanted her to remember his every touch, the way his fingers moved inside her, the heat of his mouth on her body, and the sound of his voice coaxing her. He took his time, sucking and kissing her ribs and stomach, earning more sinful sounds as he turned her over, loving every inch of her beautiful body with his mouth and hands. He lavished that brand with extra love, using his hand to pleasure her, so every time she saw the mark, she'd think of *him* and how good he made her feel and not the man who caused her pain.

When he'd left no spot untouched, he gently rolled her onto her back and kissed her sensual lips. "Ready to come on my mouth, baby?"

"Yes. I love your mouth."

He spread his hands over her inner thighs, opening her wider, and dragged his tongue along her pussy, earning more needy sounds. Her hips rose off the mattress with every slide of his tongue. "You're so fucking sweet, I want to devour you all night."

"Yes. Wait. *No.* I'll die from pleasure, and then you'll have to explain it to my family."

He laughed and kissed her thigh.

"Don't stop," she complained. "I promise I won't die."

They both laughed.

"Jesus, woman. You're killing me." He knew right there and then that if she left, he'd never be the same.

He lowered his mouth between her legs, turning her laughter into hungry moans and more greedy sounds. "God, baby, everything about you drives me wild." He kissed her inner thigh. "The way you move, the sounds you make." He dragged his tongue along her sex, earning a seductive moan that had him devouring her again. He needed so much more and knew that in a few days she might be gone forever. Pushing that awful thought away, he vowed to make it the best few days of her life. He guided her legs over his shoulders, feasting on her, using his fingers on her clit, feeling her mounting pleasure as his own as her legs trembled, her thighs tightening around his head.

"*Cal…Oh…Yes—*" Her hips bucked as his name flew from her lungs loud and untethered. Her pussy pulsed against his tongue so fucking perfectly, he didn't relent, drawing out her pleasure and staying with her until the very last pulse shuddered through her and she collapsed, breathless and boneless, to the mattress.

He kissed his way up her body, earning tiny gasps with every touch of his lips. Goose bumps chased his kisses up her breasts and neck. When he brushed his lips over hers, her eyes opened, a sweet, sated smile curving her lips.

"My beautiful darlin'," he whispered against her lips, and as her legs opened wider and the broad head of his cock pushed into her tight heat, everything changed. He felt the deep pull of their bodies, the thrum of electricity drawing them into a realm all their own. Grasping at the emotions consuming him, he covered her mouth with his, kissing her deeply as they found their rhythm. He made love to her slowly, cradling her beneath him, loving the way her breathing hitched with every thrust of his hips. When he lifted one of her legs at the knee, taking her deeper, she tore her mouth away with a pleasure-drenched moan that wound through him, making him want to quicken his pace and send her over the edge.

But she deserved more.

She deserved to *live* in a state of pleasure, and he was determined to give it to her.

He continued thrusting slowly, lifting her other knee, taking her even deeper. She moaned, clawing at the sheets. He clenched his jaw against the urge to go faster and opened his eyes, drinking her in. Her cheeks were flushed, golden tendrils spread over his pillow. She looked like an angel, and she felt like heaven. Tight and hot and so fucking good, he knew he wasn't going to last. He quickened his efforts, and as he dropped her knees, she clung to him, matching his pace.

"Come with me," he gritted out, and sank his teeth into her neck. Her fingernails dug into his flesh, her inner muscles tightening around him, and she cried out his name, severing the last shred of his restraint. Heat barreled down his spine and up from his balls, her name tearing from his lungs as he gave in to an earth-shattering release. They thrust and moaned and clawed and panted until the very last aftershock rumbled through them.

He gazed down at the breathless beauty who had utterly and completely stolen his heart and gathered her in his arms, kissing her slow and sweet, breathing air into her lungs until her breathing calmed and she made the contented sigh he loved. Then he kissed the edge of her lips, whispering, "Open your eyes, darlin'. Be with me."

Her eyes fluttered open, the tears in them gutting him as she whispered, "I'm *so* with you, I think we've become two parts of the same person."

The words could have come from his own mouth. He was a fool to have thought he could ever let her go. She hadn't even decided to leave yet, and he already missed her.

Chapter Twenty-Five

"HOW WAS DINNER with your family?" Colleen asked. The petite, energetic blonde wore her hair short on the sides and a little spiky on top and looked to be in her early fifties.

It was a simple question. A good question. If only it were easy to answer.

Sully fidgeted with the edge of her shorts. "Dinner was nice. I liked my aunt and uncle, and Jax is great, but it made me more confused than before."

"In what way?"

She told Colleen about their dinner conversations and her talk with Callahan last night. "Callahan is right. I *am* scared about what I'll find in Maryland, but I'm afraid of a lot of things right now. Jordan is sending me my birth certificate, and I can't decide if I want to use my real name, which is all over the media and could lead to me being seen as *that girl who escaped the cult* no matter what I do or where I end up, or if I even want to be Sully, since that name was given to me by a man who stole me from my family. And on top of all that, regardless of what name I use, how am I going to handle it when people ask where I grew up? How can anyone relate to what I went through? It's embarrassing, and I'm not sure I realized how angry I am at the man who took me. I wish I knew what to do with it, and that scares me. But mostly I'm afraid to walk away from Callahan, and you, and this place where I feel safe. I'm afraid I'll never be this happy again. And ever since I got away from the compound, I've been determined to make my own decisions." Tears welled in her eyes. "But I can't make these decisions. Especially the last one. No matter what I choose, I'll lose someone I want in my life."

"Oh, honey." Colleen handed her a box of tissues. "Do you remember how we talked about being kinder to yourself and not feeling so much pressure to have all the answers or to try to move forward too fast?"

Sully nodded and wiped her eyes. "But I *want* to move forward."

"You already are in so many ways, and you'll continue to long into the future. But some of the things you're questioning will take time to figure out. Why don't we talk about each of the things you mentioned and see if I can help?"

"That would be good." She blew out a breath. "Sorry to blurt it all out like that. Apparently I do that when I'm overwhelmed."

"That's what I'm here for. It sounds to me like one of the biggest things on your mind is who you really are and how you want to be seen by the world."

"Everything I mentioned feels big to me."

"And they all are, but your identity is probably the place to start. It might help you to know that many people who grow up in closed communities like the Free Rebellion have the same worries you do, whether or not their name has been mentioned in the news. There are a few different ways to handle it, but the thing to remember is that you are in control of your answer, if you choose to give one, and that is *your* choice, too. You can be vague and give just enough information to answer the question. For example, if you're asked where you grew up, you can simply say West Virginia. If someone asks where you're from, you might say Maryland, since that's where you were born."

"Actually, that's what I did when Simone and I were talking about Prairie View. I told her I'd been born there but moved away when I was too young to remember what it was like."

"That's a perfect answer. It's kind of like when a young child asks where they came from. They don't want or need all the intimate details. Keep it simple enough to satisfy the question. The rest is up to your discretion, and it's important to remember that nothing is set in stone. How you handle those types of questions might change over time, based on who is asking and how you're feeling, and that's okay. That's what I meant by seeing gray areas. Personal questions don't require all-or-nothing responses. You can opt not to answer or say *out East* or whatever else feels right to you. But I suggest you try to avoid lying, because lies can be hard to keep up with and add undue stress."

"I hate lying."

"Then that's a good reason not to do it. There might also come a day when you want to talk more openly about what you've been through. You might want to write a story about it or speak publicly or find another way to help others who have been in similar situations."

"I like helping people, but I'm angry about being abducted and held against my will. I can't imagine wanting to talk about it. I was robbed of the life I should have had when I was four years old, and there wasn't anything I could do about it."

"Yes, you were, and you have a right to be angry. Anger is part of grief." They discussed the stages of grief and what she might encounter. "You're grieving the loss of your childhood, the loss of your family, and the loss of many rites of passage that were taken from you. I know how you feel today, but it's important to give yourself room to honor all your feelings. As time goes by, you might decide to channel your anger differently to raise awareness. Or you might never want to share it with others. The choice is yours."

"*The choice is mine.* I've waited a long time to be able to live that way."

"And you made it happen, Sully. Don't lose sight of how remarkable you are."

She lowered her eyes.

"Is that hard for you to hear?"

"Yes and no. I'm proud of myself, but it's still strange to hear and accept compliments from others."

"I have a feeling you'll be hearing things like that a lot. You're a special person, and the more people you meet, the more you'll probably hear it. Not only about what you've done for yourself but about other accomplishments, too. Hopefully the further you progress with therapy, the easier it'll be for you to accept compliments. I do have a suggestion about how to deal with your grief and anger."

"I'm open to anything."

"I know you like to draw, but how do you feel about journaling?"

"Do you mean like keeping a diary?"

"Yes. Writing down what you're feeling to get it out of your system. Or even drawing pictures if you're more comfortable with that. Sometimes we don't know what we're really feeling until we get it out and uncover what lies beneath it."

"I can try."

Colleen smiled. "That would be a great start, and if you're comfortable showing me what you've written or drawn, then we can see if we can learn anything from it."

"Okay. I like that idea."

"Great. Now, let's talk about your name. I understand not wanting to be pre-judged by what people have read or heard in the media. But the name you currently use hasn't been in the news at all. That's a safe name from that perspective. But what matters is how it makes *you* feel. Who do you see when you think of Sullivan Tate?"

"I definitely don't see Casey. I see Sully. But *my* Sully isn't the cult's Sully."

"What do you mean by that?"

"It's hard to explain, but to me Sully is the little girl who fought against the things she didn't like and the teenager who tried to escape and the woman who finally made it out."

"She sounds like a very strong person."

Sully sat up taller, feeling good about that but uncomfortable with what she had to say next. "Yes, but it's a name that was given to me by people I hate."

"That's true. But you've just said your Sully isn't their Sully."

"I did, didn't I?"

"Yes, and that says a lot about how you feel. The question is, does hearing that name, and using it, throw you right back to the place you don't want to be? Or does it make you feel good about the person you've become despite their best efforts to keep you from growing and changing?"

She had to think about that for a minute. "It makes me feel

good most of the time, but sometimes when I get angry, it makes me feel like I wish I could wash it all away."

"And what name would you use if you could wash it all away?"

"I don't know. All I really know is that I don't want everyone's first impression of me to be the girl who escaped from a cult. Or the girl who was kidnapped. I want to be seen for *me*, and I don't want to use the name Casey. But I'm afraid of hurting my family, and more specifically, Jordan, if I legally change my name."

Colleen nodded. "I can see how you might think that would hurt her feelings, but her feelings are *not* more important than yours. I know that might be hard to accept, and it might bring guilt, but this is another step in taking care of yourself."

Sully swallowed hard, knowing she was right.

"Have you talked with Jordan about how you feel?"

"No."

"I think that would be a good start. From what you've shared with me about her, she seems to support your decisions and want what's best for you."

"She does. I'll try to talk with her about it *and* try not to feel too guilty about doing it."

Colleen smiled again. "That's perfect. Have you ever tried affirmations?"

"I've given myself pep talks, and that's helped."

"Affirmations can be the same as pep talks, and they're usually a good way to prepare for difficult things. Before you talk with Jordan, you might want to remind yourself that your feelings matter, and it's okay to take care of *you*."

"I seem to be doing that a lot since coming here."

"That's a good thing, Sully. It's important to remember

there are gray areas in every situation, including this one. Whatever you decide to call yourself doesn't have to be forever. You can change your name to Sullivan Tate, or Sullivan Lawler, and if you decide a month later that you want to be Casey, you can call yourself Casey. If you decide to stick with Casey as your legal name but call yourself Sully, or any other name, those are *your* decisions to make."

"It doesn't seem as overwhelming when I'm talking with you."

"You've had a lot thrown at you very quickly. It's understandable that you'd be overwhelmed. I'm glad it helps to talk with me. As we've talked about, feelings may come and go— happiness, sadness, grief for the years you missed with your family, anger, loneliness, guilt. But if you slow down and take them apart, they're a little easier to deal with."

"Except for the decision to stay or leave."

"That's also not set in stone, honey. You can make a choice, and if it doesn't feel right, you can change your mind."

"But I'll lose Jordan or Callahan."

"Do you really think you'd lose them, or are you bypassing the gray areas? Is there any chance Jordan would understand if you wanted to continue your therapy here for a while?"

Sully realized her mistake. "Probably, but I think she'd be hurt."

"And how do you think Callahan would react to you going to Maryland?"

"The same way. He said he'd support whatever I decide, and I know he means it, but I also know he'll be hurt if I leave."

"I hope you realize what that really means, which is that you are a very special person, and you have already had a big impact on both of their lives."

"I guess so," Sully said softly.

"Here's the most important question, and it's a tough one. If Callahan wasn't in your life, would you go with Jordan?"

Sully felt a stab of pain in her chest, and she teared up. "I don't know. Probably. He thinks I should go, but the thought of leaving him hurts *so* bad." Her voice cracked, and her tears broke free. She grabbed several tissues to wipe her eyes. "I've never had what we have, and I wasn't looking for it. I didn't think I'd ever want to be *near* another man, but as we've gotten to know each other, I've been so drawn to him. I've never felt anything like it. It's...inescapable in a good way. The best way. I've never known anyone like him. He's open and honest and careful with my feelings, and he's protective in ways that make me feel special, *not* owned. He's helped me in so many ways. He's the *reason* I feel safe. He started me on a path that allowed me to see people without a veil of fear and trepidation. I can be myself with him and let him see *all* of me. My pain *and* my joy. I'm happiest when I'm with him, and I feel whole in a way I never have."

"I hear you, honey, and all of that is important. Callahan is a *good* man, and I have no doubt that his feelings for you are real, but how can you know you're at your happiest if your only comparisons are the compound and the few weeks you spent with the Finches?"

Chapter Twenty-Six

COWBOY AWOKE SATURDAY to the incessant buzzing of his cell phone on his nightstand and the sweet sounds of Sully's breathing as she slept beside him. He carefully slid his arm from beneath her head and read the text from his father. *We've got a rescue at a private residence outside Lockwood. Four horses. No info on injuries.* He sent a thumbs-up emoji, scrubbed a hand down his face, and took one last look at Sully. She looked so peaceful.

But he knew better.

She was struggling with the decision about whether or not she should leave with Jordan tomorrow. Her birth certificate arrived yesterday, bringing a roller coaster of emotions, as did the trail ride with her family, which had been a great experience for everyone. Sully had been on a high afterward, but that was washed away when her aunt and uncle had come over last night to say goodbye. She'd given them a few pictures she'd drawn of their visits, and it had been a tearful goodbye for all three of them.

His emotions were overloaded, and his entire body had been knotted up for days. He climbed out of bed and headed into the bathroom. When he stepped into the shower, he leaned his forearm on the tile wall, letting the hot water rain down his back, hoping to ease his tension.

A few minutes later, the shower door slid open, and he looked up, meeting Sully's sleepy gaze. "I didn't mean to wake you, darlin'."

"You didn't. Why are you up so early?" she asked, her gaze traveling down his body.

"We got a rescue call."

Her brows knitted, and he was surprised to see her stripping off her shirt and underwear and stepping into the shower with him. This was a first, and as she wrapped her arms around his waist, pressing her cheek to his chest, his heart ached. He embraced her, turning his body so she was beneath the warm water, and ran his hand down her back. "You okay?"

"Mm-hm. I just miss you." She kissed his chest.

"I'm right here, darlin'." After her family left last night, they'd taken a walk, and then she'd asked him to hold her, as she had the night she'd found out the truth about her past. She'd fallen asleep in his arms, fully clothed, and when she'd woken a few hours later, she'd taken off her jeans, cuddled close to him again, and had fallen right back to sleep. He'd lain awake searching for answers that hadn't come.

He stroked her hair. "Are you excited to get your hair cut today?" Jordan and Sasha were going with her to the salon.

"Yes." She kissed his chest again and tilted her face up. "Do you think it'll look okay shorter?"

"You're beautiful. You'd look gorgeous no matter what you do to your hair." He ran his fingers through her hair, and she kissed a path across his chest. "That feels nice, baby."

She continued kissing his chest, running her hands up and down his torso, and brushing her soft body against him. She dragged her tongue over his nipple, sending a bolt of heat directly to his cock. He gritted his teeth, and she sealed her mouth over that nipple, pressing herself against his hard length. "Careful, baby, you're playing with fire."

"I don't want to be careful." She trailed kisses down the center of his body, warm water raining down her neck and back. "I want to feel your flames." Her eyes flicked up to his. "I want to make you feel as good as you make me feel."

Christ, she was everything to him already. She'd explored his entire body, but she hadn't had her mouth on his cock. He didn't know what that asshole had made her do, and he didn't want her to feel like she owed him anything. "You don't have to do that. I always feel good when we're together."

"I *want* to." She wrapped her fingers around his cock, looking at him with the sweetest, most hopeful expression, and he realized she needed this control, this chance to give back. "I may not be very good at it," she said softly. "I've never had a choice, so I've never *tried* to be good at it. If I'm not, will you help me?"

That cut him to his core, his feelings for her sinking into his bones. "I'll do whatever you want me to, but it's *you*, darlin'. Everything you do feels great."

She kissed his stomach again, tightening her grasp as she bent at the waist and licked the head of his cock. He sucked in air through clenched teeth, and her eyes flicked up to his, innocent, curious, *lustful.* He pushed one hand into her hair, caressing her cheek with his thumb. "Feels good, baby." She smiled and did it again, working her way around the head and up and down his length until his dick throbbed greedily. "So damn good, darlin'." She took him into her hot, wet mouth, stroking and sucking, and his chin fell to his chest. *"Fucking fantastic."*

She kept her eyes on his. Watching her loving him with her mouth and hand, taking him deep and drawing him out slowly in a maddening rhythm that had his entire body blazing was better than any fantasy he'd ever had. He fought against the urge to thrust his hips, to bury his other hand in her hair and take control, his muscles flexing with restraint. "So damn sexy, baby. I love seeing my cock in your mouth." Her eyes darkened, and she quickened her pace, squeezing tighter, sucking harder. Holy hell, she was fucking amazing.

He guided her other hand to his balls, showing her how tight to hold them, and it was all too much—the trust in her eyes, the feel of her mouth, the emotions billowing between them as hot and tangible as the steam from the shower. "I'm close, baby," he warned through clenched teeth, but she stroked even faster. "*Sully*," he warned again, fisting his other hand in her hair but still letting her lead. He closed his eyes, trying to hold back, but she was sucking and stroking fast and tight, so fucking perfectly, he got lost in the rhythm. In a last-ditch effort to warn her, he opened his eyes, but the sight of her watching him, eyes full of pleasure as she squeezed his balls, sent his climax barreling through him. His hips bucking and his vision blurring, he bit out, "*Sully. Fuck. Sully—*" He struggled to get his brain to function and his eyes to focus and realized she was staying with him despite the come dribbling out of her mouth. "*Shit.*" He pulled out, the last of his release spilling onto her breasts as he gritted out, "Sorry, baby." His body shuddered and quaked as he gathered her in his arms, their hearts thundering.

"Sorry I couldn't finish," she said breathily.

"Christ, darlin'. You *wrecked* me."

Her brows knitted. "Is that good?"

God, I love you. It took everything he had to keep the sentiment in. "The *best*, baby." He kissed her smiling lips, wondering if she had any idea that she'd wrecked him long before she'd stepped into the shower.

SULLY SAT IN the salon chair, hoping she wasn't making a mistake, and at the same time, so excited to finally get her hair cut, she could barely sit still. She'd spent half an hour poring over hairstyle books with Jordan and Sasha and had finally settled on long layers that would hang a little past her shoulders. "Are you sure that style will look okay?" she asked Becky, Sasha's feisty redheaded hairdresser friend.

"It'll look fantastic, but with your cheekbones, you could pull off any cut." Becky began combing out Sully's wet hair.

"That's what we told her," Jordan said, and Sasha nodded in agreement.

All around them, hairdryers whirred as stylists complimented their clients' appearances, and Sully realized she'd never scrutinized her looks the way other girls did. Even on the compound she'd heard girls talking about their looks, but Sully had always had more important things on her mind. She thought about the way Callahan called her beautiful and gorgeous, and even though she knew he thought she was beautiful, she always got the feeling he was talking about more than her looks, and she liked that. There were times she tried to wear clothes he'd think were cute, as she'd done today when she'd chosen the minidress Birdie had picked out for her and the boots he'd gotten her. He'd never seen her in a dress, and she wanted to surprise him with her haircut and the outfit when he got back from rescuing the horses. But she hadn't even considered her face.

That was good, she decided, because he liked her just the way she was.

"You have beautiful hair," Becky said, drawing Sully from her thoughts. "When is the last time you had it cut?"

Sully stopped herself from saying, *Probably when I was four*, and went with a more generic response, as Colleen had suggested. "A *long* time ago. It's always been frizzy."

"Don't worry about that. Once we get rid of the dead ends, you'll lose a lot of the frizz, and I've got great anti-frizz products," Becky reassured her as she finished combing out her hair. "Okay. I think we're ready."

Birdie burst through the salon door, running toward them. *"Wait!"* She practically skidded to a stop in her platform boots and wide-legged jeans, her wild dark hair spilling over the shoulders of her cropped yellow sweater.

"What are you doing here?" Sasha asked. "I thought you had to work."

"I did, but I found this picture of a haircut that would look great on Sully, and we had a slow morning, which is weird, but whatever. Anyway, Quinn's plans changed, and she offered to work so I could join you. So here I am, and look!" She thrust a picture of a pretty girl with shoulder-length hair into Sully's hands. Jordan, Sasha, and Becky leaned in to check it out. The cut was slightly longer in the front than the back and parted on the side, with a few long layers throughout.

"Thanks, Birdie. I love how natural this looks, and I think I'd like this length better than past my shoulders," Sully said. "But it looks like she has wavy hair, and my hair is pretty straight. Do you think it would look as good on me as it does on her?"

"Definitely," Becky said. "Your hair isn't that straight. It's weighed down by the length. Once we cut it, it'll feel lighter and look fuller."

"Really?" Excitement bubbled up inside Sully. "Then let's do it."

"Yes!" Birdie cheered, and whipped out her phone. "Let's get *before* pictures. Everyone, move closer to Sully."

As Jordan leaned in to Sully's left and Sasha leaned in to her right, Becky said, "I'll take the picture. Birdie, get in there."

Birdie handed Becky her phone and said, "*Incoming!*" as she climbed onto Sully's lap and put an arm around her neck, making them all laugh for the picture. "Now take one with just Jordan and Sully." After Becky took the picture, Birdie had her take more of Sully and Sasha, and then of herself with Sully. When Becky handed her back her phone, Birdie took a picture of Sully with Becky, and then she took one of Sully alone. "That one's for Cowboy."

Sully grinned, thinking of the note he'd left on the counter that morning, along with a lot more money than the haircut had cost. *Darlin', have a great time with the girls. I can't wait to see your new haircut, although I can't imagine you looking any more beautiful than you already do. Treat yourself to anything else you want while you're out. C*

"Okay, Annie Leibovitz." Sasha tugged Birdie away from the chair. "Can we let Sully get her hair cut now?"

After lots of chitchatting, encouraging words, and scissor snips, Sully sat with her back to the mirror, more nervous than when she'd arrived, as Becky finished blow drying her hair and fluffed and finger combed it into place. The girls looked like they were going to burst with excitement. Birdie had taken about a million more pictures, catching every worried *what if* and every nervous laugh.

Becky stepped back, grinning proudly. "Are you ready to meet the new Sully?"

The *new* Sully. She loved that idea. "Yes."

Becky turned the chair, and Sully barely recognized the pretty woman in the mirror. Her hair *was* naturally wavy, and the frizz was gone. The right-side part gave the left side more volume, and Becky had cut it to the perfect length, brushing the tops of her shoulders. She hadn't realized how much clearer and more vibrant her skin looked since she'd left the compound. The cut showed off her jawline, highlighting her smile, and she realized her aunt was right. Her smile did look a lot like her father's. She saw more of her mother in her eyes and brow line, and her cheekbones appeared more striking, too, giving her something in common with Jordan.

Her throat clogged with emotion, and she struggled to hold it in as Birdie said, "Girl, you belong on a magazine cover," and took more pictures.

"Cowboy is going to lose his mind," Sasha said.

Sully glanced at Jordan in the mirror, staring at her, holding one hand over her heart. "Jordan, do you like it?"

Jordan teared up, nodding. "You look even more like Mom and Dad."

The emotions in Jordan's voice caused Sully's tears to break free.

"Oh no." Becky reached for tissues and handed them to Sully. "You don't like it?"

Sully shook her head, wiping her eyes. "I love it. I just..." Leaving out the part about her past and her parents, she said, "I never realized I could look so pretty."

There was a collective "*Aw.*"

"Then you're the only one who didn't," Jordan said, leaning down to hug her. "You were gorgeous when you walked in here. You're just a different kind of gorgeous now."

BIRDIE TOOK ABOUT a dozen more pictures, and by the time they left the salon, Sully felt lighter, more confident, and a little more like a typical young woman instead of a cult escapee. Her long hair had felt like a tether to the compound and all that had happened there, and it was a great feeling to be free of it.

Birdie sidled up to her and said, "Look at you in that dress! I knew you'd look like a million bucks in it."

"Thanks. You have great taste. Can you text me the pictures you took? I want to send one to Callahan."

"I already did. Look at your phone."

Sully pulled her phone out of the cute bag Birdie had given her and looked at the pictures. She still couldn't believe she was the girl in them. She looked genuinely happy, and even though she knew she *felt* happy, seeing the light in her own eyes made it even more real.

"This calls for a celebration," Sasha said. "Let's go to the Roadhouse for lunch."

"Great idea. I'm starved for a burger," Birdie said.

"Does that sound okay to you guys?" Sasha looked between Jordan and Sully. "It's a biker bar, but not a skeevy one. Billie's family owns it, and she works there. It's not usually crowded in the afternoons. It'll be fun."

Sully felt a quiver of apprehension. She'd never been inside a bar, but she knew what Rebel Joe had been like when he'd come back from them.

"They have the best burgers in Hope Valley," Birdie added.

Birdie and Sasha seemed excited, and Sully didn't want to ruin their fun. She told herself it was only lunch and said, "Sure."

"I'm good with that, too, but lunch is on me," Jordan offered.

"It's okay. You don't have to pay for me. Callahan gave me money."

"That was really sweet of him," Jordan said. "And I know I don't have to, but I'd like to treat my sister to lunch. Is that too much to ask?"

Sully thought of how many times she'd said she wanted to do something herself these last couple of weeks and understood where Jordan was coming from. "*Okay. Thanks.*"

"See? That wasn't so hard." Jordan hugged her and turned to Sasha and Birdie. "You're so good to Sully, treating you to lunch is the least I can do."

"Hey, you had my vote at *Lunch is on me.*" Birdie grinned.

Sasha rolled her eyes. "We love Sully, and you can pay for lunch, but next time it's our treat."

As they headed into the parking lot, Sully thumbed out a text to Callahan. *I did it!* She attached one of the *after* pictures of just herself. *We're going to the Roadhouse for lunch.* As she climbed into Sasha's truck, she thought about telling him she was nervous about going to the bar, but he probably had his hands full with the rescue, and she didn't want to add to his burden. Instead, she typed, *How did the rescue go? Are the horses okay?* She added a pink heart emoji and sent it off.

Chapter Twenty-Seven

"IF ONLY ALL rescues were this lucky," Cowboy said as he, Hyde, and Kenny led two chestnut mares and an older palomino mare out to one of the empty pastures. It had been a long morning. He and Tiny had driven two hours to pick up four horses whose owner had passed away two days ago. The neighbor who had called it in had met them there and had given them the rundown about how much the owner had loved his horses. Three of the horses were fine, but one of the mares had a bowed tendon. Doc was with her now.

"Wouldn't that be something?" Hyde shook his head. "Too bad there are so many assholes out there."

"I know these horses are lucky because they were well cared for, but I still don't get it," Kenny said. "You said the guy who owned them was eighty-five. If you're that old, wouldn't you make arrangements for your horses in case something happened to you?"

"Nobody likes to think about dying." Cowboy opened the gate to the pasture.

"I guess that makes sense, but the horses pay the price, and that ain't right." Kenny petted the palomino as he led her into the pasture. "That injured horse would probably be fine if he'd made arrangements for us to come get them the day he died."

"Two days isn't ideal, but it's better than a lot of situations," Cowboy said. "At least they didn't land in the wrong hands." *Like Sully had.* Shoving that thought down deep, he took the lead off the horse. "But you're safe now, huh, Spirit?"

"Do you think they miss their owner?" Kenny asked as he led the horse through the gate.

"They were well cared for, so I'd imagine they do," Cowboy said.

As Kenny took the lead off his horse, he asked, "Will they get depressed?"

"Wouldn't you? Horses are sensitive, like people." Hyde freed his mare. "It'll take a few days for them to settle in, but at least they have each other."

"You know horses are a lot like humans," Cowboy said. "They'll grieve more than the absence of their owner. They'll mourn the loss of the comforts he gave them. These horses were well loved. They'll miss his touch, his voice, everything." He thought of Sully at four years old, scared and crying for her parents and being punished for it. *Can you just hold me?* If she went back to Maryland with Jordan, who would hold her when she felt scared or lonely? Would she ask Jordan to do it? Who would know by looking into her eyes that she needed someone to hold her hand or to distract her from her thoughts? His throat constricted.

"But we'll help them as best we can," Hyde said as they walked out of the pasture. "That's why we're pasturing them, trying to keep to their normal routine. They'll be groomed daily, to comfort them, and we'll watch them for signs of anxiety."

Cowboy locked the gate and leaned on the fence, watching the horses for a few minutes before they headed back to the barn. Kenny's cell phone chimed as they crossed the field. He pulled it out to check the text, and Hyde peered over his shoulder.

Kenny covered his phone. "Dude. Back off."

"What's up with that?" Cowboy asked sternly.

"He's got pretty girls sending him pictures," Hyde answered.

"From the neck up, I hope," Cowboy said.

Kenny looked away, a little embarrassed.

"Neck-down pics are the best." Hyde smirked.

Cowboy scowled at him. "Kenny, what'd I tell you about respecting girls?"

"Hey, I didn't ask for the pictures," Kenny insisted.

"But you gave them your number, didn't you?" Cowboy asked.

Kenny shrugged. *"So?"*

"Don't play innocent with me. We both know you didn't want to *study* with them. What does Mariah think about your extracurricular texting?" Mariah was a close friend of Kenny's. Cowboy wasn't sure if she was Kenny's girlfriend, but he knew she wanted to be.

"They're just pictures," Kenny said. "It's not like I'm messing around with them. Besides, Mariah isn't my girlfriend. We just hang out."

Cowboy shook his head. "Listen, it's your life, and at the end of the day, you're the one who has to look in the mirror and be okay with the person looking back at you. Do you feel good about getting those pictures?"

Kenny laughed. "Heck yeah, they make me feel *good*."

"Probably several times a night." Hyde chuckled.

Cowboy glowered at Hyde and shifted a serious stare to Kenny. "If you're hiding those pictures from Mariah, then it's time to cut her loose, girlfriend or not, because that girl is crazy about you, and she doesn't deserve to get hurt."

Kenny swallowed hard.

"He's got a point, kid," Hyde said. "I'm all for having fun, but if some guy was sending Mariah dick pics, how would you feel?"

"I dunno," Kenny mumbled as they neared the barn.

Cowboy blew out a breath. "Listen, buddy. I get that it feels good to be wanted. But keep in mind that there are very few things in life you can control. How you treat others is at the top of that list, and that feeds into everything else, including your self-respect and reputation. You worked hard to get where you are. I suggest you choose wisely."

"Yeah, I get it," Kenny relented, shoulders slumped.

They headed into the barn and found Dare talking with Doc by the injured mare's stall.

"How's she doing?" Cowboy asked.

"I bandaged her up and gave her a painkiller," Doc said. "It's going to take some time, but she should be fine."

"Glad to hear it." Cowboy's phone vibrated in his pocket. He pulled it out, and when he opened Sully's text, a picture popped up with her new haircut, knocking the air from his lungs. As he processed his beautiful girl's new look, he read the accompanying message, and the thought of her at the Roadhouse made his skin crawl. Despite how far she'd come, she'd still been raped by that drunk fucker every Thursday night, and he had a feeling that ugliness would come back to haunt her the minute she stepped into a bar.

"What's wrong with you?" Hyde glanced over his shoulder at his phone. "Holy shit. Is that Sully?"

Cowboy narrowed his eyes. "Keep your dick in your pants."

"Hey, why is it okay for you to get nude pics if I can't?" Kenny complained.

Dare gave Kenny a stern look. "You're getting nudes? You and I need to have a talk."

"Cowboy already lectured me. You should talk to *him*. He's a hypocrite." Kenny eyed Cowboy.

"Christ, Kenny, don't assume shit. She's *not* nude." Cowboy showed him the phone. "She got a haircut."

"Whoa. She was too hot for you before. Now she's way too hot for you." Kenny laughed.

"I've got him," Hyde said, and grabbed Kenny by the collar, dragging him away. "Let's go, loose lips. You've got chores to do."

"Let me see that." Dare snagged Cowboy's phone. "Damn, man. She looks incredible. Check 'er out, Doc." He turned the phone so Doc could see it.

"I'm afraid Kenny's right. She's jumped out of your league, bro," Doc teased.

"Shut the fuck up." Cowboy grabbed his phone from Dare. "The girls are taking her to the Roadhouse for lunch. I'm heading over to surprise her."

"I think you mean to make sure no other guys hit on her," Doc said.

Cowboy's jaw clenched at the idea of anyone making Sully uncomfortable. "That's just a bonus. You want to come?"

"Nah. I've got shit to do around here," Doc said.

"I'm in." Dare clapped Cowboy on the back. "Billie gets off soon, and you know how much she likes me messing with her while she's at work."

"Yeah," Cowboy said on their way out of the barn. "About as much as she likes hemorrhoids."

EVEN WITH THE bolstered confidence of a new haircut and a cute outfit, Sully felt like a fish out of water at the rustic bar. It was a nice enough place, not run-down or seedy like she imagined Nigel's to be, but she still felt like people were staring at her. A group of men had called out greetings to Sasha and Birdie when they arrived, and Sasha had explained that they were Dark Knights. Sully knew those men were aware of her real identity, which didn't help her nerves, but there was another table of guys who kept looking over, and a few people by the bar were, too. Could they tell she was Casey Lawler, or was she being paranoid?

She peeked over her menu at Jordan chatting with Sasha and Birdie as they looked at their menus, and at Billie, serving the table of twentysomething guys who kept looking over. Jordan, Sasha, Birdie, and Billie were so comfortable there. She felt a pang of jealousy. Colleen wanted her to gain new experiences, but Sully had to wonder if she'd feel like this with every new outing. If so, she needed to grow thicker skin. But she hadn't felt that way when she was in town with Callahan. *If only you were here now.*

"Sully, do you know what you're going to order?" Jordan asked.

"I don't know. There's a lot to choose from." She'd been excited to choose her lunch, but it wasn't as easy as she'd imagined. They made burgers five different ways, and there were three kinds of salads and a handful of other things on the menu. Everything was so expensive, too. Fifteen dollars for a burger and fries? She could make eight or ten burgers for that. "What are you guys getting?"

"I'm not sure yet either," Jordan said.

"I'm getting the Mustang Burger with all the fixings and fries," Birdie said.

"Buffalo chicken salad all the way." Sasha tucked her hair behind her ear as she set her menu down. "I get it every time I come here."

"That looks good," Jordan said. "I think I'll get it with grilled chicken instead of fried."

"Those sound good, but I'm still not sure." Sully scanned the menu again.

"What are you in the mood for?" Birdie asked.

"I don't know. I've never had so much to choose from. This is my first time at a restaurant."

Birdie's eyes widened with surprise, but it quickly morphed into compassion. "I didn't think of that."

"If I'd known it was your first time, I would have suggested someplace lower key," Sasha said.

"It's okay. I have to get used to it sometime," Sully said, not wanting her past to become the focus of the conversation. "What are clucker claws?"

"They're fried chicken strips. Most places call them chicken fingers," Birdie explained. "They have funky names for everything here." She put her menu down between them and went through each item with Sully.

Billie stopped by their table just as Birdie finished giving her the rundown. Billie had complimented Sully's haircut so exuberantly when she'd brought menus and glasses of water to their table, Sully had blushed a red streak. Now Billie was eyeing her with amusement in her eyes. "That table of guys over there want to know who the new hottie in town is."

"I think they meant Jordan," Sully said skeptically.

"Jordan's wearing a diamond big enough to see from space," Billie said. "They were asking about the cute one in the dress, and from the looks you've been getting from other customers, I'd say they're not the only ones scoping you out."

She was relieved they hadn't made the Casey Lawler connection, but before she could process their interest, Callahan and Dare strode into the bar. Callahan's eyes locked on her, and her pulse quickened, relief plowing through her, sending those ever-present butterflies into a flurry as his powerful legs ate up the distance between them.

Billie nudged her. "Did Cowboy plant a wire on you, or what?"

No. He just knows when I need him.

Callahan grabbed a chair from a nearby table and plunked it down beside her. "Hey, darlin'." He kissed her, his gaze sweeping over her face, appreciation glowing in his eyes. "I didn't think it was possible for you to look even more gorgeous, but *damn*, sweetheart."

"I'm glad you like it." She reached for his hand, holding tight, unable to believe he was really there. "What are you doing here?"

"You can't send me a picture of the most beautiful woman in Hope Valley and expect me to stay away." He touched the ends of her hair. "I don't want to embarrass you, but you could light this place on fire."

Her cheeks burned as Jordan and the girls gave her approving looks.

Callahan flashed an arrogant grin in the direction of the guys who had asked Billie about her and lowered his voice so only Sully and the friends at their table could hear him as he said, "Eat your heart out, fellas. She's with me." The girls laughed, and he leaned closer, whispering in Sully's ear, "I know it's your first time in a bar. I just wanted to be here in case you were uncomfortable. But if you want to be alone with the girls, say the word."

She was already blushing from his compliments, and now her heart felt like it was trying to climb out of her chest to get to him. "I'm glad you're here. Please stay."

He squeezed her hand, giving a single nod.

Dare slid his arm around Billie's waist. "How about some sugar, sweet thing?"

"This is supposed to be girl time." Birdie scowled at her brothers. "You guys can't be here."

"Sure we can." Callahan released Sully's hand to put his arm around her shoulder. "Sully's my girl, and this is a big day for her. I didn't want to miss it."

"Aw, I love that," Jordan said.

"Okay, I can *almost* buy that." Birdie looked at Dare expectantly. "What's your excuse?"

Dare smirked. "My girl was missing me. I felt it in my bones."

"There aren't any bones where you're feeling it," Billie said with love in her eyes. "Bobbie should be here soon, and then I can get off."

"I think you mean, *we* can get off." Dare waggled his brows.

"I did *not* need to hear that," Sasha said.

"Seriously," Birdie agreed. "Would you mind not rubbing

your lovefest in our single faces?"

The guys laughed, and Sully found herself laughing, too, because being with Callahan made everything easier.

"Hey, Jordan, you should ask Jax to come hang out with us," Callahan suggested.

Jordan glanced at Sasha and Birdie. "I don't need to add more guys to the mix."

"No, he's right," Sasha encouraged her. "Jax should be here with you and Sully."

Jordan looked at Birdie. "Are you okay with that?"

"Of course," Birdie said jovially. "The more the merrier. I just like giving my brothers a hard time. Jax doesn't happen to have any cute single friends hanging around, does he?"

"I think most of his cousins around here are married, but he has single friends back home," Jordan said.

"Time to plan a trip to see Cousin Dixie in Maryland," Birdie said.

"No, it's not," Callahan and Dare said in unison.

"I have to get back to work," Billie said. "So how about you order lunch, and then you and your bodyguards can argue about your hot-girl travels?"

They ordered lunch, and now that Sully's nerves were settling, she went with a grilled clucker sandwich and fries, which ended up being delicious. Jax showed up, and the conversation was light and fun. As they finished eating, Hyde, Ezra, and Doc came into the bar with a pretty blonde.

"Look who we found in the parking lot," Hyde said, draping an arm around the blonde's shoulders.

"As if I don't work here," the blonde said, but she looked quite comfortable beneath his arm.

"Sully, this is Bobbie Mancini, Billie's younger sister. Bobbie, this is Sully and her older sister, Jordan, and Jordan's fiancé, Jax," Sasha said. "Sully is staying at the ranch, and Jordan and Jax are visiting from Maryland."

Bobbie gave a little wave. "Hi. Nice to meet you all."

"You too," Sully, Jordan, and Jax said.

"I have to get to work so Billie can clock out, but I'll catch up with you guys as soon as I get a minute." Bobbie ducked out from beneath Hyde's arm, heading for the bar, but Hyde caught her hand.

"Don't go too far, sweetheart. We're going to need a couple of pitchers." Hyde winked.

"I will go where I please and bring the pitchers when I can." Bobbie yanked her hand free, but Sully swore she saw a spark of flirtation in her smirk.

Dare and Callahan rose to their feet, and there was a cacophony of commotion as they pushed another table up to theirs and the guys grabbed extra chairs.

"Hey, Doc, I'm glad you decided to come," Callahan said.

"You try telling those guys no." Doc nodded at Sully as he sat on her other side. "Your haircut looks great."

"Thank you." She touched the ends of it.

"More like smokin'," Hyde said, making her blush as he pulled up a chair between Sasha and Birdie.

Ezra sat between Jordan and Sasha and said, "Yeah, you look fantastic, Sully. It's good to see you out and about."

"Thanks. Where's Gus?" Sully asked.

"He's with his mother." Ezra didn't sound happy about it, and he and Sasha exchanged a look Sully couldn't read.

"Let's get this party started," Hyde exclaimed, and then everyone spoke at once.

An hour later, Dare and Billie were dancing and kissing,

Hyde and Doc were chatting with a blonde by the bar, and everyone else was cheering on Birdie as she rode the mechanical bull. "She's fearless!" Sully said over the music and the cheers.

Callahan was standing behind her with his arms around her middle, his hard body pressed to her back. He kissed her cheek and said, "So are you, darlin'."

"She must be strong. Doesn't it take a lot of strength to hold on?" Jax asked, motioning to Birdie as she rode with one hand over her head.

"Birdie's little, but she's fierce. Nobody rides better than her, except maybe your brother Zev," Callahan said. "The first time we met him, he rode the hell out of that thing and did all sorts of tricks. He impressed the hell out of all of us."

"I heard the stories," Jax said. "You ought to get my brother Nick up there. He's a freestyle horse trainer and showman, and he's twice the rider Zev is."

"Maybe we'll get him out this way one day. What about you? Want to try it?" Callahan asked.

"Hell no." Jax laughed.

Sully looked up at Callahan. "Do you want to do it?"

He put his mouth beside her ear, whispering, "The only thing I want to do is you, sweetheart." He held her gaze with a devilish glimmer in his eyes.

Her body heated as applause and whistles erupted around them, and the mechanical bull slowed to a stop.

"Way to go, sis!" Sasha cheered.

"That was wild," Jordan said.

Birdie jumped down and pointed at Sully. "Your turn!"

"Oh *no*." Sully waved her hands. "No way."

"Jordan?" Birdie offered.

"I'd fall off before I even got on," Jordan said, making everyone laugh.

"Okay, *fine*." Birdie strutted out of the riding ring. "Then let's dance. Come on, girls!"

Sully was nervously excited. "I've never danced to this kind of music. I want to, but I might be terrible at it."

"You couldn't be terrible at anything, and it's one more thing to cross off your list." Callahan winked and leaned down to kiss her. "Go have fun, darlin'."

"I'm not a great dancer, so stick with me." Jordan took her hand, dragging her toward the dance floor behind Sasha and Birdie.

Birdie twirled onto the dance floor and continued twirling around Billie and Dare, who were dirty dancing.

"Get a room," Sasha said.

"Sounds good to me," Dare called out, and Billie laughed.

"*Boy*, they can really dance," Sully said.

"If they dance like that fully dressed, imagine..." Jordan said for Sully's ears only, and they both giggled.

They joined Birdie and Sasha, and Sully did her best to mimic their moves and keep up. Other than the night when she'd danced with Callahan at the lake, she'd never danced with anyone.

"Sully, you're a good dancer," Sasha said.

"Have you really never danced before?" Jordan asked.

"Not like this. I used to dance at the compound while I cooked, but I didn't have any music, so I made up tunes in my head. I'm just copying your moves."

"That's how you learn," Birdie said. "But you should copy mine. I'm a better dancer than Sasha."

Sasha rolled her eyes, and they danced to a few songs. Sully felt Callahan watching her, but she wasn't embarrassed. She knew in her heart that it didn't matter if she was a good or bad dancer, because in his eyes, she was perfect just the way she was, and that was *everything*.

Birdie started doing silly dances, and Sully and the girls joined in, laughing and egging each other on. Dare and Billie got in on the fun. Sully looked around for Callahan and saw him feeding the jukebox. When the song changed, Birdie and Sasha squealed, and Callahan swept an arm around Sully's waist. "Time to learn to line dance, darlin'. Follow my steps. I think you'll like it."

"I don't know how to line dance either," Jordan said.

"I've got you, babe," Jax said as he joined them. "I can't ride a bull, but I can line dance with the best of them." He pulled Jordan into a kiss.

Doc, Hyde, and the woman they were chatting with at the bar hurried over, as did a few other patrons, lining up in three rows. Sully followed Callahan's lead to learn the steps. She and Jordan stumbled a few times, but they laughed with each other, and the others cheered them on, calling out helpful hints. After a few more songs, they were keeping up with the others and sharing gleeful glances. Sully might not remember her past, but this was a day she'd never forget.

When "My Girl" came on, Callahan drew her into his arms, as the others either coupled off to dance or headed off the dance floor. She looked up at him, her heart melting. "This song."

He gazed into her eyes. "I knew you'd want to hear it, and what better place than in my arms?"

She got choked up.

He brushed a kiss to her lips. "Look at you in that dress, with that sexy new haircut. You've never been more beautiful, but I know it's not about that. How does it feel?"

"My haircut?"

"Everything, baby. The haircut, spending the day with Jordan and everyone else." He held her tighter. "Being out with *me*, like this."

She wanted to say so many things, but as she listened to the words of the song talking about falling in love with a cowboy and feeling wild horses in her chest, she caught sight of Jordan dancing with Jax. Jordan's eyes met hers, and a new smile shone in them, illuminating a new connection all their own, bringing Callahan's words back to her. *Being with Jordan will add something to your life that no one else can ever give you.* She struggled against the ache in her chest, wanting to hang on to both of them with everything she had. As she looked up at the extraordinary man who showed her what it felt like to love and be unconditionally loved and cherished every minute of every day and patiently helped her learn how to cherish him right back, it was all she could do to say, "Like I never want it to end."

Chapter Twenty-Eight

WHEN THEY PULLED into the ranch, Tiny and Wynnie were on their way out on Tiny's motorcycle. Tiny pulled up alongside the truck and cut his engine. Sully noticed his hand on Wynnie's leg before they climbed off and looked at her and Callahan's joined hands, resting on his leg in the cab of the truck. Wynnie reached for Tiny's hand as they came to Callahan's window, reminding Sully of how much that gesture had stood out to her the night she'd met them. She'd been so scared that night, worried they weren't going to be as honest and good as the Finches had claimed, and they'd proven to be so much more than she could have ever hoped for.

Just like Callahan.

Tiny's beard lifted with his grin. "You look awfully pretty, darlin'."

Wynnie's eyes lit up. "You got your hair cut! It looks beautiful."

"Thank you." She reached up and touched the ends of her hair, still not used to how light it felt.

"A fresh new look for a fresh new start," Wynnie added.

Callahan's jaw tightened, and he squeezed her hand. "She

turned all the heads at the Roadhouse, and Sully even learned to line dance."

"The Roadhouse, really?" Wynnie said with surprise. "How'd you like it?"

"It was fun. A little nerve-racking at first, but then Callahan showed up, and, well, he makes everything easier."

"Thanks, baby." He pressed a kiss to her temple.

"Remind you of anyone, Wyn?" Tiny slung his arm around her and kissed the side of her head, earning a sweet smile and a nod from Wynnie. "Hey, before I forget, Simone was looking for Sully earlier."

"A'right. Thanks. Where are you headed?" Callahan asked.

"I'm taking my old lady out for a ride," Tiny said.

"We won't be too long," Wynnie said. "Sully, is Jordan still leaving tomorrow?"

"Yes." Her throat thickened.

"Have you made a decision about going with her?" Wynnie asked.

"I'm still deciding."

The empathy in Wynnie's eyes was palpable. "I know it's not an easy decision, but I'm sure you'll make the right one for yourself."

I wish I was sure of it.

"I don't envy you right now," Tiny said. "It can't be easy starting over, but family is important, and no matter what you decide, you'll always have a place in ours, whether you're on the ranch, in Maryland, or anywhere else."

Sully felt like she might cry and tried her hardest not to. "Thank you."

As they went their separate ways, she and Callahan drove down to her cabin. On the way inside, Callahan motioned to something on the porch table. "What's that?"

She picked it up. "It's a two-for-one coupon for the day spa your sisters go to and a note from Simone." She read the note aloud. "*I figured this coupon was a sign that we should join Sasha and Birdie for a spa day. I remember how hard it was to make ends meet when I was starting over after I got clean, so yours can be free. Let me know when you want to go, and we can coordinate with Sasha and Birdie.*" Tears welled in her eyes.

Callahan drew her into his arms. "What's the matter, darlin'? Didn't you have a good time with Simone the other night?"

"I had a great time with her," she choked out. "But I've never had friends like Simone or your sisters before." She clung to him, and the emotions she'd been holding back came rushing out with her tears. "All I wanted was to be *free*. I never thought I'd find *you*, much less *two* families—" Sobs drowned out her voice.

COWBOY HELD HER tighter, doing all he could to hold himself together. "It's okay, darlin'."

"No, it's *not*," she said between sobs. "Nothing is okay. I have to make the hardest decision of my life." She looked up at him with red-rimmed eyes. "I don't want to leave you, and I don't want to hurt Jordan. She was alone for all that time, too, and everyone told her I was probably dead." She buried her face in his chest, sobbing, her voice muffled. "How can I take myself away from her again?"

He felt like someone was driving an ax into his chest. "You

can't. You need to go with her tomorrow and continue building that relationship."

"*No. I can't* leave you."

Her voice cracked, and *fuck* that hurt. But this wasn't about him. Fighting against emotions bigger than himself, he gritted out, "Baby, look at me."

She shook her head.

He forced himself to lift her chin, so she had to look at him and hear what he had to say. The sadness in her eyes wound around him like a coat of nails, her every tear driving them deeper into him. "You're not leaving me, darlin'. You're finding another part of yourself. You're doing the right thing."

She shook her head violently, tears flooding down her cheeks.

"You *have* to do this, baby. You have to go with her, or you'll always wonder if you did the right thing."

She was shaking, her lower lip trembling. "But I *love* you."

Fighting tears, he held in his truth and did the right thing. "No, you don't, baby. You haven't experienced enough of life to know what true love is yet."

Her jaw dropped as heart-wrenching sobs racked her entire body. "You're *wrong*."

He hauled her into his arms, looking up at the sky as tears stung his fucking eyes. "I'm sorry, darlin'. I shouldn't have let us get this far."

She fisted her hands in the back of his shirt, and "*No, Callahan*" came out thin and so shaky, gutting him anew.

"I'm sorry. I'm so fucking sorry."

Chapter Twenty-Nine

JAX PICKED UP Sully's duffel bag, and Jordan grabbed the art box Callahan had given her. "Is this everything?" Jordan asked.

She wanted to say no. The smiles Callahan hoarded from others and shared so freely with her were hers, too. Her life was bigger than that stupid bag. It was watching the sun kiss the horizon on its way up or down with Callahan, dancing in the moonlight by the lake, and working with the horses. Did they have an extra bag big enough to fit all that? How about their late-night walks, intimate conversations, and that comfortable silence that had become so special to her? Her life was noisy mealtimes and silly games. It was hoping the girls would invite her to spend Tuesday night with them and knowing she would spend her nights in Callahan's loving arms.

And she was leaving it all behind.

"Yeah," Sully said, trying not to sound sullen, but how could she not when her heart had been shattered into a million dismal pieces?

"What about the things on the table?" Jax motioned to the Redemption Ranch information packet and the cell phone.

"That's theirs."

"Okay. We'll put this stuff in the car," Jax said.

She tried to ignore the dull ache in her bones as they walked out of the cabin, and she took another look around. *This was temporary*, she reminded herself, just as she'd done all night after calling Jordan to let her know she was going with them this morning and texting Colleen to thank her for everything. Hell, she'd been up all night reminding herself and trying to figure out why the man who had done nothing but encourage her to *feel* and *speak* and be herself had shut her down when she'd done just that.

His family was outside by Jax and Jordan's rental car, waiting to say goodbye, but the last time she'd checked, Callahan wasn't there. She was starting to wonder if he wasn't going to say goodbye. She knew in her heart how he felt about her, but after the way he'd dismissed her feelings and walked away so easily—*You're doing the right thing, darlin'. I'll get out of your hair and let you pack*—she had to wonder if she was wrong.

She swallowed hard, refusing to be weak and give in to her emotions, but it was so much harder now that she no longer had those steel walls around her heart. *Now that I know what it feels like to be loved by Callahan.*

Trying to outrun the harrowing emotions, she went into the bedroom to get the letter she'd written him. As she snagged the envelope from the dresser, she heard someone come into the cabin. Hope soared inside her, and she ran out of the bedroom. "*Calla*—" Her hopes deflated at the sight of her sister, and that brought a wave of guilt.

"It's only me," Jordan said apologetically. "I didn't see him out there yet. Did you guys have a fight or something?"

"No." She was still in a state of shock, unsure of *what* had happened.

"Are you okay?"

Sully nodded. "Fine." She took one last look around, buying time, hoping Callahan would show up, and was hit with a memory of when she'd first walked into the cabin. She hadn't been able to place the foreign scent of it. Now she knew it was the scent of safety.

Jordan went to her. "You don't look fine. Are you sure you want to go with us?"

"Yes. You've lost enough time with me. Let's just go. I'll be fine." Before she could think too hard about it, she lifted her chin and walked out the door—and her heart took another hit. Callahan still wasn't there, but Colleen and Simone were.

"Are you all set, sweetheart?" Colleen asked.

No. Sully nodded. "I can't believe you came to say goodbye. Thank you for everything."

"It was my pleasure." Colleen hugged her. "I'm so proud of you."

As she stepped out of Colleen's embrace, Wynnie drew her into her arms. "We're all proud of you, honey, and we're going to miss you."

Sully struggled against tears. "I'm going to miss you, too."

"Come back and see us, ya hear?" Tiny said.

How could she ever come back to the place where she'd found—and lost—her one true love? She kept that to herself as she hugged him. "Thank you for keeping me safe."

"Our pleasure, darlin'," Tiny said. "I have something for you."

He handed her a gold business card that read MEMBER OF THE REDEMPTION RANCH FAMILY on the front and IF LOST, PLEASE RETURN TO along with the address and phone number of the ranch on the back. Tears spilled from her eyes.

"No crying," Sasha said, pulling her into a hug.

"I didn't get to say goodbye to"—*Callahan and*—"Beauty," Sully said frantically. Why was no one mentioning him? Had he told them not to?

"We'll say goodbye for you." Birdie put her arms around both of them.

"I'll give her extra love, too," Simone said, joining in the group hug.

"So will Dare and I," Billie promised.

"Thank you," Sully choked out as she withdrew from their arms.

"I'll text you updates about the horses," Sasha said.

"I don't have a phone."

"We'll get you one," Jordan said, her own voice shaky.

Sully looked at Dare and Doc, wondering if Callahan had said anything to them about last night. But she wouldn't allow herself to ask.

"Come back so I can teach you how to ride on the handle-bars of your bicycle," Dare said, and he hugged her. For some stupid reason that made her cry harder.

Doc motioned for her to step into his open arms, embracing her warmly, and whispered, "He's on his way up."

Her pulse quickened, and she wiped her eyes, looking at Doc incredulously. He motioned over her shoulder. She turned, and her heart leapt into her throat. Callahan was coming down the road on Thunder, holding Beauty's lead. He lifted his chin and smiled, but it didn't reach his eyes.

He dismounted, handing Doc Thunder's reins, and led Beauty over to Sully. "Hey, darlin'. I figured you'd want to say goodbye to your girl."

It took everything she had to hold back her tears. She wanted to tell him how wrong he was last night and how much she missed him already, but he looked like he hadn't slept either, and she didn't know how to bridge the awkward gap between them. So she shoved the envelope and card into her back pocket and gave Beauty all the love she couldn't give to him.

The horse put her head on Sully's shoulder, and she hugged her. "I love you," she whispered. "I'm going to miss you every day, but I know you'll continue to thrive. You're going to have a beautiful life." No sooner had the words left her lips than she remembered Carol having said the same thing to her. At the time, she hadn't been able to imagine such a thing, much less hope for it. But now she knew what a beautiful life looked and felt like. She couldn't fathom the horse hurting the way she did and silently hoped Beauty would have a blessed life rather than a beautiful one, because now she knew how beautiful things could break her heart.

She stepped away from the horse and looked up at Callahan, trying to keep a stiff upper lip. "Thank you. I needed that."

He nodded, his jaw tight, those loving eyes haunted by something dark and silent and lonely, breaking her heart anew. "I have something for you." He unhooked the chain from his belt loop, pulled his grandfather's compass from his pocket, and placed it in her hand. "So you can always find your way home."

Stunned, she wondered if a heart could feel full and like it was breaking at the same time. "I can't take this," she said shakily, trying to hold back the tears welling in her eyes. "It was your grandfather's."

Callahan didn't say a word. He curled her fingers around it and opened his arms. She was drawn into them like metal to magnet. Choking back tears, she inhaled deeply, breathing him in for what she knew would be the last time.

He held her tighter, whispering, "You could be a million miles away, darlin', and my heart will still belong to you."

A rush of hot tears flooded her eyes, and she squeezed them shut, trying to pull herself together before stepping out of his embrace. But she felt like shattered glass held in place by his strong frame and feared the moment he let go, she'd fall apart. She never thought she'd want to purposely recall the horrors she'd been through, but at that moment she had no choice. She forced herself to remember the dank smell of the metal box, the searing pain of the brand, and the vileness of being in Rebel Joe's bed. It was *almost* enough to shift those walls back into place, but they refused to go all the way up, leaving room for Callahan to sneak in. At least it fortified her enough to step back and hand him the envelope.

Those haunted eyes bored into her. "What's this?"

"A goodbye," she managed.

He gave a single curt nod, the muscles in his jaw bunching.

She imagined his fingers curled around the walls inside her, pushing them down, refusing to be locked out. But he wasn't fighting for her, and she quickly climbed into the car with Jax and Jordan, breathing so hard she feared she might pass out.

"I know this is hard," Jordan said. "But I think you're going to love Maryland. Our house is gorgeous, and we have a pool, and the property overlooks Jax's family's winery…"

As Jordan went on about what lay ahead, Jax started driving, and Sully had an agonizing ache, a dire *need* to turn around and see Callahan one last time. *Don'tlookdon'tlookdon'tlook.* Why didn't he fight for her? *You have to do this, baby…or you'll always wonder if you did the right thing…You're doing the right thing, darlin'…I'm so fucking sorry.*

She rocked in her seat, telling herself she was doing the right thing. She was with her sister, where she belonged. But the need to see him was too strong, and she turned around, watching him watch them drive away until tears blurred her vision and her tenuous grip on her control shattered, and she doubled over with sobs.

Chapter Thirty

COWBOY FELT LIKE his heart was being ripped from his chest as Sully drove away. His family was talking. To him, at him, or to each other, he wasn't sure, and he didn't care. Their voices were drowned out by the misery eating away at him. He looked down at the envelope—*A goodbye*—and tore it open, finding several of Sully's drawings. Most of which he'd never seen. The first was of him standing in the Finches' living room, looking at her sitting on the couch. He looked bigger than life, and she looked vulnerable and scared. Across the top of the paper she'd written, *The first time I saw you, I thought you were the most powerful and beautiful man I had ever seen. It feels funny to write that, but it's the truth, and that scared me on so many levels.*

His chest constricted as he looked at the next sketch, of him down on one knee in front of her, holding his hat against his chest, and read what she'd written. *The minute you spoke to me, I wasn't scared in the way I had always been. I was drawn to you, connected in a way I didn't understand.*

He flipped to the next drawing, his insides shaking, and took in the image of the two of them sitting in the field by the pasture, looking up at the stars. Across the bottom of the page she'd written, *Once I got to know you, I realized your power didn't come from all those muscles, and your true beauty couldn't be seen with eyes alone.*

He turned to the next drawing, in which he was sleeping on her porch, and she was peeking out the window from behind a curtain, above which she'd written, *Your power is in the way you make everyone feel safe, and your beauty comes from the things you say and do. Thank you for sharing that with me, but you have one tragic flaw, and that's in your thinking.*

He couldn't turn the page fast enough and was met with a drawing of them dancing in the moonlight with their feet in the lake. *You said I don't know what love is because I haven't experienced enough of life, but you're wrong. I lived in a dark world for twenty years, and that felt like a lifetime to me. My heart might not be as experienced as yours, and it was definitely locked down tight, but you were right that all the love my parents showed me still lived inside me.*

Turning to the next drawing, he found the two of them lying on the blankets by the bonfire on his deck near the creek. He was on his back, one arm behind his head, gazing at her with so much love, it leapt off the page. She was lying beside him, her hand on his chest, her loving eyes gazing back at him with the same curiosity he'd seen that night. His fucking heart split open as he read her note. *I realize now that your heart held the key to opening mine. Thank you for showing me what it feels like to love and be loved.*

Tears burned his eyes as he flipped to the next drawing, of a heart with a jagged crack down the center. She'd drawn Jordan on one side and him on the other. And within that jagged crack, Sully was sitting with her knees pulled up to her chest, her cheek resting on her knees, and sad blue eyes staring back at him. Her words cut him to his core. *I may not know if I'm Casey or Sully, but in my heart, I will always be your darlin'.*

Cowboy's hands shook. He couldn't breathe as he flipped to the last page and saw her list, with most of the items crossed off, and beside each one she'd written the date they'd done it and what she thought of it. Beside ~~Be kissed like Josie Geller~~, she'd written, *Callahan blew that kiss away* and had drawn a heart, gutting Cowboy anew. On the bottom of the list was ~~Fall in love~~. Beside it she'd written, *This wasn't on my list, but since it's the best thing that has ever happened to me, it probably should've been.*

"Dude, you okay?" Dare asked. "You look like you're going to kill someone."

He was devastated and too fucking pissed at himself to speak. He'd thought he was doing the right thing, and he'd hurt the one person he'd kill to protect. He shoved the drawings back into the envelope and stuffed them in his pocket.

"You did the right thing, honey," his mother said.

"No, I fucking didn't. But I'm about to." He climbed onto Thunder's back, squeezed his heels, and bit out, *"Hya!"* Thunder bolted across the lawn. Cowboy balanced with his knees as they raced up the hill. Jax's car was nowhere in sight. He pushed Thunder to go faster—*"Hya!"*—and as they crested the hill, he saw the taillights at the entrance of the ranch. His heart hammered as the horse flew at breakneck speed toward the car, and he realized it was stopped and the back door was wide open. It took his brain a second to find Sully running down the road.

"Hya!" He leaned forward as Thunder galloped toward her. Sully saw them and ran across the grass. She was shouting, but

he couldn't hear past the blood rushing through his ears. He signaled for Thunder to slow down, but he was too anxious to wait, so he jumped off, stumbled, found his footing, and sprinted to Sully.

"You lied to me so I would leave!" she shouted. She was shaking, her nose was pink, her eyes were red, and her face was wet with tears.

He pulled her into his arms. "I'm sorry, baby. I love you so damn much. I thought I was doing the right thing for you and Jordan."

"Well, you were *wrong*," she snapped. "I couldn't breathe when we drove away. I thought I was having a heart attack. *You're* my home, Callahan. *You*, not Maryland, not Colorado. *You*."

Relief swamped him. "I'm a fucking idiot. I'm so sorry, baby. I'll never do anything that stupid again. I'll go to Maryland with you and open a ranch there, so you can be with Jordan, and work with the horses, and we'll find you a great therapist."

She shook her head vehemently, still shouting. "*No!* This is *my* decision, and I want to be *here*, with you and your family and all the people who have been helping me. With *these* horses and *these* pastures." She gulped in air and spoke in a softer, hopeful tone. "This is where you were always meant to be, and I think it's where I'm supposed to be, too."

Her tears drew his. "*God, baby.* I want that more than anything. But are you sure?" He searched her eyes as she nodded, and it was all right there, clear as day—her adamance, surety, and interminable *love*.

"*Yes.* You once told me that there was something in the way Sunshine looked at you, like she was supposed to be in your life, and that's how I feel when you look at me, and when I look at the ranch, I feel just as connected to it."

"Then we'll stay right here, and we'll go visit Jordan together as often as you'd like."

She nodded, tears streaming down her face and a sweet smile lifting her cheeks. "That's what I told her."

"You already told her?" He followed her gaze to Jax and Jordan, holding hands about twenty feet away from them. Jax was holding Thunder's reins. He hadn't even noticed they'd driven back down the road.

"We know all about falling hard and fast," Jordan called out through her tears. "I have my sister back, and I know she's safe. I want her to be happy, and she's happiest with you."

Cowboy's heart was so full, he had a hard time finding his voice, but when he gazed into Sully's beautiful blue eyes, his words came easily. "I guess wishes really do come true, darlin', because I'm happiest with you, too." He lowered his lips to hers in a kiss full of hope and love and everything in between.

Chapter Thirty-One

SULLY GAZED OUT the window at the falling snow. It had been coming down for the past two hours and had already blanketed the ranch with several inches. It was hard to believe that less than a month ago, it had been warm enough for her and Callahan to watch a movie on the lawn with the Scouts.

It was amazing how much had changed in the three months since she'd come to the ranch. She'd moved in with Callahan the day she'd decided to stay, and their home was already filled with pictures of the two of them, her family as well as his, and of Beauty, because she was family, too. Callahan had decided not to rehome her, and now she and Sully both had a home on the ranch with people who loved them. Callahan was just as wonderful now as he had been all along. He was so in love with Sully's drawings, he was always picking his favorites to frame and hang on their walls. She had thought she was comfortable and happy before making the decision to stay, but once she'd made it, a great weight had lifted off her shoulders, and she'd been able to settle in with a more permanent, contented sense of belonging without anything threatening to take her away from the man, and the life, she loved.

"*Sullivan Lawler*, stop daydreaming about Cowboy," Ansel teased, bringing her attention back to his infectious crooked grin on her new iPhone.

Her parents' insurance money had come in handy after all. She had legally changed her name, paying homage to her family without losing herself, and was able to hire an attorney to have the legal documents sealed, so she wouldn't have to worry about word getting out to the press. She'd tried to pay Callahan back for all he'd given her, and her generous cowboy had fought her tooth and nail. He'd eventually relented, only to use the money, and *more*, to buy her more gifts, such as her new iPhone, electronic drawing tools, and a laptop. As much as she disliked carrying a phone, FaceTime had become one of her favorite things. She texted and video chatted with Ansel and Jordan often. She loved the drawing tools and was hoping to start applying for illustration positions after the new year.

"I was watching the *snow*, not daydreaming. It's really piling up out there." Winter hadn't put a damper on her and Callahan's evening walks, stargazing, or watching sunsets and sunrises. They simply bundled up and snuggled closer. "Do you have snow?"

"It doesn't snow in California. I'll be eating Thanksgiving dinner in shorts, which is pretty cool." Gaia had divorced her husband after the cult was disbanded, and shortly after the sentencing had taken place, she'd moved Ansel and his sister out West to be closer to her family.

They were finding their way and getting the help they needed, as were the other girls and women from the compound. Sully had been one of dozens of victims to testify against Rebel Joe, whose real name was John Joseph Kilam. He was sentenced to one hundred and twenty years in prison for rape, sex trafficking, forced labor, and several other charges. Sully really *had* been the chosen one. She'd learned that he'd forced some of the other girls to service his henchmen, who had also received hefty sentences. That knowledge had added to Sully's guilt, but with Colleen's, Callahan's, and Jordan's help, she was learning how to deal with that.

"Not me. I'll be wearing *this*." She was in one of the meeting rooms in the main house, and she propped up her phone on the table and stepped back so he could see her gorgeous velvet minidress. It was a rich amber, with a cinched waist, decorative leather belt, and intricate embroidery around the neckline. "Jordan made it for me." Jordan had also sent her knit tights, and the outfit went perfectly with the boots Callahan had given her. "Isn't it spectacular?" She twirled.

Jordan and Jax hadn't left the day Sully was supposed to go home with them. They'd stayed for another week and had spent all their time with Sully and Callahan. They'd joined them for meals in the main house with the boisterous crew of Redemption Ranch and had gotten to know everyone, which thrilled Sully to no end. She and Jordan had a few sessions with Colleen together, which helped in ways they hadn't even known they'd needed. Jordan got to know the horses by helping Sully in the rehab barn, while Jax tried his hand at ranch chores with Callahan. But it hadn't been all work and no play. They'd gone on trail rides, played games in the recreation room, and hung out in the sweet small town of Hope Valley. If that wasn't the perfect name for her new hometown, she didn't know what was. They'd even gone to Birdie's chocolate shop, which heavenly, and in a fun group effort, Callahan, Jordan, and Jax had taught Sully how to drive. She was now the proud owner of a driver's license, a library card, and a GED certificate, all under a name she connected with, Sullivan Lawler.

"You look beautiful, but then again, you always do. Did your family make it to Colorado before the snow hit?" Ansel pushed his wavy brown hair away from his eyes, but it flopped right back down.

"Yes! Everyone's at our house with Callahan, but they should be here any minute."

"Where are you now? At the snack shack?"

She laughed at his latest name for the main house. He was always calling it something funky, like the *mingle mansion* or the *grub hub*. "Yes. I helped Dwight cook Thanksgiving dinner. He is phenomenal in the kitchen."

"Don't let Cowboy hear you say that." He snickered.

She rolled her eyes and heard a commotion down the hall. "I'd better go. It sounds like everyone's here. Tell your mom and sister I said happy Thanksgiving, and we'll catch up next week."

"I'll tell 'em. Same to your family, and tell Cowboy I'm coming to visit when it's not so freaking cold there, so he'd better be on his best behavior." He held up three fingers. "Love you, Sull."

She waved three fingers back at him. "Love you, too."

She ended the call and was admiring the lock screen picture of her and Callahan on her phone when he appeared in the doorway, big and broad and so deliciously sexy, the flutters he caused weren't restricted to her chest.

"There's my beautiful girl. What're you up to, darlin'?" His voice was low and seductive as he closed the distance between them and wrapped his strong arms around her.

"Missing you."

"Good answer." He brushed a kiss to her lips.

"I just got off the phone with Ansel, and I was looking at this picture of us." She showed him the picture they'd taken in Maryland when they'd visited Jordan and Jax last month.

"That was a great trip."

"It sure was. I'm glad we got to see everything together." She'd enjoyed seeing the town where she'd once lived, although it hadn't sparked a single memory, and Pleasant Hill, where Jax and Jordan lived, was perfect for them. They'd also gone to Peaceful Harbor and had taken a long walk on the beach, scratching one more thing off her list.

"Still think you made the right decision?"

"Well," she said with a teasing lilt to her voice, "their house *is* luxurious, and the pool and view of the winery are absolutely breathtaking." She felt his muscles tense up and couldn't continue the ruse. "But nothing compares to being loved by you in the home we've made together and the happiness we share, right here on Redemption Ranch."

"You had me going there for a minute." He nipped at her lower lip.

She giggled. "Don't be ridiculous. We could live in a tent, and I'd never want to leave your side. How about you? Still think you made the right decision asking me to move in?"

"Baby, I have never been more certain of anything in my life than I am of us." He lowered his lips to hers in a slow, sensual kiss.

"Found them!" Gus hollered, startling them apart.

"Hey, little man. What're you doing here?" Callahan scooped him up and reached for Sully's hand.

"My mom wasn't home, so we're having Thanksgiving here!" Gus said as they headed into the dining room, where everyone was gathering around the table.

Sully had learned how flighty Gus's mother was, and her heart broke for Gus, even though he didn't seem bothered by his mother's disappearance.

"There you are," Jordan said.

"They were kissing!" Gus tattled, and everyone laughed.

Callahan lifted the squirming giggler over his head. "Little man, you're giving away all our secrets."

"It's not a *secret*," Gus said between giggles. "Dare said you were smooching, and the first person to find you got an extra piece of pie for dessert! Now I *really* have something to be thankful for."

Laughter rang out around them. "Sugar! I get to eat with you!" Gus shouted, and wriggled out of Callahan's arms, running to Sasha.

"Lucky me!" Sasha hoisted him into her arms, and he hugged her tight.

"Daddy's eating with us, too," Gus said. "You better watch him! He loves to eat your pie. Remember last year?"

"I bet Sasha would *love* to have Ezra eat her *pie*," Birdie said.

All three of her brothers glowered at her, and Sully couldn't help but laugh.

"*Birdie*," Tiny warned.

"What?" Birdie feigned innocence. "It's Thanksgiving. We always have pie on Thanksgiving."

"She is really something," her aunt Sheila said with a chuckle.

"I *love* Birdie," Jordan said.

Callahan shook his head and drew Sully into his arms, his loving eyes holding her captive. "Want to revise your earlier statement about not regretting your decision to stay?"

Surrounded by both of their families and a number of

friends, she knew wild horses couldn't chase her away. "Not a chance, cowboy. This might be my first rodeo with these jokers, but it definitely won't be my last."

Epilogue

COWBOY SWAYED IN the moonlight, holding Sully in his arms, their bodies moving in perfect sync. Dozens of stars shined down on them as they danced beside the lake, their faint doubles following suit among the stars' reflections in the water. There was no music, just the thrum of their connection and the feel of their hearts beating against one another. But they didn't need music. Their love had a rhythm all its own.

It was their birthday, April seventeenth, seven months since Sully had come into Cowboy's life, and he'd fallen deeper in love with her with every new challenge they faced as they navigated the hills and valleys of her healing and their couple-dom. She and Jordan were closer than ever, and she continued to work with Colleen two days a week. In addition to her first passion—helping Sasha with the rehab horses—she'd found another love in illustrating and had created a nice niche for herself. She'd illustrated two children's books and was working on a third.

He ran his hand down her back, whispering in her ear, "Still want to sleep outside tonight?" That had become one of their many favorite things, along with late-night walks, sunrise lovemaking, massages, horseback rides, and wind therapy. Everything about Sully had been unexpected. On the surface, they'd come from very different places, but Cowboy believed in the power of love and family, and Sully had been born into both just as he had. He thanked his lucky stars that they'd found each other, and he'd spend a lifetime making sure she was never alone again.

"Mm-hm." She gazed up at him through those impossibly long, dark lashes. A different type of fierceness shone in her eyes than the little girl in the flyer had possessed. A strength that said she could handle anything and a beauty that said she wanted to do it with him.

That's what he wanted, now, always, and forever.

His nerves prickled, and his girl, who had learned to read his every breath like her favorite book, frowned. "What's worrying you?"

"Nothing, baby. I'm just happy." It wasn't exactly a lie. He was happy.

She trusted him so explicitly, she smiled and said, "Me too."

He'd never breach that trust for anything in the world, and there beneath the stars, in the place where they'd first opened their hearts, he took her hand and got down on one knee.

Disbelief rose in her eyes, and a shaky *"Callahan...?"* fell from her lips.

A nervous laugh came out as he said, "Darlin,' give me a second. My heart's never beaten so fast." They both laughed, and tears spilled from her eyes. "Sully, my sweet love, I always thought I had my life figured out, but then there you were, a little girl staring up at me from a flyer, and everything changed. Suddenly all I knew was that you were out there, and we were somehow connected, or we were supposed to be. I don't know about fate or universal signs or any of that, but, baby, from the moment I saw you sitting on that couch, I knew my heart was yours."

Tears spilled down her cheeks.

"You're not only the air I breathe. You have become the biggest and best parts of me. You're my heart and soul, and I want to spend my life watching the sunrise with you, taking long walks, and making love beneath the stars. I want to watch you soar through life illustrating and helping horses heal and be there to cheer you on for whatever passions you find along the way. And one day, if you want a family of our own, then we'll raise little overprotective cowboys and artistic cowgirls and teach them how to love the outdoors and treasure every moment just as we do. And if you don't want to have children, I'm sure we'll have plenty of nieces and nephews to share our love with."

"I *do* want them someday," she choked out.

"Then someday it is. Baby, you once asked me what it was like to know exactly who I was and what I wanted to do with my life. I've been trying to figure out an answer for you, but the thing is, I might have known who I was before we met, but now that I know what it's like to love you, I honestly don't know who I'd be without you by my side, and I don't want to ever find out." He reached into his pocket and withdrew the diamond ring he'd had made for her, with a circle of canary diamonds in alternating sizes surrounding a round white diamond, creating a star pattern.

Her lower lip trembled, more tears flooding her cheeks.

"My sweet Sully, will you do me the honor of marrying me and letting me be the man who loves and cherishes you through good times and bad for the rest of our lives?"

"*Yes*, Callahan," she said through tears and nervous laughter.

"Yes, I'll marry you!"

Gazing into her loving eyes, he slid the ring on her finger. "This star is for the little girl who had stars painted on her toenails and the beautiful woman who fought to free her and brought new meaning, and true love, to my starry nights."

As he pushed to his feet, she threw her arms around him, knocking him off-balance. She shrieked, trying to climb him like a tree as he stumbled backward in ankle-deep water, both of them laughing. "What is it with you and this lake?" he teased.

She beamed at him. "It's not the lake. It's *you*. It's always been you."

"God, I love you."

They sealed their vow with a kiss, and as their lips parted, she said, "At least now you have your answer."

"What answer?"

"About who you'd be without me. You'd be *dry*."

"Baby, I'd rather walk around soaking wet and chilled to the bone than live a single day without you by my side."

Ready for more Whiskeys?

I hope you enjoyed Sully and Callahan's love story. Please note that I took fictional liberties while writing their story. In the real world, their timeline could have taken much longer, but I'm a believer in spiritual connections and knowing when you've met the One. I have every faith that together Sully and Callahan will weather whatever storms come their way, and you can read more about them in Sasha Whiskey's book, **A TASTE OF WHISKEY**. If you'd like to read Sully's sister, Jordan Lawler, and Jax Braden's story, pick up THEN CAME LOVE, (The Bradens & Montgomerys). Their story takes place prior to FOR THE LOVE OF WHISKEY.

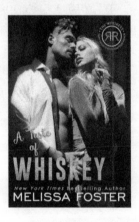

Equine rehabilitation therapist Sasha Whiskey has everything she needs right there on Redemption Ranch—a job she's passionate about, a loving family, and Ezra Moore, the sexy single father who went from trying to nail her as a belligerent teen to keeping his distance as a successful therapist and the person to whom she compares every other man. She's done with comparisons. She wants the real thing. If only dating co-workers weren't forbidden. Maybe it's time for that to change.

READY FOR MORE DARK KNIGHTS?

Meet The Wickeds: Dark Knights at Bayside

Blaine Wicked is used to women doing as he says in and out of the bedroom. Find out what happens when he meets the one woman who won't submit to his wicked ways in the newest insanely sexy, deeply emotional, and laugh-out-loud funny standalone romance.

Love Fake Dating and Opposites Attract?

Fall in love with Raz and Leni in WILD ISLAND LOVE

Sparks fly between a PR rep and an A-list actor who want nothing to do with each other.

Leni Steele might be looking for love, but she's definitely not looking to be someone's fake date. Especially not one of the most infuriatingly handsome and annoyingly cocky actors on the planet, Duncan Raz. But when the owner of the PR firm for which she works forces her to walk the red carpet on his arm, she has no choice. Neither wants to be there, much less with each other. They're like oil and water, and he gets on her last nerve. But after a few tequila shots, that's not all he gets on. What was supposed to be one date turns into a media frenzy they can't afford to ignore, and Leni has no other option than to continue the ruse. All the fake kisses, furtive glances, and seductive touches eventually start to feel very real. But Raz didn't earn his A-list-actor status for nothing. Is he just doing what he does best? Playing a role? Or is Leni the leading lady in Raz's real-life love story?

Get ready to binge read
The Whiskeys: Dark Knights at Peaceful Harbor

If you're a fan of sexy alpha heroes, babies, and strong family
ties even to those who are not blood related, you'll love Truman
Gritt and the Whiskeys.

There's nothing Truman Gritt won't do to protect his family—
including spending years in prison for a crime he didn't
commit. When he's finally released, the life he knew is turned
upside down by his mother's overdose, and Truman steps in to
raise the children she's left behind. Truman's hard, he's
secretive, and he's trying to save a brother who's even more
broken than he is. He's never needed help in his life, and when
beautiful Gemma Wright tries to step in, he's less than
accepting. But Gemma has a way of slithering into people's
lives, and eventually she pierces through his ironclad heart.
When Truman's dark past collides with his future, his loyalties
will be tested, and he'll be faced with his toughest decision yet.

More Books By Melissa Foster

Anything for Love
Trails of Love
Wild Crazy Hearts
Making You Mine
Searching for Love
Hot for Love
Sweet Sexy Heart
Then Came Love
Rocked by Love
Falling For Mr. Bad (Previously *Our Wicked Hearts*)
Claiming Her Heart

THE BRADEN NOVELLAS

Promise My Love
Our New Love
Daring Her Love
Story of Love
Love at Last
A Very Braden Christmas

THE REMINGTONS

Game of Love
Stroke of Love
Flames of Love
Slope of Love
Read, Write, Love
Touched by Love

SEASIDE SUMMERS

Seaside Dreams
Seaside Hearts
Seaside Sunsets
Seaside Secrets
Seaside Nights
Seaside Embrace
Seaside Lovers

The Trouble with Whiskey
Freeing Sully: Prequel to For the Love of Whiskey
For the Love of Whiskey
A Taste of Whiskey

SUGAR LAKE
The Real Thing
Only for You
Love Like Ours
Finding My Girl

HARMONY POINTE
Call Her Mine
This is Love
She Loves Me

THE WICKEDS: DARK KNIGHTS AT BAYSIDE
A Little Bit Wicked
The Wicked Aftermath
Crazy, Wicked Love
The Wicked Truth
His Wicked Ways

SILVER HARBOR
Maybe We Will
Maybe We Should
Maybe We Won't

WILD BOYS AFTER DARK
Logan
Heath
Jackson
Cooper

BAD BOYS AFTER DARK
Mick
Dylan

Carson
Brett

Acknowledgments

I waited ten years after starting Sully's story to finally give her the happily ever after she deserved, and I hope you enjoyed her and Callahan's love story as much as I enjoyed writing it. Please note that I have taken fictional liberties in writing this story. In the real world, their timeline could have taken much longer, but I'm a believer in spiritual connections and knowing when you've met the One. I have every faith that together Sully and Callahan will weather whatever storms come their way, and I look forward to bringing you many more Whiskey love stories.

Once again, I'd like to thank Aeryn Havens, author of SPIRIT CALLED, for her patience when answering my many horse-related questions, and Lisa Filipe, who always manages to talk me off the ledge in those hair-pulling moments.

I am inspired on a daily basis by my fans and friends, many of whom are in my fan club on Facebook. If you haven't yet joined my fan club, please do. We have a great time chatting about the Love in Bloom hunky heroes and sassy heroines. You never know when you'll inspire a story or a character and end up in one of my books, as several fan club members have already discovered.
www.Facebook.com/groups/MelissaFosterFans

To stay abreast of what's going on in our fictional boyfriends'

worlds and sales, like and follow my Facebook fan page.
www.Facebook.com/MelissaFosterAuthor

Sign up for my newsletter to keep up to date with new releases
and special promotions and events and to receive an exclusive
short story featuring Jack Remington and Savannah Braden.
www.MelissaFoster.com/Newsletter

And don't forget to download your free Reader Goodies! For
free ebooks, family trees, publication schedules, series checklists,
and more, please visit the special Reader Goodies page that I've
set up for you!
www.MelissaFoster.com/Reader-Goodies

As always, loads of gratitude to my incredible team of editors
and proofreaders: Kristen Weber, Penina Lopez, Elaini Caruso,
Juliette Hill, Lynn Mullan, and Justinn Harrison, and my *last
set of eagle eyes*, Lee Fisher.

I am forever grateful to my family, assistants, and friends who
have become family, Lisa Filipe, Sharon Martin, and Missy
Dehaven, for their endless support and friendship and Terren
Hoeksema for jumping on board to help me keep my characters' lives in order. Thank you for always having my back, even
when I'm deep in the deadline zone and probably unbearably
annoying.

Meet Melissa

www.MelissaFoster.com

Melissa Foster is a *New York Times*, *Wall Street Journal*, and *USA Today* bestselling and award-winning author. Her books have been recommended by *USA Today*'s book blog, *Hagerstown* magazine, *The Patriot*, and several other print venues. Melissa has painted and donated several murals to the Hospital for Sick Children in Washington, DC.

Visit Melissa on her website or chat with her on social media. Melissa enjoys discussing her books with book clubs and reader groups and welcomes an invitation to your event. Melissa's books are available through most online retailers in paperback, digital, and audio formats.

Melissa also writes sweet romance with no explicit scenes or harsh language under the pen name Addison Cole.